PRAISE FOR *Grange House*

"Pulses with mystery, ghostly melancholy, and young passion... Captivating."

—*Boston Herald*

"A ghost story wrapped in a Victorian romance and studded with bits of social commentary...Rich with detail and language."

—Shelly Ridenour, *Newcity*

"*Grange House* is the type of book that would be a pleasure to read more than once."

—Laura Tutor, *Anniston Star* (Alabama)

"This novel is beautifully written, a real gem."

—Lori Haggbloom, Kepler's Books & Magazines, *The Book Sense 76*

"The language, mores, and class distinctions of nineteenth-century society are faithfully rendered in this atmospheric approximation of a Victorian novel."

—*Publishers Weekly*

"Full of Gothic delights."

—*U.S. News & World Report*

GRANGE HOUSE

SARAH BLAKE

Picador USA
New York

www.picadorusa.com

Picador® is a U.S. registered trademark and is used by St. Martin's Press under license from Pan Books Limited.

For information on Picador USA Reading Group Guides, as well as ordering, please contact the Trade Marketing department at St. Martin's Press.
Phone: 1-800-221-7945 extension 763
Fax: 212-677-7456
E-mail: trademarketing@stmartins.com

Book design by Clair Moritz

Library of Congress Cataloging-in-Publication Data
Blake, Sarah.
    Grange House / Sarah Blake.
        p.   cm.
    ISBN 0-312-24544-0 (hc)
    ISBN 0-312-28004-1 (pbk)
    1. Summer resorts—Fiction. 2. Teenage girls—Fiction. 3. Storytelling—Fiction. 4. Maine—Fiction. I. Title.
PS3552.L3493 G7   2000
813'.6—dc21   00-025912

10 9 8 7 6 5 4 3

For Sheila White Blake English,
1931–1995

She is older than the rocks among which she sits; like the vampire, she has been dead many times, and learned the secrets of the grave; and has been a diver in deep seas, and keeps their fallen day about her . . . and all this has been to her but as the sound of lyres and flutes, and lives only in the delicacy with which it has moulded the changing lineaments, and tinged the eyelids and the hands.

—WALTER PATER

VOLUME I

CHAPTER ONE

I f you have come for a long stay, you must arrive at Grange House by water. The House sits at the farthest edge of the harbor from Middle Haven town, the last habitation before the harbor gives way to the open sea, and though a road runs between the town and Grange House, it is narrow and rocky—entirely unsuitable for the conveyance of large families with luggage. Rather, you must take the night steamer from Boston, which deposits you at the Grange House pier before teatime.

I like to stand in the prow of that boat, steaming farther and farther north and east, and be the first to feel the air sharpen and cool, leaving the damp heat of Boston, the shipyards at Portsmouth, and voyaging into the clear silence born in the chill air of Maine. And though I watch for it, I am never prepared for the first sight of Grange House on its point, though I know the approach, and early learned to read where the slick black shale ledges of the shoreline turn to the white granite boulders marking the entrance to Middle Haven's harbor.

If you have arrived this way, most likely you are what the native people like to call a rusticator, a city dweller come for the cooler air of the north. From the pier, the steamer's side appears lined with such visitors as she draws near, and the captain brings her along at a smart clip. Then he gives the engineer two bells and a jingle and guides her right in. You can see the mate now, waiting with the forward spring line in his hand before he tosses that hawser neatly over the piling just as the bow nudges alongside. He holds it, straining, and she's in against the pier with hardly a jar. You are arrived into a mayhem of unloading, the wharf dipping below the weight of trunks and summer guests. There you stand, surrounded by the men's cries and the groaning creak of the steamer's lines straining against the pier; and then you turn and look up the lawn to the House, set high and away, atop its granite foundation.

In such a way, I came again to Grange House in July of 1896, this place at once familiar and always strange. Long ago, my father had invested in the Grange quarry, but then the place itself took hold. When the quarryman's mansion turned hotel to a few select city families, he fixed the habit of returning every year, though Mama protested, bemoaning the distinct lack of variety in a landscape of spruce and pine. Nonetheless, the enormous old house suited the high pitch of my nerves that summer. At seventeen, I was as eager to know the world as it seemed eager to shroud itself from me, and fretful at what I thought were my bonds, I had begun to wear my white dresses like flags, a slim Crusoe signaling for the distant triangle of sails to break the flat line of what appeared to me but an endless, dulled sea.

As I followed behind my father and mother, I looked up at the top of the House to see if I might spy a figure there watching our advance up the lawn from the windows of her attic room. I never thought of Grange House without that figure standing in it. That afternoon, I did not see her, but, hoping she still looked for my return, I held my gloved hand up in a small salute.

"Maisie," Mama called from the top stair of the verandah.

"I am here," I replied, dropping my hand down to my side, but she had already swung round to follow my father across the threshold into the House, not lingering to take in the view. I cast one last glance upward, and then, gathering my skirts, took the remainder of the lawn with quick feet.

My parents were stopped just inside, next to Mrs. French, the

4

long, wide front hallway stretching past them, with its several doors to the public rooms swung open and the hubbub of teatime voices issuing into the air. It was ever so, year after year: here in the front hall the mix of salt air and cut bayberry, the branches stuffed into matching copper pots upon the table, the silvery green leaves waxy as ever against the paper roses upon the wall. It was only I who seemed to change, a knife cut in the vergeless surface of the place, my arrival cleaving one summer from the next. And that afternoon in July, I remember thinking I was like the Prince returning to the Sleeping Beauty's castle. Let the story begin, I thought impatiently, now that I am here—though what I meant by that, I had not the slightest idea.

"Well, well, my dear!" the housekeeper cried out on seeing me upon the threshold, and she beamed the compliment over to Mama, who smiled absently, pulling off her gloves.

"Are we to have our usual rooms, Mrs. French? I am quite in need of a little rest."

"Yes, of course. Please, Mrs. Thomas, to follow me."

"Welcome, Thomases," a quiet voice spoke from the doorway just behind Papa. We all three turned round, to see the cook of Grange House standing silently there, her arms crossed over her bosom. Mama gave only the briefest of nods before turning to follow Mrs. French, who waited at the bottom of the stairs.

"Cook." Papa bowed kindly to the woman.

"Good afternoon, Mr. Thomas," she answered, dismissing him as she leaned slightly back against the door frame and turned her gaze upon me. Papa never seemed to mind the cook's inexplicable command of their encounters, and I had by now grown accustomed to this woman's yearly scrutiny. Yet that afternoon, I relished the chance to consider her in turn, and I calmly lifted my eyes to hers and smiled.

For an instant, I thought she shivered.

"Maisie Thomas," she said, swiftly uncrossing her arms, "how you have grown." And without another word, she withdrew.

Never mind, I thought, a bit disconcerted, she is not the important one. For though it was Cook who ran Grange House from belowstairs, and Mrs. French who held public sway in the middle rooms and floors, nonetheless it was the topmost figure—she whom I had watched for on our arrival—who was the possessing spirit of the place. I dressed

5

quickly for dinner that evening, descending before my parents to station myself at the foot of the stairs and there await the attic inhabitant of Grange House. And long after the other guests had assembled, passing me by with a nod and a greeting, and after Mama and Papa had issued through to join them, it was she whom I now imagined descending the wooden attic stairs from her room at the top of the House to reach the servants' hall upon the third floor, then down the next stairs into the regions of the second floor, where the large rooms of her family's time had been changed to accommodate we summer people come to stay. Then on down the widest stairway, into the bright, hospitable lights of a fashionable hotel shining its face up for the rush and hum of dinner, into the clap and shiver of bodies just cased in new dresses and thin suits, into the soft mayhem of summer evenings—when our lives might suddenly thrill, and open.

"Miss Grange!" I smiled up.

She caught her breath on seeing me and paused in her descent.

"Maisie Thomas."

Though there was pleasure in her voice, the deep-sunk blue of her eyes regarded me with a touch of bewilderment. I supposed she saw what my mirror told: My cheeks now held the shape of a woman's face, and beneath the dark brown eyes turned to welcome her lay the secret longings of my untried heart. I had caught Mama watching me furtively, as though she read a hidden chapter in my familiar face, and even Jessie—who had dressed and tended me since I was a girl—exploded forth from time to time despite herself, ripping out the seams of my bodices and commenting dryly about "welcome attentions."

"Miss Grange?" I hesitated.

She recovered herself. "How greatly you resemble your father," she replied, and drew her hand beneath my arm so we proceeded together into the hum of the bright gathering.

Miss Grange was something of an enigma for the summer guests. She did not own the hotel, yet she inspired a curious respect. When she did choose to come among us, she was greeted as a visiting dignitary, or even as a monarch long exiled from the proceedings of her own court. It is not to be thought that she was important in any pertinent way. Rather, her magnificence derived from the fact of her lineage. Hers was a family whose roots were among the first to stretch down into American soil. No one knew precisely her connection to the men who had built this House, but it was commonly assumed she was a distant and poor relation who had come here to live after the main branch of the family passed away. Thus, her romance derived from her situation: She was the last Grange remaining. The history of her family preceded her into the very rooms it had built and peopled and vanished from long before the summering plutocrats arrived at the fortunes that brought them here.

And among the younger guests, there were the whispered rumors of buried wealth, the half-uttered suggestions of a lost love, of a secret pact into which she had entered when she came into the House. Once, Papa told me that she had been an authoress, yet surely none of her stories could rival the stew pot simmering at the back of the guests' imaginations. Thus was Miss Grange cast as a living character in the casual entertainment of city folk seeking simplicity under the sharp lines of a Maine sky. Simplicity, that is to say, inmixed with a good country intrigue.

"Here is Miss Grange," I said, drawing her to where my parents conversed, and Mama and Papa turned round. Mama's mouth opened into the vague and generous smile she always gave when her thoughts tended elsewhere, but Papa took Miss Grange's hand in his, visibly startled.

"But—you are not well?"

Miss Grange stiffened, and, withdrawing her hand gently, she nodded but did not reply.

"Really, Ludlow," Mama interposed. "Forgive him, Miss Grange. You look wonderfully well, as always," and she drew her hand beneath Papa's arm, turning him as the dinner bell sounded. Gallantly, he offered his other arm to Miss Grange, who did not take it but walked at his side into the dining room.

That night, several of the other guests had gone to a supper party being held in a neighboring hotel, so the dining room was laid with quite diminished table settings, and our little group joined the two solitary diners already seated at our customary table: Mr. Cutting—the illustrious and tiresome schoolmaster, whose head gleamed in the gaslight like a polished knob where he sat, starched napkin at the ready, his spoon poised in his hand, awaiting his soup—and the large and definitively unaccompanied Mrs. Hunnowell. It would seem, she informed us without prelude, that she was *utterly* abandoned. Her husband had returned to Boston for the week's business, and *where* Bartholomew might be, she really couldn't say, her eyes rolling indulgently at the empty chair beside her. I smiled. Year after year, Mrs. Hunnowell did not disappoint, remaining the kind of woman whose conversation consisted mainly of melodramas she concocted, her head tilted upward, as if the endings hovered just above us in the painted heavens of the room.

I took the abandoned chair beside her, knowing full well that Bartholomew, her son, could never be depended upon to be in the ordinary place at the ordinary time. Having penned a series of very successful travel books for those on their grand tour, Mr. Hunnowell proceeded through life, appearing and disappearing very much like the kind of train he advised young men to catch—off schedule and bound for unknown parts. Mama entirely disapproved of his unsettled behavior—a man of thirty, after all! Even as I could not dismiss him so entirely, I did find him disquieting. One never knew with him precisely where one stood—or rather, where he stood. For every summer he appeared among us, breezy and refined, playing a wide array of roles—brave gallant, avid sportsman, irreverent parlor man—and then a sometimes Bedouin intensity would flash out amongst the parts, making him unreadable, provokingly so.

"After all," Mr. Cutting's musing broke in, "the day turned out to be fine."

Mama nodded politely at him, and as Mrs. Hunnowell motioned the serving girl forward to begin, I put aside all thoughts of Bart Hunnowell and his character.

Amid the clatter of the serving of the soup, I studied Miss Grange across the table. Though she could not be more than fifty, the winter past seemed to have settled an elderly gray upon her cheeks, and a blue vein pulsed too brightly upon her hand. Papa was right. There *was* something shifted, for I do not think I imagined the heavy sadness deep down in Miss Grange's eyes, now giving them the kind of deathly beauty of a poem: *Pale beyond porch and portal,* I repeated to myself,

Crowned with calm leaves she stands. She caught my eye upon her and winked. I reddened and looked down. I have been reading too much Swinburne, I thought, and smiled to myself.

"Will you please to just look at that?" Mrs. Hunnowell breathed beside me, and I caught the erstwhile rose hip slip from behind her ear, to fall upon the broad pavilion of her bosom.

I followed her gaze out the side window, where, indeed, a fleet and incomplete tableau had formed of the sort the summer guests most appreciated. Now a man's uncovered head leaned down to whisper into the ear of a young woman. From where we sat, the woman stood too small for us to see more than just the gentle swell of her forehead, though her hand had flown up to rest upon the back of the man's neck.

And then in an instant, they had parted. But just as the young man turned, I caught sight of his face.

"Henry Brown!" I said aloud.

"But who is the girl?" wondered Mrs. Hunnowell, delighted. I did not reply. Yet something of the tilt of her head had called to mind Halcy Ames, I realized a bit wistfully, watching Henry Brown's sturdy back and shoulders advance without haste down the lawn toward his boat, oblivious to the rapt attention we paid his small encounter.

I could not think of Halcy Ames without a twinge of regret, for once upon a time we had been staunch companions, though she was Cook's daughter and I a guest. As a child, she had done light maid's work at Grange House in the mornings, filling each guest room's fireplace with new wood and making fresh the beds upstairs. Younger than I by two years, she was pretty in her way—tiny, her hands completing her tasks as efficiently as wood squirrels about their trees, and I grew accustomed to accompanying her as she went about the beds, fetching clean linens and smoothing spreads at her command.

Then one day, she was tidying my mother's dressing table, straightening the glass bottles and brushes on its marble top, and I was pulling Mama's scarves from her dresser drawer. We were busy talking, standing side by side, looking at each other in the looking glass above the table, resembling nothing so much as sisters that morning, our two small faces animated and dancing as we talked—so we did not hear Mama's hand on the knob, but when she suddenly spoke from behind

9

us, Halcy jumped so, she knocked one of Mama's perfume bottles off the table. It made a terrific noise, shattering into several tiny pieces at our feet.

"Oh! You clumsy girl!" Mama exclaimed. "Just see what you have done!"

I leapt stoutly to Halcy's defense. "But you startled us, Mama."

"A good serving girl, Maisie, must learn to be always on the ready for the entrance of her mistress without event. Fetch a broom, please, Halcy, and clear this away."

Halcy's eyes met mine in the mirror as she passed from the room. I did not understand then her face's shuttered look, but from that day on, she began to call me Miss Thomas, and though I teased her about it, she persisted. This insistence on my formal name hurt me so that gradually I ceased to search her out in the mornings, the divide between us widening to a polite silence.

Papa's elbow jostled against me as he rose from dinner. All about me there was movement and sound, and I winnowed back up into the clutter of life. Papa stood, his hand upon Mama's chair as he listened to Miss Grange recounting the terrible storm that had blown down three of the laurels out front, her combs like smooth shells held against the slick water of her hair. Mama sat poised, I could see, to detail the season's toll on her own garden. I pushed back my chair, suddenly vexed. Around me in the dining room came the same bursts of voice, the hushed movements of the maids as they cleared away the unused silver and the tiny saltcellars before setting out the decanters for the men. Above the mantel, the stilted figures of a couple embraced upon their horses in a forgotten English vale. Everything was just as it always was! I longed for something—anything—so long as it happened. I sprung out from the slow-moving throng with its discussion of winter, stepping ahead through the low-lit front hall and out, out into the night, onto the piazza, whose white columns glowed against the black sparkle of the harbor under stars. Far down the lawn, some of the men strolled, and their white collars flashed in and out of the dark like fireflies. If they turned to regard the fine old house, I would be indistinguishable, a light shadow of white against the white.

Under this blanketing velvet dark containing its faraway men and cigars, I yearned for color, a bright sweep of red flames to flare into being. It wasn't clarity or vision I wanted, no—say instead that I had come to perceive there was something I lacked. That year, I had begun to read books as though begging entry, leaning to the pages as if pressing my ear to a door. Then it seemed the pages would sing out some strange song and, slight music that it was, I'd feel an answering swell of dim comprehension, though I knew that mine was the echo of the song, not the song itself. Sorrow; Rage; even a high, vaunting Gladness—these were foreign breezes from countries to which I had never voyaged, so each book became my little craft, each page a sail set out to catch those distant winds upon which Brontë, Pliny, Chapman, Ovid, all, indiscriminate, seemed to play. And I would sit at my window and strain into the dark behind the glass, longing to see through into the heat of my life, into the knowledge that I, too, would possess something at the heart of me to tell; that there was a promise held out for me. For me alone.

"Good night, Miss Maisie Thomas." Miss Grange's soft voice stole around the column, a kind of tired laughter underneath the sound. I felt caught out. I turned to my friend.

"Good night, Miss Grange."

But she had already vanished through the dark doorway, and I could just hear Papa's muffled voice inside, pausing in his conversation to bid her good night as she passed by. In my mind's eye, I followed the tidy figure as she mounted slowly to her room, imagining the light on her table rising, seeing her draw back the curtain to stand at her window. And my eyes refocused with hers, staring out at the white collars pocking the dark lawn. One separated from the crowd with a casual laugh backward over his shoulder. It appeared he had a meeting. My heart throbbed. I strained my eyes into the dark, but the lights from inside the house cast an obscuring perimeter. I stepped around to the corner of the piazza, which ran in front of the now-darkened dining room, and peered out.

There! There was a white dress.

It waited. The collar approached. I could hear the long legs of the man switch through the grasses. The two were meeting in a near corner of one of the fields that stretched by the side of the front lawn. I watched the collar bend, like a star gliding down to the waiting sea. I watched the two white arms rise.

11

CHAPTER TWO

My father believed I should be possessed of the rudiments of a classical education. He believed so in distinct opposition to my mother, who, herself fluent in French and Italian, was certain that the duress of a more concentrated regime would constrict the development of my other "charms," thereby insisting upon small bunkers of learning to be established in the drawing room—the sewing table, the tea table, the piano—like in importance to the several Stations of the Cross.

Nonetheless, Papa had persevered, setting my reading each week and establishing himself every afternoon at the top of our house in Brooklyn, where my dolls had given pride of place to the scratched covers of his boyhood schoolbooks stacked upon the old round table in the center of the room. "Commence," he would say on entering, then seat himself in an easy chair by the window, tapping the sill with his long fingers. He carried into me the whiff of commerce—cigars and pipes and the sweet smell of his luncheon port still lingering in the air about him. And as I stood before him, reciting the Latin he had chosen, I watched him draw deeper and deeper into the old words I recited, closing his eyes and nodding to the cart-track rhythms and repetitions as I pulled him along upon the stories of another time, the brisk edges of his day falling from him as I spoke.

Having heard me, he would sit a bit in silence, until my words had nudged loose an answering scrap of poetry in him. Though he had been trained to follow first one path and then another, my course followed the accidents of his own intellectual meanderings. A reverie he sunk into while walking home across the Brooklyn Bridge would lead him backward to Schiller and then over across the waters into Wordsworth's sublime perceptions—and so he brought me the German and the Englishman as fellow countrymen in a realm of thought. He'd rise and cross to where I sat, pull a book from off the shelves, and we'd begin to read together.

One afternoon that past spring, we were bent over a piece of work in silence, my eyes following as Papa traced the words upon his page, his finger beating time upon the table so I might hear the underlying song, when Mama suddenly entered. We were both so intent, we did not hear her. And when she gave a little cough, we must have turned twin pairs of blank brown eyes upon her, blinking like animals rustled from their cave by a crack of light.

"I do believe you hardly see me," she said slowly to us, making as if to leave.

Murmuring her name, Papa leapt to his feet and led her to the table. "We were reading," I offered.

"Yes," she said, refusing to sit. "Mr. Colgate waits downstairs."

"Mr. Colgate?" Papa was mystified.

"Yes"—she looked down at me with a significant smile—"Mr. Colgate. The younger."

"Ah," said Papa. And then they both smiled down at me.

With this same unpleasant sensation of having been suddenly thrust out into the cold, I awoke the next morning at Grange House. Pulling the tossed bedclothes back up about me, I turned my head and looked out the window by my bed to see what manner of day lay in store. Behind the covering of gauzy white curtains hung a dense fog, from which the dark shapes of trees poked like bony fingers out of tattered gloves, promising a day passed with a good book downstairs upon the long settee.

Just as I turned away from the window, it seemed as though the fog billowed, a darker shade of gray surging forward for an instant, then retreating. I drew up on my elbow and lifted the curtain—there was nothing but a blank repeating quiet, a veritable sound of gray. No! It came again. Then the darker gray drifted slowly free.

I pushed off my covers and knelt upon the bed, my hands on either side of the window for balance, fixing the moving spot, a dull patter in my head. The fog blew between the dark trunks, leaving soft clumps upon the low branches like old women's hair. The foghorn called out its lonely note. I blinked to make certain of what I saw. Through the fog, the dark smudge advanced toward the edge of the trees, and then—so whole and sudden as if sprung from Mr. Collins's pen—I saw it was a figure, clad in gray.

It looked up at the House with such mortal longing, I nearly cried aloud—and for several long moments, the pale face shrouded by its gray cloak stood staring, though I could not discern the features that gazed so fixedly upon us. It remained eerily still while the fog passed cross. Then the figure lifted up a hand and simply waved. Without hesitation, my own hand lifted in reply.

The door opened behind me and there came a little shriek. "Why ever are you standing up in your bed, miss?"

"Hush," I replied, not turning from my post, though what I had seen disappeared again beneath the covering shroud of fog.

"Ah, it's that way this morning, is it?"

"There is someone out there, Jessie," I said quietly, still not wishing to turn my eyes away.

"Aye, and there's the good Lord up above, thank heavens for us all."

The fog was lifting slightly, I could see the tree line ridging round toward Grange House point, the sharp tips just freed of the covering gray. Nothing now greeted my attention, yet I crouched upon my bed in my white shift, staring through the curtains.

"It was a girl," I whispered, still watching the empty door of the boathouse. "Or was it a woman?" I reflected aloud. Jessie titched and moved from my side, but I remained where I knelt, unable to shake free the vision of that solitary gray creature upon the lawn.

After a time, there came such clatter and bang behind me, I sat back from the curtain and turned round. Her freckled brow drawn into a sharp crease, Jessie prepared my wardrobe with terrible concentration, drawing the thin white dress from out of the shadows of the armoire, bearing it in her arms gently as a child, to lay it across the foot of my bed in readiness for the lace collar and cuffs, both of which she pulled from the silken lining of the cedar drawers.

"What a lady you are making me," I remarked, a bit testily.

" 'Tis only just your clothing, miss," she answered, fastening the green-gold trim to the waist sash upon the dress, the arms dutifully stretched on either side of the cinched fabric.

"No, no. Jessie, please to look at her," I said, nearly as disquieted by this languid linen shape upon the bed as by the apparition in the fog. "How exhausted she is already." Jessie snapped two petticoats in the air beside me and did not reply. I watched the slight dust shaken free from the bouncing skirts. And with that done, she ended further discussion, gesturing for me to turn my back so she could brush out my hair.

Dressed for the day, I descended the carpeted stairs, pausing at the stairway turn to look out the vast window there, my thoughts in a jumble. The fog crossed swiftly now across the morning, and below the covering gray, the bright green of the lawn had begun to assert itself.

Several guests sat already at breakfast. An older man with enormous white mustaches I had noticed the previous night crumbled a roll into his coffee with one hand while the other traced the lines of a letter that lay open in front of him. A hideously unattractive woman sat beside him, though lively eyes peered out the window into the brightening morning from her heavyset, rather mannish features. At another table sat a tidy little mother with her two fair children and their dark-haired governess, a plain Jane of a woman.

Had none of them seen the gray figure? I looked round at the ordinary gathering. Not a one betrayed the slightest hint of the unease I felt. For though I liked a story, I reflected, taking my chair, the longing in that figure's pose rather more unnerved than thrilled—as if a character had reached out a hand from the pages of a book and pointed, direct to me.

"Shall we order a picnic for today, Maisie?" Mama asked, replacing my inborn thoughts with the airy vision of her lilac silk as she took the chair opposite. I grimaced.

"Now Maisie, you'll stretch your skin if you make such a face, and it will hang in pockets around your chin, making you jowly before you reach twenty-five."

I dutifully adjusted my face, resolving to continue my own thoughts.

"But what sort of picnic, I wonder, hot or cold . . ." Mama paused.

"Cold," I answered, and the inward door swung slowly shut.

"Yes, that is best." Mama nodded at the new girl serving coffee, accepting the Sèvres cup into her hands with an appreciative sigh.

"When I arose this morning"—I leaned forward so none but Mama would hear—"I parted my curtains and saw someone moving through the trees down by the boathouse."

"Saw someone?" Her butter knife did not pause.

"Someone ghostly," I added.

"That was very likely your own papa gone out for his row," replied Mama, now looking up at me. And then past me as her face shifted slightly, lifted a bit. "Ah, Mr. Cutting! Yes, of course you may join us."

The man bowed a thanks to her, nodded at me, then settled in the chair next to mine.

"It could not have been Papa," I pursued; "I'm almost certain I saw a woman's face."

"That is enough, Maisie," Mama said firmly, and smiled at the headmaster. Then into the consequent silence she plunged, talking of picnics. I watched my mother's animated hands outline the shape of the wicker basket needed for our party, banishing to air whatever visions I might have seen. Mr. Cutting listened with great attention, breaking in now and then to exclaim at Mama's plans, until, well into his second cup of coffee, he prodded the conversation round to his own excursions *"en plein air"* into the sublime regions of the Alps. I looked round. The other breakfasters were mopping up their crumbs, twirling their napcloths into the shining rings, and rising—papers or fancywork in hand—to set forward into the day. Mama barely noticed as I departed, taking up my hat and wrap from their hook by the door.

My boots did not make a sound as I descended the wooden steps of the piazza, pulled into the damp. Now the fog hung loosely atop the trees, and I could feel the first heat of a sun struggling to pierce that vaporous buffer.

I wandered down toward the dock and through the boathouse's weathered gray interior, passing by the unpainted boards hung with life preservers, cast-off buoys, and skeins of rope wound sailor-fashion in tight circles out onto the wide surface of the pier built up high above the wharf, where several lobster traps were stacked against the wooden railings. Behind these, the scene was a wash of gray and black, the color of trees and grass and the white flashes of birch abandoned to this ribbon of sea still overhung with the thick gray. No wind blew motion into the water, and so, though the morning was damp, it was not chill, but rather edgeless. And though Mr. Homer would never paint so soft a scene, to me, such silence entranced. To me, the gray hollow beckoned.

I heard the creak of oarlocks as oars turned in the metal cups, crossing and dipping, the water dropping off the blades in even sheets. Then advancing toward me out of that hollow, two rowboats came in slow tandem, side by side. And this time, it was no apparition, nor billow in the dense air. I could not see why the boats should be hobbled together, nor why with two men rowing they should come so slowly—and this eerie, dripping, slow, and quiet approach froze me to my spot. Two boys sat perfectly still in the bow of one boat, watching the water for rocks and calling out directions to the rowers, their small, scared voices chiming like warning bells. I saw it was Papa in one dinghy, and in the other I recognized Bartholomew Hunnowell. He had shed his jacket, and his shirt glowed against the dark band of that motionless sea. Each man had shipped his inboard oar, rowing forward with the outer, their two backs reaching and pulling together as they made their careful progress in to shore—and then, at last, I saw what they carried.

Slung across the sterns lay a man and a woman—the cold arms clasped around each other and round what must have been the snapped mast of their wrecked boat. And the length of mast and man had forced the rescuers to sling the drowned pair awkwardly between the boats— half in one, half in the other—though I saw Mr. Hunnowell's jacket was laid on the seat beneath their shoulders, looking for all the world as if he had meant to soften the hard ride.

When they reached the wharf, the boys grabbed the rings on the pilings and pulled the doubled load in. Papa and Mr. Hunnowell shipped their oars and sat a moment conferring, the boys holding tightly to the dock in silence. Still, none of them had seen me, and I took care they did not discover me now.

"We must loose them from the mast," Papa said.

Mr. Hunnowell nodded in agreement and directed the boys to tie the boats up and then to run fast as they might up the hill to the House for help. I could see the boys linger after they had slipped the lines through the dock rings, and so again, and this time more gently, Mr. Hunnowell directed them to go. I stepped back from the edge of the pier so the men should not see me if they followed the boys up the gangway with their eyes. The boys passed me by without a sound, racing each other across the pier and into the boathouse, their feet pounding upon the wooden planks and then vanishing up the dew-sopped lawn.

I drew close to the top and looked down again. Standing side by side, each still in his boat, Papa and Bart Hunnowell considered the drowned pair. I could not see the man's face, but his dark shirt had a great tear and the shocking white of his bare back reminded me of a small boy's—though I could see he had been powerful once, and lithe. I glimpsed very little of the woman beneath him, save her bare arm reaching up across his back, her hand clinging even now to the neck of her beloved. He had wrapped himself around her and then clung fast to the mast, and thus to loose them from the mast was to break the two of them apart.

Clearly, neither Papa nor Mr. Hunnowell wished to do this, for they hesitated, standing silently above the pair. At least Bart Hunowell gently touched the man's hand as if in greeting, and Papa began to pull the stout mast from the dead man's grasp so it might fall over the side of his boat. Hand over hand, Papa eased it through until the mast slid free and quietly sank back into the water.

But the mast had served to link the boats, and now the sterns of the two dinghies began to yawn apart. Mr. Hunnowell reached forward to grab the clasped torsos of the man and woman, just as Papa's boat swung wide and the bottom half of the bodies plunged into that freezing water. Suddenly Mr. Hunnowell was pitched into the sinking stern of his boat, clutched in a terrible embrace and the full weight of the dead dragging him down with them.

I gasped and stepped onto the gangway.

"Maisie!" Papa shouted to me, and I ran the remaining feet down to the dock and knelt there, reaching to grab hold of Mr. Hunnowell's shirt just as Papa caught the dinghy's side to stop the desperate tipping. For an eerie moment, we five of us, living and dead, clung together, trying to stay gravity's pull. Softly, the balance tipped.

"Are you able to hold them?" Mr. Hunnowell grunted to Papa.

Papa lay down upon the stern seat of his boat and stretched himself over the gap between the boats, to catch hold beneath the man's arms. The woman's head lolled to the side, though still her face remained obscured by her hair. Papa nodded, and Mr. Hunnowell let go of the drowned; he turned and reached up to grab my outstretched hand and pulled himself up onto the dock.

"Thank you," he said to me, catching his breath. I nodded, suddenly shy. He rolled onto his stomach, taking care to hook his feet into the iron rings behind us at the other edge of the dock, reached back down with one hand and caught the woman's wrists firmly in his grip, so Papa did not bear all.

"Get some help, Maisie," Papa said. "I do not see how we can bring them onto the dock."

I stood and ran up the gangway, and I saw to my relief when I reached the top that Mr. Coates, the Grange House boatman, was coming through the boathouse, alerted by the boys, his clamming boots still muddy from where they must have found him. He passed me wordlessly down the gangway to Papa and Mr. Hunnowell. I turned and crept back again to watch.

Mr. Hunnowell still held fast to those poor cold wrists, though he had begun to shiver.

"We cannot pull them up," Papa cried out.

Without a word to either man, Mr. Coates climbed down the

swimming ladder into the water. Keeping hold of the edge of the ladder with his left hand, he reached his right down the length of the bodies below the surface of the water, his hand discovering what his eyes could not.

"Grab hold beneath her arms, Mr. Hunnowell," Mr. Coates directed from the rungs of the ladder, and Mr. Hunnowell did so. The woman's grip was now entirely loosened upon the man, so Mr. Coates could catch hold of the man's torso, while Papa managed to keep tight grip upon his legs, and slowly the two men dragged and pushed the drowned man up the ladder until he was laid upon the dock.

I cried out at whom I saw.

Without a word, Mr. Coates and Papa helped Mr. Hunnowell draw the woman straight up from the water. I looked away, dreading who it might be. I heard the rush of water streaming from her as they set her down beside her lover. For a time, that was the only sound. I turned, and there lay Halcy Ames at my feet, her gray cloak spread wide around her poor wet body.

Mr. Coates closed Henry's eyes with two fingers, then softly combed the young man's hair from off his face, revealing an ugly wound long since stopped bleeding.

"Maisie, I think it's best you return to the House." My father's voice, so gentle then, brought tears to my eyes. And I turned to go; indeed, I did not want to stay any longer. But I heard Mr. Coates say to no one in particular, "There's a fear of more'n an accident on that face." I halted.

"Maisie," Papa's voice at my back was firm.

I walked up the gangway and across the pier, through the hollow of the boathouse and out onto the lawn. Mrs. French came hurrying down from the house, dressed already in her tea gown.

"Maisie! What has happened?"

"Henry Brown has drowned, Mrs. French," I whispered, "and—"

"And?"

"Halcy Ames."

"They are on our pier?"

"Yes, ma'am." I nodded, sudden tears filling my eyes.

"Mercy!" she whispered, one hand at her throat. She walked past me and into the boathouse.

Mama and Mrs. Hunnowell stood on the piazza and waited as I walked up the lawn to them.

"What is it?" Mrs. Hunnowell called. "We heard shouts."

I turned a sad face up to them. "Henry Brown is drowned."

"Henry? The boatbuilder's son?" Mama asked quickly.

I nodded. I could not say the second part.

"But he was to be married to Cook's daughter!" Mrs. Hunnowell cried.

"To Halcy Ames?" I asked.

"Yes," Mrs. Hunnowell whispered. "After what we witnessed last evening, I felt I must discover . . . ." Her voice trailed away. I watched her fingers hold in place the tiny row of knit work she still held in one hand as she felt behind her with the other for the wicker settee and sat heavily down.

"Oh!" I cried, and turned back around to the harbor, my mind struggling to make clear what I had seen.

Mrs. French was hurrying up the lawn toward us, her little dog barking and trotting after, but she said not a word to our group, immediately rounding the side of the House, her face bled of all its color.

"Oh," I said again softly.

Through my tears, I watched Papa walking slowly back up the lawn to us, the fog patchy now and high above, leaving room for a morning sun. The heavy burden he had carried was repeated in his gait. Slowly, he mounted the wooden stairs, then put his hands on both my shoulders and gave them a squeeze.

The front door swung open and the mustachioed gentleman and his wife came onto the piazza.

"What has happened?" His voice was unnaturally high.

Papa stepped round me to them and was outlining the catastrophe when Mrs. French appeared in the doorway. Immediately, Papa broke off his discussion and addressed her.

"How is Cook?"

"I'm afraid we've had to send for Dr. Morris."

"Why the deuce have you done that, Mrs. French? I am a doctor," blustered the gentleman beside Papa.

"Oh, Dr. Lewes, I did not think to trouble you," said the housekeeper.

"No bother. Let me just fetch my bag." And the man excused himself and entered the House.

His wife turned a worried face to Mrs. French. "Is it serious?" she asked.

"I cannot tell; Cook appears to be in some kind of stupefied trance." And she followed the doctor into the House.

"Oh dear," sighed Mrs. Lewes.

"How wonderful it is," Mama mused aloud, "to find that the loss of a local girl and boy can so affect the summer people."

"Libby!"

She raised her eyes to meet Papa's horrified expression. For a moment, she regarded him, and then she turned wordlessly away and picked up her shawl from off the arm of the settee and rose.

"Poor Cook," I said to no one in particular, recalling her greeting to me only the evening before.

Mama hesitated an instant on the threshold of the front door, her back very straight, and then she turned round. "Yes indeed," she agreed quietly. "She has lost her child."

And though she had directed her reply to Papa, he seemed not to have heard, so Mama turned again and passed into the hall. Papa was silent a moment, and then he, too, departed into the House. Only Mrs. Lewes remained behind, sunk in thoughts of her own, and then, without a word to me, she drifted past and down onto the lawn, where she took up a chair by the rocks and settled. I watched her pull a book from her pocket and, leaning, commence to write.

Halcy! my heart cried. *Halcy Ames! It was you!*

Far away, at the base of the harbor, stretched the white flank of Middle Haven. And though I could name the neat fronts of every house—Brown, Ames, Calderwood, Beverage, Warren, Vinal, names familiar as the pulls upon each door—I knew the doors would not swing open for a summer visitor such as me. House after house after house, the white faces of the town repeated upon the black harbor like palms held up to stave off my groping entry, the broad beam of the townsmen's smiles like the uncommunicative slant of sun upon those sturdy walls.

And Grange House, too, had long seemed closed to me in this

way, but that morning a deathblow was struck to the baseboard of the place, and I heard the keening brought upon a small wind through the crack. For I had been at the window when Halcy's ghost had come and stood—and waved.

CHAPTER THREE

Everyone, guest and servant, passed through the morning quietly as we could, and the hubbub at Grange House softened to a hum. Dr. Lewes, it appeared, was a mesmerist as well as a physician, and deducing that Cook would not wake without extreme measure, he spoke to her in her trance, coaxing her stunned mind back into its consciousness; Halcy's short letter remained crushed in her hand:

Mother, we have gone to be married. It could not wait, you see.

The luncheon meal was hastily set and quickly taken, and the hot hours of the afternoon stretched wider in the dreadful silence of the House. Not a guest took a boat upon the water, so it was largely still, save for the fishermen. Late in the afternoon, Mama and Papa retired upstairs, and I remained upon the piazza, where we had been sitting. For a long while, I stared at the harbor, unable to cease from watching the flat sheen of water before me, as if there lay the answers. What had happened? I tried and tried to envision Halcy and Henry in the

24

dark—secretly meeting, clasped together, setting out across the water. To marry? Marry where? Where were they fleeing to on a windless night?

And there my mind stuck—or rather, my mind could not see true. For it was Halcy as Maggie Tulliver I imagined, floating along on the treacherous torrent of the Floss; or then the beautiful, dreaming, dead Ophelia faceup among the reeds. The strange ecstasy in their dying faces settled onto Halcy's—and seemed more real to me somehow than the plain little body I had seen this morning upon the dock.

The laughter of girls burst open behind me, and I turned to see Cynthia Harrington and Ruth Barton had appeared in the doorway as if blown there by a pursuing wind.

Clad in a pale green dress, unadorned save for the pearl buttons at her neck, Cynthia dashed forward, alighting herself first beside me on the settee, then rising to perch upon the wooden balustrade. The more substantial Miss Barton chose a single wicker chair and settled herself right down. There was one moment of quiet as we sat in the light shade of the piazza and watched the seagulls trail after the fishing boats in the bright open sky.

"I would like to be married out by the lighthouse," Cynthia burst out, her eyes turned toward the tip of the breakwater, and as she turned to look first at Ruth, then at me, her hair brushed past one cheek and then the other, a very drama of revealing and concealing, which, had I been a man, I might have found entrancing.

"Outside!" Ruth exclaimed. "Why, only animals couple outside—you might just as well wish to be married in a barn!" And the dreadful girl's nose crinkled in scornful merriment. "After all, where would God be if you said your vows outside, or anywhere, for that matter, but in a church?"

"God?" Cynthia turned suddenly serious eyes on her friend. "God is the all outdoors."

"Oh, really, Cynthia—how positively Transcendental." But Ruth was not to be outdone. "When *I* marry," she ruminated, "I'll walk down the very long center aisle of Grace Church filled with lit candles and roses, so the light will be soft and bright at the same time. I'll have two little girls dressed in simple white muslin frocks trimmed with tiny green nosettes, each throwing down a carpet of petals before me." She smiled at the sight. Cynthia hopped off the balustrade and settled into her own chair, preparing for the epic recitation she must have known would follow, the two having been friends since childhood.

My attention wandered in and out of Ruth's disquisition on her wedding, watching the steady procession of lobstermen rowing homeward, their wooden traps stacked in the stern of their long dories. The men called to one another over the late afternoon's calm, and their rough voices beat under Ruth's interminable visions. What is it propels this absorption in one's own wedding? Ruth's was not the first I'd heard cataloged and imagined to the last detail. Several times in the past three or four years, suddenly a conversation would shift into this scene: one girl outlining and explaining what she saw in her head to a small crowd of attentive listeners. It is the shift I find so disconcerting—without warning, there we will be, presumptive brides declaiming, instead of the three young women we are. But today this talk of silks and laces seemed to me thoughtless. Halcy Ames had just drowned for this vision. Impatiently, I burst into Ruth's talk.

"Really, Ruth, I should think you would remember not to sift your wedding into a day of mourning."

On the instant, Ruth became a picture of sorrowful consideration.

"Oh, yes. The lovers." And she held this pose for a moment, even reaching out her hand to squeeze Cynthia's.

"Just imagine the scene," Ruth whispered. I groaned inwardly—instead of diverting Ruth's attention, it appeared I had only just tossed fresh embers atop her fire. Here again, the love story—prelude to the dress, the candles, and the little flower girls. "Halcy must have crept from her house around midnight, muzzling that old dog, and carrying a sweet little bundle of bread and chocolate for their wedding breakfast."

"Oh, Ruthie, do you think so?" Cynthia breathed.

"Yes, I can almost see it," Ruth answered. "They arranged a sign between them, I'm sure of it, and Halcy must have forgotten the sign as she approached the boat—so breathless with excitement was she—because dimly, she saw her lover waiting there at the pier. I think old man Brown must have been suspicious, for just as Halcy neared the steps to the pier, she heard his gruff hallo from the town hall piazza, where he must have gone to have a look out. Startled, she tripped, casting her bundle into the waters just at her feet, an unwitting prelude to her own dark fate." Ruth paused impressively here.

"Have mercy!" squeaked Cynthia.

"How is it, Ruth Barton, that no one found such a bundle this morning?" I spoke more sharply than I intended, but her talk made me increasingly uneasy and I wished her to stop.

Instead, she sailed serenely onward, her prow cutting in two such questions of evidence. "The waters swallowed the bundle swift and sure as though some lost soul beneath starved for the chocolate and reached out his dead hand to drag it quickly below."

Cynthia gave a little shriek. "And then what happened, Ruthie?"

"Henry, too, heard his father's call of alarm, and he flew up the intervening steps to clasp Halcy's hands and pull her down to the waiting boat. In seconds, the two had cast off, their deftness spurred by their longing hearts and willing hands."

"Ruth!" I was on my feet.

"And the father?" Cynthia prodded. Neither girl paid me heed, so wrapped were they in their fiction.

"Well, this is the tragic part. The father, thinking that the splash of oars he heard was nothing but the tides, and not being able to see into the obscuring darkness, turned away from the pier and headed homeward, back to his warm bed. Even as he tossed and turned, settling himself back into sleep, his only son sailed onward toward his dea—"

"Stop it, Ruth. Stop it at once!" I stood over her, now furious with this stupid girl and her story.

"Maisie Thomas! Whatever is the matter?"

"It's not right, Ruth. Halcy Adams and Henry Brown are truly dead, and nobody can ever know what happened."

"It is only a story, Maisie," Cynthia piped in.

"No," I began, my voice trembling, "no, it is not a story, Cynthia. It is—" But I found I could not finish, I was so hot suddenly, and confused. The greedy delight Ruth took in all the details she imagined was something terrible, and it called to mind my own imagination's flight, and I was fully shamed. I excused myself from their open-mouthed surprise and walked into the House, blindly seeking a place to put my head in my hands and think.

"Well!" I heard Ruth exclaim behind me, and I imagined her exchanging a significant look with Cynthia. What was it? What was it? I found myself drawn to the protection of the high-backed settee in the front room. Suddenly, the picture of Halcy snapping sharp her dust cloth flashed into my thoughts; she had been here, often about this very room—and that image broke open the gate around my heart. There she was; there she was after all. Alive—and particular. Not a heroine, but a girl. The one I'd chattered with, and dreamed. The one I'd followed belowstairs for buttered muffins, passing a china cup of milk between us across the wooden tabletop, the hum and bustle of the busy kitchen all around. I leaned my forehead against the back of the settee and gave in to hot, silent tears for my childhood companion.

After a bit, I heard Ruth and Cynthia's talk start up again through the open window at the opposite end of the room. My tears eased and I sat there lulled, my cheeks cooling. One of the curtains lifted and fell in the dispersing breeze of the quiet room. A minute went by, and another. Then, drifting over the wooden ridge of the settee, came a flight of smoke rings, perfectly formed and spinning in the bright afternoon air. The rings floated for an instant together and then the gay procession disbanded.

"Well said," a man commented.

I started. The wicker of his chair creaked as he rose. I struggled to press myself farther down into the pillows, listening as his slow tread crossed the room and stopped directly behind the settee.

I looked up into the calmly considering eyes of Bartholomew Hunnowell, now resplendent in white vest and trousers.

"What was well said?" I asked uncomfortably, pushing myself upright. "It is not fair to spring upon me like that."

"No, it is not," he agreed. "Forgive me." But he remained where he stood, looking down; and aware of my flushed cheeks and reddened eyes, I started up, smoothing my skirts about my hips, to move from off this tiny island of unease into the midst of the room. I reached the center table safely and turned to face him.

"What was well said?" I repeated.

He pointed toward the windows at the front of the room. "Halcy Ames and Henry Brown should not be turned into the silly tales of girls."

I followed his gaze. There sat Ruth and Cynthia perfectly framed. He must have witnessed the entire scene. I flushed up again.

"Thank you," I said, abashed. Standing there at the table, side by side, we both watched the girls a minute more. I could not think what to do. And he did not move from his spot, nor offer a break through which I might gracefully end our tête-à-tête.

"That is quite a handsome jersey," I remarked at last. He looked down at his white vest, a bright crimson *H* emblazoned across the front.

"Ah," he said, now feigning solemnity, "my scarlet letter. I wear this mark of shame and travel round the world to draw forth from hiding the infernal brotherhood."

I snorted. "A very Ethan Brand."

"Do not mock, Miss Thomas." He drew closer. "The method works! I cannot go anywhere without another one pops forward to shake my hand, speaking of fair Harvard." He paused. "On the other hand," he whispered to me conspiratorially, slipping the cigar back between his lips, "I also wear it for Mater. She thinks I am best situated with an *H* upon my breast."

I smiled. He grinned and bowed. "Welcome back, Miss Thomas," he then said softly, and walked from the room.

I stood unmoving for a long moment. Bart Hunnowell! I began to dismiss him reflexively. Only just see how the hero of the morning had slipped to patter—to become a cheerful spy upon the silly talk of girls! He was . . . I paused before the image of the two of us standing silently together. He was . . . perplexing. For there remained in him a deep, abiding quiet, a watchfulness. And when he had turned that quiet upon me, I could not rest there. I'd had to speak—or look away. The clock in the front hall chimed six. Stuff! I would go upstairs and read, I decided. It lacked only an hour until the dressing bell sounded.

As I issued from the sitting room, I chanced to hear Ruth's voice twittering away still from one of the piazza swings. I could not make out what she chattered on about, and I turned toward the stairs, until my gait was arrested by the sound of my own name rising to me from the mud of her conversation. I paused in my step. And then quite clearly, I heard, "Maisie Thomas?"

"Yes, I think so."

"But he is famously undependable."

"Nevertheless, I think they would make quite a good match."

"Stuff!" I said aloud to the empty hallway, and quickly ran up the stairs to the head of the passageway. A breeze stirred the white curtains in the windows at the end of the passage. Before me was all light and color, and the hush of shut rooms. No one was about. I stopped, my hand upon the newel post, suddenly unable to take a step farther into that silence, as though I had stumbled upon the fold between the earthly and the heavenly world, and the House around me bore mute witness. Who was I, standing there? The quiet passageway regarded me.

A door was shut somewhere in the back regions of the house. Then came a sound of footsteps that returned me to myself. Here I was, after all—Maisie Thomas. I crossed over, stepping softly down the carpeted hall, and opened the door to my bedroom. My parents' room lay directly adjacent to mine, an armoire disguising the door connecting the two rooms. The Grange who had built this house had been a thrifty man, for the walls, though numerous, were not thick. I was long accustomed to falling off to sleep in the summers to the sound of my parents' muffled conversations, and, in particular, to my father's voice, his words often unintelligible but his tone insistent and amused.

Once I overheard Great-Aunt Julia remark dryly that my father's love for my mother "certainly was lively." I did not understand her meaning and watched my parents closely to see if I might observe the nature of that liveliness. It is true that my parents were a handsome couple: Though my father was twenty years my mother's senior, his shock of white hair curled above his pleasing ruddy face like a fleecy cloud and made an admirable contrast to my mother's jet black hair and darker complexion. I cannot think of the two of them together without imagining my father pacing back and forth in front of my mother's seated figure, gesticulating as he told her a story pulled from his day, or outlining a design for some new project. Lively, my papa certainly was—and often I heard my mother give him back a delighted silvery laugh when they thought they were alone.

Jessie had already prepared the room for the change to dinner, and my sheerest blue linen dress lay stretched upon my bed. But the lingering light at the open window drew me, and the salt air bade me breathe. I put my hands upon the sill and closed my eyes, the light slanting cross my lids like a warm hand.

"Must Maisie marry?" I heard Papa ask distinctly, his question lazing in the air outside my window. My eyes flew open. Mama's reply was indistinguishable from the breeze through the pines. I pushed the window up as wide as I could without making any sound.

"I know that, my love. And she has your charms—all of them."

Again, my mother murmured a hazy reply.

"Nonsense, Libby. She shall stay with us at Two Pierpont, type my contracts, continue her studies, and live happily between us as she always has." Now I heard the teasing note in Papa's voice. The whiff of his pipe accompanied his words as they reached me there at the window next to his. A breeze slapped the line against the flagpole, and the sound beat out until it seemed to gather shape in my ear—*marry, marry*—like the hum of a distant train approaching, growing louder and louder.

Flushed and annoyed, I turned and walked around my room, seeking distraction. I picked up the hairbrush and began vaguely to take out my pins, then stopped abruptly, my eye stuck upon the blue cover of *The Mill on the Floss*. My eyes filled again, for the ghosts and the girls. I looked in the glass and started to find that I had half-undressed myself—my hair come loose from its Psyche knot and lying down about my shoulders, my dress opened at the neck and cuffs.

Leaning into this sight, I regarded the face there. Her thick hair was parted down the center and hung loosely on either side of her face before it was caught up at the nape of her neck, her pale skin shining out from amidst that luxuriant dark mass, giving the effect of a lit stage appearing from behind the parting curtains. Her dark brown eyes were round and bright, and they stared back with a hunger I recognized, looking directly at me, her hand holding her hair from her neck so the white length gleamed in the mirror. The shoulders a little high. The eyebrows a trifle thick. The soft lines of her chin and mouth below a cool eye, considering.

"And what do *you* want, my princess?" I whispered to the girl in the glass. But she broke into pieces at the sound of her own voice, and the image of beauty shivered into my flushed cheeks, my crystal earrings, the unbrushed hair curling and untidy around my face. The first dinner bell sounded below. "I renounce all of it," I said aloud and portentously, though my hands still did their business, reaching for the buttons behind, pulling my tea gown from off my shoulders, and letting the gray silk slide from me, leaving it to pool around my boots on the floor. I stepped from it and turned to take up the dinner dress Jessie had readied. Again I regarded myself, my hands fastening and arranging, my eyes steady on my task. I pulled my hair up and off my forehead, sweeping it back with a dark green ribbon upon which I had sewn three tiny periwinkles last summer. The second bell sounded.

"Maisie?" Mama called from the passage. "Are you ready?" In answer, I opened the door to them, and without speaking, turned back into the room to lower the gas by the dressing table. I caught Papa's stare as I passed by the mirror, and suddenly I wanted it all to stop—this silvery slide into men's eyes, into the story told generation after generation of breathless lovers brought into the hushed house where efficient, silent women polish the brasses of a twilight dream. I leaned and looked again at the girl in the glass and shivered. Wasn't I just like Halcy after all? For here I was—dressed to play the romantic heroine. How easily was I cast. Stop! I wanted to call to Mama and Papa. But my parents had begun to descend the stairs, and all I could do was to follow them.

The guests were assembled in the sitting room, awaiting the summons to dinner, the entire party, it seemed, now bent on forgetting, or not mentioning, the tragedy of the morning. My gaze lit on Cynthia and Ruth arranged together in the far corner in a diorama of fetching young womanhood, slowly turning the pages of one of Mr. Audubon's big picture books, exclaiming at the mysteries of the nature painted there and wondering aloud at the various names. I could see they played at a charming lack of interest in the several young men standing by the fireplace. Dr. Lewes and his wife conversed with the Harringtons, and it was to this group that my own parents moved. I drifted to the piano behind Cynthia and Ruth and stood there awkwardly, fingering sheet music with a great degree of absorption.

"Oh look!" I heard Cynthia exclaim, and I turned round.

An elderly woman flanked by two strikingly fair young men had appeared in the doorway. And much to my surprise, Papa rushed forward to greet the trio, shaking one man's hand vigorously and bowing to the woman. A brief conversation ensued and then Papa led the three over to Mama and the Harringtons.

"May I present Mrs. Lanman of Boston?" Papa said. Mr. Harrington bowed to the lady. "And her two sons, Mr. David Lanman"—the smaller one bowed self-consciously—"and Mr. Jonathan Lanman." The latter took Mr. Harrington's offered hand and nodded politely to the female members of the group.

"Mr. Jonathan Lanman," Papa announced, "is a new partner in the line. He will be the fourth man in the New York office."

Mr. Harrington congratulated Mr. Lanman on his post. "And," he continued jovially, "what a glorious stroke to join the fray down on Wall Street, rather than to continue languishing among those Boston straitlaces!"

Mrs. Lanman smiled, but her son stiffened visibly. "My father was of old Boston stock, sir, and I was proud to 'languish' there, as you say."

"Well, Jonathan, I think no offense was meant." My father chuckled. "Just another indication, I'm afraid, of how ill-mannered we southerners are in the babel of Manhattan."

Mama leapt into the breach. "And Mr. Lanman," she said, addressing the younger brother, "are you also an aspiring shipping magnate?" He blushed and mumbled, "No, ma'am." And despite Mama's welcoming attention, he did not elaborate, indeed seemed incapable of continuing any sort of conversation. Mrs. Lanman, however, turned toward Mama, asking some small question about the weather here, and Papa took the opportunity to engage Jonathan Lanman in a slight business matter.

I turned away to look out upon the twilight, the sharp tops of the trees cutting a ragged black line along the sky streaked with clouds and the leftover color of the day. Leaning my forehead into the glass, I was aware of Cynthia's figure standing beside me, shed of Ruth for a rare moment and able to rest quietly there.

There was a moon that evening, just rising, a bright white orb in the darkening sky. We both lifted our eyes to it and watched in silence as it topped the tree line of the near cove.

"Mother, I will," said Cynthia, and then she turned to me, her face grown unexpectedly solemn. "Do you remember that phrase, Maisie?"

I shook my head, mystified.

She smiled and turned back round to that moon, resting both her elbows upon the sill, her face tilted up to the light. "It is what Jane Eyre calls back to the moon, on the dreadful night where she is in danger of losing her soul."

"To Rochester?"

Cynthia nodded.

I smiled. "I detest that scene. I think she should have stayed with him the whole while, and never left."

"And never met the Rivers?"

"Never left the side of the man she loved."

Cynthia frowned at me over her shoulder. "She would have forfeited her soul!"

"Because her lover was married to a madwoman?"

"Yes."

I shrugged, enjoying the consternation I caused in Cynthia, then grandly proclaimed, "Love is love; there is altogether too much fuss made about marriage."

"Maisie!"

I had shocked her, and when the bell rang us into dinner, she hurriedly joined her parents. I lingered at the window for an instant, looking back up at the moon. *My daughter, flee temptation,* the moon had cried. And Jane Eyre had answered, *Mother, I will.* But that night, the sky appeared to me filled with motherless daughters, and the moon's face seemed to be Halcy's peering down.

CHAPTER FOUR

G range House slowed and quieted in the days following
Halcy's and Henry's deaths, the afterclap of their loss heard
in the hush belowstairs and all about the House, as if a breath
were taken but not released—until the plain pine coffin drew slowly
forward through the front door.

I watched the three women of Grange House pass by in the open
cart bearing Halcy to her grave. At opposite ends of the cart bench,
Cook and Miss Grange sat mute and frozen, struck into a strange
resemblance by their uncompromising sorrow. Between them sat Mrs.
French, who could not keep herself from leaning over to Cook and
whispering encouragements with each forward step of the horse,
though Cook stared straight ahead, unhearing. Just as the cart vanished
from sight, I saw Miss Grange look back once, as if she had been called.
Then she turned right round and placed her hand upon Halcy's coffin,
and she left it there as they passed through the trees upon the road
toward Middle Haven.

The following morning, I arose and instinctively lifted the curtain
to look down the lawn, as if I might spot Halcy there. The blue waters

shone back like shook foil. July arched overhead. I let fall the gauzy stuff.

And that day passed, and then the next, and another, until a full week had gone by since she had drowned. With slow returning life, the House started up, its meals eaten, small excursions ventured upon, the fires in the evening banked, then stirred again at dawn. Gently, inexorably, the terrible incident was carried under by the quiet force of summer. Gradually, the guests grew familiar and lazy, the city politesse thrown off and formal names, like hats and gloves, set by and left, to be taken up again in autumn. Eatons, Harringtons, Hunnowells, Havemeyers, Lamonts, Phillips, McGoverns: All became loose dots upon a landscape of summer, dark trousers tucked into high clamming boots, shell aprons tied over white cambric blouses—groups that met and formed, walked out or sat, accompanying one another across the green lawn.

One afternoon, I stood deep among the raspberry bushes at the side of the House, pulling the ripe berries from their stems, the juice staining my fingers in a vain protest. My hands ventured carefully among the thorny stems and green leaves, determined to overcome the watchdog vines in search of my prize. The heavy droning of the bees hung about me, partners in delight at the sun and the rich smell of the earth and the fruit. I knew myself to be the only picker at that hour, and I said a silent congratulation on my enterprise as the bowl behind me filled.

"But then, what is it you mean to *do*?" Mrs. Hunnowell's voice burst out upon the piazza above me. I crouched farther down so as to pick unremarked.

"Do, Mater? Whatever do you mean?" Mr. Hunnowell teased.

"With your time, Bart. Your time. It is several years since you returned from Tunisia—this letter of your father's is a grand proposal."

He snorted.

"Why ever not? Your books were a great success."

Now there came an overly dramatic sigh—still, he was light.

"They certainly were," Mrs. Hunnowell insisted. "Why not capitalize? If you don't wish to take up Father's business in the Far East, then why not pen a little collection of tales, such as gentlemen do—"

"Gentlemen," Bart broke in hurriedly, "can rarely spare the time to write."

"Oh?" Now Mrs. Hunnowell was affronted. "And what of Sir Walter Scott?"

"Sir Walter Scott wrote the same story over and over and over again." Bart had seated himself on the verandah railing. "Adventure! Romance! Country! Tra la! In any event, Mater"—the slack, teasing voice suddenly tightened with regret—"I am no writer. I cannot plot. I can only watch—and comment."

"Well, dear," his mother began brightly, " 'They also serve who stand and—' " I looked up. Bart Hunnowell had departed mother and conversation and was halfway down the lawn.

A terrific racket broke out just then upon the piazza. Mrs. French had gathered the children staying at Grange House to pick raspberries for a tea cake, and as they ran down the wooden steps of the House with their bowls in their hands, descending on the patch and on my solitude, I rose up and watched. Mrs. French stood at the front of the piazza, directing three of the children toward a clump of bushes farther down the lawn, waving with one hand distractedly as she held her dog in the other.

Hattie and Sylvia Havemeyer strayed shyly toward me, clutching their bowls to their chests.

"Do you have some berries, Maisie?" they whispered.

"Berries? There aren't any berries around here," I said firmly, and stepped in front of their view of my full bowl. They halted, nonplussed. Sylvia fidgeted with her apron; the older of the two, she wasn't quite sure whether they had suddenly entered into a game of my design or whether, in fact, there were no berries at all. She opened her mouth to ask again; then suddenly, both she and her sister shouted with laughter, dropping their bowls and clapping their hands at something behind me.

I whirled round to catch Bart Hunnowell holding aloft my bowl of fruit and making a great show of eating the berries one at a time, throwing a raspberry up into the air and then tossing his head back to catch the falling fruit directly into his open mouth. I moved to grab my bowl from him, but he nimbly sidestepped my reach and started away across the lawn in front of the House to the bordering fields, the bowl held high above his head. The girls started running back down the lawn to catch him, and the other little ones, seeing a game, ran after. Suddenly, he stopped, turned around, and waved at me, as if to challenge me to come after my own harvest. In spite of myself, I smiled—against the dulling yellows of the field grasses, his masculine form breathed color and life, and his brown arms, raised higher than the reaching hands of the jumping children, made of his body a taut and sturdy line, a mast amidst the swell of childish bodies hurling themselves against him. In that moment, and seen safely at a distance, Bart Hunnowell appeared to me to be burning with the pure flame—more, to be the single flame itself—filled with a vital warmth, of life. Of living. I smiled.

Jonathan Lanman stepped out upon the piazza just at that moment and stopped, one foot upon the top stair, arrested by the happy chaos in the fields, his hands in his pockets and his mouth pursed in what might have been a silent whistle. He stood looking at the group in the fields for a good long while, his head cocked a bit to one side, as though he were in a picture gallery, changing his stance every so often for a better viewing. His clothing abetted this appearance, for though the day was warm, still he wore his jacket and tie. But there was a passion in the manner of his gaze that belied the calm appearance of a merely appraising gallerygoer—he stared at the children as though he saw through them into a grander arrangement, as though they represented something larger than themselves. Could he see it, too? Life, sheer abundant summer *life,* careening joyous and wild before us in the field.

The sight, with its infectious joy, made me bold, and suddenly I wished to speak aloud of it to this man, for Papa clearly held him in high regard, and the past weeks had left me not insensible to the good sort he was. Often I had observed him handing his mother into her chair, or sailing with his brother, and I had noted how easily he managed the turn from family man to businessman as he discussed office topics with my father. In my presence, however, he remained quite silent, forever polite, a bit grave, and thus somewhat tantalizing.

"What do you see, Mr. Lanman?" I had stolen from the raspberry patch cross the lawn and nearly to the steps.

He started and turned to look at me below him. I must admit, I had startled myself with my question. But once tossed, it could not be retrieved—there it floated aloft between us.

"Ehmm." He colored slightly, then stepped down one of the broad stairs of the piazza as if to go join the group he had been watching.

"Forgive me," I said, "I did not mean to embarrass you."

But now his face flooded with color. "I'm not embarrassed in the slightest, Miss Thomas," and he bowed toward me. I stepped upon the lowest of the stairs. He smiled.

"I was just considering the beauty of this scene."

"The beauty?"

"Yes, how fine these old grasses are and how vibrant the man and then the children surrounding him—how the sea around them also serves to remind us of our own short lives, the sea eternal and man ephemeral"—he chuckled ruefully—"or something like that."

"You have quite a terrible idea of beauty, Mr. Lanman," I declared.

He crossed his arms, playful but attentive. "And what is so terrible in that?"

I climbed two more of the steps between us. "You indicate that what is beautiful must remind us of our insignificance."

He did not smile. "I believe it must."

"Then she is a very schoolmarm." I smiled, but I, too, was serious. "Yet I do not think beauty need teach us anything."

"What, then, is its function?" And now his tone condescended, just slightly, to me.

I shook my head and pursed my lips, then drew a large circle into the air with my finger.

"Nought," I whispered. "Beauty—"

"Beauty is never for nought, I hope," he interrupted, and then, indeed, he smiled at me, raising an eyebrow. "You should know that better than most, Miss Thomas."

I felt a tiny shiver of pleasure at what was clearly meant to be a compliment, and I returned his smile. Indeed, what did it matter that I did not quite agree? I turned to look again at what he saw. But now the scene had entirely altered, and its comfortable distance was soon to vanish, for Bart Hunnowell was walking back up the lawn directly toward us, my white bowl in his hands.

"Miss Thomas, I believe this is yours?" Bart advanced to the bottom of the steps and stopped there, holding out the bowl. I looked quickly back over my shoulder.

"Yes, Mr. Hunnowell, you know that it is."

Following my glance, Bart smiled and drew an inch closer, addressing Mr. Lanman above me.

"Excuse me, Jonathan. I do not mean to interrupt, but you see Miss Thomas and I have some small business matter to attend here."

"*We* were just speaking of beauty, Mr. Hunnowell"—I took one step down to him, the quicker to end this little encounter—"never business."

"Ah, Beauty." He grinned up at me. "Do you wish your raspberries back?"

I crossed my arms over my chest, determined to pin him down. "No. I wish to know your views on the subject."

He looked at me and then at Mr. Lanman, raising a hand to shield his eyes as he considered us. I had caught him.

"Beauty is genius," he answered seriously.

"Ha!" Mr. Lanman guffawed behind me. "Rossetti! I detest Mr. Rossetti."

"*Rossetti?*" I asked.

"Mr. Dante Rossetti," Bart answered, "a man—"

"Who wrote this about his mistress," Jonathan broke in, and then began to recite dismissively:

> "*Beauty like hers is genius. Not the call*
> *Of Homer's or of Dante's heart sublime,—*
> *Not Michael's hand furrowing the zones of time,—*
> *Is more with compassed mysteries musical;*"

There he halted, his disdain a bit heavy in the air.

"I have not heard that poem," I mused.

"And what is so detestable in that, Jonathan?" Bart Hunnowell set down the bowl.

40

"Detestable? He sets the creations of great masters beside a single woman and finds *them* wanting."

"But he is right: Beauty is caught—it is not made." To my surprise, Bart had come to stand quite close, drawn intently to the conversation. "It is but a glance, quicksilver—the flash of fire before it is gone." He had both hands on his hips.

"Yes, but that quicksilver, as you call it, does not understand itself."

"I beg your pardon?"

"Rossetti sets a standard for beauty based on mystery—on the incomprehensibility of a woman he loves."

"And should the beloved be other than incomprehensible?" Mr. Hunnowell had shifted the talk, his whole body gone quite still.

"I should hope," Mr. Lanman declared, "to know and understand thoroughly the nature of the beloved."

"I should never wish such a thing," Bart Hunnowell replied quietly.

"Why?" My girlish voice sounded a little odd cast in between them.

"When my beloved is incomprehensible, she is endless," he said. "And I would follow her into that blank unknown."

"Oh," said I. Mr. Hunnowell had answered me as if I were not a marriageable girl whose head might spin at such talk of love. He had answered me with passion, with passion for an idea. I felt suddenly that I stood alone in a quite capacious room and the air was lovely.

Jonathan Lanman coughed. "Perhaps Miss Thomas would like her berries, Mr. Hunnowell."

It broke the spell. He looked at me and smiled. "Miss Thomas"— he stooped and picked up the bowl—"answer me this first."

"What is it?"

"How many berries are there in this bowl?" He spoke quite low, as if we were in secret negotiation.

"What does it signify?" I did not look at his face, but kept my gaze upon his hands around the porcelain.

"Ten? Thirty? A score?" There was laughter in his voice.

I did look straight at him then. "What is it you wish, Mr. Hunnowell?"

"A single one." Something soft crept forward from his tone.

I raised my voice and waved my hand grandly. "You may have one—choose your pleasure."

He reached into the bowl and picked out a large berry. Then he bowed and put the whole bowl at my feet, and as he rose, he took my hand in his and peeled open my fist to put the raspberry in the middle of my palm.

"For you, Miss Thomas, a keepsake from my morning's harvest." And then he turned and strolled down the lawn toward the pier.

"He is something of a puzzle," Jonathan Lanman observed from the top of the stairs.

"Yes," I said, my eyes on Bart Hunnowell's retreating back, "he is." And I did not turn immediately round, my hand still holding the berry at its center.

"Hunnowell," Jonathan continued. "I have done some business with his father."

I glanced back at him, determined to return to the conversation we had begun earlier and clarify what I had meant about beauty. But his head was now tipped back in reflection, his fingers playing among his blond whiskers, and I saw he had vanished from this scene, become suddenly an office man. Disappointed, I crossed my arms over my chest and scraped the toe of my boot upon the stair, not unused to this masculine habit of disappearing from intelligent conversation at the first mention of business, as if a pair of well-shod heels had clicked smartly together in the man's head.

"Though he does not hold a candle to your father," he said aloud.

I stared at him, pleased and surprised. The man had not vanished at all.

"Of course not," I answered. "My father is the greatest of men."

He smiled at my hyperbole. "How fortunate for you."

"Indeed," I replied. And then, not liking to lose this easy informality, I pushed forward. "Tell me of your own father."

Jonathan Lanman turned back to face the water. "He died when I was very young—too young to have but one memory."

"What is it?"

He shook his head and then looked at me. "It is nothing, an insignificance."

42

"Surely not if it is your only recollection." Still I probed, though I could see the questions pressed a bit too hard upon him. Again he shrugged.

"He stood against the window, very tall. And he was holding out to me a piece of sugar candy."

"And did you take it?"

Now he smiled sadly at me. "I do not recall."

I did not speak again, flooded suddenly with the image of my own father seated across from me in the schoolroom and then, peculiarly, of the warmth of his breath as he leaned across me, pointing up mistakes in my translations.

"I should very much like to live up to his name," Jonathan said quietly.

"His name?"

"Yes. My name."

"I am sincerely sorry for you, Mr. Lanman," I said softly.

Now he turned right round where he stood to face me squarely. "Why should you be sorry?"

"A name is so little." His eyes widened and I hurried to explain myself. "Such a small thing to have of your father's, compared to his guidance and his"—I looked away—"warmth."

"You are entirely mistaken, Miss Thomas. A name is never small," he said hotly. "My name is my father in me. It is him restored to the world through me."

I nodded, stirred by his vehemence, though I chafed at his dismissal of my remark. Before I could think what to respond, he took my hand in his and gravely shook it.

"Names are like hands, Maisie Thomas. When I proffer mine to another, I am sure it speaks of a good grip, of a manly character."

"Well, I cannot take up your metaphor," I said breezily, "as women's hands are often gloved—and our names are more like frocks."

He grinned, easier now, and released me. "A womanish thought, if ever I heard one. For you will put yours off before long, I should imagine, and take up that of a husband's."

I did not look at him. "No, you mistake me. I did not mean that at all."

43

"No?"

"No. I merely meant that a name is nothing but words—like cloth, like gauzy stuff. It is nothing."

He coughed. "Perhaps you might feel differently once you have entered your married name?"

"And why might that be?" I asked him somewhat crossly, unable to tease any longer.

"It is the name with which you face the world in full possession of all your powers." He smiled at me, his meaning unmistakable. "Of all your considerable powers, Miss Thomas." And then he bowed and excused himself.

"Stuff!" I said to his departing back. I turned round to face the lawn once more, took hold of my skirt, and curtsied to the view; we had had our little conversation. "Stuff!" I said again.

"What brave words, Maisie Thomas."

I looked round to find Miss Grange standing in the shadow of the door.

"Hello," I said, made suddenly shy and glad all at once. She pulled her shawl more closely round, her hands remaining in the wool crossed at her neck while she regarded me with a bemused expression. *She* would understand what I had tried to explain to Mr. Lanman.

"I have missed you, Miss Grange," I blurted.

She stepped out of the shadow and onto the piazza, and I saw the terrible toll the past two weeks had taken. Now, indeed, she was paler than ever I had seen her, and shrunken slightly. My heart constricted for my old friend. Though she had been no relation, clearly Halcy's death was deeply felt, and I thought such grief to be yet another testament to Miss Grange's great spirit. I crossed the few feet between us and took her arm. She patted my hand, and we walked to the top of the piazza stairs and looked companionably together upon the view.

Down on the great rocks at the end of the lawn stood three or four guests idly fishing, their uneven heights a ragged echo of the chopping waves beyond. Scraps of their comments blew backward and up to us in single words, the only movement among them the lift of a wrist as a man shifted the angle of his line. Bart Hunnowell stood at the end of this line of men, neither fishing nor speaking, just regarding the water. Perhaps the flash of our dresses upon the piazza had caught his eye, for he turned round, and seeing us standing there together, he took off his hat and waved it in greeting.

Miss Grange lifted her free hand briefly in reply. And then, her eyes still upon the men, she said to me, "Come walk with me tomorrow, Maisie Thomas."

"Gladly," I answered, looking across at her, pleased she had not forgotten our little ritual, uncomfortably aware as I spoke that Bart Hunnowell still faced us, watching.

CHAPTER FIVE

It was always with Miss Grange that I took my first walk into the woods behind Grange House, and it was a satisfaction to find myself behind her, following her strict back, remembering the path once again as I stepped along it, carefully, and studiously, as if it were a line I retraced with my copybook pen.

Though Mama quailed at the dark overhung silence of this interior forest whose bosky corridors appeared to her unhealthy, I was not so faint. In here grew an utter disregard for place or decorum—the bright grass blazed from the backs of rocks and small roots sprung up through the dank mosses. A man on horseback might never find his way through, as the trees above leaned low and heavy across the path. Witches'-broom hung from the balsam boughs, which cast off pine-cones tiny as a child's thumb. Yet in me, the hush of these summer woods refrained—as the trees shifted, creaking in a slight breeze, the inner strings in my chest quivered back a reply. Familiar and foreign all at once, each shift in the path's direction thrilled, as one thrills to the sight of a thing forgotten come round once more. Again and new, I trod on the damp moss thick as the best Persian spread upon granite.

When I was a child, the great delight in Miss Grange's company had derived from the mysteries of the woods she unlocked before me. Few of the other summer guests ventured to penetrate the back regions of the woods behind the House, preferring instead the yachting pleasures of the open, startling waters of the sea. For some fortuitous reason, I had been singled out as one who could walk alongside the quiet familiar of these trees, and my childish self-regard puffed greatly at the unexpected sympathy grown up between myself and my older companion.

Yet, I admit that in the past few years I had accompanied Miss Grange more and more in order to fathom *her*—the secrets of the woods grow hushed before this woman whose character I could not mark. Though she was quiet, she was not unforthcoming. Though she was solemn, she was not severe. Try as I might, the older I grew, the less certain I was that I could correctly read a particular smile she gave, or a confirming nod of her head. I had begun to watch Miss Grange with the degree of quiet anticipation one usually reserves for a mummer's sleight of hand.

That morning we walked silently along, Miss Grange's basket slung upon a strap soldier-fashion across her chest and back, lending her slight frame an added heft. And though we did not speak, my companion often paused at several spots upon the way and pointed, as if to recall us to the previous journey here, each place a stitch picked up again and knit anew into the continuous correspondence between us. She seemed disinclined to pause in any spot for long, however, as if her finger tapped impatiently upon the page while she waited for me to turn it as I read. I did not mind her lack of attention; indeed, I welcomed it, sensing that though she did not inquire into me, still she watched alongside, her clear, unstated sympathy the very essence of my pleasure in our friendship.

But I could not stop from exclaiming aloud at the violent curve the winter wind had caused in a line of spruce. Trees that had stood new and clear and proud last summer now veered at slant angles one from the other—still living, but unalterably shifted, one blown sideways so relentlessly, its newest branches grew round its neighbor in a lateral crutch.

Miss Grange had stopped beside me. "What is it?"

47

"I cannot say," I whispered. And at first I did not know why I had started at the sight. But then I saw the trees had called to mind how Halcy's arms were wrapped round Henry's neck just so, tight and small around his sturdy frame. I pulled my linen wrap tighter round the light stuff at my shoulders.

"Look there instead." She pointed to a small pine sapling growing at a slight remove from this stand, its trunk grown straight up from a granite boulder, its small roots coiling down around the rock in snake-like fashion to seek the plenishing soil below. I considered the comparison Miss Grange had forced, thinking she meant me to see the old adage about bending with harsh forces played out here among the unsuspecting pines.

"And I am meant to take hope from this one?"

"Hope!" She swung round at me with a laugh. "Heavens above, Maisie Thomas. There is no hope to be found in the spectacle of a sapling struggling for nourishment from a rock—separated from its own soil—" She broke off.

I took her on, playful and serious all at once. "But it has adapted to its situation, Miss Grange."

"Adaptation—yes." Miss Grange stepped backward. "A very woman of the woods," she muttered, as if in converse with a prior thought.

"Miss Grange?" I turned to her.

" 'A woman will be loved' "—my companion's voice had risen and ordered itself into the swayback rhythms of a pedant—" 'in proportion as she makes those around her happy; as she studies their tastes, and sympathizes in their feelings. In social relations, adaptation is therefore the true secret of her influence.' "

"I beg your pardon?"

She smiled at me and performed a slight bow to the tree before us.

"The immortal words of Mrs. Sandford, Maisie—written for the edification of girls, these sixty years past."

"I see," I offered lamely.

"Adaptation"—Miss Grange signaled the poor sapling now become but an analogue for Mrs. Sandford's unfortunate opinion—"is well for a tree, Maisie—never for a woman."

And with that, she adjusted the basket strap, which had slipped down upon her arm, and stepped on.

"Well," I said, and fell in behind.

Far into the heart of the woods we walked, a silent pair, arriving at the old blacksmith's shop around midmorning. Leaning slightly to the left and more derelict than the previous summer, still it stood, defiant and skeletal. From the outside of the shop, one could look straight through the walls into the trees behind, the past winter having blown through the structure, widening the gaps between loose boards and opening holes. I hovered somewhere between a laugh and a word of condolence.

"Poor place." Miss Grange sighed.

"How long has it stood here?"

She shook her head. "My mother brought me here as a child, and it was abandoned even then."

Now this intrigued. Once or twice, Miss Grange had spoken of her childhood, but I had always imagined she had spent it elsewhere. "What an uncanny place to bring a child!"

Something flickered over Miss Grange's face.

"She sat us down here"—she pointed to the threshold stone—"and told us stories."

"What type of story?" I asked.

She drew off her shawl and folded it, then without looking again at me, sat down upon the flat rock in the doorway, closing her eyes as she leaned a cheek against the lichen-covered frame.

"What type of story, Miss Grange?" I repeated softly.

She started, then opened her eyes and fixed me an instant, neither of us moving. Then she shrugged.

"Simple stories. Often, however, she would drift off behind the shop in search of some new mosses for her terrarium, commanding me not to move beyond the shadows in the doorway."

"But shadows move!"

Miss Grange smiled, a bough released from the weight of a perching gull as it lifted.

"Yes, Maisie Thomas. Shadows move. And once I followed a shadow beyond the perimeters of the doorway, and I found there was another shadow just to the side, and so thought to follow that, and then another. And before I knew where I was, I had stumbled on my mother, deep in shadow. . . ."

Miss Grange's voice faltered here. I wasn't looking at her face, watching instead the trees scratching against the worn surface of the shop.

"And was she angry?"

Beside me, Miss Grange blew out her breath.

Unsure of the portent of such a response, I turned my gaze from the shop to the woman. She was still and very white. For an instant, I had the sensation of having been abandoned. Miss Grange had pulled into her own memory so deeply, I could not follow even the traces of her familiar face. Instead, I thought I saw the girl she had been—darting after shadows, the summer wind playing about her in the thick inner woods. I thought I followed her little form around the corner of the shop and saw another woman, younger than Miss Grange and terribly beautiful—her fine spun hair escaping a simple cap of years ago. This woman was on her hands and knees, digging into the mosses with what looked to be a dinner spoon. Frightened, I took a step backward so quickly, my boot caught the hem of my skirt, and I fell. Miss Grange rose up and came quickly to my side, holding out her right hand to pull me up—and her hand was warm.

"Are you hurt, Maisie?"

"No."

We stood together like the trees, stiffly apart but rooted by my vision. For, though I did not ask—would not—I sensed I had imagined something true, a slight scene that the place had planted in my brain, made large, made sightly, by this moment and my companion, as if imagination were servant to suggestion, as if what were real had been pushed aside. Miss Grange said not a word. Passing above us, from far away, a gull cried, and the ordinary world folded in again around us, the sound repeating all the reassurances of a day in the woods in the summer in the sixth year of the last decade of the nineteenth century. The tips of our boots triangled out from under our white-and-gray skirts. We were two women, young and old, standing in the warmth of a July shadow, two light spots between the trees, a human clearing. Around us, the woods chattered and leaned. Between us, there was only silence.

50

"My mother made a terrible mistake once."

Without thinking, I whispered, "I know, Miss Grange. I could see it."

She turned her face to mine, brushing her gray hair back from her forehead distractedly, then rubbing the sides of her dress with her hands. Finally she crossed her arms over her chest and turned away from me.

"So," she said. "You do possess it, Maisie Thomas."

Her assurance made me slightly fearful.

"What is it I possess, Miss Grange?"

Still speaking to the air in front of her, she drew out the words slowly as a catch being pulled from the ocean.

"The capacity to see."

"To see?"

"To imagine"—she turned now to look at me directly—"and so to recognize the hidden story, the hidden life that speaks in charms and whispers and will not show its face, save halfly."

And without looking again at me, she stepped over the rocks that lay strewn between this place and the faint start of another path, where she turned. "Come," she called to me then. "Come, Maisie Thomas, let us go on to the quarry."

"Our task is finished here?" I meant to be playful now, not understanding my old friend's sudden shifts in temper. She smiled and raised her stick. "Our task is finished here."

And though I had the uncomfortable sensation that my playful comment was party to her own design, I fell into step behind her once again, reflecting as I followed upon the Miss Grange who seemed today twin-featured, her known and unknown parts walking before me in plain view as never before. But what she had meant by "our task" remained a question for the trees.

After a little distance, we arrived at the abandoned quarry that lay between Grange House and Middle Haven at the center of the woods. Long before my birth, quarrymen had worked its cold innards, tapping the granite veins until they were sure of the weak spot in the stone where they'd wedge open a seam and cut great chunks of the rock to ship to Boston, New York, and farther south to Philadelphia. It was to the financial promise of this rock that Papa had been drawn so many years ago, and he described once how the granite dust blew upon the sea breeze, and he recalled the small Sicilian men whom the company had hired to work the rock, appearing weary but spruced up in bowler hats and stiff old-fashioned collars, promenading the streets of Middle Haven.

I, however, never stood at the lip of this deep hole without thinking of secrets, for cold water had surged up through the rock with a bottomless green so dark, a stone thrown disappeared immediately, as if grabbed by a lost lady's hand. The spot held about it the cool damp air like to castles and cathedrals, and whispers seemed to sound along the windy and abandoned walls.

It was here at the edge of the quarry that Miss Grange motioned for us to sit, our backs against the natural stone bench made by an old cut in the rock. From her basket she pulled the makings of a country luncheon, bread and hard cheese and two small blueberry tarts, and we settled companionably into our meal. The water lay very still in its granite bowl, the white rock across the way seeming to shine in the sun that penetrated through the surrounding trees. I brushed the crumbs from my skirt and leaned back against the rock, its old warmth stealing through my thin muslin blouse.

"Halloooo," I called out suddenly. Miss Grange started, but she smiled as my smaller, hollow voice returned to us across the water: "Hallooo."

"Surely, Miss Grange, this place is peopled," I remarked gaily to my companion.

"Of course it is peopled," she retorted.

I turned to face her, but she spoke out directly to the water. "There are other stories beside the one we live," she said. "And I intend that word—beside—to be understood quite literally, Maisie. When we walk, the others we might have been step in and out beside us."

I looked down swiftly, thrusting my boot into a clump of moss and upending it. When I looked into the quarry, I saw possibility— of wild imagined occurrences. Instead, it appeared, she saw lost souls.

"The only other story I'd like to hear," I said, deliberately trying to alter an atmosphere that I felt began to border on the lugubrious, "is the one in which the heroine is not directed straight into marriage and then onward to the birthing room. I wish for someone to tell me another story. Tell me *that* story, Miss Grange," I challenged, catching up my skirts and rising from my seat to stand at the lip of that great hole. "For I am sick unto death of mere love stories," I pronounced.

"Good girl," she said swiftly.

I looked back over my shoulder to see my companion's expression and found she stared directly at me now, the words cast down like a glove between us. I turned right round to face her, now fully discomfited by her tone and manner.

She scrutinized me a minute. "The time has come to tell you one of my own stories," she said at last, her gaze still fastened upon me. "And I hope that it may lead you to——" But here she broke off, as though she had said too much.

"Lead me! What do you mean?" My voice sounded cracked in the soft air.

She did not move, but continued to watch; and I did not know if a beast had sprung, or still sat, coiled and waiting, so peculiar had she grown.

"Slant, not straight—for it is truth and phantasm combined," she finally answered, "as are all good stories." Then she raised her arm and motioned me again to come near.

But I stayed my distance from this unfamiliar smiling woman among the rocks. The entirety of this morning, Miss Grange had addressed me as if she thought me to be like her: a woman who had chosen an attic solitude rather than a first-floor life among her kind. And suddenly, this proximity unsettled. "It is late, Miss Grange," I said. "Let us return."

A moment passed, as if my words had lost their way in the air between us.

"Just so," she replied at last, and rose up from her seat. "The tale can be told only in the House." She came to join me where I still stood at the quarry's edge and looked down. Our two forms wavered upon the black water. She reached down and touched the point of her walking stick to the glassy surface, setting us quivering; then she turned to look at me and gave her old smile.

"Come," she said. "I shall tell it to you this afternoon after tea." And then she stepped back from the quarry, turned, and, without looking again at me, started back down the path to Grange House.

CHAPTER SIX

That afternoon, the promise of a story beguiled, hushing the little voice of disquiet summoned up by Miss Grange's odd intensity, and I climbed the stairs into her attic room.

"There!" she said as I paused upon the topmost step. Her voice clattered in the hollow of her room, sounding the depths of that stillness around her. Few entered here but for her, and the room had acquired the pale demeanor and unpenetrated quiet of its single occupant, the attic chamber hanging above the House's lower gaiety like a distant memory. I had been invited up here only twice before, and long ago, when as a child I delighted in visiting an "attic"; but this afternoon I walked the length of the wide chamber and drew in my breath with the sudden unexpected pleasure. Suffused by the afternoon light, the filmy curtains at the windows lifted and lowered as if keeping time to someone's breathing. Here was a room in which a thought could hover and remain.

It ran the length of the house, a pair of high windows at either end where the roof came to a peak, so that when one looked out, one had the sensation of standing in the crow's nest of a clipper ship. Indeed, standing at either of the windows gave an onlooker the full glory of a sweeping view: Out the front pair, one saw the wide swath of green lawn reaching down to meet the white rock of the shoreline, and thence to the sea; and out the back, the constellation of color shifted as the sky crossed the tangle of pine trees that formed the perimeter of the woods behind Grange House, the road to the town running along this edge like the crooked parting in a small child's hair.

Against these back windows, and interrupting the oaken line of bookcases that formed the windows' lower casings, was tucked Miss Grange's writing table. On it lay a red copybook, her inkstand and blotter. There was a large dictionary open to the side. Four blue-and-brandy-colored rugs lay like little woolen pools upon the dark gray of the floor. At the center of the room stood the simple oak bed on which she slept, flanked on either side by the two chimneys of the House, dividing the attic into three separate spheres—beginning, middle, and end—three stations in which to pause: here to write, there to sleep, and, at the end, a place from which to stand and watch.

"Once on a time," Miss Grange began, and I smiled. Sunlight flecked the slant wall behind her. I took a step toward her chair. "There was a family by the name of Grange."

I halted. "This is a story?" I asked.

She nodded, her eyes never leaving my face, gesturing me forward, and I drew cross the distance between us to settle myself at her side.

"Once on a time," she repeated, her hand dropping down to her lap, "there was a quarryman by the name of Roric Grange, a man adamantine in both his passion and his fury, a man who could be gentled only by his wife, of whom he was inordinately proud. Yet his pride seemed to many to be oddly placed, for though the gentlewoman had lived among the townsfolk of Middle Haven for over thirty years, by them she was still considered somewhat curious: 'Fremd,' they called her—the old word doing best, as there was not a new word for her. That she had strode off a boat from Ireland, that she had soon after married the son of the richest man in town, that she had borne him two daughters and a son, that she had, furthermore, been midwife at many of their own children's births did little to soften the stiff fabric of the town's reserve.

"And her husband had done nothing during his lifetime to bridge the gap between his wife and his fellow townsmen, delighting instead in bringing back for her all the newest fineries from New York and Boston, to which he traveled often, and indulging her taste for printed matter of all type, feeding a voracious appetite for books and journals, even the odd almanac so she might chart—or cheat? some wondered—the weather."

Miss Grange paused for a moment as outside a man shouted a greeting to a passing boat.

"Go on." I spoke low, but I think she hardly heard me. Leaning her head against the chair back, she closed her eyes and continued.

"The son, George, had died tragically in a railway accident while down at Harvard College, and then less than one year later, Rorie Grange himself drowned one January night. The house appeared to retreat in its grief, and as the vital link that had stretched between this family and the town had snapped, the women of Grange House were rarely to be seen in Middle Haven, though often a fisherman sailing by the house on the point might catch a glimpse of one of them passing between house and sheepfold, or see a flash of one of their dresses crossing through the trees.

"Yet there were some who now suspected that a slow and fearful rot had gripped the foundations of that manse, creeping cross the sturdy granite. It was too silent suddenly, the fishermen remarked to their wives upon returning home, too strange. Then, too, the good doctor of Middle Haven had been said to receive a visitor to his surgery, and now a subsequent summons to Grange House itself. All in all, the good people whispered, the signs were not favorable.

"Their suspicions were not ungrounded. As Dr. Bates approached the house early one June evening, he regarded appreciatively the fine, hard beauty of the house, classical in its spare lines, though ample in its proportions, regretting once more that he had not been a more frequent visitor to the hearth of his old friend Rorie Grange—or more exactly, to the hearth of his widow. Women should not be too long without the steadying influence of a man, he reflected, and hobbling his horse, he thought uneasily what he meant to say to the daughters who had summoned him to their door. He had little knowledge of the two young women's characters; however, he had hit upon a pre-liminary observation to soothe: Though the Widow Grange's removal of herself and her belongings to the attic was singular, it was not entirely out of the ordinary, given the nature of her circumstances.

" 'When the female of the species undergoes the change in life,' elaborated Dr. Bates shortly thereafter, settled before the Misses Grange, 'she can drift free of her moral compass—and if she is allowed to fix her mind too long on one object, her inner guide may smudge, as when the bodily eye dwells too singly on one color and so cannot see the world but through the taint of that dominating hue.'

"The doctor spoke low and kindly, though he was, if it need be known, not a little embarrassed to be sharing so intimate a meditation on the delicate constitution of the female with that very same female's own daughters. Indeed, there was nothing in the situation to put the poor man at ease. The room in which the conference was held, usually cheerful and warm, had been left to grow quite cold, the servants having fled the House, and the two young women before him too aggrieved by the behavior of their mother to tend to the trivial—what some might call the essential—tasks of sustaining a commonplace in life.

"Nonetheless, the man of science persevered, rubbing his hands together for a spot of warmth and observing to himself as he did so that he had been the only one to have spoken for some many minutes. The two women before him listened—the one upon the sofa directly across, the younger in a chair at a little remove from him and off to the side—neither one taking her eyes from his face, as if to capture every nuance, every slight vibration of small meaning left unsaid but heard in the pitch between his words. The effect being, as I have indicated, that the good doctor wished nothing so much there in the capacious sitting room of the great house as to be firmly ensconced before his own fire, his tattered ottoman beneath his slippered feet, with the glory of distance and a good brandy and soda to put between him and these transfixed girls.

"But now, with their troubled gaze upon him, the doctor could not for the life of him think of a word to say—appearing every bit the speechless suitor rather than the older man of rationality he was to represent.

" 'Why not believe what Mother says,' came a quiet voice from the chair at the man's side. 'That there is someone—'

" 'Hisst, Nell!' cried the elder, startled into motion by her sister's words.

"Thus wrested from his speechlessness, Dr. Bates looked to the younger woman almost thankfully. But what he saw there yielded little comfort, for upon her small, pale face lay the stamp of a fixed idea, her eyes staring and wide from out the mass of her thick hair, left free.

" 'Nay, Susannah,' this one pursued, 'the doctor should know.' And she turned back to address the man. 'Mother has heard voices calling to her.'

" 'Voices?'

" 'A voice.'

"Susannah Grange had buried her face in her hands, but she did not protest again, and, keeping her eyes upon her sister's bent head, Nell proceeded.

" 'In the past week, our mother has complained that she must get higher in the house—higher up, to reach this voice.'

" 'What is the nature of the voice? Does it speak words?'

" 'No.' Susannah's head shot up. 'There are no words, Nell.'

"The younger looked at the elder. 'There are no words,' the elder repeated firmly, and then, as if possessed again of herself and the situation, she turned her full attention upon the doctor, though she pressed a nervous hand to her brow. 'Last night, we heard Mother calling out in great excitement. We ran to the top of the house and found her standing in the middle of the attic, her arms raised up as though she were pleading with someone in the eaves.'

" 'Was there someone else there?'

"The question was met with a disquieting silence it seemed neither daughter wished to break. The intrepid man attempted another question. 'Now, think, if you would, whether there has not been some idea your mother has fastened upon—'

"Low and swift, Susannah interrupted.

" 'She believes she is to be punished now for undetected sins— that is her word, Doctor—sins that she committed when she was quite young.'

"Dr. Bates chuckled. 'That is a common-enough alarm among women at her time of life.'

" 'But she holds great stock in the idea,' said Nell gravely.

" 'Come, come, my dears. What has your good mother to be punished for, eh?'

" 'Precisely,' said Susannah, looking at Nell. 'There is nothing for which Mother need be punished.'

" 'But that is not all.' Nell paid her sister no mind, fixed instead upon the doctor.

" 'Yes?'

" 'She believes that someone has returned.'

" 'I see.' The doctor reflected on this. 'And when did this fixity begin?'

"Susannah Grange blanched and looked down at her hands. Nell Grange looked hard at her, as if to force her sister to raise up her head again, but the elder remained in a mute and frightened silence.

" 'You see,' said Nell Grange at last, 'how we are all affected.'

" 'Aye,' replied the doctor, and he rose to his feet. 'Why not show me up to your mother, then?'

"Nell nodded and moved toward the door, and, taking his leave of Susannah, the doctor followed, crossing the wide hall to the bottom of the stairs, where Nell waited with a candle in her hand. Slowly, they ascended toward the landing at the turn of the wide oak stairway, and as they did so, the doctor could not help but notice that the old house had fallen into some disrepair: The blackened chimneys of the sconces gave assurance the lamps had neither been cleaned nor lit for some time, and from the ceiling of the stairway landing there hung several loose strips of rose paper.

"But the walls themselves spoke of more than disrepair, for upon the paper seemed to sprout small white blotches of mildew here and there, ascending in a sorry pattern of the house's neglect. He shivered. Perhaps it was the chill and the quiet, but he could not shake the sense that he moved slowly within an unquiet mind, and that there on the stairs, the house watched his advance and had begun to call him softly to remark.

"Tonight, through the great window upon the landing, bright clouds streamed across the lowering dark of twilight.

" 'This is my favorite spot in Grange House,' the doctor com-

59

mented, pausing to stop before the window, where below, the dark calm of the harbor lapped upon the rocks. Beside him, Nell Grange had stiffened.

" 'You do not like the water?' he guessed.

" 'How might I'—she did not face him—'when my own father drowned down there? And he the one who had raised us on stories of other children falling into fissures in the granite on the shore, bashed and drowned by the turning tide; or when from here we heard for ourselves the terrible calls from the sailors on board the granite sloop *Mary B.,* who foundered off the breakwater in winds so strong—do you recall?—no aiding boat could put in to save them.'

"He shuddered. 'Yes, I do recall.' An unnatural vehemence marks this woman, he noted—her slight figure turned, as if to punish herself, toward this sea, her face lost in that obscuring mass of hair.

"*In my Father's house are many mansions,* she began to recite softly, and then stopped. He waited. 'But if those mansions do look upon the sea, Dr. Bates, then heaven keeps a view directly into sorrow's rooms, for no frame can protect against such sight as would make the eye wish itself blind instead of seeing.'

"And with that, she turned, gathered her skirt, and began to ascend the rest of the stairs.

"For an instant, the doctor considered that the sickness he had been called to attend within the House was not contained, as it were, to the attic story, but that it crept lightly long the halls and spoke through the teeth and lips of young women.

" 'Dr. Bates?'

"Nell Grange had paused at the top of that short flight, holding her light high. The doctor was forced to follow, and as soon as he had gained her position, she turned and illuminated the long, wide passageway of the second story. Stretched away from them was a hallway, richly carpeted and lined with several chamber doors, pulled to, their china knobs glowing in the dusk. At the far end of this passageway was the entrance to the third story, where the servants slept, and then from there a smaller set of stairs to the attic at the top of the house.

"The doctor needed a bit more time. 'Before we proceed, Miss Grange, may I remark that you seem to differ with your sister about what has been taking place here?'

" 'Yes,' Nell said.

" 'Has your mother ever heard anything—'

" 'Voices,' she corrected.

" 'Yes. Has your mother heard voices before?'

"She set the candle down upon the hall table and crossed her arms. 'Yes. Before this latest, there was a first. Six months ago.'

" 'I see,' said the doctor, sitting himself down heavily upon the hall bench to pursue his thought. 'Near the night your poor father drowned?'

"Nell nodded her head. 'That very night.'

"The doctor sat looking down at the carpet under his feet, unable to train his mind on the problem.

" 'Dr. Bates,' Nell Grange prodded.

"He lifted up his eyes and stared. For she had pressed her two hands against the wall, thumb-to-thumb, so the fingers spread out upon the paper. He started up.

" 'So you *did* note the smudges on the wall downstairs,' she said slowly, and nodded as if satisfied. 'One must stare down one's horror, stare at it straight and look it in the eye, Dr. Bates. It is when one glances away that one is lost, for then the thing is loosed and it can creep round, playing in the mind with its soft, insistent fingers.'

"He forced his voice to speak. 'And what is your horror?'

" 'There *is* something here.' She looked up at the ceiling above their heads. 'Someone.'

" 'Who?'

" 'I cannot say.'

" 'Why, then?'

" 'I do not know.' And then, without another word, she picked the candle from its place and walked the length of that second story, pulling open the door to the stairs. The doctor and the daughter rose another flight in silence, then walked the deserted length of the servants' quarters to the final stair. She pushed open the door at the bottom of the attic stairs and with her candle pointed him up to this last story.

" 'Mother,' she called into the darkness at the top, 'Dr. Bates is here to pay a call.' And then, with a little nod to him, she left him where he stood.

"An answering light moved quickly to the top of the stair, and he proceeded uncertainly up the dark passage toward it. But something caught his attention in the middle of the stair, and he paused, leaning to examine what looked to be a blotch upon the wooden walls, like the ones he had noticed below. He leaned closer and a chill ran down his spine.

" 'Dr. Bates?' A frail voice with a hint of impatience came from behind the lamp above him.

" 'Aye,' the doctor whispered, his eyes still on the spot before him. But it was not what he thought. It was not, not at all, the tiny hand-prints of a child, splayed thumb-to-thumb across the grain. It was a blotch after all, like all the others.

" 'Come up, Morris Bates.'

" 'Aye, I am coming,' and reluctantly he cast one more glance at the spot and proceeded slowly upward once again.

"Beside the candle glow, the widow's face was high and lovely— for her beauty was the light that flares just as darkness falls, hallowed and yet magnificent all at once, though her eyes regarded him wearily.

"But seeing her thus, the doctor had finally landed upon firm ground now, for he recognized the symptoms of what was this woman's final illness. And now he thought he understood the nature of the secret put before him: Death had come to sit upon the woman's heart, and soon, soon his weight would cause her life to slow, then stop. The heightened color in her face, the glitter in her eyes as she watched the doctor approach trumpeted the Old Man's certain advance.

"She gave Dr. Bates her hand, and he took it in his, feeling the chill in the stiff joints. 'Come into my parlor,' she said lightly. And she led them down the huge expanse, lit at the end by a row of single candles. The high pitch of the roof was cast into cathedral heights, it seemed to loom so far above the table. All other parts of the room were darkness, and the two walked to the seating arrangement the widow had fashioned before the attic window.

" 'I am glad you have come,' she said simply.

" 'Yes. It has been far too long since we have met,' he replied.

"They sat awhile in silence. Perhaps his old friend, her husband, was called to mind just then and shared between them in the candle-light.

" 'I am not well,' she began.

" 'I see that.'

" 'In spirit.'

" 'Yes,' he said, and thinking he would not hurry her into speaking of her trouble, he regarded the eaves above her head. But what he saw there upon the wood caused him to start yet a third time that evening. She turned her head and followed where he looked. 'Ah.' She smiled.

"Etched into the eaves behind her, in line upon line like another layer to the grain of the wood, were written what looked to be names. He rose to his feet and drew a step closer, aware the widow watched him. Yes, they were names. The names of women. Lines of women's names carefully written, and scrolling down the roof above the widow.

" 'It is my slight attempt at history,' she said, 'to pass the daylight hours up here.'

"He took one of the candles up from the table and read the names of women in town. *Molly Gowan. Elizabeth McGean. Heather O'Hanian. Frances Drake. Betty. Cecily. Mavis. Ivy.* And away down the slope of the roof they stretched. Women long dead, others still living in Middle Haven, and some merely girls. There must have been three score. Scratched there into the soft wood at the top of the house, these women hung above his head like leaves.

" 'Do they trouble you?' the widow asked.

" 'Hm? No, no. Though there are a few I do not recognize.'

" 'They are Irish girls.' She cleared her throat. The doctor could not keep his eyes from the lists. *Alexandra. Catherine. Diana. Claudia. Faith. Fern. Harriet. McGee. Caroline.* All the names of girls born to the women whose childbeds the widow had attended—he saw it now.

" 'But where are the boys?' he wondered aloud. She stirred behind him but did not answer. After a longer moment, he turned round with the question on his lips. She was fixed upon an empty—an un-marked—place farther up in the eaves.

" 'There is only one,' she whispered. 'And I do not need to write him down. His name is scratched too deep in here,' and she placed her hand upon her chest, though her eyes remained trained upon the roof above them, her head tilted as though she listened past the doctor.

"Despite himself, the doctor glanced quickly where she looked. There was nothing. 'Who?' he turned round and asked.

" 'My son,' she answered. The blue vein at her throat throbbed, and the doctor leaned forward to take her hand in one of his, reaching with his fingers past her palm to the wrist to take her pulse, which raced beneath his touch.

" 'Cassie Grange,' he said gently. 'Poor George lies buried upon the hill in the churchyard.'

" 'Aye, but I had another son—him that I bore before coming. Him that I left for dead.'

"The hand in his trembled slightly.

"And though he did not believe what the widow told him, Dr. Bates did know the best physic for an unquiet mind was understanding, so he asked her gently, 'How came it you left him for dead, Cassie?'

" 'In my mother's arms.'

" 'Ah, that was hard on you.'

" 'Aye.'

"The man and the woman sat together, hand in hand, her pulse beating between them.

" 'The babe was weak unto death with the typhus. I knew it. And the ship was leaving. "You canna bury him at sea, love," my mother said to me. "He is a Gilroy; he should rest by me in Irish ground." And then she took my baby into her arms.'

"Could this tale be true? The doctor thought not, yet it had the raiments of an old hurt the widow yet wore, and so, still thinking as would a physician, he asked another question to ease the imagined hurt further from off her shoulders.

" 'Did your mother force you away, then?'

"The widow looked at him and whispered, 'Nay.'

" 'Ah.' He waited, now growing uneasy.

" 'Nay,' she repeated, a little stronger. 'Nay—I wanted to go. I was frightened'—she paused—'of death.'

" 'No mother can bear to see her baby die,' he began soothingly, but she shook her head.

" 'Nay! I was not such a mother as that yet,' she said softly. 'It was my own death I could not bear.'

"Again she lapsed into silence. Still the doctor held her hand in his, though this was growing to be a bad story.

" 'I turned and looked down the hill to the ship in the harbor, then took a step toward the door, though I knew I'd not see my mother's face again in this world, and never more see that little mouth pipped for my milk, his hands batting at my hair falling cross his face.

" 'My mother's hand fell on my shoulder. "It is right you should do so."

" 'And so I leaned down and kissed my tiny boy and placed both hands on either side of his little face so as to carry the shape of it with me. Then I picked up my satchel and left.'

"She lifted her face and looked at him. 'I left!'

" 'Cassie,' the doctor soothed, seeing her eyes growing wide.

" 'I never buried him, I never wrapped the winding-sheet about his face or eyes.' She withdrew her hand from his. 'I saved myself, but I left my self behind.'

" 'Cassie,' he began again.

" 'And now he is tired of waiting.'

" 'Cassie!'

" 'He wishes to pull us one by one across with his little hands.'

" 'What hands?' the doctor asked sharply, despite himself.

" 'The hands I laid on him in parting, he mimics now—he mocks! For never do I wake without I feel his little hands upon my face. And never does the morning start without I hear him calling "Mama!" just as I open my eyes.'

"The doctor watched her closely, but she hardly addressed him any longer. 'And now he has stepped a little closer. Now he has appeared in the very flesh!'

" 'The flesh!'

"She looked at him through the candles and smiled a patient smile. 'A stranger has arrived into our house who maintains himself to be my nephew—cousin to my daughters—born to my sister back in Ireland years ago.' She stopped, waiting, it seemed, for the doctor's reaction. And when he could give none, she burst out. 'Doctor, have you not guessed the secret?'

" 'What secret?' The doctor was stern.

" 'Think, man! *The stranger below is my son!*'

"He stood and tried to take up her hand again and feel her pulse, alarmed by the sudden drop of color. But she pushed his reaching hand aside and put her own upon his chest to steady him. 'And he wants my girl Susannah also,' she whispered, smiling almost proudly, 'and why not, after all? She is the very mirror of myself—as I did look, the day I left him!'

"He stared at the woman. For a gentle instant, she returned his gaze, until what she saw there was enough, and she raised her body up from the chair and moved past him down the attic room.

"The doctor looked a long while upon his patient. Often he had been the unwitting confessor of the dying, and still more often he had heard this dreadful pain of the mother leaving behind her children, but never had he heard, pulled from the stretched nerves of the soon to die, a story such as this one.

" 'You are overtired, Cassie Grange,' he finally said to her. 'You must rest,' he added more softly, though she did not turn round. 'I will sit beside you, tomorrow.'

"And taking up one of the candles, he made his way silently down the stairs, not pausing to examine the walls, nor bethinking himself of the speed with which he descended silently down through the third and then the second stories until he'd gained the peopled regions of the bottom floor. And there he caught his hat up from off the stand and stood before the candle burning beneath the front hall mirror, where he saw a shaken old man reflected.

"Suddenly, within the verge, there appeared beside him the younger reflection of the woman he had just left.

" 'Dr. Bates,' whispered Susannah Grange. 'How does my mother?'

"He turned to face her. 'Not well.'

" 'Is she dying?'

" 'Yes, my dear.'

"She put a hand upon his arm. 'I knew it. I have felt it in my dreams.'

" 'What dreams?' he asked wearily.

"She drew close to him and lightly placed her hands on his cheeks. He stiffened. 'Like that,' she said, withdrawing. 'Right upon waking, there comes the briefest touch of her hands on either side of my face, as though she wished my attention somewhere, as though she made ready to leave.' Susannah stared at him. 'I am frightened, Dr. Bates. I am frightened of what is to come.'

"The old man could not find voice for a moment.

" 'Help her to rest, Miss Grange,' he managed at last. 'I will return again tomorrow.' And with that, he made quickly for the door. But the door opened with his hand upon the handle and there upon the threshold Dr. Bates was met with the handsome face and steady form of a stranger.

" 'Good Lord, man!' Dr. Bates cried, his heart pounding uncomfortably fast.

" 'This is our cousin, Dr. Bates,' Susannah said at the doctor's side. 'He came to us just two weeks ago.' And turning to gaze at her, the doctor noted the delicate flush that had stolen upward into the woman's pale face.

" 'How do you do, sir,' said the man, offering his hand.

"Dr. Bates turned back to face him. 'Well, thank you,' he stammered, noting the steady warmth of the hand he shook. Then he bid them both a good night and sought the outer door."

Miss Grange's boot scraped against the brass fender before the fireplace as she pushed up to shift her position within the chair. I reached forward to help her and saw with a start that tears had fallen upon her cheek.

"Could you ever imagine a mother such as that, Maisie Thomas?"

The question caught me off guard; I had been flush with the unexpected vision of that stranger. "Miss Grange?"

But she continued on again without further comment.

"Now, Dr. Bates was a Harvard College man, an educated man of reason, and though his reason was wed to a strong belief in the sublime, he was troubled not a little as he pulled the door closed behind him on that dark house, a house of death. He had thought the widow's mind merely to have slipped loose its mooring on the truth, and yet the appearance of the man gave her story a strange kind of dreadful credence.

"And as he caught up his pony's reins and mounted, the phrase Nell Grange had recited swum up again onto the surface of his mind: *'In my Father's house are many mansions: if it were not so, I would have told you.'* Though she had hideously twisted its meaning, he was struck by the coincidence of hearing his own pet phrase upon the lips of the young woman. For though it was unorthodox, this was the phrase the doctor himself had most often used to imagine the unimaginable, especially considering the female sex, plucking this doctrine from its proper place and making of it a gentle reminder of the female body—a promise, as it were, from God. Housed within a woman, the doctor thought, were rooms of undisclosed shapes and sizes, and a woman may live a life and never open but two or three, and live within them quite happily. But there were those who twisted and turned within the windy stairwells of their selves, opening doors to rooms and peering in upon possible worlds unmatched in the exterior.

"But who was the woman who would abandon her dying child? Worse still, who was the mother who would exhort such a breach? That was a room he had not seen before; nor had he supposed it existed within. Yet he could not believe Cassie Grange could possibly have told the truth. It did not stand to reason, he thought, for she had been tireless in her youth at the bedsides of young mothers; hers had been the quickest catching hands, hers the gentlest touch upon the babe newly dropped to our world. How could such a one have left behind her own to die? He dismounted in his stable yard.

"Yet her strange preoccupation bespoke an unquiet conscience. And he thought again of Cassie appearing over and over, often unbidden, to help a laboring mother. As if she wished to be the first to welcome each new soul, he thought uneasily. As if she stood at the gate hoping to see her lost little one come through once more. His hand paused upon his own home gate at such thoughts, and—it must be said—he turned round and stared into the gloom behind him down the road upon which he had just come from Grange House.

"There was nothing. And when Dr. Bates did finally lift the latch upon the little gate and saw the merry face of his own wife appear at the front window at the sound, he stepped lively up the path, eager to push open the front door and enter straightaway into the home region, his own full of warmth and chatter and the distinct possibility of a late-cooked stew. And the good doctor imagined that after the last dish had been dried and replaced upon the shelf, and the simple Annie let go back to her mother with a hot bit of pie, that he and his wife might sit right down next his sister and make a good hash pot of the day.

"But such a happy ending was not to be. For no sooner had he gained his entrance hall, then his sister Agatha appeared, fairly colliding with him in her excitement.

" 'We've Mary Ames here waiting for you.'

" 'What? Abby's daughter?'

" 'Yes,' Agatha said, her knowing eyes upon her brother's face, ready to catch any hint of trouble, 'lately of Grange House.'

"He turned aside and carefully placed his hat upon his own hat-stand, though the trouble of the evening seemed to have followed him home, so it did not appear to matter one whit in which hall he hung his hat and coat.

" 'Well, Mary, what can I do for you?' he asked the girl who waited for him in the snug front parlor, casting only the briefest of glances at his ottoman by the fire. His wife rose and brought him a pipe, good woman, which he took thankfully and walked to his chair.

" 'Have you seen her, sir?' Mary Ames was frightened, and she as steady a girl as he had ever brought into the world.

" 'Whom, Mary?' he asked.

" 'Widow Grange,' the girl said. 'I had heard you were called there.'

" 'Yes." The doctor drew on his pipe. 'I have seen her.'

" 'And?' his wife prodded.

" 'She is not well.'

" 'Nay, sir. She is worse than that,' said Mary.

" 'What do you mean, my girl?' Agatha was sharp in her brother's defense. 'If the doctor says the lady is not well, then that is that.'

" 'Go on, Mary.' Dr. Bates looked at the girl.

" 'It's the whole house, sir,' she whispered. 'The whole House is not well.'

" 'Go on,' he said again.

" 'Have you seen the smudges, sir?'

"His blood ran cold. 'What smudges, Mary?'

"She covered her face in her hands. 'Oh I cannot bear it!'

"The doctor rose immediately and went to the stricken girl. 'There, there now, child. Tell me about the smudges.'

"She took the hands from her face and looked into his eyes. 'Oh, I could not stop them, Doctor. She walked and walked, up and down, up and down the stairs, and up and down and up and down our long hall upon the third story, and behind her as she passed sprang up the marks of tiny hands upon the walls.'

" 'Mercy!' cried the doctor's wife.

" 'I tried to clean them, sir. I did. But there grew to be so many, and then I felt I were cleaning her very inmost parts—'

" 'Mary!'

" 'I cannot help it ma'am. I think that woman is become the house!" And then Mary buried her face upon his shoulder and wept. The doctor patted the girl and nodded at the shocked face of his wife. But his own heart beat loudly in his chest, and he was troubled indeed. Had he not seen what she described with his own eyes?

" 'There Mary,' he said finally. 'Widow Grange is not well. That is all. Do not be frightened.'

" 'Oh, sir, I am frightened for the sisters.'

" 'There now. If I tell you that I have promised to look in upon the House every day, will you quieten?' And though at first the girl seemed inconsolable, after more soft words and several more reassurances, the doctor was able to soothe her and walk her to his doorway, then watch her hurry down the lane toward her home as he stood there in the cool of that June evening. But down the harbor, across from the tip of the breakwater, the light at Grange House landing did not shine where it ought.

" 'Aye, but the house is a beauty,' Dr. Bates remarked as he returned to his hearth.

" 'Bad bedrock, I would say, for beauty,' Mrs. Bates retorted.

" 'When there's a one can build beauty from this rock and pineland, unforgiving as a bad judge, I say, Godspeed.'

" 'Agatha!'

" 'Yes, my dear. I do believe it.'

" 'There was a stranger there,' remembered Dr. Bates suddenly.

" 'A stranger!' both women cried.

" 'Aye, a nephew.'

" 'A nephew,' Agatha repeated. 'There is no such thing. All the Granges rest up the hill.' She nodded in the direction of the cemetery.

" 'Of hers,' said the doctor.

" 'Humph,' said his sister.

" 'Oh,' said his wife.

"The fire popped.

"The next morning, several other calls kept the doctor from his promise to sit with Cassie Grange. After he had finished his dinner that afternoon, he saw the mercury had dropped, and as he stood in the window of his front room, he was of two minds about venturing forth to Grange House—whether to beat the storm or follow after.

" 'It looks dreadful, Morris.'

" 'Yes, the weathervane's just turned to the northeast. I'm afraid the blow will be mighty.'

"There was no rain, but a terrible moaning wind had sprung up, and it banged open the front door, causing the two of them to start. As the doctor went to close it, he noted a dense cloud lowering over the harbor. The dinghies bobbed wildly at their moorings. He slammed the door to, though he felt the wind buckle the wood beneath his hand, as if a heart beat back through the board.

"The sky had so darkened around the house that suddenly they were cast deep into shadow, and Agatha called to Annie to come quick and light the candles in the front rooms. Still the doctor remained where he stood in the front hall, looking through the windows at the violet sky undercut by a menacing shadow seeming to advance from across the bay directly into the harbor. And, from where he stood, he made out the black roofline and two chimneys of Grange House above the trees at the edge of the water. He watched the roof, though for what, he did not know, but suddenly he felt he had been drawn to his post at the window, as if called there by some unseen voice.

"Just then, a crash of thunder split open the heavens directly overhead, the *crack* brimming over the thick sides of the clouds, repeating all the long way down the harbor. There was a preternatural burst of a sickly green, followed by the echoing crack of the companion thunder. Another crack came, this one louder than the first, and longer—as though two enemies waged battle overhead, the one shaking and snapping the very bones of his opponent loose.

"And then a blinding light sliced down through the center of Grange House's roof. Not stopping to give word or explanation, the doctor grabbed his cloak from off the hook, flung open the door, and began walking fast as he could down the road to Grange House. There came another crack, a horrible sound.

"The trees above him bent and scraped and the wind still keened a high note in the air. He scurried forward, his heart racing, his eyes fixed on the distance. He had been walking nearly twenty minutes when he spied a cart and cart horse galloping down the road toward him, and the doctor saw Nell Grange whipping the creature to a furious pace, so fast that he worried she might not be capable of stopping. But she had seen the man and slowed to a canter, then a trot, and stopped before the doctor, panting with her horse, and bent to reach down a hand and pull the doctor up.

" 'Come!' she cried.

"As the pair made their frantic way back to the House, the skies pealed louder and louder overhead. 'I fear I have done a terrible thing,' she gasped out into the wind, whipping the horse faster, tears streaming down her face.

"Dr. Bates clutched the side of the cart. 'What is it?'

"Nell shook her head to clear the tears from her eyes, her hands holding fast to the reins. 'Mother wished us to carry her tub to the attic, and Susannah protested on account of the storm.' A sob strangled in Nell's throat. 'But then Mother insisted. She was frightful in her panic for the tub—and I do not know what I did anymore, Doctor. I grabbed the thing and dragged it up the stairs and called to Susannah to bring the water for a bath.'

" 'With this storm?' Dr. Bates could not keep the dismay from his voice.

"Nell nodded grimly. 'I could not bear it, Doctor. I followed my mother's orders, and pushed the copper tub directly beneath the highest peak in the roof.' She sobbed again. 'And then, Doctor, I came for you.'

"Thunder crashed about their heads. Nell stifled a moan and

whipped the horse with a fury, though they could see the white of the house appearing through the trees at the end of the road. But now the wind had shifted again and the smell of smoke and the ruffling sound of a great fire assaulted them upon the road. The horse reared up at the smell, nearly throwing them from the cart; never had the doctor seen a woman so intent and so terribly calm, for she handled the horse and compelled it forward again, nudging it and gentling it all at once. So, more slowly they drew closer to the house, where it seemed the storm had concentrated its full fury.

"There was a drop of wind suddenly, as though the world rushed away before turning to deliver one last mighty smack—and just as the doctor and Nell Grange appeared in sight of the House, the first great towering flame shot straight up through the roof and into the sky. Nell screamed and threw herself down from the cart, running up the lawn. But another flame burst from the third-story windows, and the woman was pushed back from the house by the wave of heat.

" 'Susannah!' Nell shouted. 'Susannah!' The roar of the wind and fire was her only answer. And she stared upon the ghastly spectacle of her mother's and her sister's bier, raging above her head like one of the Furies, the flames reaching out through the holes in the roof in determined bursts toward the sky.

"Behind him, the doctor heard the church bells ringing.

" 'Thank God!' he said. 'The town's alerted!'

"Nell turned hollow eyes on him.

" 'What does it matter?' she cried. 'Everything will be gone if they are.'

"The spine of the roof cracked suddenly, and one of the chimneys fell into the open mouth of the burning story, while the other half of the roof swayed in the gust of the fire, slowly dancing above its end.

" 'Look!' Nell shrieked. And the doctor saw the stranger standing in the gash in the attic the fire had made, the two women slung on either shoulder. He wavered there above their heads, at the lip of the opening in the house, his face and clothes entirely blackened by the smoke. For an instant, the doctor imagined he could be of help to the man and stretched his arms up. For an instant, it seemed the man looked down where the doctor stood, considering.

7 3

"And then he stepped off into the air and plunged the four stories to the ground.

"The doctor closed his eyes as if to clear his sight, then opened them upon the three fallen bodies before him. And, his heart racing, he approached, one small corner of his mind appraising the desperate angles at which they were flung, calibrating the slim hope of survival. Dimly, he was aware of Nell Grange still standing behind him as he reached the bodies; so it was for her that he tended first to her mother, gently rolling Widow Grange over and brushing the hair from off her face.

"He sprang back in horror just as Nell gave out a shattering scream. For a mad moment, they both regarded the thing. And then Nell, wordless, bent down to draw her sister's hair from off her face.

"And there indeed it was repeated. Like the smudges on the walls, on her cheek were stamped the marks of two tiny childish hands."

CHAPTER SEVEN

A long while after she had finished speaking, my eyes and ears were full of the crackle of fire and the gasp of silence that surrounded Nell Grange as she gazed down upon her mother and sister, and I had the sensation of having fallen through Miss Grange, into a hidden world, into the throng of voices contained within. And how vast, how wide a view of human character she possessed. No longer frightened by her urgency, there in the thrall of her voice and of the scenes she had spoken before me, I knew a gift had been bestowed upon me by my old friend—a gift, indeed a kind of grace. That is what she had meant by the rocks. She must tell it to me because she could see that I would take up this strange, fantastic flower and recognize its sorrow and magnificence. Never before had I glimpsed the multitude inside her, or the wild imagination that roamed free, burning down the very house. This very house—but there I stopped.

I fancied the air before me shimmered as I swam back up, my eyes refocusing upon the attic room in which I sat; I could not resist casting my eye upward at the eaves above me, and as quickly looked away.

Of course there were no names scratched there. Nor was there a trace of fiery damage upon the slanted walls. After all, it was not a Gothic chamber, but a writing room—a room where Miss Grange now regarded me, as if she watched a sleeper awaken.

"That was a tremendous tale, Miss Grange," I said, still in its grip.

"Aye." She folded her hands upon her lap.

"But who was the stranger?" I put my hand upon her arm. "Was he meant to be real?"

She looked down at my resting hand with a queer expression. Then, cautiously, her own hand covered mine and pressed it. "He *was* real."

"What do you mean?" I looked at her, startled. "I thought you said it was a story!"

"It is a story, Maisie. One of many I wrote"—she hesitated—"but born from a single truth."

"Something like that happened here?"

"Yes."

"But . . ." My mind raced. "To whom? To relations of yours? Is that when you came to Grange House?" Here was an answer at last! Here was a part of Miss Grange's history revealed!

"No," she said, "I was born here."

"Oh!" I said, confused

"I am Nell Grange."

I raised my face to hers, horrified.

She reached forward in her chair, touching my sleeve. "You see why I told it to you now, do you not?"

I looked at her long hand upon my arm; at last I shook my head.

"There are two kinds of stories to tell." She tapped my arm. "One of love and one of ghosts. You did not wish to hear of love, so I told you the tale of a woman in the grip of ghosts—in the dim land of half-truths."

"The Widow Grange?" I asked. "The mother?"

"And the daughter," she answered swiftly, and then looked direct at me. "The daughter, too."

"But"—my voice quavered—"which daughter?"

"Maisie?" Papa's voice came from the bottom of the attic stairs.

Miss Grange sat back quickly in her chair. "She is here with me, Ludlow Thomas."

"Maisie?" We heard him take one step but then remain where he was at the bottom.

I rose up and went to greet him at the head of the stairs.

"Mr. Thomas," Miss Grange called from where she still sat, "I have just finished telling your daughter one of my stories."

"Ah," said he, looking up at me. "What sort of story?"

"A ghost story, Papa," I blurted, wishing he had not interrupted.

He looked a little perplexed. "Yes. Well, I know Miss Grange is full of stories," he remarked.

"It is Grange House that is full of stories." Miss Grange had risen and crossed the room and now stood beside me. And so we both stood at the top of the stairs, looking down. For a minute, Papa seemed transfixed at the bottom, gazing back up at us, and then he stretched out his hand.

"Come, Maisie," he said.

"I fear"—Miss Grange regarded my father—"the stories of Grange House have begun to repeat."

"You don't mean that," Papa said evenly, and beckoned me again, his eyes fixed on me.

"Aye," she said, "I do."

This time he could not quell the shudder that overtook him. "Come, Maisie," he repeated quietly. "Come."

As I put my foot upon the top stair, Miss Grange said low and almost desperately, "It is urgent I tell you more."

I nodded to her quickly, not certain I understood what she meant, and descended to where Papa waited, then followed after him down the hallway to the next flight of stairs. He did not speak, and neither did I ask why he behaved so strangely. But as Papa and I returned to the inhabited floors, it seemed the story had reached past the borders of a tale. And for an instant, as I recalled the look of dread in Papa's eyes, such power repelled, as if I had looked upon the glittering face of the enthralling Christabel.

But it was a fleeting instant, and for the remainder of that after-noon, I gladly gave myself up to the voices of those other Granges living in the phantasm of this House still hovering all about me. Though Miss Grange had called it a story, Widow Grange and her daughters had come forcefully to life through her telling—their characters so real, I vowed I would know more. If that had been a story, what, then, was the truth? But then I recalled Miss Grange's whispered plea upon the stairs, and an unnamed dread accompanied the thrill. For my newfound resolution appeared too closely held in the hand of her intentions. A hand I wished both to clasp and push away.

That evening there was such a wildness of revolt and desire in me, as if the fictive fire continued, and I wanted to shake loose the very air and break open the House about my head. Gladly I gave myself to the giddy preparations as Grange House bulged and primped and grimaced, its merry guests readying themselves for Mrs. Strong's annual midsummer party. That night indeed, I wished to laugh and sport and fill my dance card full. Yet as I followed Mama and Papa down the lawn behind the others to meet the boats, I could not help from turning once and looking back up the grass to her window, where a single lamp glowed.

The dark backs and bare shoulders of men and girls greeted us upon entering the dance. Papa and Mama and I stood on the polished steps of the entrance hall before descending, and oh, how I wanted to plunge in, to feel the glances on my bare arms, to greet the nodding heads among the sudden spray of laughter and bright conversation. The butler bent to hear Papa's whispered instructions, then called out into the crowded room.

"Mr. and Mrs. Ludlow Thomas. Miss Maisie Thomas."

I noted the Misses Peabody and their confederate, Miss Nash, turning in unison to get a better look as we passed through the room, and I imagined they thought Mama to have stepped clear from a milk bath, so soft and fresh she appeared. In a rich cream silk, she flowed at Papa's side, nodding hello, the diamonds sparkling in her dark hair.

I felt a little stiff, a new birch beside my mother's dancing beauty. I caught a glimpse of Bart Hunnowell walking among the white-clad girls like a shepherd. And as if he had heard my inward comparison, he stopped to tend to some remark of Cynthia Harrington's, holding her dance card while she prettily pointed out the names.

Bart smiled and then excused himself, walking through the crowd toward the darkened verandah steps and the night. The room shivered in the light of a hundred tapers. Suddenly, he was caught in the twirling patterns as several couples eddied around him as though he had been pulled into a quickening current, and he propelled himself through the swirl and out into the cooler quiet of the hall, out to the darkened verandah steps, where he vanished from my sight.

And now the gaiety behind him surged forward, racing us toward midnight on the wave of the dance. A combination was proposed in which the men danced the part of the ladies and the ladies took the lead, and the result was a laughing excuse to trip over one another while the men's ungloved hands rested on the bare shoulders of the girls. There was an outdoor supper on the verandah at twelve o'clock, and the moon glanced between the silver forks and knives and sparkled in the punch, all the while dancing also in the darker harbor waters. All the windows in the front rooms were thrown wide to the night and as the air chilled into the early morning, the music played there grew more heated, as though Mrs. Strong's fiddlers had exchanged their bows for pokers dipping again and again into their music's lively fire.

Though the three spinsters never missed the yearly dance, the Misses Peabody and Miss Nash seemed untouched by the music and stood, ready at their positions, to make all manner of commentary as the couples whirled by. The three old women are like geese, I reflected as I watched them over Mr. Lanman's shoulder, and I thought of the smooth surface of the sea at midnight. The geese broke their circle and floated along the side of the room, their heads bobbing together nervously at the crowd, picking their skirts up as if to avoid being splashed by an unseen wave.

He had asked me to dance, and after our small exchange upon the verandah yesterday, I looked forward to a turn with him, wishing to test him on other interesting topics. And yet, though he remained perfectly correct in his manner, nodding and smiling at me as we chatted through the first movements, there was of a sudden a touch of the suitor about him, as if our conversation and my free opinions had sent a flag up to wave along his horizon. As we swirled, I felt the gentle pressure of his hand at my waist, and it seemed as if that guiding care held all the future in it. the door held open, the easy bow before he left for his work in the city, the silent room in which I sat, composing little messages on thick white notecards, the calls of our children far away at the top of the house. I could see it so clearly, and for an instant the known world beckoned, a sweet comfort in the picture. I glanced up and saw he'd watched me all the while. My foot faltered, catching my hem. He pulled me closer to steady me.

"I must have some air, Mr. Lanman."

"Certainly, Miss Thomas. The moon is growing full tonight, as well."

There was a brief panic in my heart in response to his talk of the moon. I gathered my dress about me and glided through the swaying couples, aware again of his hand now at my elbow, steering me toward the open doors that gave straight onto the verandah. I wondered if he expected a certain kind of conversation. Ah God, had he thought my plea for air a sentimental ruse? I was irked at the thought.

Thankfully, we were not alone. Others clustered along the wide verandah that wrapped around the house. We walked toward an un-tenanted spot where the vista before us stretched far into the harbor. I was not quite prepared for the calm that lay outside the warm festivity, and within the instant, I longed to return.

But he spoke.

"This moon is nearly full. It lacks four days before its apex."

"How can you tell? It is so difficult for me to know the difference between a waxing and a waning moon."

A burst of laughter from a neighboring group broke around us like bells. Mercy! I thought. Are we really conversing about the science of the moon?

"When the moon is growing full, it marks a *C* in the sky; as it wanes, the shadows on it make it mark a *D*."

"But that's wonderful! However did you learn that?"

"I read *The Farmer's Almanac,* Miss Thomas."

"Ah."

He smiled at me through the dark.

I was, inexplicably, struck dumb. Perhaps he sensed my discom-fort, for he stepped apart as though to peruse a better corner of the night. Several moments passed by in silence, and I could not help but note the strong line of his jaw set there against the white column. He placed both hands on the piazza railing, leaning forward.

"For how long do you plan to stay at Grange House, Mr. Lanman?"

"We leave tomorrow."

"Tomorrow!"

"Yes." He turned round to smile at me. "Your father has been kind enough to allow me this respite before my family removes itself to New York, but I must begin to earn the trust he has so far placed in me." An unmistakable urgency coursed through his voice, deepening it.

"I did not know your mother moved with you."

"She is originally from New York. I think she is pleased to find herself back amongst familiar sights, and also"—he coughed—"Boston perhaps has too much of my own father about it."

"Ah," I said again, not wishing to sink into intimacies shared in darkness. Out from the house drifted laughter and conversation. Quickly, I must find a reason to leave this piazza full with its confidences and its moon.

"Miss Thomas?"

I started. The voice behind me was perilously close, indeed so close, I felt the breath on the nape of my neck.

"Miss Thomas," drawled Bart Hunnowell, "may I have this dance?"

"You may, Mr. Hunnowell." I took his extended arm, and, turning to adjust my skirts, I curtsied to Mr. Lanman. He had moved into the light cast by the open door, his face shining into mine without shadow, and upon it sat a stiff smile.

The house swayed as I entered back into the smoke and luster of the late hour's frolic, the tune for this last dance having already swept several couples into its music. Without speaking, Bart Hunnowell guided me into the center of that swirling lace and linen, into the bud of the dancing flower, right into the circle of his arms, never pausing. I closed my eyes an instant and fell into the sway and turn of our dance, his hand upon the base of my spine, guiding me across the floor.

Round and around we whirled, until it seemed the room spun down to the single point where his hand touched my back. Other couples danced alongside, and they were but the flashing light and color of a backdrop, not the spinning center of the world, not this circle of sheer motion in which we clung. Faster and faster we moved, in and out of the others and around with a wild control, for I do not think he led anymore nor I followed, but still we moved as one, our feet impossibly certain of the marks, and with each swift turn, I felt a bubble of mad hilarity rising, until finally, just as the music finished, I could not bear it and I burst into high, gay laughter, breathless and free. I looked up at my partner, smiling, and for a brief instant Bart Hunnowell pressed me once still closer, and then he released me, as though casting off.

"Thank you for the dance, Miss Thomas."

I nodded. I couldn't trust myself to speak. For I felt I had just danced upon the lip of the world: Music and light and the low sound of human laughter coursed through me now as if my skin, my very body, were a portal to it all, all small and glorious, every gesture suddenly precious to me. Something indeed had broken open.

Beyond the rim of Mr. Hunnowell's shoulder I could just see my father bending to better hear something Mrs. Strong seemed to be whispering. They had not noticed our dance. Papa's face was flushed and intent on his conversation. Mama sat in shadow. And, as he accompanied me toward my parents, I had the curious sensation of returning to a house I had not known I had left: a house that blazed its bright light into the surrounding darkness.

"Maisie!" Papa drew me from the arm I held. "And Mr. Hunnowell."

Mama looked up in surprise. Bart Hunnowell paid her his compliments and, with a tiny smile to me, retreated back into the crowd.

"Maisie, I had no idea you had made him your partner. I thought you danced with Mr. Lanman."

"I did, Mama. But I grew faint, and we went out to the verandah for a breath of air, and while we stood there, Mr. Hunnowell came to ask for the last dance."

My mother exchanged a glance with my father. I turned away to watch the festivities breaking up. The party guests gathering in their last groupings seemed to form brilliant constellations in a new sky, and I longed to throw open my arms and grasp the bright moment to me. A young man draped a light woolen shawl around his mother, and a girl watched him surreptitiously, all the while fanning herself with her dance card. Beside me, Mr. Strong burst into song as he bid farewell to a collegiate man, and, half-jesting, the younger man placed a gloved hand upon his heart and raised his eyes heavenward. Yet he added his higher, sturdier voice to that of his host's and soon the men divided into parts and the song's light melody stole above the steady, gruff bass.

> *Teasin' teasin',*
> *I was only teasin' you.*
> *Teasin', teasin',*
> *Just to see what you would do,*
> *Of course you knew that I was*
> *Teasin' teasin',*
> *To find out if your love was true.*
> *Don't be angry,*
> *I was only, only*
> *Teasin' you.*

And as the men slowed and held the last beautiful note, both their faces now turned to the ceiling, drawing forth the song from their open throats, I felt a rush to tears. For here we all were—all of us. And the song. Mr. Strong clapped his partner on the back and now in the rush of *huzzahs* and farewells, the song stopped, the party broke off and away, and the sound of boots sounded on the wooden floorboards of the Strongs' verandah. I caught sight of Jonathan Lanman advancing upon us and swept him into this opening.

"Ah, Mr. Lanman. Will you ride back with us?" Papa called.

"Thank you, sir, but I shall walk round. I wished only to say my good-byes."

"Your mother told me you were leaving early in the morning. Good of you to bid us adieu." Papa's tone was jovial.

"Yes, that's right, sir. Mother and Dave retired long ago."

There was a tiny pause. "Good journey, then," said Papa. "I'll see you in the office on my return."

My mother leaned forward. "I do hope our paths will cross this autumn, in the city."

Mr. Lanman bowed quickly to her. "I expect so, madame."

He cast one brief glance at me and I curtsied. Again he bowed, and then, without another word, he was gone.

Papa's arm drew around Mama's waist, and we departed the party ourselves, passing out onto the verandah and down the narrow path to where the last boat for Grange House awaited. We were the din- ghy's only passengers, the other guests having left the Strongs' long ago. Guiding by the bowsprit lantern and by the near moon, Mr. Coates said nothing as he rowed us along the shoreline toward the answering light hung at the Grange House pier.

The oars flashed as they dipped, shivering the bright curtain of reflected stars that lay upon the sea. A second light appeared the closer we drew, casting its glow into the night. Miss Grange's window stared out upon us, a quiet beacon for our return. And to my exhausted, exhilarated senses, it seemed to shine out for me alone.

CHAPTER EIGHT

R uth and Cynthia possessed themselves of the verandah the following morning and, carefully as any pickers, were examining all possible hard shells for the rich meat of Romance inside.

"What do you think of Maisie Thomas and Mr. Lanman?"

"Well, what are his prospects?"

"Eldest son of a father who'd gone off—a bit loopy, Mama says." Cynthia's voice slowed.

"Loopy!" Ruth remarked with not a little glee. "What does she mean? Is there madness in the family?"

(At this—I could not help it—I nearly stood upon the bench where I had been reading, the better to hear her reply.)

"Well . . ." Cynthia paused. "Mama says the father studied rocks out in the Arizona desert and, so the story goes, was overtaken by Apache warriors who squatted round him in a circle for one whole day watching as he dug, and polished what he dug. I imagine that's unnerving for anyone, but he had some idea about the rights of savages and he offered them what he'd found—whereupon they spat on the ground before him and faded as silently away as they had come."

"Mercy!"

Cynthia laughed a little shrilly, unaccustomed as she was to being the one with the tale to tell. "Mama met him once, I think. At the Cabot Cotillion."

"Last year?"

"No, no. Years ago. He was very tall, she said, and with long white curls left free. Most attractive, but utterly—" Her voice broke off abruptly and then started up again in a tone of delighted surprise. "Oh! Good morning, Mr. Hunnowell!"

I looked up to see him upon the verandah.

"Ladies," he drawled as he passed by, then went down the stairs, where he stood upon the lawn for a moment, considering. I fully expected him to continue toward the water, but instead he wheeled round, and so caught sight of me. I ducked my head down into the book.

"Good morning, Miss Thomas." He now stood before me.

"It is," I replied, glancing briefly up from my page, then casting my eyes quickly back down. How to conduct an ordinary conversation when he had seen me laugh so? But he turned back toward the water and, without another word to me, stood near, his arms crossed. And glancing up again, I saw there was harbor all round in this silence. Nothing moved. Nothing sounded. The lobster buoys upon the water held the view in scattered dots.

The Grange House dinghy rounded the edge of the cove, and we saw Mr. Coates rowing swiftly toward the pier, with Miss Grange his only passenger. The bow of the boat disappeared as it drew within the shadow of the boathouse, though we could hear the loose phrases of the two cast up by a bit of wind. Upon the verandah, Ruth and Cynthia had recommenced their patter. After a time, the small figure of Miss Grange appeared in the door of the boathouse and we both watched her advancing toward us, coming over the grass with some difficulty, with a frailty about her I did not like to see.

"Beauty like *hers* is genius," Bart remarked. I flashed up at him in surprise, but there wasn't a trace of foolery in his expression.

"I beg your pardon?"

"Yes." He shifted round and nodded. "Yes, you see, don't you, Miss Thomas, how much of the world Miss Grange carries in her?"

He stretched wide his arms to take in the bright blue of the day against the stern beauty of the House, the chattering maidens upon the white verandah, the deep woods behind, their thick scent reaching even to where I sat upon the bench, looking up at him. "All this," he said quietly—and the moment held.

She carries more than this world in her, I reflected, and did not reply.

Bart brought down his arms and folded them across his chest in one swift movement, calling to mind the suddenness with which a shot bird drops from flight. I was unaccountably sorry.

"Yes," I said hastily, not wishing him to misunderstand my silence, "I think Miss Grange is very great."

His face softened, and he smiled as he watched Miss Grange make her way toward us. "Just so," he said. He waved to her. I held my hand up to shield my eyes and marked with a start how slowly she came.

"Though I do not think she is well," I whispered more to myself than to Bart.

"No, she is not at all well," he agreed, and moved forward to accompany her up the remaining part. And as I watched the two advance toward me, with Miss Grange leaning heavily upon Bart's arm, I felt a slight foreboding suddenly, as though welded to the tip of an arrow and speeding I knew not whither.

At luncheon, Miss Grange appeared beside my chair and asked if I would come and gather mushrooms that afternoon.

But Papa rose to his feet as she entered, and before I could answer her myself, he exclaimed, "You must not tire yourself, Miss Grange. Are you certain you are well enough?"

Mama broke off midsentence what she had been explaining to Mr. Cutting. Papa's manner verged on becoming impolite, so personal was he.

But Miss Grange gave Papa a steady smile instead. "If you would be so kind as to lend me your daughter's helping hands, I can manage an admirable harvest."

I leapt up, chagrined at Papa's behavior. "I will just be a minute, Miss Grange," and I left the dining room in search of my shawl.

We entered into the cool afternoon, directing our steps over the yellowing lawn toward the dark hem of pines that rung round the back of Grange House. Miss Grange walked slowly but with renewed strength, the mushroom basket bobbing against her hip, her gray figure a ship pointing us into those woods, and I was nothing but the dinghy following.

We proceeded side by side and at a measured pace, though as always, Miss Grange spoke little to me as we passed through the trees. The sound of the waves slapping into the shore receded, so I knew we pierced inward, deeper into the woods, though I had lost all trace of direction. This was a path I had not walked before, and I saw now we were bound for a mushroom patch other than the one that grew in the rocky ledges around the blacksmith shop. All about us, the broken limbs of trees lay like whitened whalebone on the mossy ground, the woods repeating the underwater life of the bordering sea, several granite boulders pocking the pine-needle surface like the sudden gray reefs of an inland ocean.

As we ventured farther and farther in, I grew aware of an old stone wall running alongside us, and looking down, I saw that we walked on a type of road, almost an alleyway of the sort one might find in a formal garden, stretching through the trees, though the long roots of the pines had grown cross the clearing, poking beneath the moss like interwoven fingers. I stepped over them with a little shudder.

After a time, we reached the end of the wall, and I slowed my steps then to gain my bearings. Miss Grange, however, continued straight on. I thought I heard the slap of water against rocks, though how we could have walked so far inland and still hear the ocean confounded me.

For a moment, all was hush. I was aware of feeling quite flushed suddenly, my curls damp on the back of my neck, my forehead hot. Though I did not look at her, I heard Miss Grange's footfalls stop. I heard her set the basket down. I imagined what she did, though I still stood in the middle of the pathway, not wishing really to venture forward, nor yet backward, content to rest a little in this invisible quiet.

"Maisie Thomas?"

"I am here." I swung wide my arms then to her voice and to those trees. I am here, I repeated silently. After a moment, I drew down the path toward Miss Grange, who stooped, then plucked and carefully stowed the dank masses in her basket, intent on her harvest. Though I was quite warm from our walk, she had not thrown off her light cloak, and her long hands slid in and out of the loose gray sleeves as she picked. She did not speak to me again, and so I simply watched her.

Did I dream? I think I did in a fashion. She had halfway filled her basket, and I suddenly wished to tell her something large, something to show that her trust in me was not misplaced—how the story had lodged in me and grown—

"Maisie?"

Miss Grange had stood, and she regarded me now with her level blue eyes, a mushroom cupped in her palm. There was a streak of dirt across her forehead.

I took a step forward, then halted.

"What is it, Maisie?"

I shook my head, unable to speak. She looked at me, then bent again to her collecting.

I did not know how to say what had suddenly surged over the confines of my thoughts. "I—"

She looked up.

"There is such a wild longing in me," I blurted out.

"Ah." Her hands burrowed in beneath the domed heads. "And what is it you long for, Maisie?"

I was silent, reflecting. She looked up again.

"Not for, Miss Grange, toward."

"Toward?"

"Yes. Toward. As if—" I stopped. "As if I am pressed up against the window in my room, my whole body straining to reach past the glass, to see—"

"To see?"

I shook my head. "To see. To see. I cannot name it, but I know

89

it lies just there—some idea, some vision past what is framed by the glass, some place past this."

She did not answer.

"What is a longing such as that, Miss Grange?"

She stooped again and did not look at me.

"You are opening, my dear."

"Opening?"

"Yes. Readying to begin." She stood.

"Begin? What is it I am to begin?"

She was quiet for a moment, and then she raised her eyes and looked straight at me, as if she had made a decision.

"Your part in the story."

"*My* part?" I regarded her. "In what story?"

"Come." She was almost impatient with me now. "Come," and she walked still farther down the path from me, the stone wall running by. Without thinking, I followed, just able to keep her figure in my sight, so quickly now she moved. We drew near a thinning in the web of trees. And with a shock, I realized where she had brought me. I stopped dead in the middle of the path and watched as Miss Grange proceeded through a break in the wall, into the middle of the clearing, and came to stand over the leaning granite marker of a single little grave.

She turned right round to me and said, "The last story, the un-written story. It begins here."

"In a graveyard?" I could hardly speak. The loneliness of the thin granite slab, the chiseled like of which made wilder the trees and swift branches ringing round, frightened me beyond reason. Indeed, all was made crooked about this little granite moon.

"Every story begins in a graveyard." She beckoned sharply, so intent was she now. "Come—step through the wall. Read the legend on the grave."

But I could not move from where I stood still in the middle of the path.

"Why have you brought me here?" I could not quell the brief panic in my voice, and I crossed my arms for comfort.

"I wished to show you—" she began, but seeing my agitation, she drew closer, stopping just across from me and leaving the wall between us. "Here," she said, "give me your hand."

I hesitated.

"Come, give it me," she repeated more softly. I lifted my hand from my side and reached it across the wall, and she clasped it in hers and gave it a little squeeze as if to reassure.

I shuddered and Miss Grange looked up swiftly. "Why are you frightened?"

"I never thought to see a grave," I whispered.

"Listen to me, Maisie." She squeezed my hand once more in an effort to turn my stunned attention elsewhere. But all round us the trees leaned, and the tiny gravestone rose up behind her shoulder.

"Listen, Maisie." Again, there was that strained urgency in her voice. And perhaps it was that insistence, that new tone in her voice, that forced my eyes to look up at her once more.

"Some stories are only fathomed in the writing of them."

I watched her.

"And the one I told you yesterday was one of many I wrote, again and again—to bear what had happened. But this one"—she pointed to the earth—"this one I never could write."

I waited, my heart scarcely beating. She looked straight at me across the wall.

"And I fear that is why Halcy has drowned."

"Halcy!" I stared wildly back at her. Now Miss Grange appeared to me gripped in the same strange madness—some gray dream of truth—as the widow in the attic of her own ghost story. I made to drop my hand from her grip, but she held fast.

"She drowned because this tale was never told. So the old story of Grange House has repeated once again!" She squeezed my hand. "Can't you see, Maisie? It must be stopped! Someone must write the next story to replace the old—and I cannot, though I have tried. So"— she paused and smiled—"I pass it on."

"Pass it on?" I repeated, sick and afraid.

She regarded me, and several answers seemed to flit across her lips. "To you. To write it," she said at last. "I have chosen you, Maisie Thomas." She smiled at me. "All these years, I have watched you grow proud and lovely, stretching your arms out to the world. You are the one to do it."

I stared at her, transfixed.

At last, she let go my hand. "I am not well. You have seen it yourself. I do not need to tell you." Then she brought her fingers gently beneath my chin and tipped my face up to look into her eyes.

"Now, what else do you see there?"

I looked. Miss Grange's face bent to mine like a tending star. But what I saw there, I could not say. Her eyes held mine for a moment before I searched for answers along the ridges and hollows of her face itself. I was acutely aware of her slow breathing, and of the small throbbing at her temple. Her fingers held my chin firmly, and as I did not know what I should be seeing, I felt only that she was too close to me, that her face might lean down farther and blot mine out.

I blinked. "Your face, Miss Grange."

She dropped her hand from my chin and stepped backward. Light reasserted itself between our figures.

"If you wish to see past yourself, you must learn to see the world through the veil, Maisie Thomas; you must learn to see the blots through the obscuring patterns of perfection."

I stared back at her. My own words in her mouth now seemed twisted and malformed. "Miss Grange—" I began, careful not to seem too hasty.

"I am asking for your help, Maisie," she broke in calmly.

A guilty flush stole up my throat. "My help?"

"Yes, I brought you to this spot," she said quietly, "so you might see it—and so begin."

"But—this is a *grave,* Miss Grange." I was close to tears. "What is there to begin?"

"The story," she repeated as if I were simple. "The story of this grave." Then she turned to catch up her mushroom basket. Through the open top, the pile of white and fleshy masses attached to their thick stems seemed like hands.

"Come. Let us go back."

But now I was stuck to the spot. Though I could not cross the wall and read the legend on the granite marker, neither could I leave the place. "I cannot," I said. "I do not understand."

"Yes," she said a little unkindly, "now I see that you cannot."

And she stepped over the stone wall and headed directly through the trees behind me, following no path that I could see. I watched her slow departure in a torment of contradiction. I was horrified by this lonely, well-tended secret. Who was buried here? I shivered, remembering Miss Grange's face stooped so close to mine. And what did she mean, "the story of this grave"? How might a grave hold a story? It was but a marker for the dead. And surely she who was possessed of so many stories, surely she knew who lay beneath. What had she need of my help? She is too elliptical now, I thought. I did not like her thus.

And yet she had placed me next to that hidden grave, had studied me, and then had found me wanting. It was I who had failed some type of test. I set off after her. A branch caught my shawl and I yanked at it, glad to hear the fabric tear.

CHAPTER NINE

O nly Mrs. Lewes, the doctor's wife, sat upon the piazza when we arrived back at Grange House, and inside all was still. I parted company from Miss Grange in the front hall and climbed the stairs up to my room, where I lay down upon my bed, determined to read until teatime, but I fell instead into a sound sleep.

A late sun stretched long shadows upon the front lawn when I awoke, and three fishing boats stroked slowly down Middle Haven harbor, crossing my window with the steady pace of the homeward-bound. The sound of a teaspoon clinking against the thin sides of a bone china cup and the low murmur of voices reached up to me where I lay. I rose quickly and dashed water onto my face and neck, then refashioned my hair up into a tidy bun. I looked down at my dusty petticoats. Never mind, I thought, and opened the armoire to reach for my simplest tea dress.

Masculine voices burst into laughter as I descended the staircase, and then as suddenly hushed, cut over by a bright feminine exclamation, which only set the men to laughing harder. My pace quickened and I passed down the front hall toward the entrance, stepping out onto the bright glare of the piazza, across which the lowering sun illuminated the little group of guests in an orange glow.

"Maisie!" Mama called, and I turned toward the sound of her voice to find her seated with Mrs. Hunnowell at a small side table, Papa standing round them holding a cake plate awkwardly in his hands.

"Ah. Here is my daughter, returned to us over the distance of one hundred years," Papa remarked cheerily.

I blushed. "Hardly, Papa."

He winked at me, then turned round to fetch another chair, only to discover Bart Hunnowell had already found one from a little distance down the way. "Ah," said Papa, taking the white chair from him, "there we are."

I sat next to Mama and, unthinking, took up the teacup full of the hot tea she poured me, holding it between my hands. "Maisie!" she remonstrated, and motioned with her eyes toward the abandoned saucer upon the table. For the second time, I flushed up, and not looking at her, I replaced the little cup onto its proper resting spot; then, as carefully, I tucked my feet up beneath my skirts and folded my hands in my lap, immeasurably comforted by custom and teatime and conversation.

Toward twilight, Papa rose to stand at the balustrade and look out over the darkening harbor, his fingers drumming the wood abstractedly.

"I think I will row out, my dear." He turned to Mama, who looked at him, surprised. With a quick shove against the table, I darted up also. He smiled and held out his hand to me.

"Run get your shawl," Mama instructed from behind.

"Will you come?" Papa asked her.

"No, Ludlow," she answered. "It is late."

We pushed off from the dock into the evening calm of the harbor and Papa rowed us for a time, almost soundlessly, his strokes cutting through the still water, the high tide brimming the rocky shore, the pink sky reflecting below the oars—so it seemed we were an arrow shot by Papa cleanly over the sea.

"When Henry Brown's father came for his son," Papa said without preamble, "he placed the boy's hands in the pockets of his trousers before wrapping him in sailcloth and laying him down on one of the wooden seats in his boat."

"Why in his pockets instead of over his chest?" I asked.

"I cannot say, Maisie. Perhaps it is a custom among the fishermen here—something to do with . . ." His voice trailed away as he tried to imagine the reason.

I shivered. "It is curious, isn't it, Papa?"

"You'd not have known what the old man carried," Papa continued. "Another fisherman returning to harbor might have thought the burden but a bundled sail in the prow of his dory."

"No, Papa. Another fisherman would never have made such a mistake."

He regarded me in the dimming light and nodded. "You may be right." And then, more to himself than to me, he said sadly, "If only I might have carried Father's body home."

I sat silently and waited. But Papa did not speak again and rowed onward toward the darker shore across the harbor through the intermittent pop and ripple of a school of mackerel jumping to the surface of that dark sea about us.

"Were you very sad to lose him, Papa?" I whispered.

He took one more stroke and then straightened up to look at me. "I was very sad, yes, Maisie."

"What age were you?"

"Nearly thirty, my girl. But I had spent a long time away from my own family—on business for the line—and when I returned at last, he was already gone, already buried—and but a grave." He splashed the water with one oar, lightly. "There was much I never told him."

I watched as one of the lobstermen maneuvered heavily toward us, his stern weighed down with catch.

"Papa, when you were my age, what did you wish for?"

His mood had shifted. He crinkled up his face. "Wish for? Why, I wished one day I'd be in a rowboat with a girl like you—mind, I did not say little—looking at me out of my own brown eyes and asking me what I wished for."

"Papa, I am serious."

"Serious, my own girl?"

"Yes, Papa. Answer me." I looked down at the water skimming beside us. "Please."

He took a few strokes without answering.

"Papa?"

"Ho! Maisie I had great visions for myself." He smiled at me, and choosing not to see the smile as a warning, I persisted.

"And what did they consist of?"

His voice when he answered was so sorrowful, I looked up in surprise.

"Of quiet conversation with great men—"

"And did you not fulfill your wishes?"

He shook his head.

"What stood in your way?"

"There came a time"—he paused—"when I no longer considered myself fit to stand beside the great."

We were silent for a bit. The low shadows stretched longer along the water. Papa began to row again, slowly guiding us back around toward Grange House. It was a high tide and the harbor seemed a bowl brimful with its waters.

"And Papa, what should I wish for?"

He looked directly at me then. "Maisie, my girl, do not ask anyone else what to wish for. What is it you see when you close your eyes?"

How could I answer such a question? The longing in me had no form. I saw shapes and movements, patterns without whole cloth, scraps of a history; my wishes like harbor markers anchored and voiceless save to those who knew how they might be read. Without thinking, the words tumbled out: "Quiet conversation with great men."

My father looked at me sharply then and turned his face away, beginning to row again with great concentration. Nettled, I added in a whisper, "Like you, Papa."

But he did not hear. He had fallen into the rhythm of forward motion, the dinghy sliding effortlessly through the twilight toward the House. Two more solitary lobstermen approached, their work continuing even as they pointed home. I sat silently, feeling the boat surge beneath me, my back swaying slightly with each stroke. The water lay very still around us, still as the great quarry pool, calm and imperturbably deep at the center of the woods. Lulled by Papa's steady, thoughtful strokes, I let the afternoon's scene return, and saw the sorrow upon Miss Grange's face beside the little grave, and saw her wish to have had me see, and I felt ashamed of my fright.

"I do not understand Miss Grange." I sighed.

"Miss Grange!" Papa's head rose up with a jerk, and he stopped rowing.

Startled, I put out my hand to his wrist. "Forgive me, Papa, I did not mean to stop you."

He fixed me then. "What do you know of Miss Grange, that you should speak of her like that?"

"Nothing, Papa." I trembled in the evening chill. Something had cracked a whip into my father's mood. "When I walked out with her this afternoon, she took me to a sad spot."

"What spot, Maisie?"

I looked down.

He shipped his oars and now addressed me with his full attention. "Tell it to me," he said slowly.

I thought for a moment of her hands clasping mine above the narrow band of the wall beside the lonely grave, and I shivered.

"Maisie." Papa did not look at me, but at the shoreline behind me. "I do know that Miss Grange once suffered a great loss."

My head jerked up.

"Something grievous . . ." He paused.

"What do you mean, Papa?"

He shook his head and did not answer.

"What do you mean, Papa? Do you know something about Miss Grange?"

But he shook his head once more, this time more softly. "No, Maisie. I know nothing of her."

One of the traps fell backward into the water with a soft plop, the lobsterman's line playing out between his gloved hands.

"Tell me, Papa," I blurted, "did she lose a child?"

I thought at first he had not heard me, so still did he remain. Not a flicker of life crossed his face. Then, straightening, he drew in the oars and regarded me.

"No," he said. "No, she did not lose a child."

"Well, I am sorry for her," I mused into the water.

"No, Maisie. Never sorry." Papa's reply was rapid, almost hot in her defense. "You should not ever think of Miss Grange as a sorrowful figure." And now he looked at me in earnest through the twilight. For the second time that day, I grew impatient. Papa was elliptical as Miss Grange herself, speaking out without saying a substantial thing.

"She was once a talent of great promise."

"As an authoress?"

"Yes," he said simply. "She had published several stories that attracted much attention. Even Mrs. Stowe had corresponded with her, and then the great Thomas Higginson came to see her himself and took away her manuscript with him."

"And then what happened?"

Papa seemed not to have heard.

"Papa, where is that book now?"

"It was never published," he answered.

"But why?"

"Because—" He caught himself. "Why? Why, I haven't any idea." He ran out the oars, their double splash heralding an ending. "But you see she need not be considered sorrowfully," he finished.

"Nonetheless, you should not like me to be like her?" I flashed out hotly.

Again he fixed me, and this time I thought he meant to speak true, but there was something in my face too eager, perhaps, too stirred, for he dropped his gaze from mine and answered strangely, "You must marry, Maisie."

"Surely, Papa, one need not marry as an anodyne to sorrow!" I was provoked indeed.

He smiled faintly. "My dear, marriage puts solid ground beneath one's feet: ground, walls, rooms. You must have a house, my girl. A place. You cannot have a history without a place."

"History, Papa!"

"Yes, Maisie. History is a place." The boat swung round and the roofline of Grange House appeared. "A place one returns to, again and again."

I looked at the black edge of the House behind Papa's head, and I was suddenly and inexplicably melancholy.

"You are most contradictory this evening, Papa. I thought I was not to train my sights on wishes set by others."

Now he was impatient with me.

"No one, especially a woman, can build a life in open air. There must be forms. There must be vases. Wish all you might, your visions will shrivel and die if you have no place in which to set them. The most beautiful bloom is that which has been forced upward through a narrow casing."

I crossed my arms. "No one, I think, Papa, ever said such a thing to you."

"It was entirely different for me."

"Why was it?"

"You cannot understand," he answered me swiftly.

"No," I replied bitterly for the second time that day. "I do not."

He did not speak further, but busied himself by bringing the rowboat briskly into the pier in several clean strokes, shipping the oars as we drew alongside the wooden pier, blackened by twilight and the thick, silent sea.

But, I reflected, walking back up the lawn beside my father and looking directly into the great white frame of Grange House, stern and stark in the soft dusk, Miss Grange does have a place. I raised my eyes to her window. And she had never married. A stab of irritation rose up once more. Now indeed I wished I had not shied from reading the name upon that stone.

CHAPTER TEN

The following morning struggled into existence, the bleary call of foghorns crossing and recrossing the harbor. When I rose, the fog was close in at my window, heavy and insistent in its thick silence. We were to make the trip to Leadbetter's Island, one of the string of islands extending the granite spine that stretches out from Middle Haven harbor down the reach of Hurricane Sound to the east, sprouting above the black water into a pale sky. It was a favorite journey, but I knew the day would prove difficult now, for Mama's fear of the fog would dampen the spirit of the voyage, and Papa's cheery dismissal of that fear would only clamp shut her lips.

The sound of Jessie busy at the dressing table called me back into the room.

"The blue or the white this morning, Miss Maisie?"

Ah. What did one wear to visit a tower in the middle of an island in the middle of a bay? If I wore the white dress, I could slip in and out of the fog like a ghost and give Papa a start.

"The white, Jessie."

"The white? On a day such as today, miss? And if there's a rough crossing out to that tower, won't the white be in a pitiable state after the trip? Far better the blue."

"Oh, very well, Jessie, you dress me as you please. But why give me a choice to start with?"

I was answered by the smart snap of the brush through my hair, the heavy weight pulling me down to sit at my table.

"Jessie?"

The strokes punctuated her powdery breathing.

"What age were you when you married?"

Was there a change in the brushstrokes? Did they become fiercer, more insistent? Jessie's breathing shuttered open and closed, not pausing an instant. I closed my eyes, waiting for an answer. Each time the brush drew down through my hair, it pulled my head back into Jessie's body, rocking me softly against its aproned warmth. When Jessie answered, her words came as if from a great distance.

"Eighteen. And a widow at twenty."

"Oh, Jessie," I said. "I am sorry."

She did not reply. I imagined a bright and hopeful Jessie, unaproned, standing next to a thin boy whose whiskers had just started sprouting on his soft cheeks. Then I saw Jessie and her husband walking down a lane, his arm awkward around her waist, his mouth bent close to her ear to say a little something. I saw a dark horror between them, a little grave on a hill, and then I saw the larger grave that was his own. My eyes flew open, frighted by the ease with which my mind could summon such things.

"Oh, *Jessie*."

"That's the hundred, miss. And the breakfast bell sounding. We've to hurry with the blue's buttons."

I descended to breakfast in a strange turmoil. To think I had never asked to hear Jessie's story.

I must have entered the breakfast room with my musings on my face, for Mrs. Hunnowell stared at me with a particularly annoying expression, as if to say, Ah! Ah! I know your secret. You dear little thing. She turned to Mama and said, "Mrs. Thomas, do you and your husband take to the opera down in New York?"

My mother paused, aware of my quiet form passing behind her to take my seat.

"The opera, Mrs. Hunnowell. We do, yes, enjoy it very much, although I must admit a preference for light opera. I prefer my passions leavened by spots of gaiety. By contrast, upon leaving one of Mr. Wagner's operas—meant, I am sure, to cure what ails me—I am often besieged with a heaviness, as though I'd spent all night straining to see into the darkness behind a window, to find after all that it is only dawn that lies on the other side."

"Really, Mrs. Thomas. How prosy a thought. It makes one despair. Quite. In these strange times, often the opera is the only place in which to find unmixed sentiment."

"Strange times, Mrs. Hunnowell?"

"Strange and dreadful. There is no longer such a thing as sentiment these days, my dear. Last night I lay reading one of that sunflower gentleman's new plays—"

"You don't mean *Oscar Wilde,* Mother?" Bart Hunnowell's velvet voice curled up from the cushioned depths of a sofa on which, evidently, he had been lying the entire breakfast.

"Just so. Thank you, dear. I lay reading Mr. Wilde—"

"Really, madame," Mr. Cutting broke in, "I cannot believe I have heard you correctly."

With a polite sigh, she turned her attention upon him. "Why, Mr. Cutting, I said I was reading Mr. Wilde."

"But that is shocking, Mrs. Hunnowell. How came your husband to allow such filth into your house?"

"I am the arbiter of taste in our household, Mr. Cutting." Again came the delicate and patient little sigh. "Women are far more able judges than men as to what is and what isn't worthy literature."

Mr. Cutting wiped his mouth carefully and put down his napkin. "Perhaps, Mrs. Hunnowell, the feminine taste for literature is more easily able to disregard the harder facts of life. Mr. Wilde is in prison, madame, for unspeakable crimes committed against decency."

"Well," Mrs. Hunnowell parried, not in the least undone, "the man ought to be in prison who would write such a love scene in which the hero says, 'Please pass the butter dear' to his lady love."

A delighted guffaw rose up from the sofa.

I turned in my chair to regard the old lady.

"Butter!" continued Mrs. Hunnowell. "Where is the sentiment in *butter*? The most unromantic thing I ever heard of."

"Why is that, ma'am?" I interposed.

"At your age, my dear, whenever Cupid shot his arrows into my soft heart, I could hardly stomach a morsel."

Mr. Cutting snorted.

Undeterred, Mrs. Hunnowell turned her full attention to me.

"My child, when I was in love, I never ate at all. I lived"—and here she paused, exhaling the next words carefully—"I lived on air and love. A thought of *butter* would never have entered those spirit regions."

"Ah. Love," drawled Bart Hunnowell, the words dragging him up from the sofa. I felt his eyes on my back, and my face answered with a hot surge of color. For some reason that morning, I wished to provoke him into the more interesting silence of his—this lounging parlor man I thought beneath him.

"I don't know," I commented aloud, "I'd rather wish my life to be full of incident and feeling, with a love that gives purpose to life—not air, Mrs. Hunnowell—and sets a flame to burn with the pure clarity that heats a day."

"Why that is beautiful, Maisie." Mrs. Hunnowell clutched a hand to her bosom.

"How aptly your daughter describes the hearth lamps burning in the home," Mr. Cutting said approvingly to Mama.

"And what might that purpose be, Miss Thomas?" Bart asked quietly.

I turned round to face him. "I beg your pardon?"

"This purpose love would give your life—this *flame,* as you call it—what would it be? Musn't you burn *toward* something? Musn't there be a goal in mind?"

"Must there be?" I stabbed back, uncomfortably aware that we were the only two who spoke.

"If you do not wish to be consumed—if you wish your life to have its own inviolable core that burns but does not perish in the burning—then, yes, I think it vital to seek a purpose."

He had turned on me, upending the very image I thought he would most approve. Caught out, I cast back hotly, "I do not notice you, Mr. Hunnowell, to be heavily encumbered by the pursuit of a purpose."

The color drained from his cheek. The shot had met its mark. He stood up abruptly. "Then you have noticed far less than I thought, Miss Thomas." And with that, he passed from the room.

"Oh, my dear!" said Mrs. Hunnowell, staring after her son.

Mama said nothing. But I gazed at the doorway miserably. I had not meant to hurt him. The dull thrum of the kitchen bell vibrated below our feet, causing me to start.

"Libby? Maisie? Are you ready?" Papa's cheerful figure appeared. He wore about him the sharp pine scent and cool air of the morning, and his mood was expansive, determined to breathe in the day with great gulps. Bidden to don my things quickly, I raced to the coat closet and searched among the layers of wool and fur for my own cloak, slipping into my leather long boots at once. Papa was wrapping Mama into her pelisse as I returned, while they waited for me outside on the verandah. And glad I was then to escape this disquieting House with them.

"Will the fog thicken still more do you think?" I noticed my mother's gloved hand creep into Papa's.

"It very well could do."

But the seemingly unaffected words covered his squeeze of her hand, and he kept it in his as we proceeded to the boat, the lawn glowing beneath the fog. The sky held no height, so we walked in what seemed a type of soft tunnel, a green shot to the blackened sea. Against the white rocks on the shore, the water lapped, but then beyond where one could see, a blank mist erased the border between atmosphere and liquid.

The excursion boat bobbed slightly at the float. Mr. Coates waited, his expression clouded by the smoke of his pipe. I remembered a whispered remonstrance to Mr. Coates that Papa had rendered years ago upon his smoking before ladies—lady *guests,* my father emphasized. And I recalled the respectful way in which Mr. Coates had regarded my father, agreed, "Ayuh," and continued to smoke. It seemed the man's response had endeared him to Papa, for I could not fathom my father's summer happiness without including there the hours he spent smoking on the float with Mr. Coates, the men's twin silence rocked gently by the waves of passing craft. As we approached, he raised his hat to Mama and grinned at Papa. "Thickafog."

The *Posy L.* had a handsome wooden hull, sleek and gray. Papa and Mr. Coates stood on either side of the wooden mounting box set upon the float and handed Mama and me up into the boat. Then Mr. Coates hopped aboard and cranked the engine while Papa cast off, leaping onto the gunwales as the boat slipped away from the float. I drew to my favorite seat, at the side of Mr. Coates in the stern, and turned to watch the disappearing land as the boat nudged into the harbor and its envelope of fog.

There reigned a tense expectancy in the boat, all of us straining to see through the fog and silence, as if to help the prow better push through the thick air. The spindle tops of painted lobster buoys popped into view, bright spots against the blank black of the sea. At times, Papa called out the colors of the lobster buoys we passed, determining which lobsterman had left these signs, knowing Mr. Coates did not heed nor mind the summer visitor's sleuthing. Behind us we could hear the low throbbing of another engine and just make out voices from another boat. I turned in the direction of the sounds, and for an instant, I caught the white prow of the following boat emerge, then disappear as quickly back into the fog. The ghostly crew remained unseen, though their chatter bespoke several cheery men, a cheer that seemed misplaced in that atmosphere. I turned from them and faced forward into the dense mist. Mr. Coates's great brown hand lay easy on the tiller, his mouth pursed in a soundless whistle. We pulled forward into it, deeper and deeper, until the sound of the other boat dimmed to a hum and the buoys gave way to the single red and green channel markers. The rocky line of the harbor breakwater stretched into view and we left it, passing farther on into the quiet.

And then the dark outline of the island loomed into view. Long fingers of granite stretched forward into the sea. As the boat drew closer, the granite line was softened by the enormous boulders, almost womanish in their roundness and covered by dull green lichen. Mr. Coates navigated the prow up the island's narrow cove, over the sunken rocky ledges that lay like teeth at the entrance to this watery mouth. Although I knew this coastline well from previous visits, a chill swept down my frame as I espied how close-knit lay the rocks below us and how near they seemed, though covered by the interposing feet of water. When we could go no farther, Mr. Coates cut off the engine. In the sudden absence of sound, the single cry of an island bird called its warning.

Papa took up an oar and side-rowed the boat, pulling us to within a few feet of what had been a wharf, built and abandoned some years back by the quarry workers who had plumbed this island for the granite. He then drew a broad plank from the *Posy*'s aft and lay it across the gap of water between the boat and the rock wharf. Having secured the plank, he stepped up to the makeshift bridge and crossed it, swaying as the boat released his weight, causing the water to slap against the rocks. He beckoned me, and I put my hand on Mr. Coates's shoulder and lightly stepped across to Papa's waiting hands. I climbed past him up higher onto the enormous square-cut boulders that still held the plan of the wharf, though many had tumbled off and down, upending, so I could see the deep gauges where the men had cut into the rock, the thin lines still left by the iron nails that had split the rock face open.

I watched below me the spectacle of my mother's struggle between her pride and her fear. She turned stony in her concentration, her jaw set and jutting. Gaining the plank, Mr. Coates held on to her hand as she edged out over the water and Papa's hand reached to grab hers as soon as she neared him. There was coming the moment when Mama would have to drop the old pilot's supporting hand in order to move forward to grab Papa's, but I saw that she could not. Hovering over the few feet of water, her arms stretched between the two men, my mother appeared stricken into place.

"My love," Papa whispered. His eyes on hers, he waited.

Mr. Coates let her go. She shut her eyes and walked, and Papa's hands were on her elbows, leading her to him like a small child. But the next instant, she turned to the man in the boat, smiled her kindest smile, and squared her shoulders. Blood surged into my face, the front line to the quick jab of shame I felt as I turned from the finale of this drama. Mama's strength was a thing put on or taken off, depending on my father's nearness: I had watched the swift shift in her face at the sound of Papa's approach, a bright, determined shield replacing blank, I thought.

The woods drew around me. Even here, the fog had entered, so the moving vapor crossed between the trunks of leaning trees and the blackened wet of the living pines. There was a green in here that glowed with such intensity, I imagined I was on the inside of some immense wood body, and the bright spots of color like to the forest blood. Mama and Papa were behind me, but far enough behind so I felt I walked alone, stepping over the thick-coiled roots and wrapped in the inner damp of this wood's sweet wet. The Spanish moss had grown thick in here, great skeins of it hanging over the path like shook hair. I had to push it aside to stay my course, and I walked to the tune of my own breathing, my eyes tracing the ground, careful to follow the tricks and turns of the path. Walking this way, I stumbled into a thick riot of upturned trees obliterating a clear passage. The winter winds had swept through in a fury, leaving the bases of great pines upended and exposed, or split down the middle so the trunks caved in as though made of clay. Stretched over two of these fallen trees was an enormous cobweb, spun like a banner at the level of my head. I stepped closer to see the dew upon the sticky threads, my face looking through the web into the wreckage of trees behind.

Something spectral moved between the trees. I dropped my out-stretched hand and stood still, my heart pounding. There. It took a step forward. I heard a rustle. A gaunt white face stopped directly behind the gossamer web, its eyes staring directly into my own, their pale wildness holding me to that spot as tightly as a snare.

And then, as if she would cross through the web, the ghost of Halcy Ames stepped toward me and held up a moving bundle in her arms. She opened her mouth to speak and the tiny bundle cried out— though it was my voice I felt in my throat, and I flung myself away from the web and that figure, racing back down the path. But even as I hurtled away, I heard a pursuing tread, as if my footsteps now were doubled.

My parents were in sight ahead of me. They had not been so far away. There they were after all, crowned by the soft fog casing, watching my hasty approach. Papa stepped forward to meet me on the path and so, in my haste and panic, I stumbled straight into his chest, nearly knocking us both to the earth. My father's body was firm and hot. I could hear his heart beating and I wrapped my arms around his neck and pressed my face into his shirt. He neither moved nor asked a question, but held his ground and stood against me.

"What is it, Maisie?" Mama asked.

I raised my face to hers. Below her hat, my mother's face was calm and soft, whitened with concern, but a warm human blood coursed through her, the faint rose glowing through the skin's veil.

"I saw—" The terrible face appeared again in my head. A gull screeched.

"What is it, Maisie?" Mama repeated. "You are quite white. What has happened, child?"

"I thought I saw . . ."

"What, my dear?"

But now she asked with a faint shadow of impatience around her mouth.

"I thought I saw Halcy Ames," I blurted.

"Maisie!" Mama put her hand upon my arm.

Papa said quickly, "Halcy Ames is dead, Maisie."

"It was her," I said softly, "and it seemed she wished—"

"Hush, Maisie, you have only oversparked yourself," Mama said firmly.

But Papa crossed his arms, his silence beckoning. "What did you see exactly?"

I told them then, without missing a detail, though Mama's face stiffened as I spoke of the tiny moving bundle.

"And she meant to speak to me—"

"Speak!"

"Yes." I put my hand upon Papa's chest. "To speak a warning."

"I do not believe it, Maisie." Mama had grown quite pale. "Ludlow, talk to her. Tell her she saw nothing."

Instead, Papa turned and cried "HALCY AMES!" But no one answered. "HALCY AMES!" he repeated into the dense surrounding, this time with greater force. "SHOW YOURSELF!"

A distant bird called through the trees. We three stood together listening in the afterclap of Papa's shout. Still there was nothing, and no one stirred. Mama adjusted her hat with a tense absorption. Her hands shook slightly as they threaded the ribbon.

Papa exhaled a soundless whistle.

"Do you know, my dear, you are not the first to see ghosts in these parts?"

Mama's head snapped up. "Pray, Ludlow, don't. You only encourage her."

"No, no. I've a story for our girl."

"Ludlow." Mama was not smiling. "It hardly makes sense to dispel one ghost by invoking yet another."

"It is altogether a sound proposition, my dear, and I have had the story much in mind since our row last evening. Clearly, Maisie's ghost bids me tell it."

"You are bidden to tell it?" Mama's hands were tight upon her parasol.

"Yes, my love," Papa said firmly.

Mama arched her eyebrow and turned away from us to proceed farther along the path alone, putting some little distance between us while we watched her go, in silence.

"See how easy it is to think even a living person ghostly on a day such as this, Maisie."

I looked, and indeed Mama's step was smooth, gliding along the path and moving slowly through the trees.

"Your mother has no disposition for the uncanny," Papa said fondly.

I could not bear it. The vision I had seen had seemed so real, and both Mama and Papa were bent on having me think otherwise. "Papa," I interjected one last time, though halfheartedly, "I am sure I saw her."

"Listen to me, Maisie," Papa said, his manner suddenly abrupt. "I must tell you—"

"Of ghosts?" I was in no mood to be treated like a child, and balked at Papa's tone.

"Of the Granges," he began.

"The Granges, Papa? Miss Grange's family?"

He hesitated an instant. "Indeed," he confirmed, and rushed on. "At the middle of this century, the Grange family—the very

Granges of Grange House—were prosperous and well-respected citizens of Middle Haven. It's said that theirs was the money that laid the foundation stones beneath the church, and theirs, too, the money that raised the roof upon the schoolhouse. The eldest son was a tall and well-built man who looked throughout the county for a wife to take. Many a young girl was pushed forward into his view at market by clumsy mothers' hands. Many a girl gazed at him pacing on his fine horse through the one street of Middle Haven. Many a soft pair of hands closed in prayer for a share of Rorie Grange's heart."

"Papa, stop. This does not sound like you. Where did you come upon all this?" My hand trembled on his arm.

"I read it once, my dear." Evading my gaze, he continued on.

I dropped my hand from his arm. It could not be, but it seemed my father was telling me the story of the Widow Grange's arrival in Middle Haven—the story before the tale Miss Grange had told me.

"There came a day, a sad day indeed for the native women of Middle Haven. Into the harbor sailed a ship, a mighty vessel that had crossed from Ireland, and though tending to Portland, it was blown off course in a fierce nor'easter that carried the unwitting crew into Middle Haven harbor. On board the ship were a dozen families who had left their bleak prospects and the weary search for food in time of famine to set sail for the verdant and bountiful promise of New England. Arriving in so unexpected a fashion in a town and harbor not marked on most maps, the ship's crew and passengers took it as a sign from the heavens that indeed they must stop in Middle Haven and settle there.

"The Granges were among the first families to greet the weary ones on board, and, hearing of the Irish determination to stop and settle, they offered the shelter of three of their fish houses, the small snug huts the fishermen drew their nets into at the end of a catch, to three of the newcomer families. Among these three families, chance had it there was a family in great sorrow on account of its overabundance of girl children."

"Papa!" I exclaimed. "*When* did you come to hear this?"

"On account of its overabundance of girl children," he continued, determined as a broad-beamed vessel cresting a troublesome sea, "the mother and father were in desperate need of guidance as to what kind of employment they might find. Rorie Grange's father contrived that one of the girls might find employment in Grange House's kitchen, thereby alleviating the strain of five daughters packed together in one small fish house. The father beamed at the plan and, it's said, he turned to his wife, winking at her in that particular Irish way, and said, 'Choose the one, then.' Whereupon the good wife chose.

"And choose well she did, for that canny woman marked the bent of her husband's thinking and chose the girl who indeed ended the story by becoming the young Rorie Grange's wife. Cassie Grange was a proud girl and fine, and the two made a handsome pair; like great steeds, they cut a swath through the timorous grasses of Middle Haven society. They were given three children—George, Susannah, and Nell."

Here Papa stopped suddenly, lost in thought.

"That is not the way it was," I protested. "Cassie Grange arrived from Ireland all alone—"

"The way it was?" Papa looked down at me, though his tone remained unreadably light. "It is a story, Maisie."

I considered him awhile. How had Papa come to read one of Miss Grange's stories? "Nonetheless," I continued at last, "you have told me a love story when you promised me a ghost."

"All love stories beget ghost stories, Maisie. Sure as fire," he said quietly.

And then he walked away from me along the path, his pace quick, as if he strained forward, away from the story he had started. I watched him go. How well did he know Miss Grange after all? There was nought to do but follow his departing back, though I meant to stick him with the questions when he stopped.

But he did not speak again. For in a short while, we arrived at the tower, which now surged upward through the clearing at the rocky center of the island, its high white figure rising straight up from the granite plateau upon which it rested. An old Martello tower, it was built by the Sicilians who had come to work the quarry on this in-hospitable northern island. As the island's granite cache dwindled, the workers grew inexplicably mournful, though their misery at the severe Maine climate had been loudly proclaimed. It might have been in answer to the emptying island that the men began to build the tower over the first of the quarried cavities, a southern shrine to the northern hole. And now it seemed a finger held up in urgent proclamation, debating, with its solid casing, the soft tendrils of fog drawn close around it.

And I saw that for today, I would hear but that preface to the ghost story, for Papa had begun to climb the broad granite slabs that constituted an outer stair to the base of the tower. I turned to see what Mama did, and finding her bent to examine a clump of mushrooms, nosing the tip of her walking stick in between the furry heads, I spun to follow my father.

He had already disappeared through the squat doorway. I stepped up each stair in the dull vacuum of fog, my heels clicking on granite as I rose. Halcy's white face flashed into my mind's eye. Why did she appear to me now? Her wild visage confronted me again; she had looked at me, opening her mouth as if to call my name. I stopped on the stairs, my legs quivering beneath me. I closed my eyes, remembering Papa's voice sounding the silence in the woods—it had been imagination. Her face sprang up beneath my lids.

A deafening crack split open the air. Another sharp crack sounded in the terrible high pitch of snapping wood, as if the backbone of heaven had broken. Papa screamed from inside. And then there followed a tremendous rain of sound, great crashing splinters falling in dull thuds into the hole beneath the tower.

Then, only silence. I could not move. A figure scrambled past me, racing to reach the door and pull it open, but it seemed the dreadful shift that had taken place inside had wedged the door anew in its casing. As I watched Mama tug at the slim handle, it came away in her hands.

"Papa?" I whispered, unbelieving. "Papa?"

I hurled myself up the stairs and pounded on the thick wood. I thought I heard Papa struggling on the other side of the door.

"Papa, wait! I'm coming."

We were tearing at the door now, trying to pry an opening around the latch, the two of us frantic, clawing at the unforgiving wood. I whirled around and called back into the trees, "Help. Help us! Someone help us!"

But there was no one. My mind shied away from what it imagined on the other side of the door. Then I thought of Mr. Coates waiting in the cove. Mama seemed to have the same thought, for she pushed me away. But then, in a spasm, she clutched me back again, holding me to her so hard, I felt the edges of her heart beating through our two thin dresses.

"I will hurry, Mama."

And she put me from her. I tucked my dress up around my waist and ran back into the darkened quiet.

3 August 1896

Dear Mr. Lanman,

Mama wished me to write someone at the firm, and as I know Uncle Alec is abroad just now, I am taking the liberty of addressing you. We are in a good deal of trouble. Yesterday afternoon, Papa fell through the floor of that old Martello tower on the island in the bay, twenty feet down into an abandoned quarry, onto some jagged rocks.

Forgive me, Mr. Lanman, I cannot stop there—it would rather relieve my mind to use the few minutes before the mail goes in telling you about it. You see, there was no passable opening of any kind on the ground floor of the tower, and we had to enter it by climbing a ladder to a window. Fortunately, some gentlemen arrived soon after us, raised the ladder, and lowered it inside—the floor consisted of nothing but beams some distance apart—and succeeded in dragging Papa up. Then he had to be lowered on the ladder to the ground, carried a long way to the water, and then rowed to Grange House. Dr. Lewes tended to him, and another doctor came in the evening and has been here ever since. Papa has not been unconscious or delirious, but last night he suffered frightfully. Today he is better, and the doctor says he thinks that while the injury to the spine is most severe, it is not fatal and that he will eventually recover. He must have fallen directly on his back, as the back of his head is dreadfully gashed. He will have to lie quite quiet for a fortnight at least. Just try to fancy how awful it was when he was down, away down, under the floor, and we could just see him but not get to him.

This is the most beautiful place I know, and the people are so kind—but oh, it is so far from home and everyone. I hope you haven't minded this chapter of horrors, but it has eased my heart considerably simply to write it all out.

Yours,
Maisie Thomas

14 August 1896

Dear Mr. Lanman,

Thank you very much for your letter of the seventh, which came on Monday and cheered me a great deal.

If only you knew how miserable we are. Papa is much worse. Since Tuesday night, he has not been rational at all. He has been very restless but is a little quieter now, and is in a sort of stupor most of the time. Beside the concussion of the spine, one lung is now congested.

We are expecting a house surgeon from Boston tonight who is sent by Dr. Hayes (the husband of a very good friend of Mama's and a very fine physician), who has not much opinion of the local doctors, Dr. Lewes having regretfully departed on Wednesday morning. It will be a comfort to have someone always here and we shall feel we have done all that is possible (we have had a surgeon from Rockland for a day and the doctor from Middle Haven three times)—beside which, he cannot fail to be an improvement on the present incumbent. You could not believe anyone could be as utterly without tact as he, and he adds to our alarm in every possible way. We have a lovely nurse, however, and Jessie is a great help—but we are so far away and so unhappy.

Yours,

M. L. T.

33 Broad Street
Thursday, 20 August 1896

Dear Miss Thomas,

    I only just heard of the death of your dear father, and I can't express in words how shocked I was, or how I feel for you. Although I was quite young at the time, I remember my father's death and the horror of it all. I have always felt myself that one should try to be thankful when a dear one is taken from this poor, wicked old world of ours to a better one, where there is no more sorrow. Please let me know, if you can, what I can do for you. If I can be of service to you in any way, I should be grateful, if you would let me.

Yours sincerely,
J. T. Lanman

VOLUME II

CHAPTER ELEVEN

W e buried Papa upon the hill in Middle Haven churchyard
on a brilliant August morning. Mama would have none
at his grave but we two, and for the first time I stood
alone beside my mother and watched our vital third depart from us. I
did not listen to the minister's words save to mark sadly that he bid
my father to heaven as he might offer directions to a stranger. Though
his manner was all it should be, nonetheless he knew us little—as
summer people only—and laid upon my father's coffin but a ritual
hand in farewell. How lonely Papa would be, I reflected, watching the
minister bless the soil; for there was none familiar to stop beside him
as the first rain fell upon his face, and none to share the chill of autumn's
coming winds.

It was this fresh, unexpected sorrow that made me stay my steps
when it came time to leave Papa behind. Mama, too, could not leave
the spot, and I stood beside her and looked across the rooftops of
Middle Haven and out to sea. In all the land was a heavenly clarity,
the long arms of the shore stretching forward with the running tide,
the sharp pine forest pointing up from the white rocks to the sky.

"I detest the state of Maine," Mama remarked into the silence the clergyman had left behind. Startled, I slipped my hand beneath her arm and watched as he descended, nodding to the diggers, who waited farther on down the hill at a respectful remove, their brown-clad backs to us, passing a little pouch between them. Mama's veil lifted slowly in the light breeze. I could not look down into the neatly filled hole before us.

"But Papa loved it here, Mama," I tried to comfort.

"I never understood that love of his," she answered tiredly, and without another word to me, she put off my hand from where it rested in the crook of her arm, as carefully—as distantly—as if she removed a restraining vine that caught at her clothing. Then she leaned forward and whispered tenderly to the new-made grave, "Good-bye, my darling."

And she proceeded down the hill between the stone markers, a slowly diminishing black form, stepping resolutely farther and farther from this spot I could not leave.

"Mama?" I called after her, but she did not turn, and the sound of my voice hung round me in that perfect sunshine, my only companion save the dead. As I watched my mother's departing back, my heart stuck. The harbor waters below glanced back the air in little dizzying specks of brightness upon the waves. A fishing boat sailed slowly past the breakwater. My heart tocked once. Who was there now to call me *child*? I looked down, here lay Papa. I looked up, there was Mama—and I the sad pivot between. I stood still, watching as she grew smaller and smaller, until, just as she reached the gate of the churchyard, I picked up my skirts and ran down.

All through the mournful long train journey down from Boston, Papa's mahogany cigar box upon her lap, Mama uttered not a word. Farther and farther through the green countryside we traveled, the outdoors flashing by as the maples of Massachussetts waved into the blue air. In Providence, we changed locomotives, and Jessie came up into our compartment with the basket Mrs. French had thoughtfully prepared, handing boiled eggs and salt chicken round while the men shouted one to the other above the train's silence.

There lay atop the packets of food a note addressed to Mama and myself in Miss Grange's careful hand. I reached for it instantly and opened the gray paper to find a characteristically simple message: *My heart travels with you both.* Tears sprang to my eyes and I passed it to Mama, who did not lift her veil but regarded the note in silence. Then, to no one in particular, she said softly, "Well, he is with her now."

"Mama?"

And edged by a chill I had never heard, she continued, "Her heart need not travel far to find its rest."

I tried to see past the black gauze to her expression, but she turned her face quickly and bid Jessie leave us alone. Jessie nodded and slid shut the compartment door behind her, just as Mama burst forth querulously.

"Why is it, Maisie, you did not see fit to worry about my heart?"

"Mama?"

"When you told me of your father's last wish."

"Would you not have wanted to carry out his wishes?"

"I would rather not have known his wishes."

"But Mama—"

"And why is it, Maisie"—she raised up her veil with one shaking hand—"he spoke that wish only to you?"

"Mama," I murmured, "you know he could barely speak at the last. He would have"—I stopped and put my hand upon her knee—"he would have told you the same if—"

But she closed her eyes against me then and said simply, "Well, you are your father's child."

Stung, I leaned back into the cushions. Neither of us spoke. With a jolt, the train moved forward and slowly began again its shuddering journey to the south. Mama's face through her veil remained rigid; and glad I was then, glad I had not told Mama all that Papa had said before he died. It would remain our secret, his and mine. Indeed, I reflected, I do not think she could have understood those strange words, and would not have tried. Hers was never a questing spirit.

Like his, I thought sadly. Like mine. I shut my eyes to blot the unwelcome orange gaiety of sunshine, and was again beside him on the bed. For a long hour, I had knelt there, my head against his side, his wasted hand stretched out and resting in my hair. Behind me, the nurse sat asleep in her chair, the lamp turned quite low. Mama had finally dropped off to sleep herself in the adjoining room, though through the open doorway I could hear how fitful was her sleep. My father's touch seemed nearly weightless, and nothing stirred in the shadowed room but the hand upon the mantel clock ticking away indefatigable time. Toward the dawn, I felt him move, and raising my head, I saw that Papa whispered into the dark, his lips working and his poor dry mouth framing words I could not hear. I stood quickly and dipped my handkerchief into the pitcher by his head, then dabbed a bit of moisture around his lips and onto his tongue. He paused and his eyes looked up into mine.

I could not bear the sense I had that he stared at me from across the widening gap between us, and I leaned my face down close to his to whisper, "Papa." He shut his eyes slowly and then opened them. He looked at me for a long while and then began again the effort to speak.

I leaned closer and laid my ear near his lips, and heard now, faintly, "Bury her."

"Who, Papa?" I asked softly.

He closed his eyes. "Words."

I placed my head upon his chest, the tears starting to spill slowly over onto my cheeks. "Words," he whispered again.

"Bury me." Then he seemed to strengthen and put his hand upon my head as if to hold me to his heart, and the dismal beat I heard chimed against those two strange words he had whispered. I wept steadily against him, my hands wrapped around his neck, my ear, my cheek, my very being listening to the life within him fade.

"Bury me—"

I raised my head and a great sob burst free, my tears now falling upon his blankets.

"Here," he said at the last.

Only that.

Neither of us, I think, was prepared for the shock of our front windows on Pierpont Place already darkened by the heavy drapery marking his death. As the carriage drew to a stop, the front door with its knocker wrapped in black crepe opened slowly inward and the sad figures of our people ranged in the doorway behind Papa's man, Mr. Tish, who walked down the steps to greet us. But Mama emerged from the carriage with her head held high and took Mr. Tish's arm. Up we passed and into the house, through the long entrance hall and into the sitting room, where a cozy fire cast back the morning damp. Mama smiled her thanks at the murmured condolences of Miss Matchless, Hope and Ruella James, Cook Parsons and her little girl as one by one departed, until we were left alone. Mama took off her soft black bonnet and patted her hair, looking around. "Well," she said quietly, then burst into tears.

That night, she walked from top to bottom of the house, flinging wide the doors of every chamber to pause on every threshold, her lamp raised high, shining the light deep into the wintry rooms, regarding the familiar arrangements of furniture and whatnots, of goods upon the pantry shelves, of small dressers and bedsteads in the servants' attic rooms. And though I followed behind her, she did not seem to notice, nor was she aware of the women's frightened faces as they stood in their doorways to gaze at our two figures illumined by a single lamp as we passed along the servants' hall. That night, the living glided about the emptied house; and it was we who were the homesick ones, though home.

At my door, I left Mama to her silent wandering and entered into my own snug room. The curtains hung massive against the far windows, darkening what was normally a cheerful chamber and competing with the little fire left to burn in my grate. Wearily, I threw myself into the chair and stared at the embers burning like so many watchful eyes behind the iron bars, flaring into life, and I nodded back, drifting off into a half sleep, and then it seemed Halcy's face stared back at me in the fire just as she had on Leadbetter's Island. Again her wide and frightened eyes begged me, again her mouth slowly opened as if to speak, and there was seaweed in her hair and the deep dark scent of damp ground round her. I stared back at her, and when she offered me her tiny bundle, I took the little moving body into my own arms and looked down into its scrawny red face—but Papa's eyes looked up at me, blinking, his mouth opening and closing in an effort to speak. I dropped the baby and turned and fled, terrified, back to where I saw Mama and Papa waiting for me through the trees. But when I reached them, I ran right through them.

"Mama!" I was on my feet, my heart pounding in my chest, the fire sunk to a dim glow, and the room gone quite chill. "Mama?" I whispered, shaking. I felt my way over to my bed, where I sat down heavily, the tears streaming down my face. The clock chimed one. I wept, fully clothed and unable to move. I heard a rustling in the hall, and then the knob turned and Mama herself walked in.

"Mama," I sobbed.

"What is it, Maisie?" She drew to my side. "You have frightened me terribly."

I could not answer her, I was weeping so.

"What is it, Maisie?" She put her hand on my shoulder and brushed the hair off my hot, wet cheeks, only making the tears come faster.

"There now," she whispered, and setting her lamp upon the table by the bed, she turned me gently round and began to unfasten the buttons at my back. "Hush, Maisie." Her fingers were firm as they eased the fabric loose, and eased my shoulders from the cloth. Still I wept, but the squall had begun to lessen. "Hush, Maisie," she said again, and I leaned my head against her and raised my hands to my tearstained face.

When I awoke the next morning, Mama's hand lay upon my shoulder, the fingers curled peacefully over the curve of my arm. She breathed deeply in a good sleep behind me, and for a little while I lay there upon my side and listened to her breathe and stared at that protective hand. Long and beautiful, the shapely fingers were ringed by Papa's many demonstrations of devotion; the deep green of an emerald flanked by diamonds rested upon the snowy field of her smooth skin. My mother prided herself on her hands, and the happy similarity between her own long hands and mine had often been remarked. I raised my own up above the coverlet and held it for a moment next to hers. But for the rings, we seemed to share the same hand: a pale skin covering the slender curvature of bone. Gently, I laid my own over hers.

"When you were born," she said softly behind me, leaving her hand where it lay, "you came before your time, a tiny seven-month child." She paused. "Dr. Skillings took you away, fearing for your little life, and when I regained consciousness after some while, the room was empty. It was as if you'd never been born." I sat up and looked down into her face. But she lay upon my pillow, staring up into the hangings, not seeking my eyes nor turning to me, as if the memory were imprinted there.

"Then followed a terrible time, for it was my life that nearly flickered out, not yours, and few believed I had many days remaining. I remember a long, long while spent upon my pillows when all the world seemed gray and worth a feather. Night after night I called and called for you, begging the nurses for a glimpse of your little face."

"Why would they not bring me?" I wondered for my poor young mother.

"They dreaded that you might catch my fever," she replied quietly, and then closed her eyes. "Papa went to Boston to fetch a specialist, and I vowed I would not die until he returned. Day passed by night into day and I lay with my head turned always toward the door so that if he were to arrive even as I died, his figure should be the last image my eyes should hold of the world."

Still immobile upon the pillows, the tears had begun to slide sideways down her cheeks, but she let them fall, and I did not wish to disturb her.

"And then one day he did! He did come through that door carrying you in his arms, so pink and healthy—such a brave, dear thing." She covered her face with her hands and wept, her tears flowing between her fingers, and I laid my head down upon her breast and wept with her. "For a long, shy moment, he stood there in the doorway bearing you, with such a strange smile upon his lips."

"Strange?"

"Yes, almost bashful—as if he wondered whether I would accept the gift he held for me in his arms!" She laughed through her tears. "So silly, when he held my child: my life restored to me, then. It was your papa gave me back my life—you, Maisie."

I put my head upon Mama's breast, envisioning my young papa standing in the door. She stroked my hair. Her head turned upon the pillow as though she listened intently. I raised up.

"I can almost hear him come again," she whispered.

"No, Mama!" I said brokenly.

"Almost." She smiled and closed her eyes.

Far longer than I can measure, my mother's face bore the stamp of her bewildered grief. I had thought Mama childlike in her behavior, inordinately dependent upon Papa, deferring to and addressing him exclusively in all manner of her expression. But the great silence of the first few weeks upon our return seemed to make of her a majesty, with a terrible power in her sorrow, and my small stilled heart seemed mewling by compare. After that first morning, she did not mention Papa again to me, as though she wished to lock him away, and seeing it was her best consolation, I did not speak aloud against the magnificent fortress of her grief.

Outside the house, autumn drew close about us. From my window, I watched the tilting glory of bright yellow in the sycamores give way to the umbrella spires of bare spindled trunks and darkening afternoons. The woolen mantles slung upon the front hall settee gave way to fur-lined greatcoats, and Parsons sent up stewpots thickened with brandy for our quiet dinners.

Of visitors, there were plenty. And for these, Mama rose to appear suitably adjusted to her state of mourning, sad but not melancholic. *Grief*—the very word, let alone the feeling—had a touch of fever in it, too hot and furious for the resigned matron Mama was expected to be as she received the well-meaning consolations. I would watch the light rise in her cheeks as she bent her head and listened, her gentle voice plying social questions of the caller, her fingers at work upon a tiny pillow. But as their voices faded away in the hall and the heavy front door shut behind the bustle and the interest, the work would fall from her hands. I became accustomed to these abrupt descents, the curtain having lowered upon the stage, and knew just how to pry the work from off her lap without her noticing, tucking it gently into the basket at her feet, then taking up my post in an opposite chair, the house quieting round us once again.

At the end of that September, I turned eighteen, and Mama insisted we seat ourselves to a formal dinner, and drink a toast. But as we stood across the table from each other in the candlelight, and Mama tried to speak what Papa ought, I could not keep my glass raised, nor keep the tears from spilling over—and both of us sank back down into our chairs. So that day passed wordlessly into the next.

Out of that quiet, our days marched in leaden procession. As though God had gripped Time's clapper and would not let it swing again, the hours rolled forward soundlessly, without color or light, a blank after blank after blank repeating. There was nought to mark, nought to note, but the quiet tedium of waking and watching Mama grow dimmer, as if her soul were shaded. Yet all that long autumn, I watched her, and listened, though there were no words between us save the most mundane, and no sound save the swish of thread pulled through fabric, or her footsteps pausing in the passage outside my room at night. Pausing, and then stepping on. I grew to be an aficionado of still life, my mother's face a field of sorrow so infinite in mute variety, I could not look away.

The quotidian matters of our house pressing too heavily upon Mama, I began to answer Miss Matchless's inquiries as to menus and linens. And though the housekeeper sorrowed for my mother, I watched the woman's sympathy begin to founder in the servant's need for order. The house must run. The place must continue.

"Look at Miss Maisie," I'd heard her mutter belowstairs, "she needs a husband. Who's to see to that?"

"Hush up, old woman," Jessie snapped. "You've not lost a soul you ever loved."

"Me?" came the astonished reply. "Why, I've lost everyone." A dish was put back on the shelf. "But there was none of this . . . mooning." Another dish replaced. "One goes on. One must go on."

For whom? my own heart clamored as I climbed back up the kitchen stairs and stood, my foot arrested upon the threshold, listening to the ticktock of that empty house. Nothing material had altered with Papa's death: Uncle Alec had ably taken up the stewardship of the firm and our fortunes, having worked at Papa's side all his life. Nothing in the wide front hall cried out the difference, not the thick carpeting upon the stairs, nor the burnished mahogany banister twining its languorous way up into the morning quiet.

Yet the world had grown insubstantial. I crossed the front hall soundlessly and entered Papa's library. The smell of leather mixed with the chalky scent of old paper and the deep-laid whiff of his cigars. But the wide desk had been cleared of his daily business, and the human stuff of the man had disappeared into the horror of this final tidiness. He was gone. There was his desk.

What am I to do? I asked the mute books lining Papa's study walls. But they spoke no more to me; their work was done, it seemed. I had lost my passport into that country; the avenues I had strolled along beside Papa were grown over with disuse.

Indeed, I had lost the capacity to recall a time before this time. Once this room had been filled with the warm hubbub of the many interlacing voices in the books upon the shelves, and just last summer Grange House had thronged with strange beginnings and I had glimpsed an opening and danced with Bart Hunnowell upon the very ridge of the world, extravagantly glad. But now the room before me was a cold cathedral of bleak spines, and Grange House—a place to which we would never return—closed up in my mind to become nowhere other than the place where Papa had died. And Bart Hunnowell? I could not summon any other image but that of his hurt and angry figure departing wordlessly from the breakfast table.

And so the winter days descended and swept by, each as mutely unchanging as the last, my mother's black-clad form stretched on the sitting room sofa, and I seated in the corner by the window, my head bent over a piece of fancywork, turning the stitches up to the weak sun. One bleak day in late January, I sat as the wind hurtled against the panes, the glass shuddering at my shoulder. Outside, passersby were bent against the driving weather, their hats and bonnets but frail shells around their heads and shoulders. I watched as the schooners behind them sailed slowly down the East River, their masts dwarfing the snow-covered city buildings of Manhattan across the water. A woman laughed, and the sound was caught up into the carriage jingle and carried past my window in the horse's hooves passing by on the pavement below. The world came to me now in meaningless pieces. And I had lost the beat of Papa's fingers upon my hand, tapping out the underlying song. The song that bound it all as one.

Behind me, the room was cheerful, though my mother sat at her writing desk, pen poised on her page for longer than was natural. I had a rapid glimpse of what the future held for me, curious captive between this inner and outer weather, and I but eighteen. I turned to regard my mother, but my movement warned her and I caught the swift replacement of the blank look on her face by the smile that stood for bravery and resolve.

"What is it?" she asked.

The thud of the muffled knocker sounded against the street door in the hall. There were callers. Mama rose to adjust her combs in the mirror, and the glass held us both for that instant, held us together as we must have appeared: a mother and her daughter in mourning. But she would not return my gaze in the mirror.

A weary sob started in my throat. "Oh, Mama," I said, my voice catching, "the world has broken into pieces."

"The world was ever in pieces, Maisie," she said quietly to my reflection.

"That is dull comfort," I said ruefully through my tears.

But she did not smile.

Dear Miss Grange,

How does the new year find you? Well, I hope. Often I have thought of you this bleak winter, for my thoughts seem to run upon tired boards, and the last two weeks at Grange House are all that my heart recalls. And there, you come to mind as you were in Papa's sickroom, so kind and patient with us all. I fear I may not have thanked you for your kindness to us in those last days—or your care.

Oh, Miss Grange, how am I to bear this? What shall I do? I miss Papa so. The world has stopped its speaking, stopped breathing, and my own voice has stuck in my throat. Mama manages one day after the next by writing letters.

Tell me—what is the view from Grange House in snow?

Yours,
Maisie Thomas

My dear Maisie Thomas—

 There is nought for you to do but remember and recall. Bring your father to mind as often as you can, Maisie Thomas, and let him rest there. His was once a vast and roving spirit. Let that spirit return to find its place in you.

 And once he has gathered there in your mind's eye, set him down in writing. For well I know the silence in the heart that settles after a death. You must set him walking again, and talking. And do so upon your pages. Long ago, that was the only way back to the land of the living for me.

 If you like, think of me as you would a companion by a quiet fire. Imagine me leaning forward a little to listen. For I will listen, and well. Your papa was a friend to me—long ago. Twice he came up to Grange House on quarry business—the first time to work with Father. And the second—well, the second time, he walked cross the threshold of our sad household and breathed new life into us all.

Ever yours,
Nell Grange

CHAPTER TWELVE

T here. There it lay—a purpose. Miss Grange's letter pressed
upon the spring and a hidden drawer popped open. I climbed
the stairs to my schoolroom and unlocked the cabinet in
which I had neatly stacked my copybooks last June, and I pulled one
out. It fell open to a Latin translation heavily marked by Papa, and my
eyes blurred. *Come back!* my heart cried. *Come back!* I looked down at
my words and at his corrections, and I sniffed.

I brought the book to the round table and, sitting down, turned
to an empty page. Where should I begin? With his death? My hand
hesitated, stunned by the sudden image of him lying bent and broken
at the bottom of that jagged hole. No, I thought, with his name.

LUDLOW THOMAS, I wrote at the top, and began:

*The Ludlow Thomases trace their forebears back to a still-extant castle
in England. When the young John Milton staged his masque, the bright
scenes played across the faces of the Ludlow family. Some callow, intrepid
Ludlow left Shropshire in the seventeenth century, following fast behind
the* Mayflower, *to settle first in Massachusetts, then in the wide, rich*

*Connecticut River Valley, to end at last among the elms of Brooklyn
Heights, whose vistas opened out into New York Harbor. It was 1815
by then, and the father of this story's Ludlow Thomas, son and heir of
the Black Ball shipping line, was pulled crowing into the Brooklyn clamor
of the new century. The rise of the early years of the century expanded
his fortune; the older he got, the more his familiars dropped away: The
brighter, it seemed, burned his star, and one evening he bent over the
head of his new son, Ludlow, pulled into the year of 1838, august as—*

I hesitated, smiling already, the spell of my writing broken—*a
muffin.* I put down the pen, remembering Papa roaring aloud when he
arrived at Mr. Dickens's description of the tiny Paul Dombey just so.
Papa! I smiled down at my handiwork. Even though I had written
little about him, there he was. I lowered my head again and this time
began to write him down in truth. That morning in January, I felt my
life commence to beat once more, faintly at first and then stronger as
I determined to take up Miss Grange's proposal. I made a pledge to
draw the world round me, and hold my papa close, in tiny blackened
scuff marks upon this page.

Thus increasingly, throughout that bleak January, then February,
the household's silence stretched from top to bottom story, its occupants intently putting pen to paper: Mama, enwrapped in her letters,
spent long afternoons at her table in the sitting room, and I upon the
third floor, in my old schoolroom, installed at my pages, each day
notching Papa up inch by inch from where he had lain for so long in
my mind.

Yet I soon found my page loosed its margins, for as I set down
the smell of uncovered earth telling of spring advancing even beneath
the winter chill, my mind might recall an afternoon upon a bench
in the park with Papa. I would write the conversation, the bent of his
body as he spoke, my blue gloves folded, and, word for remembered
word, I'd call him to me, recalling him through the rich blue-black of
my own ink, and falling further back in time to childhood, quickly
rendered, until I arrived at the moment when Papa first began coming
home in the afternoons to give me lessons, when my narrative grew
quite complicated. Writing Papa in this way, I found him first here
and there in the crannies of memory, not stuck upon a single thread

with a beginning and an end. And so I carried him carefully now, with small deliberate hands, weaving myself upon the page with he whom I missed.

February passed away without incident, then March, and by the middle of April, spring had begun her gay unfurling in the parks. And on one day, Mama nodded when I asked if I might walk out, and then another day, and a third. The blast of the old ferry, the sweet smoke from the sugar refinery blown into the air above the river—life! I recalled what Mr. Hunnowell had said a little bitterly to his mother— that he could only observe. And with an unexpected surge of sympathy, I wished I could tell him how mighty I thought it was to be an observer after all. For one could lose oneself in the aimless city tide: its people and my footsteps merging and convening, and then one could see best. All seemed to swing wide round me. Wide and sad all at once, for though I had grown accustomed to Papa's absence in the house, out-of-doors, he became an everywhere: a man turning the corner out of sight, a catch of a favorite tune of Papa's whistled between a taximan's teeth, the rain falling upon the slack waters of the East River, and then the great bridge stretching away from me toward Manhattan, magnificent in the late afternoon, the steady approach of city men crossing to where I waited, as I used to do at this time for Papa. And there was Papa striding toward me once again. His top hat gleamed in the spring light, though the angle blotted out his dear face as he came through the bright spot toward me with a grave smile upon his lips.

"Oh," I whispered with a start. "Mr. Lanman."

"Miss Thomas." He smiled. "How nice." And he held out his arm. He appeared very tall. I had forgotten. I took his proffered arm.

We spoke little on that spring afternoon, but it was a comfort to rest my hand upon his arm, just as an ordinary girl might do; a comfort to answer his quiet questions as he steered us expertly through the streets homeward. And, I remembered, he had been a kind correspondent during the days before Papa died.

And when, on the following evening, Jessie appeared at the door to ask whether we would receive a Mr. Lanman and his mother, I smiled at Mama; it would be a pleasant change from our solitary evenings. "We will indeed," my mother pronounced, slightly stressing the final word, and followed Jessie into the hall to greet the Lanmans and direct the drying of their damp garments.

"Hello again, Miss Thomas." He smiled. And before I could reply, his mother took my hand and pressed it hard between her own. "My dear," she whispered, "I have been so sorry indeed for your poor mother and yourself."

"Please. Sit down. Mrs. Lanman, come sit here by the fire across from me."

My mother indicated Papa's leather chair for Mr. Lanman to sit in, as easily as if it were only another chair. I took my accustomed place at my mother's side, a bit overwhelmed by our configuration, for we were exactly paired: The mother and the son faced the mother and the daughter. Mrs. Lanman broke the awkwardness, and Mama's ready answer bespoke a genuine willingness in her, an active part, I had not seen for months. The two were shortly engaged in a series of comparisons between this spring and the last, Mrs. Lanman insisting that she had not seen the like of this one for harsh and unforgiving weather.

Mr. Lanman gazed at the painting hung in the alcove behind my chair.

"Would you like to see it, Mr. Lanman?" I asked.

"Very much."

We rose and drew into the alcove. And suddenly, the evening of Mrs. Strong's dance flashed before my eyes, stopping at the moment when this man beside me had come up to speak to Papa, and what had Papa said to him then? With Jonathan Lanman before me, I could not remember, and despite myself, I felt tears well up at this lapse in my own memory.

"This is exquisite." Mr. Lanman had stepped quite close to examine it, his whole form leaning toward the small painting. I blinked back my tears.

"Yes, Papa bought it for Mama while on their honeymoon in London; I don't believe Papa imagined the painter would become so notorious, but the curious mood in it always beckoned to my father."

"He had a good eye."

Yes, I agreed silently. We turned back to the *Mariana*, where a young woman in deep blue velvet stood at her window, stretching out the stiffness of an afternoon spent at her needlework in front of the casement. In glorious disarray, several autumn leaves had fallen in onto her embroidered panel of flowers; and upon her face as she regarded the out-of-doors lay a kind of melancholic apprehension, a beautiful melancholy nonetheless, as if she has just then understood something, something grand. Here was the portrait of a lady thinking, in luxuriant privacy—and yet, she had been watched: She had been caught, for Mr. Millais had rendered her mood too exactly to have imagined it.

"Do you ever wish that one's life might look more like this?" I asked his black back.

"One's life?" He turned to regard me.

"Yes. To live amidst such abundance—and to be so thought-fully understood by another being—to have one's sadness appear to be so—"

Full! I finished to myself. I had faltered beneath his gaze. Foolish, foolish to speak such thoughts aloud.

"Miss Thomas, you begin to sound like Walter Pater." He was smiling. That was good then.

"Walter Pater? Is he a friend of yours?"

"I should hope not!" Mr. Lanman gave an embarrassed chuckle. "He's a bit of a questionable character; or rather, what he proposes is questionable—but his words often blaze a pathway straight to the heart." He smiled more quietly now.

"What makes his character so questionable?"

"Now your curiosity is aroused, and I'm guilty of having intro-duced you into distinctly unfeminine company."

"But please tell me of him, please do. I know so little."

"Indeed, Miss Thomas. You have never struck me as knowing little." His voice had softened, and the look he gave me then, I valued more than the loss of an answer.

Behind him, our two mothers stirred into action as if sensing the newly risen heat of the scene between us.

"Jonathan, my dear. We must leave these busy ladies. Mrs. Thomas has just told me of their plans to go abroad this spring."

He started at his mother's voice but did not, I think, register what she had said before I myself had uttered a little gasp of surprise.

"Ah," he said, turning to smile at my mother. "I am afraid the lights of the Brooklyn season will have lost their brightest orbs."

Mama bantered him. "Hardly, Mr. Lanman, when your own mother stays behind. Shame on you for such hyperbole."

Jonathan Lanman bowed in reply. "At least grant me the privilege, then, of calling upon you and your daughter in the intervening days between now and partial darkness."

"We would be delighted," Mama responded in her old manner.

Mr. Lanman nodded good-bye to me, and his mother took my hand again in farewell. The door closed behind them, carrying out into the hall the bright vistas and fresh prospects of a newly discovered landscape. Mama did not look at me, but seated herself back at her desk and commenced to write.

"Abroad, Mama?"

She lifted her chin, keeping her eyes on her page, and smiled. "Yes."

One hand upon the top of the page, she scribbled several more lines, blotted her work, and finally looked up.

"We must make you scarce in the face of someone's certain interest," she said quietly.

"Mama?"

But she did not reply.

Nor did we travel abroad, for, on second thought, Mama decided it best to fling wide the doors to "someone's" interest instead. And glad of a direction, I floated along in the wake of her excitement, pleasantly caught up in the change of scene.

In the following weeks, Jonathan Lanman paid us regular visits. Often his mother accompanied him, her wide-browed face a merry second to his more composed visage, and there was gentle laughter in the sitting room again. And there was surety in the hand he rested upon the mantel in the sitting room. And comfort in the easy clarity of his opinions. Indeed, his steady, pleasant conversation with my mother recalled the row of white oaks that lined the entrance to my grandmother's house in Oyster Bay: beautiful, immovable sentries that promised some permanence upon a mutable earth. I chatted and watched, as if playing a piano, the one hand crossing over to play the high notes while the other remains steady below, for I saw that Jonathan Lanman was paying court.

As April crossed to May, gradually small renderings of Mr. Lanman found their way onto my pages—as if I had begun writing *to* Papa rather than *of* him.

And Mama grew familiar, her dark brown eyes dancing in the candlelight, her white hands animated again as she conversed with our new friends. Indeed, one unseasonably cold evening in the middle of May, Mama returned to the sitting room after having seen the Lanmans to the door, a bright smile upon her face.

"What lovely people they are," she mused, drawing close to the fire, "and it is marvelous to find pleasure in company again. I feel the Lanmans to be so *sympathetic*."

"What was the story he spoke of, Mama? I don't remember Mr. James having written a vampire tale."

"Oh, no, Maisie, it was not a vampire tale at all."

I shook my head thoughtfully. "A story about a woman's vitality being sucked dry from the bite of a man's marriage proposal does deserve, I think, Mama, to stand on the shelf alongside Mr. Stoker's."

"You have not read Mr. Stoker?" Mama's glance was swift and alarmed.

I shook my head. "Of course not, Mama. Where would I have procured such a book?"

"Really, Maisie, I haven't the faintest idea, but you often speak so forcefully upon things about which you know nothing."

I pursed my lips.

"Furthermore," she said, rubbing her hands together and holding them near the grate, "Mr. Lanman was referring to the De Gray 'Romance' of Mr. James."

I nodded, remembering his fine hands receiving the cup of tea from Mama and replying in answer to her question, "No, no, Mrs. Thomas, I confess I am on the side of old Mrs. De Gray in the story, who took life as she took a cup of tea, weak, with plenty of cream and sugar, and—"

"Surely not weak!" I had interrupted.

"Maisie, let poor Mr. Lanman finish out his thought."

"I do not mind interruption in the slightest, Mrs. Thomas. Indeed, it is in this sitting room where the interruption is usually of the most stimulating kind." And he looked directly over his teacup at me, causing me to blush.

"Yes, I see." Mama smiled at him rather conspiratorially, I thought. "But do go on, please."

"I have always believed, Mrs. Thomas, in moderation—not to be temperate merely for temperance's sake, but because this way one might try all the world has to offer. Moderation allows for an enormous range of experience and tastes"—he held up his teacup—"without possible damage to your parts."

"Go on," I prodded softly as he took a sip of tea.

He grew earnest. "I believe in living a life that rests upon a wealth of experience, that comes from having known and seen all the shining face of the world."

"Yes," I answered, smiling at the picture that had risen in my mind, "but that does not sound like a weak life to me."

"*Weak* was only Mr. James's word. I prefer *moderate*. Experience! Travel! Encounter all! Yes, yes! But within bounds. How might the mind fully relish all it has digested if the stomach rebels at too great a quantity or too overspiced an encounter?"

At this, his mother clapped her hands together merrily and said, "Jonathan, my dear, you make me positively long for the supper table. We must leave these ladies to a less gustatory conversation!" And then she rose, nodding her head amiably at Mama and giving my hand a little squeeze as she passed me by.

And he? He gave my hand his own farewell, a touch that lingered just a hair beyond where it should, leaving me with a new picture to feast upon in my mind's eye. For he, too, longed to see the world and take in the full glory of what life might offer. His words sparked my banked imagination and fanned it high again. I knew he had said what he did for my benefit. I knew he meant me to link his vision, if I wanted, to my own.

With each day, it seemed the light in Mama's eyes grew higher, and now she took great interest in my appearance, and finding me at my desk would take the pen from my hand, with a titch! and rub the calloused spots smooth again with linseed oil and rose. At first I protested, for I had prescribed myself all the lives in the *Encyclopedia Britannica* and had just arrived at Carlyle. Simple, blunt, and truthful, I found him a most rugged and refreshing sensibility, one from whom I did not like to be pulled.

"I do not like veils. I do not like vermilion prosing about a death," I pronounced to Mr. Lanman one evening. "Men die in dramatic, ridiculous wastes of lives, all the time. And the prose should render it simply."

"Yes, but there is no meaning to be gained simply from the statement 'Men die.' "

"The meaning lies around the words. Think of your father—or mine," I added hastily, seeing his jaw stiffen. "Every time I read 'A man died,' I think of Papa. And there I am amid the smell of his sickroom, and standing near that mannish nurse who nonetheless held his head so gently while I poured the medicine down. Men die, and I think of Papa. I plunge back down into those hours, the words carrying me to my own meaning."

"You give away all power of description to the word itself."

"Yes, I think words hold a very ocean in them, and we can but dip down and pull up the tiniest cup."

"I don't think you ought to speak in such a way to Mr. Lanman, dear," Mama chided after he had departed.

"I am sorry, Mama." I turned to her. "You are distressed about my talk of Papa."

"Papa? No, I wasn't listening to any talk of Papa—I heard only something to do with oceans—but your tone was rather too straightforward, most contentious."

"I did not think so, Mama."

"Men do not like to be told straight out what you think; it is too blustery for them from a young woman."

"My words should fall about him like a gentle rain?"

"Now there it is, Maisie. That"—she mused, careful to describe it, proud of her exactness—"irony."

"Yes?"

"It is quite deflating."

"I do not think Mr. Lanman feels deflated by his visits, Mama."

"No," she agreed. "Nonetheless, you speak too directly for my tastes."

"I am sorry for it, Mama." And I rose and patted her cheek, but the gesture did not convince, for she grasped hold of my hand and looked up at me.

"What people think of you is important, Maisie."

I withdrew my hand gently.

"We are nothing without the good opinion of others," she pursued. "When I looked at your father, I could see in an instant what type of woman I was." She smiled.

"But Mama," I protested.

"Did I ever tell you how it was your father and I began our courtship?"

I stopped abruptly where I stood. "No, Mama."

She laid her head back against her chair. "One ordinary afternoon just at the end of the season, I found myself sitting upon the edge of a white settee at the Morgans' cotillion and looked across into the laughing eyes of your father, who had taken his seat upon the opposite chaise. Between us was set an enormous and odious arrangement of lilies, and I believe my dislike lay unmasked upon my face."

I smiled at the scene Mama had painted, beguiled by this early history.

" 'You do not like flowers?' he asked me.

" 'I do not like this arrangement,' I replied, shy of him. 'There is no expression in it. Just—'

" 'Just?' He was tamping down his pipe, but he looked at me in his sideways fashion.

" 'Just quantity,' I finished.

"He nodded. 'Precisely, Miss Haskell. I absolutely agree.' Then he came round the lilies and stood beside me where I sat, and we talked a little."

"About what?" I breathed.

But Mama shook her head as if startled to find herself seated before me with the dwindling day around us. "I do not remember." She shrugged, the memory still light on her face.

"Why did you never tell me that story before?"

"There was always Papa, before."

I nodded, a lump in my throat.

"But within a month, he had asked for my hand." She looked up brightly, though tears threatened. "Then he left."

"Left? Where did he go?"

"To Grange House."

"Oh!" I said, thoughtfully. This must have been the time Miss Grange had mentioned in her letter. "And for how long was he gone?"

"It seemed ages, though it was but three months." Mama smiled wearily. "I nearly drove your poor grandparents to distraction, so anxious was I for his return."

I sank down beside her.

"But then"—her voice hardened—"when he did return at last, I wished him gone again."

I sat up on my heels. "Why, Mama?"

"He made me frantic. . . ." She tapped at the arm of her chair. "Or, I was frantic—now I cannot tell the cause. But once he had returned, he seemed incapable of remaining, needing to dash off here and there on business for the line."

"Perhaps he grew shy as the wedding date approached." I warmed to this picture of Papa.

Mama's eyes rested on me, as though she had only then recalled to whom she spoke. "Perhaps," she said, and it seemed she meant to halt the conversation just there.

"But you do not think so?" I prodded.

Still she gazed at me, considering. I patted her hand. "There was no wedding date," she burst out at last. "We could not agree to one. Every date my parents proposed, Ludlow would turn aside with an objection. May was too chill. June was far too ordinary. July too hot, and—" She sank back in her chair.

I took her hand, startled by the vehemence of this recollection, and the evident distress my poor mother had felt. She pressed my hand, then shook her head as if to clear the memory.

"Then all of a sudden the dreadful prelude was done. One bright morning in January he knelt before me with happy tears in his eyes and declared he could wait no more!" Now she smiled. "And two weeks later—we married. I became Mrs. Ludlow Thomas!"

I looked at her for a long minute. "How happy you must have been," I said fervently.

She flushed. "I was." Then she reached out and clasped my hand. "As will you be."

She had pulled the present round us, and I noticed with full force the color in her cheeks and the lilt in her voice. It was clear that my "romance" might call Mama back across the threshold into life. And my heart grew full.

Like a seamstress, I saw a way to mend the great tear, and in no unnatural manner, for it was what Papa, too, would have wished. Jonathan Lanman was a man I knew he approved. And, in these past weeks, I had come to like the careful formality of his manners myself— the easy way in which he took Mama and me in charge—it was restful. I could do as I pleased while he chatted. Think as I pleased. That evening, the world's pieces seemed to gather forces round again, and I felt right and happy, as though I heard my father's voice in my ear, singing out the underlying song once more.

CHAPTER THIRTEEN

I found myself drifting along upon this gentle current, being pulled nearer and nearer to some type of declaration. It was pleasant to float along so, comfortable in the knowledge that a marriage was right and good for Mama and thus myself. Our lives would broaden with the addition of Mr. Lanman. Like the pages I had written all throughout that winter, Jonathan Lanman appeared to me a vessel in which I could mingle both the past and present. He had known Papa. He, too, would wish to carry my father forward.

Yet these peaceful visions of my future were tinged by the sad realization that we would never return to Grange House, and thus I might not see Miss Grange again in this world. And so one morning toward the end of that spring, I began to copy all I had written and recalled of Papa for Miss Grange, thinking she might like to read what had given me such solace to write. The part of me that would no longer return to her longed to spend the cozy hour by the fire she had conjured and pour my recollections into her imagined ear. I made a tidy package of my writing, tied it neatly up, and sent it off.

Within a week's time, into my hands was delivered an answering packet, wrapped in a dark green oilcloth and postmarked from Middle Haven.

Mystified, I tore it open and saw to my surprise that Miss Grange had sent me what looked to be a diary of her own. A letter lay atop.

Maisie, it began. *After all, it is clear you are the one I had hoped you to be.*

I quickly lowered the page, my mind balking. Those words thrust aside the woman who had comforted me in my sorrow. Here instead stood the woman by that lonely grave in the woods. I shuddered. How Miss Grange had frightened me that day—insisting I had a part to play in her unfathomable tale.

Then the image of her pale, importuning face, and of the pain in her voice as she spoke of the grave, returned to me. She had clasped my hands. She had looked directly into my eyes. And on that day, I had looked askance.

Forgive me, Miss Grange, I said to her pages neatly piled before me. I did not know Sorrow then. I took up the letter and its companion pages and began to read.

Maisie—

After all, it is clear you are the one I had hoped you to be. You have the gift indeed. On your own, you have managed to write your father down, just as I should have liked—slant, not straight. Now you must help me, Maisie. It is within your powers so to do. And though I never thought to show you what you have in your hands, I see now it is the place to start.

Here are several portions of my diary—the storeroom of life's detail in which I found my fictions. The first two I send merely to give you a glimpse of my ambition, long before the sadness overtook our house. (Forgive me this vanity!)

The latter contain sketches of your father. And for now, let us say these are sketches I made of him for a love story I never finished.

Read these carefully. Consider what you see there. And, when you are ready, write me what you think.

Yours,
Nell Grange

3 August 1872

This shall be no diary. For what is that but a little coffin, a life laid down into several single narrow pages—yet such a leaky vessel! If I am to succeed at all in this profession, I must cast off the mooring of the everyday, for does not Memory herself blur the lines between what occurs now and what occurs later? And is not my aim to take memory as my muse? How she appears quick-sudden at my side and overtakes me, so I may be sitting there in Mother's chair, my two hands up and stiff as spindles while Sue winds the yarn around and around, and still be in another time, also in that chair—when a child perhaps, and watching the snow falling into the dreary ocean—so Sue leaning toward me as she twines becomes that snow descending, softly breathing.

This book shall be bigger than a single grave; let it be the very yard!

Reader (for so I hope someday to have), reach in your hand to lift the old iron latch and give a little push against the gate. Step cross the stone threshold with me tonight, then follow toward the Grange family plot. Cast your eyes upon these five granite moons anchored to we who lie below the summer grasses.

Lean down and read with me:

CASSANDRA GRANGE, *Wife of*
RORIE GRANGE, *Father of*
GEORGE GRANGE, *Brother of*
SUSANNAH GRANGE, *Sister of*
NELL GRANGE, *Self*

"The stone'll speak the story," says old Abby in the kitchen, but my long fingers round this pen deny it. What is a stone to the smell of this night pulled close about me as I write alone by my candle, my pen scratching into this empty book, my yellow room a dark cave cupped around this center point, this pen point into which I now begin to pour all the waters of my twenty-four years, the foghorns lowing side the wharf, my right foot placed upon my left for warmth beneath this table.

5 August

Do you wonder about me, Reader? That is good. I should like to have it so. I should like to have another—wholly unknown—read what I have written late into the evening, finally casting down the book to say, "How thrilling!" I should like that—to reach my hand across the sill and shake yours. Surely, even here, I might feel the tug upon the line between us—the crossing breeze of my reader's gently exhaled breath as he looked up, having understood.

To be an Author, Reader!

(Now the rest follows five years later—N.G.)

10 September 1877

We have a cousin, it would appear, come to us from Ireland without warning; and though another man at table disconcerts, he is not disagreeable: rather silent, with a shock of black hair, and hands that are kept firmly in his pockets—save when they emerge to take up knife and fork. True to fashion, Susannah has coaxed some particulars from Mr. Hayden Gilroy: He was raised by a stonemason and his wife after the death of his own parents. Poor man, it must seem to him that Susannah is the only woman among us able to speak, for in the past two days since his arrival, Susannah alone has played formidable hostess, as I prefer to let her do the talking so I might best watch the scene; and Mother, unaccountably, appears incapable of direct address to her nephew. Seemingly distracted by infinitesimal noises, she bears her attention fixedly upon us, but with her head slightly turned, as if an extra sphere is newly laid around this ordinary one of humdrum conversation.

"Whatever is the matter, Mother?" Susannah asked tonight.

Mother turned round upon the landing to look at the two

149

of us stopped upon the stair below, each of us shielding the candle flames with one hand as we waited for her answer.

"Why do you ask?" Her hand crept to the banister.

Seeing the bleak expression upon our mother's face, Susannah shook her head.

"No matter."

Mother looked again from her to me, and then, for answer, turned round and took the rest of the stairs, moving along the passageway without another word to us. We followed her to her room, stirring the fire in the grate a bit higher to take the chill away and laying out her night things upon the bed, but Mother stood in the middle of the room and paid us no heed, listening instead to some inner conversation.

"He does not take after my sister," she finally said, and motioned me to her table for her drops.

It is four months tomorrow since Father died.

20 September

What is the trouble with Mother? If I watch her any more closely, or with any more disguised suspense, I may overstrain my own senses of perception. Nonetheless, all is not well with her: Color flushes into her cheeks at the oddest moments and as quickly vanishes, leaving her slightly shaky and frequently abstracted. I could wish to write something about a bellows pump and memory—how my mother flushes up and dies away, old thoughts respiring in her, and suddenly illumining what is otherwise a steady pallor.

Now we are positively overrun with men.

Mr. Ludlow Thomas is come again, and we are all in a strange flurry—he has brought a portmanteau full to bursting with books and magazines and tiny fragrant sachets from his betrothed. He is much changed since Father's funeral: less Macassar, less city, less silly conversation. I suppose the thought of his impending marriage has burnished him to this softer, more reflective man.

Nonetheless, he remains a man of commerce come to oversee his investment; though he is delicate with George, and clearly taken with Cousin Gilroy's hard knowledge of the matter, it is his resolve that will provide the necessary tinder to keep Grange Quarry active. Twice already, they have all journied out to Leadbetter's Island, only to return and sequester themselves in Father's study. Indeed, Father would have reveled in the scenes now playing round the house—the whole of the Eastern Seaboard is parsed and paved by Grange granite in our conversation. For Mr. Thomas sees the winning of the war as a boon to the granite business: Northern pride will raise a fury of great buildings to itself, he proclaimed, to which Mother replied, "Then there will be blood upon our stone."

I see she means to be evenhanded in her displeasure with both new men.

Mr. Thomas appears quite intelligent (though he *is* fair), with a ready laugh that, I surmise, belies a more serious character altogether. Of the two newcomers, I prefer him, though our cousin is by far the finer animal of the two—sleek and hungry; continuing to be unnervingly restless.

(30 drops today)

23 September

The men are gone to the quarry for two or three days, as Mr. Ludlow Thomas wishes to speak to the workers. What does one do with such a man? He gives me his confidence—indeed the very contents of his heart—in womanish fashion, rather than pocketing it without comment like most of his sex.

"What is this one named?" he asked me, pointing to the tiny white shell in his palm. I leaned down from my perch upon the ladder and brushed away the sand from the surface of the shell so I might see the markings.

"Nothing," I replied, and wet my cloth again, preparing to climb up a rung farther.

"I do not believe you, Miss Grange." He held his palm up so it drew even with my waist above him. "Look again."

There was a particularly salt-encrusted spot I concentrated on, rubbing fiercely against the windowpane in tight circles, the motion warming my hands. I felt a tug upon my apron strings.

"Stop!" I could not help smiling down at him. He was ridiculous, insisting that he must learn all the names of the shells and crawlers before he returns to New York, where he means to deliver a lecture on the life unremarked among the rocks of Maine.

"Spat," I said without looking at him.

"Spat? And what is that?"

"An oyster baby."

He looked into his hand. "And why not call it merely oyster?"

"Is a child a man?" I asked him.

He shook his head mournfully, as though I played with him; and he a man of business, a man of consummate intelligence and self-worth. He drew out his handkerchief and made a great to-do of wrapping the tiny white creature. "Well." That was all he said before he turned and proceeded down the lawn. I turned back to the window, the autumn sun welcome upon my shoulders and the back of my neck. I'd the whole first-floor side windows still to do.

"You are magnificent, Miss Grange." I jumped and nearly dropped my cloth. He spoke low and stood at my elbow, looking up at me quite earnestly.

I stepped down from the ladder and dried my hands upon the grass, entirely perplexed as to a suitable response.

"Because I know the names of shells?"

"Because there is such knowledge in you"—he tapped his chest—"in here."

I looked past him to the apple tree in the meadow. "Oh, and how is it you have come to know that?"

"I have listened to you"—he stopped—"next your sister."

"She is a mighty one."

He did not answer for a moment, and I glanced at him beside me. He was studying me and smiled when he saw my eyes upon him. "She is pretty," he admitted. I nodded in agreement. "But, may I say it?" he continued. "You are beautiful."

I colored, suspecting a joke immediately.

"Do not tweak me, Mr. Thomas. Susannah is the beauty in

our family." I picked up the bucket, wishing nothing more than to leave, but he put a detaining hand upon my arm. I looked at him.

"Stay, Miss Grange, I do not . . . tweak you."

"Then why say such a thing when it is so preposterously untrue?"

He looked away impatiently. "Very well."

I was pricked by his impatience into raising what should have been silent.

"What would your fiancée say if she heard you were paying compliments in plain view?"

He colored, then said quietly, "It was no compliment, Miss Grange."

Well! What did one do with that? We stood awkwardly side by side in silence. But he did not move away.

"Tell me, Miss Grange." His tone was lighter. "I have none, and you are so sure of yours—what is it to have a sister?"

I turned to face him, surprised. But there was no laughter on his lips, and I wished to step free of where we two had been, so I answered him, directly.

"A sister is one's other half," I offered.

He was silent, waiting.

"Or, say," I continued, more for myself than the city gentleman beside me, "she is at once who I am—and am not"—I paused—"made visible."

"And who are you not?" He watched me.

"Who are you who should know so much about me?"

"Nobody." He held out his hand. "A friend."

(Again, 30 drops)

27 September

When he appeared at first, I did not trust my eyes, for he was clothed in a suit the color of fog, and he moved through the leaning trees as easily as I.

"Stop a bit, Miss Grange," he called to me. I waited for him to approach and amused myself by thinking him an apparition who, the closer it stepped, stepped into its living, breathing body;

so when he arrived before me now fully clothed and slightly flushed, wan ether had turned to flesh.

"Hello," I said. "For an instant, I thought you were not mortal."

He burst out laughing at this, and the sound shivered the casings of the fog—what was dim become clear: We were a man and a woman in the middle of the wood.

"Where are you going?"

"Nowhere in particular."

"No destination?" he exclaimed in mock horror, his face alight. "No clear path? You undermine to the core what I thought to be the chief characteristic of a Yankee."

"I am not a Yankee," I replied breezily, and set off in the direction of the last gull's cry.

"Ah," he called to my back, "yes, I have forgotten. You are a figment of my imagination—the touchstone of my imagination—called into being by the fog."

I did not turn, but spoke a little louder to send my words backward to him. "Your muse?"

"No, let us say my heroine." He had fallen into step right behind me on the narrow pathway, and I could hear him dodging the pine boughs that snapped backward after I passed.

"A heroine? I detest that word, *heroine*."

"And why is that?"

"It is only just *hero* with a little tail stitched on."

He was silent. We walked forward for a bit, until I heard the osprey call and circled toward the cove, following its shrill cry. I could hear him step after step behind me, his hand brushing back the cobwebs in regular time to his even breathing. I found I enjoyed his company—he did not talk needlessly to pass the time as we walked.

"I do not think I understand your meaning, Miss Grange." I paused and looked behind at him blankly.

"A little tail?"

"Oh." I frowned. "I do not think a feminine character should be described in similar terms to a masculine character."

"But surely *heroine* connotes its own meaning, distinct from *hero*?"

I walked on again, uneasy. I did not know how to answer him—and the distinction was of vital importance. It was as if my mind stubbed up against the borders of itself, like a rock wall suddenly risen at the edge of what had seemed a limitless and broad spring field. I knew what I meant, but I did not have the tongue to say it out loud. We were nearing the cove, and I could hear the soft washing of the water onto the flat rocks. Hearing our advance, the osprey began a shrieking that caused me to stop dead and wait for the next sound to beckon me in a new direction. The osprey shrieked again, then was answered by another, the call coming from deeper into the woods.

The birdcall and its answer suggested the manner of my reply. I stopped walking and looked at him as I gathered my thoughts and set them clearly upon the sill.

"Say aloud the word *hero*," I instructed him.

He did so, and the wonder of it was he did not question me by look or word.

"Now say the word *heroine*."

Again he did what I asked.

"Do you hear?"

He shook his head. "What is it you mean me to hear?"

"Hero. Heroine. Hero. Heroine." I repeated the words slowly and carefully, the fog brushing across the place we had stopped, as if to soften the very edges of my meaning.

Again he shook his head.

"The echo. The lady word is nought but a softer, longer version of the man word."

"And are not man and woman versions of each other?" He was not light as he asked this question.

"If the similarity might be signified in another fashion," I answered, "so that the one is not the other with an addition—I do not like that addition: It speaks of fainting couches and lilting voices and cast-down gazes."

"Why not think instead of hero as a heroine cut short—as

one cut off from that lengthening echo? The man lacks the extra—for the echo is what recalls a self back unto itself; thus the man seeks it in a woman."

He had brought us to familiar ground now, and it was most irritating. What I had meant was not a disquisition on why the sexes needed each other. It had a thing or two to do with a woman not being a man, but then not being an "—ine," either. And now, I thought, my silence has handed him the trophy. He would think he had settled the point, had finished it off nicely, so ending—and winning—the conversation.

But I misjudged him, for he did not proclaim victory in his demeanor or his actions. Instead, he had started to walk once more, plunging still farther into the ghostly woods, where, I sensed, he walked to think. And I followed, raising my eyes every so often to see where his shape tended. Again we were silent, and we walked now in single file, now in tandem as the trees made a little clearing between them, passing farther and farther backward into those woods. As we moved through the familiar places, I grew distracted by his direction and by the evident ease with which he found his way about in the center of these woods without the bordering shoreline as a guide. In here, all compasses save memory are of little avail. Yet it seemed he knew where he stepped, and the closer on we drew to my sister's and my spot, the more agitated I became, though curious to see if he would find it.

Within an hour, we were upon the old quarry, where Father first tried to mint the rockbed beneath these woods. The granite walls of the great hole rose above the deep black water that had risen when he had cleaved the rock down too deep.

My companion stopped and looked down into the dark obscurity. I also gazed into the place. Far beneath that surface lay castoffs from childhood—some shells thrown in for wishes, a whittled stick of George's, and an old doll of Susannah's I had tossed in to see if it might swim. I'll not forget how fast it sank, nor how quickly our noisy gaming became shocked silence. The memory still causes me sorrow—I would raise that doll to this day to give back to Sue, she mourned it so, and I the instant villain.

"This place is haunted, I feel it," he spoke into the water.

I sniffed to break the spell of his romantic nonsense, telling him instead of Susannah's doll. "She's what haunts the place, more likely."

His face had altered. "Poor girl," he said.

But to which "girl" he referred, I still have no idea. Perhaps the doll had called to mind someone of whom he was fond, for a faraway smile slanted out beneath his mustaches.

28 September

"Who was it you walked with yesterday?"

"Was I walking, Sue?"

She flushed. "I saw you leaving from the stair window. I wanted to catch you up, but you disappeared so fast, it seemed, as if you went to meet someone."

"I did."

"Who? Tell me, Nell." Her hand held fast to my arm.

"Myself."

"Ha! I do not think so."

"Well, it is so." I stepped from her grip and walked the rest of the way down the staircase toward Grandfather Reuben's library. But she ran quickly down beside me and drew her arm beneath mine, pulling me toward the open, sunny door. I let myself be led by her, half-loving being taken in this way, and also curious to see where she meant us to go, what new plan she had for us to follow.

We crossed the threshold and stepped out onto the porch's protective cape. Sue meant to sit outside, her sorting basket already placed just to the side of the painted bench by the front door, and I noticed she had brought me a book to pretend to read by. I looked down the lawn and saw a brave scene indeed, for there they all were, clustered about a crop of rocks beside the boathouse. Hayden Gilroy crouched down at eye level with the rocks, and above him stood George, paying rapt attention, his hands on his knees, bending down to follow something our cousin explained. Mr. Ludlow Thomas stood a little to one side, his arms crossed, listening to Hayden but looking out to sea. For a time, we two sat in silence, watching this masculine tableau below us.

"Who is the better man?"

"George, of course."

She slapped at my dress beside her. "Nay. Answer me."

"Who is the better man, do you think, Sue?"

She squinted and tipped her head, looking for all the world like a holiday painter there by my side.

"The one is very tall and handsome, and seeming wise, I think. And, of course, with a considerable fortune."

"And a fiancée," I put in flatly. "What about the other?"

"The other is . . ." She did not continue. I watched the men.

"If he weren't engaged, Mr. Thomas would suit you nicely, don't you think, Nell?"

I answered contrarily for the fun of watching her color rise. "Nay, Sue." I leaned over and whispered in her ear, my hand resting upon her neck. "The other suits me more."

She whirled round her head to face me.

"Was it he you walked with yesterday, Nell?"

"How can you know there was a he?"

She colored.

Susannah, dear, are you reading this?

29 September

Last night, a new story woke me from my bed, and I could not sleep for the importuning voices of the characters, engaged as they were in some strange dialogue I do not choose to record: It sets the man as too excitable, the woman too cold.

30 September

In the house tonight, we ladies await the men's late return from the quarry: I for the scene, and Sue for the company.

Mother has retired; Abby has left a light supper by the fire, but it remains untasted, for both Sue and I are hard at work. There she sits in her corner, and I do not need to turn round to see her hand hesitate above the black page of her scrapbook, or the manner in which she sucks thoughtfully upon her lip, surveying the arrangement she has prepared for each page.

Piled at her feet are little labeled boxes full of things she has saved: a sliver cut from a letter of condolence sent to Mother from a person in Belgium; leaves and shells, feathers, scraps of dresses we have cut down and given away. All our lives are held there upon the pages of Sue's black books—senselessly, I should add, for she has made no effort to explain, merely to record.

"Why paste that in?" I had turned round to see her holding up a steamer ticket of George's—for a trip he never took, mind.

She placed it carefully down upon the page. "Because it happened."

"Nay, Sue. George never went."

"Exactly."

The men burst in. I accosted the first to enter. "Mr. Thomas, what do you think about saving every little scrap, every little thing connected to the events of a year?"

"Why I think it should make quite a stockpile!" he replied cheerfully, crossing to the fire.

George, however, came to Sue and looked over her shoulder at what she did. "Well, look at that. I had forgotten it was the same day." Both he and Sue were silent. "Poor Father," he said suddenly, and she looked up at him and smiled.

"What does the ticket say about your father?" Cousin Gilroy had also drawn near to Susannah. She rubbed the paper flat with a tiny board and leaned down to blow softly upon the page.

"The ticket says nothing about our father," I replied, and turned away from them to see Mr. Thomas give a good kick to the center log.

"Not true," said George soberly. "I did not use the ticket because Father had just died."

Mr. Thomas's foot stilled.

"Nonetheless," I pursued into the silence, "Susannah's book is full of things without explanation. The ticket itself does not describe what happened."

"It does not describe," Susannah remarked, "it stands for."

Cousin Gilroy leaned over her to the box beside the open book and picked up a deep green leaf rimmed by a bit of orange.

"And what does this stand for?" he asked.

Susannah flushed. "Oh, that leaf is inconsequential."

"Then why press it into your book?" Our cousin was curious, and he held the leaf up to the lamp flickering upon the wall above Susannah's head.

"Yes, Sue. Of what is the leaf a representative?"

"Of a walk I took, that is all."

"Autumn, I'd say, by the mixed coloring," Mr. Thomas mused.

"Yes. It was the eleventh of September to be exact."

"Ah," remarked Hayden Gilroy. "Three days after I arrived."

Susannah bent her head, letting the shadow hide her cheek.

"And what does it signify, then?" I pursued.

"Autumn," she murmured, lightly pressing her palm against the ticket pasted firm upon the black page.

"Autumn," I mused aloud. "How many words must I use for that one? What story might I tell?"

"A walk in the woods," said Mr. Thomas.

"The cool and damp——" George began.

"Upon a corner of the lawn," I cut in, "under the branches of the spreading birch tree, an old man waited in the dappled color, watching as a village child progressed to where he sat, welcome as a small breeze, her petticoats blowing about her chubby ankles." I paused.

"And how are those words better than the leaf to say autumn?" Susannah asked before I could begin again.

"A leaf is too private a system of expression," Mr. Thomas put in unexpectedly.

"Yet, there is no strain in regarding a leaf," Mr. Gilroy responded.

"That story sounded fairly easy upon the ears, I'd say." George laughed. "Go on, Nell."

"Nay. Susannah is right." I crossed my arms, suddenly melancholy. "My words are no better for telling."

And though he asked once more, I remained silent. Silent as George and Hayden and Susannah began to chat again about another page in her book. Silent, and melancholy as the tomb. What were my words after all? For every leaf Susannah found and pasted, I'd need to write pages upon pages—and still who would ever know who we had been? Below my companions' chatter, below the fire's pop, came the steady ticking of that clock upon the mantel. I looked at the flash of color in Susannah's cheek now raised to Cousin Gilroy's as he spoke, George rocking back upon his heels, impatient somehow. The foghorn tined the night. Here were we all, casting after our own dooms with miniature rods. Nothing can represent us—nothing satisfy.

(35 drops)

CHAPTER FOURTEEN

I sat for a long while without moving, rehearsing the scenes I had just read, the pages still clutched in my hand. So few pages and yet a world. And there was comfort in that world, for well I understood the profound distraction of Miss Grange's mother and, too, the sister with her scrapbooks, pasting in the ticket the brother never used. As if the ticket might somehow signify the whole abysmal horror of their father's sudden death. A ticket. The tears rolled down my cheek. And there in the room with them all was Papa. I could see him distinctly, the character was writ so true. There in her hands, my father walked and spoke in flashes I recognized; and reading him, having him so quietly to myself before me, was a heaven of a kind. Though I did not comprehend what she wished me to do with it, her diary gave me a *great* sufficiency, a gift indeed. Here were pages from a book that did not sit upon the shelves downstairs in my father's house. Here, indeed, was a papa I never could have written on my own.

Was Papa—and then the very same characters as those in the wild gothic Miss Grange had told me last summer. Here was the mysterious cousin arrived, the elder sister, a brother (though here he was alive) and their troubled mother—with her drops. I shivered. Something in the creeping increments of those drops recorded recalled the smudges climbing up the fictive walls of Grange House. Were the drops real indeed, or just a bit of embellishment to aid the scene? But they must be real, I reflected. What was in my hands was a *diary*. I stopped short.

A diary. Was everything recounted here true, or merely true enough? And what did she mean by calling these "sketches" for a love story? A love story she imagined, or—

I stood up. A love story in truth? Papa had told me he knew nothing of Miss Grange. And there he was again, in my mind's eye, saying it, seated across from me in the boat, and the oars stretched out into the calm harbor. Yet there was he now also, standing below Miss Grange upon a ladder, and smiling up into her face.

I heard Jonathan's voice downstairs. And still in the clasp of her pages, I descended to meet him. I do not remember anything of what we spoke that evening, simply that the vision of my younger papa seemed to follow Jonathan everywhere. And I could not resist comparing Mr. Lanman to Miss Grange's rendering of the man in the woods. Would Jonathan ever have said such a thing about heroes and heroines? Indeed not, I reflected as I sat observing him playing cribbage with Mama, his fine brow concentrated above the board. Indeed, nowhere that evening, nor the next, could I find in Mr. Lanman the easy movement of mind and spirit so clearly set down upon the pages of her diary. Did it matter? No, I asserted to my now-habitual page. But then, almost guiltily, I returned to read and reread the sections she had given me. And thus, the following days found me bent to her pages, listening to their secret tune.

Often I found myself speaking the woman's lines aloud in the privacy of my schoolroom—a woman I should like to be: a woman unafraid to show the sometime contradictions of her mind. And then, once or twice, visions of Mr. Hunnowell sprang up—standing before me with my bowl of raspberries in his hands, or waving from the rocks. He might have fit the part of the man far better than Mr. Lanman. But then—in order to be fair—hastily, I searched my memory instead for a more provoking image—the inexplicable and contradictory parlor man at breakfast, for example—thus banishing him as a mere pretender for the role.

Though no man could fit the part as neatly as had my young father, still I welcomed these sketches of a love story, gladly taking them as a kind of primer. For the conversations between the man and the woman suggested what I would like to see of love. So Miss Grange and my father became unlikely characters in the romance I would choose to follow—more, to echo. And I took their words to heart.

Had I recorded the many voyages I traveled up and down the stairs of our house, my mind struggling to put the diary in its place, one might have thought a new geography was mapped. Up to the top, and what I sought for myself—the soaring freedom of Miss Grange's mind—beckoned me; then down I'd march—down to where Mama sat, or Miss Matchless stopped me with a question, or where Jonathan looked up as I entered and rushed to draw me to his side.

One morning, I sat at the round table in my schoolroom, idly flipping through old lessons. Upon the reverse of a dictation, I wrote, *Shall I marry Jonathan Trumbull Lanman?* My hand cupped the pen and rested on the white page. There was a comforting pleasure in writing out all three of his names—such round solidity displayed before me. Below them, I wrote, *Shall I be Mary Ludlow Thomas Lanman?* Our two names stared back at me, mute testimony to a future I might call my own. I put the pen down. A spring breeze blew in about my shoulders. I looked out the schoolroom window, following the line of roofs to the ribbon of river beyond. The ships passed by. High tide. My fate remained undisclosed.

At last, the answer seemed to me to lie with Miss Grange. What had happened at the end of her "love story"? And in a state of mingled dread and anticipation, I wrote her thus: *If there is more—if this is not a fiction, I must know. And I must see the end.*

Six days later, as though it had been poised and ready to descend, I received into my hands a second packet, wrapped like the first in a dark green oilcloth. I cut the string around the cloth and carefully drew out from their wrappings a stack of pages. A note lay atop:

Very well, Maisie Thomas—

It is better so. The best way forward is through the past—through these words—so you might see, and so begin your part.

Yours very truly,
Nell Grange

This time I did not dally over her hieroglyphics; I snatched up the pages and read.

4 October 1877

It is a bright blue morning, offering a domed sky so high, you might think it called itself to mind of summer, the clouds sluffing across to weave heaven's white upon the blue. I am sick and feverish and am forbidden the downstairs, and so I must content myself up here with little visits from Susannah and the slow movement of this daylight across the room. There are such blazes of pride to an autumn day, all fierce color tilting against the dun land advancing, Quiet Conqueror. Ah, Lord, I cannot harness my mind—she would prance a bit and not approach the mounting block.

ON DRIFTWOOD BEACH

The wind came up strong from the west and blew the waves sideways, though the whitecaps hurled straight in on the coming tide. George walked far ahead of us, searching out new wood. The sun had begun its lowering and, I think, it was that slant and the wind that set a weird light bouncing on the rocks covering the beach—noticeable enough for Hayden Gilroy to stop his walking and crouch, sifting stones through his fingers and holding up the smooth globes to the wind. Susannah walked onward on some pretext after George—it would not do for her to rest all the time with Mr. Gilroy, he might think her forward, or, worse still, an interested party. Mr. Thomas was stopped at the water's edge nearby.

I regarded the random collection of rocks splayed along the line of my boot tips. Next to my right boot lay a perfect stone egg, mouse gray and flecked with tiny spots of bluish green, battered smooth—so smooth, I fancied I could feel the waters that had made it still slipping from the face. Return, you must, I thought, and with a single motion grabbed it from its resting place and turned and hurled the stone straight out into the broiling water, feeling the weight of that stone still in my hand even as it left me.

"Bravo." Mr. Gilroy was standing beside me.

I smiled. "Let us see if your arm surpasses mine."

Without answering, he bent and chose a like stone in weight, this one round as a newel post and again as smooth; then he leaned back, his arm behind his head, and took a running step toward the sea and then shot out his arm so the stone hurtled far past where mine had sunk, to vanish in the deeper water. He turned for my applause. I shrugged.

"The target does not hold. It is far too difficult to discern whose has fallen where."

He grinned at my gaming and motioned up the beach where Susannah's back grew more and more distant. I nodded.

This time I chose a round rock also, and one of smaller heft than my first. The wind was in my favor, but I wanted all advantage. "Show me," I ordered, "that little step and toss."

He raised his eyebrows.

"The little throwing jig you did just then before you hurled it to the sea." I could see he meant to extend the game to suit himself, so, quickly as I had asked for help, I turned from that direction and set myself to aiming instead for Susannah, far from us, but providing me with a point to imagine hitting. I rocked a bit, the way I had just seen Mr. Gilroy do, and drew back my arm, when suddenly he was all round me, his one hand at my waist and the other upon my throwing wrist, detaining its free motion.

"Like this." He spoke to the back of my head and moved my arm with his hand so I could feel the easy motion of my arm bent and then extending with the throw, while his hand at my waist pushed me forward and backward in a kind of windmill dance to set my arm in steady motion.

"Now. What is it you want to aim for?"

"Susannah," I said, smiling, for there she was, standing stock-still, having turned around to see perhaps what we did behind, and seeing our two figures so, she had stopped dead in her paces. Just then, she began to wave. Gilroy dropped his face to mine as if he sighted with my eyes. He stood so close, his cheek nearly rested on mine, and his whiskers grazed my own chin.

"Yes. That is good. She is the most perfect of targets." But he did not move his face from mine, and I could feel the bunch of his cheek as he smiled.

I put his hand from off my waist. "You aim to disadvantage me," I said.

"Nay"—he took a step back—"never."

I looked at him once, then down at the stones beneath my feet, and then up again at Susannah now advancing toward us back down the beach. I took three running steps forward, then hurled as hard as I could, my body following the arc of the stone; and when it fell, I heard the clatter on its brothers like applause. Susannah stopped again, and I could see she frowned.

I cupped my hands around my mouth and called, "Susannah!" but the wind stole half her name, and unhearing, she gave her beautiful head a toss and continued advancing on our position.

"You might have hit me!" she said as she reached us.

I laughed and pointed to Mr. Gilroy. "You must thank him for that."

And oh, such a tumult crossed over Susannah's features then as made the ocean lakelike by compare!

Mr. Thomas had watched the whole fandango and approached behind Susannah. "Best watch how much range you give a lady, Gilroy—teaching her to throw is kin to putting the apple into Eve's plump hands."

Our cousin laughed. "Sure enough, what you say is true."

"That is the kind of thing men like to say to ease themselves of worry," I said lightly, "but the serpent in the garden was a fiction."

"A fiction? Ha! Created by whom, pray?" Susannah laughed a little edgily.

"Eve," I answered.

"Eve!" My sister meant to gather the men into her mockery.

"I am not speaking to amuse you," I replied, suddenly testy.

Mr. Thomas cleared his throat and waited for me to continue.

"The serpent in the garden was Eve's first fiction."

"I see," said Mr. Gilroy doubtfully.

"There was no snake. There was only Eve." I chose to address him. "When she stretched out her hand and took the apple, the first thing she knew with that bite was she must cloak herself."

My cousin stared. I did not look at Mr. Thomas, but continued to speak what I had never said aloud.

"She conceived of the snake, to give her desire a frock—just as carnal love is now habited in wedding dresses."

"Nell!" Susannah gasped.

"And what was Eve's second fiction?" asked Mr. Thomas evenly.

I turned to him.

"Having been broken open by them, that she loved her children."

"But surely every woman yearns for a child," he admonished.

"Nay," I said. "Not every woman. I, for instance, do not wish for a child."

"My sister is not so hard as she sounds," Susannah said softly to the group.

"What appears to be fondness in a mother's eyes as she follows her child toddling about the room is her longing after that part of her the little hand grabbed hold of passing through."

"What an extraordinary idea!" Mr. Thomas broke out.

I smiled at him, for I saw he was not off-put, but, rather, stirred.

"But a mother lives on in that child."

"Nay. *That* is God's fiction. For what are children but a windy grave? From the moment they are born, they look upon their mother's face with eyes that can see past her, and mark the lonely spot where she will lie."

Hayden Gilroy turned and tossed a rock. "I do not understand you."

"Aye? Well, there is the fig leaf dropped down between us, then."

5 October

Women—like words—are useless. There lies between what is in my head and what I can put upon the page so vast a gap—like dying.

(35 drops)

6 October

A small new story begins to struggle forward. And today, I think all the world is found in this room. Here is hope, and longing; here is sorrow. Spots of joy. Incident? Thy name is a woman wrapped in shawls at her small desk.

(40 drops, an increase)

8 October

Mother excused herself early tonight, and George and Hayden were not yet back from Middle Haven, leaving Susannah, Mr. Thomas, and myself around the fire toasting cheese for a late supper upon their return. We looked a cozy group, but the house drew too close about me, and several times I had stood to leave, only to have Mr. Thomas ask me yet another question, and thinking it rude not to reply, I had sat once more and considered aloud with him. He had wheeled us round to a discussion of the places in which we felt most happy.

"Content?" Sue asked.

"No, Miss Grange," he said urgently, "I mean happy. Joyful, if you will."

She settled back into her chair to think.

"I am most joyful in the windy regions of my own mind," I blurted, turning the long handle of the toast rack in the low

fire, "whereas my sister prefers the smaller confines of her"—
Susannah looked up at me, startled—"room."

"You are drawn to the limitless, Miss Grange?"

"Yes."

He shivered. "I must confess I find that much possibility
thoroughly unnerving."

"Possibility?" Sue broke in. "My sister spoke only of the
inside of her mind. A place severely, and deplorably"—she
turned to me in mock sympathy—"limited—"

"I should never have used such a word in connection with
your sister, Miss Grange!"

"—by our library and by our cloistered circumstances," she
finished.

I recognized my sister's mood tonight, a pussycat on the
prowl, her little bell tinkling as she stalked.

"Some of the vastest reaches of the human imagination began in the cloister," Mr. Thomas replied.

"Surely you do not advocate limitation, Mr. Thomas."

"No, I do not. But let me tell you, Miss Grange, that I have,
like all good young gentlemen, climbed into the Alps with a
stout companion—but what I found there at the summit was
not, I think, what is often prescribed."

"What did you find?"

"A distinct sense of unease, a longing to find a place for me
to curl up and take a nap."

"A nap?" I laughed out loud.

"Yes." He smiled, but with his lips only; the memory disturbed him even now. "Such vast unbroken nature was alarming."

"I quite agree, Mr. Thomas," said Sue. "One likes to be
surrounded by one's things."

"One's clutter, Sue." I sniffed, seeing without looking the
unlit corner of the room behind us, where the old settee lay
covered in the piles and bundles for her scrapbooks; and nearby
the two red chairs facing each other, flanked by the broad-backed
sofa, in "conversation"; the three portraits hung at intervals upon
their gold ropes from the lintels between the intervening windows (heavily curtained tonight); the mantel before us, upon

which sat Father's pipe stand full of polished stems and the tiny china figurines my grandmother so favored. "Where might I stand alone for a bit of thought?"

"Really, Nell."

"But does it not make far more sense," he pursued, turning right round to face me, "to understand, as does Darwin, that the chair does not—can not—exist without its table: things, if you will, in their relation?"

"Sense, yes. But I am speaking of something to imagine—a life without its accompanying shrouds—"

"But why diminish our things, Nell?" broke in Sue.

"Who might you be without these things, Miss Grange?" he asked, seeming not to have heard what I had just uttered.

I smiled at him. "Who indeed? Precisely." And then I put the toast rack on the hob and rose to stand beside Susannah. "All night, Mr. Thomas, there has been an echo in this room: Miss Grange, Miss Grange, Miss Grange. We knew whom you addressed, but the name rings round and round, the same tone regardless of the difference in bells. And I ask you now, push forward your metaphor: What might I be if considered without proximity to Susannah? What might she?"

Sue flushed. "Hush, Nell. Now you embarrass him."

"Embarrass him? I do not think so." I leaned my face down so it was on the level with hers as she sat, then tilted her chin toward mine. "Look here at her strong, clear beauty, and look at my own barbish complexion. Beside her, I am nothing to look upon. Beside me, she is a paragon."

Sue brushed my fingers from off her, stood up, and pushed past me to the high table tucked to the side of the fireplace. I listened in silence as she struck the flint and lit her candle, but I did not turn my head. I watched him instead.

"Things in their relation," I finished.

"I see," he replied uneasily, shifting in his chair.

15 October

" 'Here,' Father said to me gruffly, and stuck the book out, 'for your scribbles.' "

"Excuse me—you were what age?" Mr. Thomas tamped the tobacco down into his bowl with deliberate fingers.

"I was eleven," I answered quickly, not wishing to lose the image of Father seated at his desk, his glasses folded upon the stack of ledgers at his elbow, and the triple candles burning high upon the shelf behind his head. I had stolen into his room to obtain my usual ration of his cast-off papers in the wastebasket beneath his desk. Carefully closing the door behind me, I turned, and there was Father, staring straight at me. I whirled back to the door just as he called my name.

" 'Come here, my girl.'

"I turned slowly and walked to him without taking my eyes from off the floor. I stopped at the edge of his great desk.

" 'What are you after, Nell?'

"His voice was not unkind. I stole a look upward as far as his hands, which were placed on either side of an open accouting book.

" 'I am sorry, Father,' I whispered.

" 'That does not answer the question,' he replied.

"I looked a little farther, to his shoulders. 'Paper,' I answered.

" 'Paper.' He cleared his throat. 'For what purpose?'

" 'To write.' I ducked my head down again.

"He closed the book before me. 'What is it you write?'

"I could not answer.

"He stood up impatiently then, came round the front of the desk, and pulled the book from his pocket."

Mr. Thomas struck a match and held it into the bowl of his pipe, inhaling deeply, the air whistling down that tiny chimney. I found I was smiling at him. At him, and the memory.

"But you did not answer my question," Mr. Thomas exhaled. "Why do you write?"

I looked at him standing by the mantel, his hair brushed surely back from his brow, casual and earnest as he waited my reply.

"It allows me to vanish."

He drew upon his pipe but did not comment.

"Go on."

"When I sit down to write, at first it is as though I am descending downward through the fleecy coverings in my head, and down I go, down I go, all the while staring out the window, in the attitude of someone at study, my pen in my hand. And the soft procession of my thoughts floats past me as I fall, until I am suddenly stuck upon one that will not fall past, something solid, a voice perhaps or a scrap of conversation I do not know the beginning of, or the end. And then I take up my pen and I begin to listen."

"Ah, it is your pen that does your writing."

"Hush. It was you asked the question."

"I beg your pardon. Continue. Please."

But I could not. His lightness had noosed my explanation. He waited for me to begin speaking again, and then, hearing my silence, he looked up, a rueful smile upon his face.

"I suppose I have ruined it."

"Yes," I said simply. "You have made me feel foolish."

"Why is it you should wish to vanish?"

"Why should you wish to remain here?" I challenged.

He smiled richly. "To stand before you and hear your voice crossing to me in autumn."

But I wanted him to fathom me. Unthinking, I rose and crossed the room to him.

"When I vanish, I can see."

22 October

Tell me—what is the distinction between what one imagines and what one remembers? How often my memory, or my recording of events, slips the leash—and I wander just a bit further outward—into Possibility—where what Was and what Might Be are twin sisters on these pages. For I have set down here all the doings of our days, and see, my dear Reader, how easily the little scenes crawl forward, as though drawn to being by the bright clarity of fiction?

Nay, not fiction exactly. For, of course, what I have written here is what did happen.

Isn't that right, Susannah, my sister, my best reader?

173

"Close your eyes, and I will tell you a story."

He sat down swift as a pupil and crossed one long leg over the other, his black boot shining on the carpet at my feet. Then he closed his eyes.

"Very good," I said, then I closed my eyes also and began. "Behind Grange House, there is a long, long path, overgrown slightly and shadowed by the old trees that grow either side, whose wide boughs cover the air above the pathway. It is a damp day, and the path holds all the moist in it, so you must travel in your stoutest boots and step around the bogged-down center of the most inland place."

"And where is it the pathway leads?"

Irritated, I opened my eyes. "Do you wish to follow where I see?"

"Absolutely."

"Then you must give over asking questions that skip you to the end before you have set one foot upon the path."

He nodded. "Right you are. Continue, please." And he folded his arms once more across his chest and closed his own eyes. I watched him a moment to see he did not sport with me, but he remained dutifully so, eyes closed and his head tipped slightly to the left, as though he waited for the story to be poured directly into his imagination. I nodded, closed my own eyes, and continued.

"It was perhaps twenty-three years ago, a woman walked alone through the trees, dressed simply and with no eye to pleasing anyone but her own comfort, her lithe grace easy to see beneath the dark blue wool of her dress. She knew the path well, but she did not walk on that day with any determined sense of direction; rather, it seemed, she drifted with the slight breeze between the spruce boughs, stopping here to rest and watch the sun slanting down to the understory growing up beneath the higher, older trees."

He coughed. My eyes flew open, and I had the sense that he had watched me while I spoke, not keeping his own eyes closed to listen. "What is it?"

He smiled. "Excuse me please, Miss Grange. The under-story?"

I looked at him blankly.

"Just now you spoke about the understory. Growing beneath the trees. I wondered had we departed the path for another place entirely?"

"It is a figment of speech—it means undergrowth."

"Ah, that is good." And he closed his eyes again and waited. But I was chary now of his posture and folded my own arms across my chest and calmly watched him, waiting to see what he did. He remained silent.

"What is it you want?" I asked him.

His lips curled into a little smile, but he did not open his eyes. "The end of the story. What is it this woman in the woods is after?"

"What should she be after?" I retorted.

"Well, if she is an ordinary mortal, I expect she should be after love."

I sniffed. "Exactly."

He opened his eyes then. "Is she after love?"

"Nay."

"Why not?"

"Are you after love, sir?"

I believe he colored slightly. "No."

"Exactly."

"Come, Miss Grange, step down off the horse named Exactly and speak to me plain."

"I do speak plain." And I rose then and moved toward the door.

"What is it *you* want, Miss Grange?"

I turned to him, my hand on the knob. "A story."

He chuckled. "I would say that you had one."

"Would you?"

"Yes. Let us review." He rose and, with his finger pressed to his lips in a dramatic fashion, crossed to me and gently pushed shut the door once more and led me back into the room.

"Here we are. A man and a woman, alone in a room on a

beautiful cloudless day. What could we be doing in here? Your readers have their ears pressed to the door to discover, and indeed, there are several possibilities for the scene."

"Which are?"

"Well." He took the chair I usually sat in and drew my closed book to him as if to open it again and write, but seeing the alarm rise swiftly on my cheeks, he smiled at me and did not do so. "Let us make a list of chapter headings for this story taking place right here."

"The Conversation," I obliged.

"The Plot," he countered.

I raised my eyebrows.

"Let us say," he continued, "what is happening here in this front room of an old house on the coast of the northernmost state between a man and a woman is"—he paused and looked at me—"thick with intrigue."

"How so?" I moved closer to the table where he sat.

"How so indeed?" he responded, studying me. "You are the writer. Prod us forward gently"—he smiled—"into the plot."

I regarded him in silence, this man sitting so very still in the chair, waiting for me to answer. And then there was Mother walking toward us slowly through the woods, her skirts kicking around her boot tips as she came and her tall form gliding effortlessly along toward us. I remember we were hiding from her, Sue and I, and had crept behind the great boulder that had come to rest beside the old well where we played. And the moment stretched before me again in all its lovely silence—how rich we were just then before her voice broke open the air between us— to be hidden, yes, but soon to be found—Mother's laughter cleaving open the thick green glade. I felt the strings—this man, the table where he sat, and Mother and Sue in the woods, the sunlight stretching between the two scenes from now and from another time—tremble tight in me, who held them all together.

"What is it?" he broke in.

I shook my head slowly. But the dual moment shivered and fell away.

"How full the world is." I smiled. "How wide."

He did not reply, but stared openly at me.

I walked past him to the window and thrust aside the lace—and there the green lawn lay sunstruck by midafternoon. Hush, I thought to myself. Hush, said back the scene through the glass. Next to me at the window, he lifted the opposite curtain.

"My plot," I said without looking to him, "would take me past the knob on that door, past the door, past the bourne of this house into . . ." I paused.

He had turned to listen, his hand resting between us on the sill. "Into?" he prompted.

"I cannot tell exactly, but I have a thought that if I listen low enough to the murmurs on a page as I am writing, I might push open a hidden door, an entrance into—"

"A better world?"

"No." I faced him. "Do not tease, now."

"I am sorry."

"Well, I have no words for it." I shrugged. "That is the struggle—it is not a romance, it is not a war, it is not a better world. I wish to write down all the possible layers."

"All the layers?"

"Yes, all the layers of the world," I said haltingly. "In them lies all that is true."

He had moved very close to me, and I looked up into his face. What I saw there made me step backward, away from him.

"Close your eyes," he instructed me. But I shook my head nay. We were quiet. And then he said again, "Close them. Please."

I did so. Slowly. And I heard him approach, heard him stop very near. We were quiet. He drew in his breath then and said softly, "There are still other ways to travel past that bourne." His lips were almost in my hair. Then sudden footsteps away from me, and the soft click of the latch as the door closed after.

30 October

The wind came up so fierce today, we could not walk, but sat in the front room all the long, droning afternoon, facing out on our dark Atlantic, while down at the water's edge the pine trees bowed nearly into the sea, thrust over by this wind. Not a thing outside escaped this dry fury.

Mr. Ludlow Thomas said his mother would take to my un-orthodoxies quite nicely.

"What is it about me brands me unorthodox?"

He turned and pointed through the glass. "When you look out this window, what do you see?"

The restless clouds roamed the sky. "Possibility," I said.

"Precisely."

"Why, what is it you see?"

"The evening star." He craned his neck to catch an angle on the harbor. "That returning fisherman."

"It is the same."

He leaned his forehead against the window. "Would that it were, Miss Grange."

We were seated on the broad window bench on the stairway landing, deep in the shadows of that place. Below us, I could hear Susannah and George laughing about something, and then, just under their voices, the deeper, slower voice of Hayden Gilroy.

"But it is the same," I continued. "Carry what you see for-ward—the fisherman passes by the breakwater and looks up into the friendly yellow eye of the lighthouse, and in that eye he sees his own wife setting their table for supper, and around her the warm lights lit in his own house, and then perhaps he remembers what he had forgotten to tell her that very morning when he took up his cap on leaving."

"And what was that?"

I poked him. "What was it indeed?"

He was silent. "That he loved her."

I shifted on the seat. "Nay. That he would have soup for his supper, more likely."

Mr. Ludlow Thomas stared back into the glass. "Yes. That is more likely."

I shivered beside him. We neither of us spoke again, but watched the bleak weather pelting around. Only after he had unbent his tall frame from the cushion and risen to go downstairs, only after I had heard his step firmly descending from where I sat and then his quick crossing of the front hall to the library did I turn from my seat and look at the place where he had sat, so close, and said he loved me.

1 November

Today winter's white eye stared unblinking down into the jet-black sea. No matter it has just turned November. Down at the landing, the dinghies have each their various small dances, slapping against the cold, wet wood of the supports holding fast the float to the shore. I wandered down there with a high, wide happiness about this story I am weaving. The hard-edged sky, a block of white above the waves, braced in me the knowledge of my growing power to envision a scene and to tell what I have longed to tell in my soul—truthfully. So long my pen has stood humble in the face of my stormy visions, unable to form what is so clear to me, and yet so unutterable. I felt this morning as though I had been cast clear of the broiling tides, pulling behind me the neat lines of a slim craft able to crest the waves and carry within it a cargo others can see.

(50 drops)

I HAVE COME TO UNDERSTAND A LITTLE ABOUT TIME

In every room, upon every mantel, or standing stern and boldface at the end of the front hall, Time talks, talks, talks. And we tend to him with our delicate fingers, reaching in between the chains and pulling lightly, gently upon the weights inside to set him up again. There is no place in this house free from tock, tock, tock, just as, Reader, there are few places free from the dismal view of water.

One morning, Ludlow Thomas stood before the mantel in the dining room, the others gone to their tasks and I clearing away what remained of breakfast. I knew he was aware I stood behind him, staring at the smooth finish of his head, at his arms stretched wide along that white mantelpiece. And the clock ticked out between us, the only sound. Tick, tick, tick.

He opened the little door beneath that round white face, reached in, and took the tiny clapper between his fingers. And in that enormous silence, I heard my heart. I could see the clapper twitching in his fingers, only making the absence of the ticking more enormous, as if muted time became a character.

"What would you be now?" he asked. "In this space I have just made—where time has stopped. Who would you be?"

"That is foolishness," I found the voice to say.

"No." He did not turn round. "Imagine it." I gazed at his long fingers delicately pinching the clapper as though it were the stem of a glass, holding this moment.

"I would be . . ." I began—and I imagined it. I could cast my words out—and they did not fall from off my mark. They stuck, and, sticking, set the souls I traced in motion, cross the past and present, beyond Time's corset and my poor imagination into—

"I am not free, Nell," he said softly, still not turning round. "Free?"

"In that place without time, I would be free. In that place, I would come to you and take you, and you might be mine."

I heard the words he said, and we neither moved. Neither did he let his fingers loose their firm hold upon that clock. I watched him stand before the mantel, watched him turn his body toward me while with one hand he still held that slender ticking time.

"It does not avail." I whispered then. He shivered. I walked cross the space between us. "It need not be holy to touch each other."

"But it is holy," he protested, taking my hand. "It is—" But then he broke off, blushing, and would not look at me.

I put my hand on his arm. "It is—"

"It is pure meeting."

"And why should we not, then, meet in such a way?"

"Yes, of course." He smiled down at me. I could see he was uneasy, however, and soon enough, indeed, he looked past me to the painting behind my head. After a time, he looked back down into my eyes.

And then he let the clapper go, and Time started up again between us.

6 December

A heavy misting rain all the day, and by midafternoon, I feel I might stifle inside. Mother sits restless, as far from the fire as she can, complaining of fits of heat. Susannah walks and walks, to the fire and back, then around the room, around the room, her steps keeping pace with time advancing, until she grows near elemental in her motion. However, when I look up and catch sight of her eyes, they are soft and hopeful, as though she sees, spinning by her in the air, the glass ball containing her future, that pretty trinket garlanded all round by love and bonaventure.

Haven't I a heart? Don't I imagine also a happy, glowing chamber into which I enter and find love? Though no man before this one has shown me any interest, I, too, have my visions.

I have a vision, yes, of a comfortable room and of a man who sits near me while I write. When I look up, he is there across the table, looking down, absorbed in his own affairs. We are mutual.

7 December

I was aware of his legs against the back of my chair as he bent over and reached his hand down to cover my own where it rested on the page.

"Put up your pen and kiss me." He gentled me, pulling loose the pen from between my fingers and softly laying it down before he took both my hands in his, turning me round in my seat. I looked up at him, directly into his smile, his happy eyes, which drew now down to my own level as he knelt beside me, and loosing my hands, slipped his arms about my waist and tipped me to him, pulling my face down to his waiting mouth. Down, away down in my chest, a trapdoor opened and a warm light flooded into this newfound chamber.

After a time, he pulled me from the chair and we lay alongside, our lips still seeking. I closed my eyes then and wandered with him, his hands stealthy guides into this terrain, and my hands, too, loosed their moorings, slipping lightly cross to open waters. On and on we sped, past harbor to the ocean, until at last I cast off the lovely twining fabric that bound me to my shore. In that moment, I opened my eyes and saw the shape of this new land—wide and free, he calling and I an answer, as if I were cavern ringing round.

For a moment after, I thought I still heard my name in the open air, but listening, I found instead it was him breathing beside me, his lips now caught in my hair like a strayed bird. I pressed my cheek against his. He smelled to me of new grasses and tobacco.

8 December

He has gone.

(87 drops)

11 December

The house is strange, strained. George's departure with Ludlow on quarry business has left a larger hole around us. It is just we four, but Mother does not come downstairs.

16 December

Filled with words today pointing toward but not dwelling in my story. This morning I wrote as though I'd cast my body out into a sudden rain, arms outstretched so the whole five feet of me was open to it, drenched by the plash and thunder of the water. I have learned to be very quiet, the way the blank ground in new spring quiets a busy lane, holding what it knows in its dark, damp soil.

*   *   *

The very last page in Miss Grange's packet was the original of a letter, and it lay on my lap like a leaf fallen out of its season. For several minutes, all I could do was stare at the familiar handwriting, the thick black ink whorling round the words.

2 Pierpont Place
Brooklyn, New York

Nell,

    I am returned to her to whom I had pledged my heart before I saw you. She loves me, and I—I thought the history of my heart was written upon her dear face, and yet I see my history cannot be written. If I were to speak a lesson of my life this moment, I would utter to the breezes: A man's history is not the course of events told one after the other; it is a place he returns to. A place he circles round and round but cannot, perhaps, ever enter.

    My darling, I think you are become that place.

Ludlow

16 December

CHAPTER FIFTEEN

Papa!" I whispered, and swept the pages from off my lap. Though the diary raced forward like a fiction—indeed, in places I could see Miss Grange longing to slip her leash—Papa's letter rose up at the end, firm and final. Firm as was my living hand clutching the page. "Oh, Mama," I whispered now, and gathered the rest of the scattered pages to me. For the story of the grave was a love story, after all. I could read the last chapter, though it lay unwritten here. Below that little marker must lie a brother or a sister. That is what Miss Grange wished me to see. This was the tale she wished to pass on to me— I stopped.

By the side of the grave she had asked me to write it. But here were the pages she had already written in my hand. What more was there for me to do? I could not think. In truth, I wished to do nothing then but read again. And oh, how Maine was come down unto Brooklyn now, the attic story loosed and roaming free. From start to finish I reread the whole wide arc of the tale. I saw clearly the true matching of the lovers upon the page, their characters giving me then the closest lesson I had yet had in the wild strangeness of the human heart.

That evening when I heard Jonathan's voice in the hall, I rushed downstairs to greet him, overwhelmed by a great desire to bring my life into line with the pages I had read, and make real what I had learned somehow.

"I am glad you are here, Jonathan," said I softly, my hand outstretched.

He put down his hat, seeming a little taken aback, and took my hand. "And I, too," he replied, softer still. Then, more loudly, "Your Mama proclaims that she is ready for gaming. Are you also?" I shook my head no, suggesting instead that we stroll out the windows to the edge of the garden. Mama looked up at us as we passed through the sitting room; her face turned from the lamp and smiled.

The twilight air promised rain, and the night shadows had begun to gather deep among the leaves. The evening birds were grown silent in advance of the damp. We walked companionably to the end of the lawn until we reached the end of the garden, and then, when he would turn round to return, I drew us instead to sit upon one of the stone benches within sight of the house. Still we had not spoken.

"Jonathan," I began.

"This time is only a half-life," he broke in, and turning to him, I saw he must have been preparing this speech the whole way down the garden. "Incomplete. I imagine a new canvas—one in which the hues will deepen and the pattern of our life will become manifest—directed. Certain."

I watched his toe trace a pattern in the damp grass, my mind in a jumble.

"I hope, Maisie, this little story of ours will soon have an ending."

"But Jonathan"—I turned my face to his in the twilight shadows—"I do not like endings."

He laughed at my serious face. "Maisie," he whispered, "in our end is our beginning."

I sprang up, longing now for a place to go. "Let us walk a bit," I said.

"Ah, what a restless angel," he said, standing as well. "All the future," he spoke behind me, "stretches away from this garden where we stand. Your life has not yet begun, Maisie. I know it. I know it with such certainty, I can make you a promise."

I closed my eyes and listened to him. Was it so? Perhaps what I had read had nothing to do with me. It was an old story, one perhaps best forgotten. Agitated, I stepped away from Jonathan and bent down to examine the roots of a lilac bush I had picked from that morning.

"Maisie," he began.

But I was not ready for the declaration.

"I was thinking just then of Miss Grange," I said, straightening.

"Ah," he replied, "poor creature."

"Why ever name her poor?"

He drew nearer to me. "She is all alone, my dear." He put his hand upon a branch of the dogwood tree above me and said again, "Maisie."

"She may be alone"—I could not keep myself from mention of Miss Grange—sharp pines were newly risen in the midst of this city garden—"but she is not a sorrowful figure."

"No?" He shrugged. "I should have thought she would be." We were silent awhile.

"I have been reading sections of her diary," I blurted.

"Oh? How is that?"

"She sent them to me."

"Ah? I did not know you were so familiar."

Then, seeing I wished to speak more on it, he hurriedly asked, "And what is in this diary?"

He must know. If he was to be the one at my side, then he must know what Miss Grange had asked of me. Further, he must know of Miss Grange's link, I thought wildly. He should know what happened before I was born.

"A love story."

"Ah." His lips were very pink beneath his brown mustaches.

"And—" I looked up at him. He smiled in reply. "I am to do something with it."

"Why ever would you do anything but read it?" he broke out cheerfully, but seeing it weighed on me, he grew serious again.

"Because it—" I could not bear it. I could not speak it. He waited for me to finish, ever attentive to the rushes of my conversation, but I had stopped. We were quiet.

"Maisie?" Now his voice seemed to strain round my familiar name.

"Yes." I had bent once more over the flowering bush.

"Maisie. Dear. I must ask you a question."

We had arrived. I straightened up but kept my back to him.

"I have already asked your mother for the right—"

I did not wish to hear the words. Nor did I wish to say them. The gap was so wide between us—all I could think to do was stop it up with my mouth. I whirled round instead and pressed my lips against his. There came a little moan of surprise from him and his hands fluttered down to my waist. Then, more assured, he drew me in against him and kissed me now, thoughtfully and long, as though committing my lips to memory. I stood still and closed my eyes as we kissed, and into the depth of his embrace I fell, and for a long delicious minute, we might have been kissing or dancing, dancing as I had once on a time with Mr. Hunnowell, my breath exhaling wild and free.

I descended to breakfast the following morning in a curious condition. It is good Jonathan must be gone for a time on business, I thought. For the kiss had been a kiss, yet not. The grave was a grave, and yet my sister or my brother. My papa was my father, and yet not. And I had nearly sealed my fate last night, though I had not spoken aloud.

Yet the joy upon Mr. Lanman's face betokened a sweet certainty. And Mama's expectant smile as I entered the breakfast room was that of a child on the verge of having a secret shared. I took my seat across the table from hers and wondered what I should say.

"Mr. Lanman forgot his hat last night," Mama began. "I found it upon the settee in the hall."

"Oh," said I noncommittally.

"I noticed it needs a little brushup," she continued, "and so I've had it sent down to Mr. Martin's."

"Mama," I said, and then stopped.

"Yes, Maisie?" She was delighted.

The postman's bell rang and then our own bell sounded in the front hall. I quieted, trying to think of how to represent to Mama what had transpired.

"Yes, Maisie?" she repeated.

But Jessie appeared in the doorway just then. And I looked up to see she carried a thick package wrapped in the familiar dark green oilcloth, and I sprang to take it. But before I could reach her, she had put it on the table directly in front of Mama. I stood stock-still in a panic of confusion. Why had Miss Grange sent Mama a copy of her diary, as well?

"Whatever is this?" Mama asked. And before I could reply, she had taken it up in her hands and had begun to unwrap it.

"Mama." I nearly leapt toward her, but she had torn the protective paper from the bundle of pages inside.

"Oh," she said abruptly. "They are from Grange House."

"Yes," I said, bewildered, looking down upon what seemed to be a stack of black-bordered letters.

She swept the broken packet to her chest, then she looked up at me and said, "Leave me, Maisie."

"Mama?"

With an effort, she focused her gaze upon me and gave her brave smile. "Please."

For an hour or so, I left her, until in an agony of curiosity, I reentered. Mama still sat where I had left her, sunk awkwardly into a dining room chair at an angle from the table.

"Mama?"

She jumped at the sound of my voice, so absorbed was she in reading what she held in her hand.

"Yes, Maisie? What is it?" And as she turned to me, she casually laid her arm across the stack of envelopes before her, so I could not see to whom the letters were addressed.

She had never done such a thing before, never hidden something from me in such plain sight, and I turned away, startled, and walked to the window. Not a leaf, not a blade of grass, not a passerby stirred. Coyly charming, the June morning turned a placid face to the warming sun. Troubled, I took a turn from the window, walking to right the painting between the side windows, and then round once more, to stop at the other side of my mother in her seat.

She looked at me and down at the envelopes, and then up at me once more, in such silent agony, I drew immediately to her side and put my hand upon her shoulder. "What is it, Mama? What has happened?"

She shook her head for answer and then there erupted from her such a violent laugh, such a whip crack of harsh sound that I stepped back, frightened, only causing her to laugh again, harder this time, and higher, until the sound kicked free into the air of the room like a girl at the top of a swing. And then down she came, my poor mother, down again, and she covered her mouth as the terrible laugh turned to a thin wail and then a sob, though through her tears there still seemed to be a jagged smile upon her face as she held her hand out to me to come near. I went to her again, and held her against my waist, awkwardly patting her shoulders and hair.

"Look, Maisie. These are all my poor letters, returned."

I glanced down and recognized her handwriting upon the envelopes, though she did not move her arm. Were these the letters she had written this winter?

"Go along, my girl," Mama said sadly, lifting her arm from off the stack, "just see to whom your poor mama has been writing all this time."

Still frightened, I leaned over her and read the name scrawled upon the top envelope: *Mr. Ludlow Thomas.*

Without looking at Mama, I pried up the corner of that first envelope to see if the second was also addressed to Papa. It was, and the third, and the fourth, and the last. There were fifty or sixty letters in front of me, and all were directed in Mama's bold round script—to my dead father—in care of the postmaster of Middle Haven.

Was she mad? I turned over the many pictures I had of her silent form moving through our house, but too quickly these gave way to the more indelible one of her at her desk, her head bent as she wrote. I shuddered with the realization that all through the lowering darkness of the winter, she had been writing to Papa.

Mama held up the letter she had been reading, and I took it nervously, unable to look at her, and read:

My dear Mrs. Thomas,
Postmaster McGovern arrived yesterday with your letters and begged that I return them to you, wanting them to arrive, he said, with a friendly,

rather than official, hand. I have taken the liberty of tying them up in a ribbon I wore after my own Fredrick passed away. My dear lady, do not think I am insensible to the sorrow these letters bespeak—and, I pray, do not think me forward if I say this sorrow, madame, never vanishes. I pray for your sake that it lessens. Mr. Thomas's grave is well tended in the churchyard—I have seen that your directions were carried out exactly. Though he is gone to our God, he remains in some way up here, and perhaps instead of resting in Brooklyn this summer, as you had indicated last year, you might pass it here. Come and stay for the full season rather than the two months you have been used to. Come and see that the nearness of his grave will ease, rather than heighten, your grief. Yours very truly—

Anabelle French

I was struck by Mrs. French's kindness, and further by a depth of sentiment I would never have envisioned in the woman I was used to thinking of with a slight ridicule—the plump little body, with her dog and her flushed cheeks and officious air, was now irretrievably complicated by this rich voice of understanding. Then the sorrow of it all flooded in, the awful sorrow in the stack of Mama's letters: written and stamped, then sent and now returned, unopened and silent as himself.

"Mama," I said miserably to the letters in front of me. She picked up my hand and stroked it, and my tears rose up at her touch. We sat together for a while without speaking, her hand covering mine.

"We will take Mrs. French's advice, I think," Mama said, a deep calm replacing the tempest of sorrow in her voice.

"To do what?" I turned to her.

"To return to Grange House," she said softly. "To him."

And her, I added to myself. *And so begin*—came her words, unbidden.

CHAPTER SIXTEEN

We arrived late on a chill night that June, traveling for the first time overland, as Mama had insisted she would never again set foot in a boat. Having met with Mr. Coates in Middle Haven, we traveled the remaining miles sunk in obscurity, the moon shuttered by thick clouds. I remember how soundless the night appeared to me, as if the various clicks of the horse's hooves were a pebble cast into a still pond, the tiny noise drawing attention to a fathomless silence. Mama leaned her head against the rim of the carriage door, exhausted.

The hoofbeats sounded to me like muffled voices, and as we drew closer to the House, my heart seemed to clatter about in its casing. I had read the diary and reached its ending—I knew the secret of the grave. Yet I could not shake the conviction that somehow I was now riding still further into the tale, where the living Miss Grange stood waiting. But what more could there be? I resolved not to think about Jonathan Lanman while I was here at Grange House, wishing no distraction, and I determined that our kiss, our small beginning, should remain quiet next to Miss Grange's earlier secrets. It was better so; we need not rush—we need not act; indeed, nothing need be said about it to Mama. The last mile or so, I rode with my head stuck out the carriage window, holding my hat on with my hand, letting the small breeze from our movement cool my cheeks. It was this way that I saw the House glowing through the trees as we rounded the last bend. The lights of Grange House cast their own nimbus out into the dark night, and in that instant I had the distinct impression that the place we were entering was almost preternaturally charged.

Her slim, familiar figure waited on the back piazza, though the lights were so bright around her, she appeared at first a silhouette painted on the glassy clarity of that House. As our carriage slowed to a stop before her, Cook appeared from out of the shadows beside her and helped Miss Grange toward us.

"How unnecessary of her"—Mama sighed—"to await our late arrival."

But I hardly heard Mama's words, so shocked was I to see Miss Grange's slow approach. She was grown quite thin, and though the light was not good, her eyes seemed to me wide and too big for her face. Still her voice, when she spoke, held the old rich warmth.

"Welcome, Thomases," she said, and patted the side of the carriage. I saw Mama shake her head slightly before Miss Grange opened the latch upon the door.

"Hello," I said with an uncertain smile from the carriage's dark interior.

"Welcome back, Maisie Thomas," she answered, but her gaze did not stop upon me longer than the instant, as Mama had held out her hand for aid in stepping out. And Miss Grange took it up. Thus following behind my mother and Miss Grange and Cook, I came back again into Grange House, the gray interlude of the dismal winter crossed over.

Inside, there was the general din of companionable and aimless chatter. Several of the guests were up late over their brandy and water, and there was a clutch of women in the writing room, though none seemed to be writing. Mrs. French rose from her seat to greet us, her dark green skirts skimming the painted gray floor.

"Welcome, dear Mrs. Thomas, and Maisie. I am so glad to have you here with us again."

Mama smiled. "Thank you, Mrs. French."

"Do you wish anything after your journey? A cordial? A bit of cold supper?"

Mama looked at me and I shook my head in answer, too overcome by finding myself back in this House once again. I had forgotten the beauty of the place—how simple it was and how satisfactory all at the same time.

"I've made sure to place you in the rooms you always occupy, and Jessie will be next door for your convenience." Mrs. French and Mama were moving toward the staircase up to the second floor.

"Thank you, Mrs. French. I think we shall retire straightaway."

"Certainly. You must be quite tired after such a long journey."

Just for an instant, standing there amidst the ordinary conversation, I thought Papa would come in behind us, his cigar box safely dispatched to the pantry, as if the year we had lived between his death and this moment had been suddenly tipped and poured away. The bayberry still shivered in its enormous copper pot on the long hall table. Might he not walk in?

Mama turned. Written upon her face I saw at once the tremendous effort to withstand all this kindness. I stretched my hand to her and said softly, "Come, Mama," and we proceeded together up the stairs.

At Mama's request, Mrs. French had the door taken from off its hinges between our adjoining rooms so there was an easy, open passage between us. Mama's room was soft with the reflective glow of the gas on the rose-paper walls, and it gave such a restful appearance, Mama sat down on her bed and smiled. Then she lay back upon the pillows where Papa had died and spread out her arms. I walked past her to the windows and stared into the dark behind the glass, straining to see the harbor, but instead, the reflection of my mother stretched upon the bed floated in the blackness before me. I watched her in this uncanny way, seeing her and seeing past her into the dark outlines of the trees, so she appeared almost to hover above the rim of the night. Had she spoken at that moment, I would not have known whom to answer: the apparition in the window or the voice behind me, issuing from the white face on the bed, her black-creped form lying like an echo of a body.

I was bone-weary, and I walked through to my room, noticing the neatly made bed snugged up against the three windows, the white linens appearing to shine beneath the sheer white organdy curtains. Jessie shuttled between us with towels and scented water, but Mama bade her go herself to bed. Minutes later, I climbed between my covers, turned my face to the damp, salty night behind the window, and was asleep before Mama had lowered the lamp.

Sometime before dawn, a low moan broke into my dream. It grew louder and more insistent and I struggled awake into the shadowy room filled with the first wan light of morning. From far off in the bay, the foghorn sounded a single lonely note across the waves. I heard Mama stirring and knew she lay in her bed listening to the foghorn's cry, as did I.

"Mama?" I called.

She stilled.

"Yes, Maisie."

"What does that sound bring to mind?"

There was no answer at first, and I thought she had fallen back asleep, but then, as if uttered from a long way away, she sighed and said, "Papa."

I turned my head on the pillow and dimly perceived through the doorway Mama's form humped below her covers. I sensed she hovered somewhere on the border between sleeping and waking and that she listened to me breathing just as I listened to the silence that stretched across the room after Papa's name. I crept from beneath my covers at last to cross the room to her bed and slid in beside her, curling my back into the cupped cave of her soft front. Her arms drew around me and we rested there without speaking until I felt Mama's breathing slow, her arms slackening. Then she slept once more.

And did the well-loved dead also wake to hear the foghorn's low cry? I thought of him, lying in the curve of the hill above the town, and of his face turning cross the distance toward my own. Perhaps that note, that lonely note, was the open O of his call.

Thinking so, my eyes rested vacantly upon the ridge of my bed through the doorway. Against the spare white of the room, the intervening door frame appeared more massive than it was, making of the door less a portal than a marker. My mother's arms still hung around my shoulders. Papa! How I wished he could find his way back to us, lying here.

Dawn gave way to the yellow light of a sickly morning. I watched as the room around us grew more distinct, the dark brown furniture contrasting with the rose-patterned wall. Upon the wall before me, several smudges marred the paper. Sliding back the covers, I slipped my feet onto the cold floor and crossed closer. Some child had been let free in here and had pressed her dirty hands upon the wall. I passed through the doorway and back into my room, where I stopped and turned slowly back around to regard that wall.

My heart raced. *Some child?* I crept back to the smudge and stared.

At last I placed my own hand over the mark upon the wall. And heard the House then—half truth and half phantasm—so full of its multiple vanished chorus who sang and sang—and never ended.

We were to visit Papa's grave that very morning—an appointment I dreaded on Mama's part, as I thought she should rest from our travels before setting out toward certain tumult. Thus, it was with great discomfort that I came out of the breakfast room and onto the piazza that morning, to see my mother dressed and ready for the ride.

"Go find your hat, Maisie. Mr. Coates is willing to take us into Middle Haven right away."

"But, Mama," I began to protest.

"Is it in your trunk, or does Jessie have it?" She smiled at me, though there were tears in her eyes.

Reluctantly, I turned toward the front hall.

"Hurry, Maisie. I don't want to be late."

I wheeled round to look at her again. Late? But she had turned away and was already proceeding around the House to meet Mr. Coates and the Grange House wagon.

Late? I thought as I retrieved the hat from Jessie's room, crossing into mine. Late? I dashed some cologne at my neck and wrists in a rising impatience with her tone. Mama flew to see Papa's plot as though to an assignation.

And what did I want? I grumbled to myself as I marched down the stairs, through the hall, and out the door. I jabbed the tip of my parasol into the grass, leaving behind tiny punctuations. Stop. Stop. Stop.

"Good morning, Miss Thomas." Mr. Coates smiled as he helped me into the wagon.

"Good morning," I began, but my throat had closed over his name. It was too much. Where was Papa? I stepped up into the seat and sat down next to Mama, turning my face toward the trees.

The road to Middle Haven passed by the old quarry, and I looked through the trees at the great amphitheater of white rock, blasted open, the giant chunks of quarried granite shining through the trees, now left cast about like a god's toy blocks. Last summer we had picnicked there, Miss Grange and I, and somewhere past it, in those woods, lay that hidden grave.

We left Mr. Coates and the wagon at the green, as Mama wished to walk the rest of the way to the cemetery. We walked through the bustle of a market day, past the mackerel and cod on beds of wet seaweed laid out in barrows, past new lettuces brought from inland to this town where nothing grew in the rockbed soil but pavement blocking, church corners, and the markers for Middle Haven's dead. Then we bent our steps onto the road that led up a small hill to the cemetery. We were alone as we followed it, and Mama walked, I realized, with a gladness about her, her shoulders cast wide as she stepped quickly upward. The white and green tops of the new summer grasses bent about us, whispering into the fresh breeze that blew from off the water. Here in town, farther removed from the bay, the sun beat back the fog that hovered still at the edge of the breakwater and hung over Grange House point.

She leaned down and opened the little iron gate suspended between two great granite pillars that marked the entrance to Middle Haven's simple graveyard, and we climbed up the hill through the rows of Ameses and Browns, Calderwoods and Carvers, to come to Papa, who lay singly amongst those native families.

A peace came over me then such as I had not looked for. There he was after all, chisled into the gray stone.

LUDLOW THOMAS, *b. 1838 d. 1896*
Beloved Husband of Libby. Devoted Father of Maisie.

As I grew accustomed to the granite letters, I felt oddly comforted. There we three were, twined in his death and marked that way for both the curious and the devoted. How necessary it was to be able to have him here in one place. How restful after the past months, in which he slipped in and out, speaking through the dumb language of his things—this pipe, a red slipper, the black stylo—and through the pages of Miss Grange's diary. But here, beneath this stone, I could address him; here he could not move, could not shift. Here was my father where we had placed him, and I knew because I had watched him lowered down.

"After you and Jonathan marry, I would like to bring you both here to stand before Papa," Mama mused aloud.

I started. "Marry!"

"Yes, next summer, when you are married."

"What do you mean, Mama?"

Mama turned a querulous face to me. "What do *you* mean by such a question, Maisie?"

"But Mama, nothing final has been said."

Blankly, she repeated, "Nothing final said? But Jonathan disclosed to me his intentions the night before he left on business. He asked for you in the most earnest fashion, and I was certain he had proposed. . . ." Her voice trailed off as she looked at me.

I could imagine the scene. Up here, above the harbor, and next to Papa, the parlor drama I could see played out between Mama and Jonathan suddenly appeared to me foreign, as though it did not refer to me at all.

Mama repeated, "Maisie, do you mean to say that you are not securely engaged to Jonathan?"

I thought of the kiss and of his words. Until this moment, I had known that kiss to be a loosely binding stitch between us. But then, too, I had stopped him from saying aloud what would make the kiss into a promise. I had merely kissed him. This morning before Papa, that was all that I wished the kiss to mean. Two hearts in a garden amidst that lilac silence. Jonathan might take that kiss as a seal, but I could not.

"That is right, Mama, I am not securely engaged."

She drew in her breath at that, then turned back to Papa, as if he might help her to understand what I had just said. Agitated, I followed her gaze, but now the tombstone did not comfort.

How little it seemed now—how insufficient! Ludlow Thomas— the beloved Husband, devoted Father. There the man lay beneath the scant phrases, no different from those on the tombs beside him. Father. Husband. And yet, how those words winged backward away from him, ringing hollow around him. For he had lived far more than in his relation to us. And the pages of Miss Grange's diary now asked the stone, *Who, after all, were you?* And all the stone replied was, *Husband, Father.* I struggled to understand. Where, then, did the man go? Where were represented all the complexities of his life? All—it was all come down to these few implacable words written above him.

In that moment, on the hilltop, with my mother beside me and the question of my marriage hanging in the air, the lesson of my father's tombstone began to speak. For was I not standing here, nearly accepting Jonathan and our marriage, yet not wanting it, all at the same time? How might a stone hold upon it this humming in my chest, this winging indecision, this moment where I stood and gazed down the corridors of my life and all the doors appeared thrown wide?

Would my stone read only *Maisie Thomas, beloved wife of* _____? Only that? Never the story of this full-throated longing beyond. I looked across the tombstone, over the roofs of Middle Haven, and outward to the harbor: who I was—all that I was—cast up into the bright air. Nothing can represent us—nothing satisfy. Indeed, Miss Grange, I admitted sadly, you are right.

CHAPTER SEVENTEEN

Mama and I settled into a quiet custom of visits to Papa's
grave, often venturing separately to see him. I liked to walk
there by myself along the green alley of the road to Middle
Haven. Indeed, his grave became a punctuating constant, a place to
which I returned and rested from the strain of waiting for Miss Grange
to summon me, as I imagined she would. I longed to tell her how
much I could see now; how I had understood what she wished me to.
I considered writing her a note, but then in a mix of cowardice and
politesse, I decided it best to wait for her to seek me out. Perhaps she
did not know quite how to approach me, with her diary now between
us.

But she never called for me, nor did she descend after that first
evening. Neither was I aware of her in her customary position at the
window. Often I would look up, thinking to catch her there, though
nothing but the blank eye of glass returned my stare. And this present
silence folded round the vibrant character of the past, until the firm
line between the diary and the woman upstairs wavered in my mind
as a hot day shimmers over water.

Save for me, the silence in the uppermost regions went entirely unremarked below, for the *Boston and Maine* had recently proclaimed Middle Haven the "watering hole for the decided and unpretentious wealthy," thereby drawing all the decidedly pretentious to watch how old money was handled. The Maconomo House, which loomed at the opposite end of the harbor, accommodated ninety people, though they charged the exorbitant price of four dollars and fifty cents a night to stay there (without dining). J. J. Sullivan, the manager, demonstrated his talents as host to celebrities by planning weekly follies, sometimes importing a singer from Boston just for the weekend evenings. In town itself, there were three other guest establishments, the Manchester House, the Stanley Cottage, and a boardinghouse kept by Miss C. E. Brown, and all three appeared positively to hiccup with people, they were so full.

Simplicity is difficult to teach, however, and much of the gaiety of the season drew from the meretricious and boundless excesses of the newcomers' spirits. Mama was quite put out at first, complaining about the tuba orchestras that one could hear bellowing over the water—"like mating cries," she'd sniff as we mounted the stairs to retire.

The irrepressible desire for show suited the clear bright blue days that summer sported. For the days having reached their fullest bloom, the open throat of the season was now held bare to the glorious mornings and cooler evenings. The hours beckoned through the lovely trees. Never do I remember so many uninterrupted days of sun: The sky seemed to have emptied itself of fog and rain, to hang like a perfect porcelain bowl above us. Rows into the harbor at twilight were planned, and picnic lunches staged on nearly every large outcropping of rock. Day after day passed by in this way, slightly mad with fun, while the nights shivered with lights sent out across the still black water, carrying chatter and laughter like a velvet-backed butler filling glasses in a crowd.

Even Mama yielded, each day drawing closer to the bonhomie, until one morning I saw her smile again in the old way, her lovely head held high while she positively bantered with Mr. Cutting.

Indeed, it seemed a curious camaraderie had sprung up between Mama and Mr. Cutting. In years past, Mama had drooped beneath the deluge of his words, none of them particularly inspiring, meant rather to crush the air from any original thought struggling up into the room. But this summer, I noticed Mama smile at his effulgence; indeed, I thought there were times when his conversation actively interested her.

And so it was that the man had lately become a consistent third: offering his opinions, holding Mama's sewing bag while she stepped down the piazza stairs, and generally clouding my horizon.

He was kindly, but he had very little imagination for anything other than all the catastrophe and disorder of the past, prefacing most comments with a confounded shake of the head.

"What is it Mr. Cutting?" Mama turned to him upon the verandah after luncheon.

"Imagine, Mrs. Thomas," he began, gazing down the fine length of lawn toward the dinghies setting out for an afternoon sail. "How little the young understand their fun; why, only fifty years ago, those same dinghies would have been the cold refuges of families struggling to fish for their livelihoods."

"Excuse me, Mr. Cutting, I do believe there are still fishermen upon the seas," I interposed.

"Yes, Miss Thomas, but the general quality of life has so improved. There is duck cloth; there are galoshes. There is light, for Lord's sake, when the men return home. Just imagine the cold and the dark." And he shook his head in amazement. I merely regarded him. History appeared to him as a series of marvelously dispatched incidents of progress overcoming nature, delivering us at last into this perfect present. I conceived of his mind as a museum gallery, where imagination hung gilded and framed upon the walls. He scoffed at novels; he scoffed, indeed, at writing anything down.

"Although," he conceded, "newspapers do hold their value; there is always something to be got from them at least—something real."

"More real than true, I think, Mr. Cutting."

"What a curious distinction, Miss Thomas."

"Oh, she means nothing by it, Mr. Cutting."

"Don't fret, Mama; someone far greater than I made that distinction long ago."

"Yes, but what did you mean to say about it, Miss Thomas?"

"I think"—Mama motioned to me—"Maisie is restless." I rolled my eyes at her and she smiled in reply. "Go on, dear, I can see the chafe marks around your mouth."

I bowed low to Mr. Cutting and suggested, if he really wished to know what I meant by the distinction, he read Mrs. Gaskell's *Life of Charlotte Brontë*. "Poor girl," he answered, shaking his head. "All of them dead in a moment."

And with that profound aesthetic comment in my ears, I left them upon the piazza and wandered down the steps, quite troubled. Mama's manner toward Mr. Cutting had begun to alarm me. She did not seem to mind the fact that he was an outrageous bore. Instead, it appeared his very stolidity attracted her, and she leaned into the man when he spoke, as though he were a rare flower, and not the old black umbrella he far more naturally resembled.

I stared out upon the familiar harbor, anxious and annoyed. Jonathan was to come at the end of a month to collect us—and nothing had begun here. Nothing save Mr. Cutting's attention and Mama's discomfiting lack of clarity.

And thus two weeks passed by, and I spent my days in a state of rising agitation. Had not Miss Grange meant me to play a part? I was ready now to do whatever she asked. Still she had not called for me, and my hours were passed instead with a book beside Papa's grave, or in reluctant observation of Mama's folly—or flummoxed before the daily ardent letter from Jonathan, to which I tried to fashion a suitable reply.

One evening, with yet another one of these unanswerables in my hand, I emerged from the writing room and stopped short. There was baggage in the front hall, the gleaming leather valises of a large family lined in a tight row by the door. As we passed through, Mr. Coates brought in three hatboxes awkwardly piled in his arms. Whose arrival did these announce? I wondered, a vague hope stirring. Faintly, I heard Mrs. French above us in the upstairs passage, showing the new guests to their rooms.

"The Hunnowells are here," Mama ventured, pointing to the ornate *H* embossed on every valise.

"No, Mama, surely not; there is enough luggage here for eight people!"

She smiled and answered, "And how many would you count Mrs. Hunnowell as being?"

"Rather, it is Bart Hunnowell I would . . ." But my voice trailed off at the sound of footsteps behind us.

"Good evening, Mrs. Thomas." The voice was quiet, almost chaste. We turned to greet Bart Hunnowell, who bowed over Mama's hand and then raised his eyes to me. "Good evening, Miss Thomas."

I smiled at him shyly. "Good evening, Mr. Hunnowell."

"Madame"—he turned back to Mama—"I have thought often of you throughout the winter and hoped you were well"—his voice faltered—"after Mr. Thomas's fall."

Mama smiled at him, her eyes suddenly bright. "Thank you, Mr. Hunnowell. You are kind." And she looked away from him, toward his bags. "What lovely valises you have," she said softly.

"How was your journey?" I asked a trifle loudly, and made a move toward the sitting room, forcing Bart Hunnowell to keep step beside me while Mama composed herself, and in that moment he gave me a smile so unexpectedly kind, it cut me to the core. I stared at him an instant. Where was the raillery? But then he dropped back again into his old, easy habits of address.

"It is one of the distinct and several wonders of this world, Miss Thomas, that after nearly a year apart, you still remain so raptly interested in my welfare."

Here was safe ground reached. Here was the sitting room with its marked terrain—there the chair for us to sit in, there the divan for Mama to lie back in—here the room for conversations signifying nought but companionable time. My chin cocked, I smiled back at him, affecting the coquette.

"The House has awaited your arrival, sir, with anxious and repeated forays to the window to sight your first approach."

"Ah, and were you among these nervous sentries?" He had thrown his head back against the antimacassar, striking the pose of a weary saint, his dark hair framed by Mrs. French's pearly white laces. It could not be helped. He was lovely.

"Certainly not, sir." I was suddenly discomfited, and I walked without thinking toward the window facing the harbor.

"No, Miss Thomas?" The laughter lurked around his drawl. "You certainly seem to take up the part of the watcher at the window quite naturally."

Oh! He had pressed too close upon me. And I had wished to think of him kindly. I whirled to stab him with a home truth.

"I do not watch for *you,* Mr. Hunnowell. I am nearly en—" But I could not finish the thought out loud.

"Enraptured? Endangered?" He had stood up as well and stepped toward me at the window. "Enfeebled by your—"

"This conversation, if one might call it that, has gone far enough, I think." Mama broke in quickly here, and thankfully so, for I was at a loss. This drawing room banter had sudden teeth.

"Yes," Bart agreed, his eyes upon me. "We were caught unwitting upon the very shoals of a confession."

"Mr. Hunnowell"—Mama's tone was a little dangerous—"what tales have you of your travels this past winter?"

Bart left me at the window and came to stand before Mama, who was seated upon the sofa.

"I did not travel at all this winter, Mrs. Thomas."

"Ah? Then what did you find to do?"

Bart smiled down at her. "I performed the difficult and costly experiment of remaining right where I was."

"How very brave!" Mama answered without a smile. "And how is your dear mama?"

A light trill of laughter from the front hall answered for him. And then the lady in question appeared, clapping her hands in delight at the sight of our little gathering. I drew forward to greet Mrs. Hunnowell, then stood silently by in a profound confusion. Under the greetings and the exclamations, I slowly drew away, until at the door, I turned round—nodding briefly to Mama, curtseying my good nights to the Hunnowells—and then escaped.

That night I dreamed such wildness—of two lovers who rowed out into the middle of a black lake and drowned there while I watched them sink. And the lake suddenly spread beneath my boat and floated me away from the scene and onward out and out, until the lake became a sea; and there the water ended, and instead I felt myself falling down, away down, into a soft darkness. Where my spirit took me then, I cannot tell. I sensed a woman falling beside me. I had never seen her in this world, but as we fell, she held her hand to mine and uttered my name. But I had the peculiar sensation that I was reading a book all the while, that I read the story of the lovers in the dream, turning the pages of their adventure even as I saw their ending played out in front of my eyes, the words of the story floating in the air above their heads, and I was strangely aware even while I dreamed that the story I was reading was a story I had written, the words appearing just seconds before I read them.

Sunday, 5 July

Dear Maisie,

I dreamt last night that I received two letters from you at once, and took that as an omen that you were disgusted with my last and wouldn't write again. Ho! Though I was disappointed today not to hear from you and although you have told me you wouldn't write often, I shall be disappointed every time a letter fails to come when I want it. (Which is every day.) I have become a chronic kicker!

I went to the wedding last night with the fixed purpose of remembering the gowns, etc., so that I might regale you with an account of the show, such as girls love. But alas, when the bridal party came up the aisle and the ceremony began, it was kind of solemn, and I got thinking of less frivolous things and don't remember a single gown. The church was very prettily decorated with some sort of white flowers (I never was a botanist) and lots of green. That is a perfect word picture. The church was very well filled and the crowd was polite enough to keep its seats, so everyone could see very well, the procession going up one aisle and down the other. Prescott Slade was best man and looked so woebegone in the march out that I couldn't resist murmuring, "Cheer up," which had a good effect, as he smiled the rest of the way. Nannie Fricke looked very well, I thought, and it did me good to see how happy they both were. You probably know who the bridesmaids and ushers were, so I won't fill up the letter with such details. Howard Slade spent the night with me, and he and Dave and I went to the reception. I tried to be attentive to one or two girls, but Dave persisted in hanging around till he cut me out, which wasn't brotherly. The bridal couple departed to the usual accompaniment of rice and old shoes. I was in the hall at the time, well in the front rank, and the rice thrown by those behind lodged in my back hair. It might have been the shoes, though. I didn't get a very good look at the presents, as there was quite a crowd in the room where they were displayed, but they seemed to have some very pretty silver and glass and there were a few etchings or engravings. You know they have taken a house in Hicks Street—near Bedford Place—and I suppose they had some furniture. After Herbert and Nannie had gone, there was dancing, but as Slade has also renounced the world, he and I dragged Dave home at eleven o'clock, so we only got two dances. I had the pleasure of con-

gratulating Miss Noyes and Roller Salthis last night. Poor old Lloyd is sort of frozen out, isn't he?

Slade was telling me today of a freight line of steamers that runs to Boston, upon which he could get me a pass. A boat sails every evening, I believe, but does not reach Boston till one o'clock the next day, so I don't think I will go that way. I don't want to be away from you any longer than I can help, and this route would get me to Middle Haven at least four hours later than if I went by train. I did not hear from the hotel today, but I expect to soon.

I don't want to spend any more than I can help on board, but I do want to be in the same house with you. Don't you think it would be much nicer?

Would you like a bull terrier pup? I could get you one if you like. Just think, Maisie—how soon I shall see you!

Yours,
Jonathan

CHAPTER EIGHTEEN

I n the days that followed, though my furtive glances upward at
Miss Grange's windows had grown habitual, I did not expect to
see her there. And, in truth, my eyes were wrested more and more
from the topmost window to regard the figure of Mr. Hunnowell
reading, draped upon a chair by the rocks, or disappearing into the
woods with his sportsman's gun upon his shoulder. His manner toward
me had remained light since his arrival, absorbed, as it seems he was,
by other enjoyments. But his enthusiasm for each blue day grew catching, and I found myself lingering later and later in the breakfast room
to witness the explosion of breath and life that was Bart Hunnowell
on entering the morning. Each day curved in his mind with one question: How were we mortals, he asked me earnestly one morning, to
best serve the day? I suppose he was only half-serious, but I answered
him as though he were catechizing me.

"As though we were breaking through the tape."

"The tape?"

"Yes."

"What kind of tape?"

"Of a footrace." I smiled. "I love the way the runners come to the finish with their heads flung high and their arms outstretched and their chests thrust forward into the end."

Bart drew in his breath and rose from his chair, then stepped around the table and knelt at my feet.

"Miss Thomas," he said, "you are a poet."

"Stuff!" I answered, and pushed him backward onto the carpet, where he lay in mock distress while I picked my path serenely around him and withdrew.

Thus noting his hyperbole, yet liking him more and more, I was happy to acquiesce one morning in July when Bart suggested I take a rowing lesson with him. The morning's tide suited a rowing lesson: The currents, which were usually strong enough to pull a boat the right way round, lessened at low tide, and I relished the chance to learn how to handle the oars more adeptly. We set off in one of the House dinghies, Bart placed in the stern so he could watch my form, he said; and I took the oars, choosing not to smile at this. The day was not yet hot and the slow tempo of my rowing drew a little breeze into play about us. I leaned forward with both hands, almost touching Bart's chest as he faced me, and then pulled back, catching as much of the flat waters as I could. Bart was teaching me how to feather my oars—the part I most loved when Papa rowed—the long oars stretching across the water, the blade sinking in and pulling through, popping up at the end of the stroke, and then the swift turn of the wrist that flattened the blades, feathering as they sped backward, readying for the next dip. The oars had fit snugly in Papa's hands, and they seemed to gather the sea in easily, unlike my choppy attempts, which shot us forward and then left us stopped dead while the oars slapped the water as I drew backward and forward upon the seat.

"Why do you think it is called feathering?" I asked Bart, pausing.

"What do you imagine flying to feel like?" he replied.

I looked up at the gulls above us, hectoring one another with great raucous shrieks and then in an instant becoming sublimely silent, turning and diving and riding the air on their long gray wings.

"Smooth," I answered. "Like sliding down silk."

He grinned. "When I feather my oars, I have the impression I am riding water as if it were air."

"Like a bird?"

"Like an arrow, shot clean from its quiver, feathering across the water. Like this—" He stood up, rocking the boat terribly, and put his hand on my shoulder as he climbed over me to sit in the bow seat behind mine, where he slipped the second pair of oars into the water.

"Now, put your oars in." I did, and we took a long stroke together. "Turn your wrist now," he ordered, and I obeyed, my blades gliding flat across the water as I leaned forward to take another stroke. "In again." And both our oars slid in at the same time. "Out," and we pulled out again. And this time, I felt the motion of the boat dictate when to feather my oar and when to put it back into the water. "In" and "Out," his voice repeated. "In" and "Out," like a chant; and we pulled and rose to the beat of his voice, pulled and rose, our bodies silent and attuned as they worked together, until the words dropped away and we pulled past his voice, my arms and back taking his rhythm inside. We stroked together, the boat shooting forward into the harbor, away from the shore, and I could imagine us at the tip of a slim shaft winging through air toward its target. Farther and farther out we rowed, the tiny O's the oars made as they pulled out of the water spinning in widening circles behind us, and I stared after them in a trance, pulled by the sound of the oars moving in the locks, over and over and over the water.

After a bit, my wrists grew tired and clumsy again and I caught some water, which caused the oar to jerk up out of the oarlock and throw me off my seat. I caught the oar before it slid away, but then I realized I could not pick myself back up onto my seat without loosing my grip on the oars, and I was uncomfortably aware of Bart behind me and the view I presented him of my awkward helplessness. But he reached forward without a word and grabbed hold of one of my oars so I could push myself back up. I looked behind and smiled my thanks at him, taking up the oars again. He remained silent, however, and did not commence rowing. I turned again, wondering why he stayed his stroke.

Bent over his crossed oars, he was staring thoughtfully into the water.

"What are you thinking of?"

"How I could never have plotted this," he answered.

"Plotted what?"

He looked at me then. "A man and a woman, alone beneath a summer sky, rowing farther and farther from shore—"

"That is an old plot," I hastily interrupted.

"Nonetheless, one cannot write a good story without one," he answered swiftly.

"Stuff!" I flashed out. "Of course one could."

"Well, I cannot," he said.

"What need have you of a plot, Bart Hunnowell?" He was being perverse, I thought, and blind. "What need have you of any of that, when you have—" I struggled to put to words what he had shown me. "Pure motion."

"I beg your pardon?"

I looked away. "You can travel. You can feather—fly—" I trembled. "There are far too many plots. *You* have no need of plots."

"But—"

"You see so much, Mr. Hunnowell," I finished, "isn't sight enough?" I was near to tears, though I did not understand why.

He stared back at me, then said very softly, "Thank you, Maisie Thomas."

We were both quiet.

"I had begun to tell you, however, that the man and the woman have found themselves stopped above a haunted spot."

I stared. "This is where you found Halcy and Henry?"

He nodded.

Startled, I turned my face away from him. I did not want to recall Halcy Ames.

"I have thought of them all this past winter," he continued softly.

"I have seen poor Halcy's ghost." I blurted it out, and then turned to see the manner of his reaction.

"What do you mean?"

"I have seen her—twice."

"Where?"

"The morning she drowned, and on Leadbetter's Island. Last summer. On the day"—my voice shook—"Papa fell."

Bart put both hands on my shoulders and bade me turn all the way around, until we sat face-to-face, our knees touching in the space between the seats, our oars shipped and crossed behind us and pulled into the boat.

"Tell me what you saw."

So I did, leaving nothing out. I told him how it came to be that I walked the path so far ahead of my parents, and of the place where I stopped, and of the figure I had seen and of what she held in her arms. I told it all to him in a great rush and then, unable to stop, I kept right on speaking and told him the whole sad tale of Papa's accident and of the moments when we stood over his fallen body, unable to reach him and unable to move. And then I ceased, suddenly as I had begun. But the words that had flown from me seemed to gather like rope in the air between us.

"Maisie, let me tell you what I heard last summer." Bart spoke very gently, grabbing light hold of this line newly cast between us. I looked up at him.

"After your father was carried into the House and up to his room"—I closed my eyes against the memory Bart's words recalled—"I lingered in the passage by Miss Grange's stairs for some while. I had the hopes"—he swallowed—"of being of use to you and your mother." I opened my eyes. He tapped an oar upon the water.

"Go on," I whispered.

"Late that night, after the House had gone to bed, Miss Grange came down her stairs and passed by me without noticing I was there. She was dressed for the outdoors, and I was seized by a desire to talk to her, to ask if she thought your father's case was grave. Sometimes just the sound of her voice reassures."

I smiled, knowing precisely what he meant, and stared into the water beside us.

"So I followed her," he continued, "down the stairs, through the hall, and out onto the piazza, where I stood hidden by one of the columns, watching as she moved toward the boathouse."

"Why didn't you call to her?"

"There was something so intent about her movements," Bart said, "and at first I didn't want to disturb her, thinking she might appear, at some point, to welcome conversation. But then"—he paused—"then I grew curious—where was she going? And why in so secretive a fashion? So I slipped down the steps and along the lawn after her, only half-thinking about what I did. After all, if she saw me, so much the better—I was seeking her out."

"And did she?"

"No." His voice was strained.

"What happened?"

"As I came to the boathouse door, I heard her voice and someone else's, mingled in low conversation." He spoke now with his eyes on the water, slowly calling forth what he remembered, as though he were seining the ocean's bottom, casting a net and pulling the words up with great care.

"Who was the other person?" I asked, half-forming a picture in my head of the scene.

"I cannot say for certain, but Maisie—"

I looked straight at him.

"Their talk was of Halcy."

I shivered, knowing. "It must have been Cook she spoke to."

"You may be right. It was another woman."

"Could you hear what they were saying?"

"Miss Grange was insisting to the other person that 'the girl had lost the child.' Then there was a dark sound, like a sob choked back in the other person's throat, and then the question: 'Aye—but where is it buried?' "

I picked at the paint around the oarlocks, thinking about what Bart had overheard. What had Miss Grange to do with Halcy's baby? I looked past him toward the islands, whose black humps ranged like a child's drawing of hills sticking up from the water, raggedly uneven but distinct. Leadbetter's Island lay straight off our bow as we were now pointed.

He followed my gaze. "Halcy Ames wished to tell you something."

"Halcy is dead, Bart," I whispered. "You pulled her body from the water."

We sat in silence. "And why should she appear to me?" I asked miserably.

"Come." He put in his oars once more. "I must take you somewhere." And without waiting for me to set right, he took a long stroke and set us forward again. I fell in with him and rowed, my heart glad to work, my back and shoulders pulling and yielding in time as my mind turned over the pieces of conversation Bart had overheard. *Had* Halcy born a child before she drowned? She had held one in her arms on Leadbetter's Island. I rowed and rowed. I saw we had rounded the end of the point and were heading down the other side, the ocean side. The current grew much stiffer and I found I had to fight my oars to continue.

"Where are we going?" I asked after what seemed an endless time.

"Not much farther," Bart answered between breaths.

Several more minutes of hard stroking against the current brought us to the head of a long cove. I turned round and saw the rocky remnants of an old pier still piled above the shallower waters. Bart nosed us forward and several strokes landed us alongside one of the broad granite foundation blocks.

"What is this?" I wondered aloud.

"We are on the far side of the old quarry," he said. "This must have been a loading dock for the workers."

He leaned down and offered his hand. But I looked up at him, suddenly uneasy. I thought I knew the spot he meant to show me.

"Come," he said softly.

I shook my head.

"You have been here?"

I nodded. "With Miss Grange."

"She was a very little girl," he said sadly.

At that, I pushed myself from off the seat and gave him my hand.

Quite close to the old quarry dock, a path led away into the woods, the old stone wall alongside. And there, not far beyond, lay the little headstone marking Miss Grange's secret grave.

Almost defiantly now, I reached out my hand and brushed the hanging green tendrils of moss from off the marker's face. It bore the legend:

PERDITA GRANGE
Pray for Her

"I think she is the sad explanation for Henry and Halcy's death," said Bart, looking down upon the stone. "They lost her and buried her. And then, distraught—"

What he did not finish struck me cold. "No!" I whispered.

He was silent.

"How could you say that?" I turned from the grave to face him.

He looked back at me gently. "We all of us thought as much. Why else had they tied themselves to the mast?"

I started to shiver. "All of us? Which all of us?"

"Your father. Mr. Coates. Myself."

"But no one ever spoke of that! No one ever suggested such a thing. Surely Papa would have brought that up with me."

Bart remained quiet, watching me.

"I suppose he meant to protect me!" I said hotly.

"You were also on the dock, Maisie. You saw us untie them."

I glanced away from him, feeling at once mutinous and betrayed. He was right. My eyes settled again on her name. Could this be Halcy's child? I looked at the tiny grave through poor Mama's eyes and a faint hope surged up. I had been a poor reader of that scene on the dock, perhaps I had misread Miss Grange's diary after all.

The stone stared back.

"But—if she is Halcy's, then why is she named Grange?"

"I assume Miss Grange put up the stone," Bart answered thoughtfully. "And the name must be her way of protecting Halcy's name."

For several moments we stared down together at the grave. And, almost, almost I would have followed Bart Hunnowell along to his conclusion. Yet, though I did not remark it aloud, to me the moss-covered grave and well-worn stone spoke of a child buried long before last summer.

"No," I said at last with dread conviction. "This cannot be Halcy's child."

And then I turned and walked away. Bart never said a word, but followed. And followed still as I crossed the broken, tumbled rocks and took my seat again in the stern, when he gathered up the rope, stepped in, and pushed us off.

He uncrossed his oars, slid them back through the locks and into the water, taking a few short strokes while waiting for me to do the same. But I could not. Bart began rowing again in earnest, and my idle oars slapped against the water's surface as we drew around and headed back homeward, my heart heavy.

"You might speak to Miss Grange to be certain," he remarked quietly in between strokes.

The roof of Grange House appeared through the tops of the trees, the chimneys crenellating the air. I had a sudden vision of the place in deep winter, the sharp pitch of the roof shrugging snow from off its black face.

CHAPTER NINETEEN

As Bart rowed back to the dock, the sight of her windows staring out at us from under the eaves of the House strengthened my resolve. The time had come to ascend to Miss Grange's room.

"Promise me something, Bart Hunnowell," I demanded as he leaned to help me step out of the dinghy. I looked straight up into his eyes. He nodded and remained there with his hand outstretched, sensing I did not ask lightly.

"Tell no one else about this grave."

"I will not." His eyes were steady on me and I saw he marked the promise.

I put my hand in his and stepped up onto the pier, leaning on his arm as I did so. For an instant, he did not release me and I did not withdraw, so we stood together on the pier, our hands clasped. But I could hear the cries of several boys racketing down the lawn, and smiling, I disengaged my hand from his.

"You are wanted, Mr. Hunnowell."

"Make me a promise as well, Maisie." Onshore, my given name

on his lips unsettled me, and I took a small step away from him. "What is it?" I asked lightly. "That I practise my oarsmanship?"

I was surprised by the struggle I saw in his eyes.

"Pray do that first, Miss Thomas," he answered.

"And second?"

He turned in the direction of the boys fighting to open the gate at the top of the gangway, then turned back and gave me one of his open smiles.

"Second?" He bowed elaborately. "Come row with me again."

I gave him a deep curtsey and followed him up the gangway, at the top of which he was pulled into the hubbub and wheeled away by a frenzy of white shirts and knickers and the rampaging bluster of boys.

As I walked up the lawn, where Mrs. French and one of Cook's girls were laying out the croquet course between the rocks, I thought I spied Miss Grange, heavily wrapped, walking slowly through the grasses as if bound for the woods.

Mrs. French broke into my observation. "Will you bring your mother down to play, Miss Thomas?"

Annoyed, I did not reply at first, trying to follow Miss Grange's progress, but when she vanished into the trees, I said politely, "Mama does not like croquet, Mrs. French."

The broad-beamed woman exclaimed, "Well then, something in the air up here must have changed her opinion of the game."

"The air?"

"Why, yes, Maisie, only just this morning your Mama asked if I would be so kind as to set up the stakes."

"Did she?" Here was something strange.

"Indeed, she did."

"Well, then perhaps we will play after lunch." I smiled at her and continued on my way. Despite myself, I could not hold long to the favorable opinion I had formed of Mrs. French, the letter writer, when the woman herself was so distracting. Instead of the wise widow that had shone through her words, here stood a woman who seemed shamelessly to consider herself still in the late bloom of girlhood, dressed as though she were sugarcoated, rather than substantial.

I watched all that afternoon for Miss Grange's return, stationing myself with a book in the stairway window seat, and when I heard her voice proceeding toward me from the front hall, I stood up so as to catch her on the landing as if by accident. But I saw she was otherwise engaged, for she rounded the bend with Cook behind her, carrying a tea tray laden with the makings of tea for two people.

"Maisie Thomas," Miss Grange greeted me. "At last."

Cook stopped so abruptly on seeing me upon the stair, she caused the spoons to clatter upon the tray. "Your mother looks for you, Miss Thomas," she informed me unceremoniously.

"Thank you, Cook," I answered, watching as Miss Grange held tightly to the banister and half-pulled herself up the intervening stairs to where I stood.

"But Miss Thomas will take tea with me," Miss Grange said over her shoulder, and reached the top of the stairs. Cook looked at the two of us standing there, and she grimaced. "Very well," she muttered, but she stuck out the tray and gave it into my hands to carry. "Do not," she added quite fiercely, "let her tire herself by talking."

I nodded, quite liking Cook's adamance. I would not tire her, I could see myself how weak she was. And I turned and followed Miss Grange, all the questions in my head hushed by the woman before me, now laboriously ascending the two remaining flights of stairs. When at last we arrived into her attic chamber, Miss Grange sank down into a chair pulled near the stairs, and as she rested, she motioned me to set the tea tray upon her writing table, then instructed me to pull two chairs close by.

When I had done what she asked, Miss Grange rose and slowly crossed the room to where the tea things lay ready. I sat down with mingled pleasure and discomfort. Here I was, alone with Miss Grange—and now what should I say? I watched her one hand dip and measure while the other moved slowly round the cups and saucers, holding them in place, her fingers alighting first here, then there. The foghorn at the tip of the breakwater announced a coming shift of weather. I stole a glance at my hostess as she poured the tea, and it was only Miss Grange after all, though illness had sharpened her familiar face and shaded the light in her eyes.

"Milk and sugar, Maisie?"

I nodded and accepted the hot cup into my hands. She did likewise, lifting her cup daintily in a salute toward me. I bowed my head in reply. I felt the old sense of peace I shared with her return—a peace now deepened by the pages I had read; and what I had seen in the woods did not seem dark as it had in the bright, unforgiving sunlight. For up here resided—I struggled for the words to describe the light, the opening silence, this feeling I had of expanding—something like: Severalness.

"Of what are you thinking, Maisie?"

Of what indeed? I opened my mouth to answer her, to tell her I felt I had begun to understand something. But what was I seeing? And how did it matter, when she was asking me perhaps for something I was not thinking at all. I strained against this harness: Mouth that could not say what I saw, Mind that could not speak, but only see.

"About your room. How glorious it is up here."

She smiled, and I saw something other than my words had sent its arrow from the shaft. We drank our tea. I could not think how I should mention the diary. So the last thing I thought to speak bolted free.

"Miss Grange, I am nearly engaged."

"Ah" was all she said.

"What do you think of that?"

She smiled. "What might I think?"

"You might think it strange."

She regarded me in silence as I lowered my cup to my lap. Then I raised it up again, looked at her, and almost desperately pronounced, "It all seems so . . . final."

She put down her cup. "What is final?"

"My life," I answered helplessly.

She thought a minute, then leaned forward. "Tell me, Maisie. What is it that you wish?"

"I wish—" Again sounded the foghorn's soft remonstrance to the incoming weather. "For someone to point me toward a place where I may go, where I might put down all this yearning in me."

"Toward what?" Her eyes were fixed on me.

I looked at her. What? What indeed? "I do not know. I cannot say. Papa might have told me."

"I doubt your papa ever would have told you what to do."

"No, but he taught me, introduced me to other minds."

"That was good."

"He would have shown me how to grow to be like them, to fit into the shapes they held open."

"What shapes?"

"Shapes, shapes, Miss Grange. Shapes of possibility. For a life."

She sat back. "Your father could never have shown you that. Never," she finished softly.

"Because he died?"

"Because he could not show you what to be—only your longing, that precious longing, can show you."

"No, Miss Grange," I uttered miserably. "It seals me: I yearn and yearn and end with wordlessness."

She put down her cup upon the table and clapped her hands as if to clear the air. I watched as she lowered her hands back onto her lap, the echo of the clap still extending past me into the long room. Then the quiet.

"There are no words," she spoke carefully, "because this longing is your self, Maisie, your self speaking."

"But what am I to do?"

"Grab hold," she urged, "grab hold."

"But of what?" I was growing still more desperate. "What shape shall I grab hold of?"

She shook her head at me. "There is no one shape for a woman to fit."

I thought a moment, then pursued. "Papa would have said a woman should fit into her house."

She pursed her lips. "Oh, well for that matter," Miss Grange remarked dryly, "a woman should fit the shape of her mother."

"Her mother!"

"Yes, you see I was wrong just now, Maisie. There are very clear shapes, as you call them, held up by the world for a woman to consider. Two of them, in fact, beckon to you always: the upright, comforting shape of a man and the eternally present shape of your mother."

"I think you tease me now."

"No, my dear. I am in earnest. And I say to you, Maisie Thomas, that it is all nonsense. Think past, think further out than this house,

220

those curtains, the trees. You might marry, or not, but nothing will alter this wordlessness, this longing."

I watched her grow more and more agitated as she spoke, drowning my own unhappy confusion.

"Listen to me," she continued. "I failed someone once, a young woman like you who wished, like you, past the bourne of her body, and who carried that longing like a child she could not set down."

"I do not understand."

"She was defined by her longing. She did not let her longing shape itself, delighting instead in a restless melancholy, an acuity of vision and of heart upon which she prided herself."

"And what happened to her?"

"She was buried."

"Buried?" My head jerked up, and I was reminded why I had come. "Miss Grange, I have seen Perdita Grange."

Soon as the words fled my mouth, Miss Grange's warm intensity dropped from her, the chill so sudden, I feared they had done her grievous harm. I started forward, alarmed by the change in her complexion, and as I reached to touch her, her gray face turned to meet mine.

"So . . ." She looked at me wearily. "You have read her name. Now at last you can begin her story."

"Begin?" I stared at her. "But the pages of your diary have already told it."

Now it was her turn to stare.

"Isn't your love story the story of the grave?" I asked testily.

"No," she whispered, slightly surprised. "Of course not."

I nearly stamped my foot, so confused and unhappy was I. "But Miss Grange, if that was not the unwritten story, then why did you send me those pages at all?"

She reached forward a placating hand. "Maisie. Did they comfort you in the beginning?"

Tears threatened. I nodded.

"That was all I intended," she said, "at first."

"And then?"

Her hand clenched upon the chair and a spasm of some deep pain crossed her face. Carefully, she adjusted her weight. "And then I saw the love story might draw you . . . nearer."

"Why?" I could barely breathe, knowing what she would say.

"Because, Maisie, once you had a sister."

I nodded, the tears now spilling over onto my cheeks.

"And it is her unfinished story that now must be told."

"Oh, stop this!" I cried, bolting from my chair and walking unseeing the length of the chamber, tears running freely down. "I cannot bear more!"

"The love story ended, Maisie," she continued softly; indeed, she would not stop. "It was fully told. I loved your father. He chose"—her voice shook—"your mother. Perdita was born. And your father never knew she had lived. There," she said, "there is the sad ending." She fell silent.

I could not stop my weeping. I could not move toward her; neither could I speak.

"Maisie," she uttered. Still the tears came.

"Maisie," she said more softly.

I looked up, sniffling.

She smiled and pointed to a captain's chest behind me, pushed back beneath the eaves. "Go, Maisie, and open the chest."

As in a dream, I did as I was bidden. I threw up the lid upon the chest, and then stood back, a bit horrified. For the chest was full of loose paper, the capacious grave of page upon page upon page of writing, now spilling over the opened top and onto the floor around my skirts. I picked a handful and regarded the jabs and feints upon the page, scraps of dialogue, dismembered scenes written on the backs of old accounting ledgers, the numbers bleeding through.

"What is it?"

"The tales," she replied softly. "Born of what happened—to us all."

"Who?" I whispered, gazing into the mess.

"Myself, my sister, my mother"—she paused—"even Halcy." She lifted her hand to take in the wide room around us. "And we are, every one of us, all up here. Ourselves the very haunting. Ourselves the very house. What was longed for and did not come to pass, that is the stuff of haunting—that is the stuff of age-old fictions." She nearly rose from her chair. "Oh, I had such glory in my head, Maisie. For years, I could take life and shape it as I willed—upon the page. I thought my life was vast and grand—our lives become art in my hands. And I grew proud"—she smiled bitterly—"proud with a craftsman's pride at my renditions of our house. So proud, I lost myself in their making. So proud, indeed"—her voice was low and ragged—"I could not see the truth before me!"

She stopped abruptly. "And so the glory I took in weaving broke this house open."

I turned slowly round to her, uncomprehending.

"Aye." She trembled. "Aye, it broke open. And then it stuck."

"What stuck, Miss Grange?"

"Every story of this house stuck; every voice began to stutter," she answered, her eyes in the middle distance between us, "after her little grave appeared there in the woods."

The attic barely breathed.

"Appeared?" I said, a dark fear rising in me. "What do you mean, 'appeared'?"

"Maisie." She swallowed and looked at me. "Maisie, I do not know how or why Perdita came to be buried there."

I stared at her, horrified. "You do not know?"

"I do not know!" she repeated in a savage whisper.

"But . . . how can that be?" I struggled to make sense of what she told me. Even if she had fallen into some lunacy of forgetfulness, she had been surrounded by her family in the diary.

"You had a brother and a sister and your mother. Surely they—" I broke off, for my words had brought tears to her eyes. And I saw then that the fire in the ghost story she had told must have been nothing—a painted scene—next to the cataclysm that had clearly happened here, and my heart constricted for her. Quietly now, I crossed the room and came to kneel at her side.

"You love your mother, I think, though she is not like you?" Her voice was unsteady as she looked down at me.

"Yes."

"Then you must help me," she pleaded, "for I am certain that the reason Perdita died has to do with my own mother and"—she searched for words—"her confusion."

I shuddered, vividly recalling Widow Grange gripping the hand of the old doctor as she told her tale in this very room. I looked up. A shaft of evening sun slanted upon the eaves. This room, and not. My gaze descended to Miss Grange, and she leaned back in her chair as if satisfied. "You do see it now, then."

"No, that is just it." I shook my head sadly. "I do not."

"Until it is finished, this story is bottomless."

"You are too cryptic, Miss Grange. It seems the world is but an echo to you and ourselves but repetitions."

"Aye," she said. "So it seems to me."

"But *I* shall not repeat." I raised up on my knees. "I shall not."

"Aye?" She gave a long, slow sigh. "Good. Then it is settled."

I stared up at her. It did not matter what I said anymore; my words only sank into the deep pool of her longing.

She hurried forward. "Everything you will need is right here." And she made a grand arc in the air around her.

"In this house?"

"Of course." She fixed me. "It is all right here. All these years I have listened for what happened—to the voices of all those gone, who are here—yet I cannot but circle that grave, round and round. I cannot cross the gap to finish—" She touched my shoulder. "But you, Maisie, you can."

"I?" I wished the width of the attic still remained between us. "Forgive me, Miss Grange, but *why* would I?"

She smiled oddly, then looked at me, suddenly nervous.

"Because Grange House will be yours, Maisie Thomas."

"Mine?"

"Your own." And she leaned forward then and took from a drawer in her table a second red leather copybook, this one secured with a slim blue ribbon; carefully untying the book, she opened it, fingering the pages till she arrived at one. For a full silent minute, she regarded that page. At last, she looked at me, held out the book, and pointed to a spot. "Read here."

I looked down at the page and read the words: "Ludlow Thomas is come again, and we are all in a strange flurry."

Bewildered, I looked up at her. "But I have read this."

"No. You have read only the love story. Here lies the understory." She closed the book. "When I call you again, I shall give this to you, and then you must shape it, Maisie Thomas."

"I should take up a pen and write what you have written, again?" She nodded.

"But how should I finish what is already written?"

"Seek the answer to what happened to cause Perdita's death. Close in the gap and the grave and then"—she smiled—"begin at the beginning and write us anew, all of us—my mother, my sister, Halcy Ames. Start up the story, Maisie; start it up again and carry us forward. Begin it again and finish it—so it will not repeat."

Slowly, she took one of my hands. The drawing on of evening cast long shadows into the room, and we sat between these shadows in the intense light that evening sometimes shines. Chafing my wrists, she started a tuneless singing. My head leaning against the high back of the chair, I felt flushed and powerless, but calmed by her cool fingers. A current passed through me, like sun stealing through a shaded patch of forest. Much of what she had told, I couldn't fathom, but resting there, I *saw* what she told, as with some new faculty of apprehension. In me, the wild tale at which she hinted—the silence of her relations and the girl—developed shadow, line, and a dim but definite perspective. Her fingers on my wrists were soundless bargainers, but it was the promise of the tale itself made its pact with me: a tale of sorrow that held Papa in it, and my sister.

Her voice drew me, a lantern set out for the storm-tossed returning. "Let you not be another buried by a mother's tale, Maisie. Write us all down, child. And write us new—seek past the lovers and the grave."

"Yes," I heard my slow reply, "I will try."

CHAPTER TWENTY

Though I descended Miss Grange's stairs that evening, I had the distinct sense that I pushed upward with each step, back into the light and air of the lively regions of the House, returning to its noisy surface as though I had lain below the water longer than my breath could hold. How could Miss Grange not know what had happened to her child? And how was I to finish a story that was not mine? A story, the outline of which I did not understand? Never, I think, was any child so glad to see her mother as I was catching sight of her just rounding the second staircase dressed and on her way down to the cocktail hour.

"Mama!" I called, and hurried over the intervening passage toward her. The distress on her face was made manifest by her weak smile.

"Maisie, I have only just discovered where you were. I had been quite frantic with worry until Mrs. French suggested you were upstairs."

"I am sorry, Mama," and I took her hand. "I took tea with Miss Grange."

"Yes, Maisie, but when I went to look for you this past hour, your book lay on the window seat, and you had vanished."

I smiled up into her worried face. "I would not have disappeared before telling you."

Her agitation seemed to increase with my smile, and drawing me to her side, she wrapped an arm around my shoulders and walked me into her room. There, she sat me down in front of the mirror, her hands on either shoulder. Surprised, I looked up at her in the glass, but she did not catch my eye, intent as she was on drawing the long pins from my hair. I searched her face as she pulled each pin, carefully lining one by one upon the dressing table, her one hand gently shaking out my curls as they fell free; and because I knew she meant to tell me something, but could not at present, I closed my eyes and gave over to the comfort of my mother's hands. After a time, she began to brush out my hair—almost languorously, one hand on my forehead, pulling me softly back into her chest, each slow stroke catching my long hair and moving down from root to tip. For several minutes, she brushed in silence, and I was lulled by the quiet and by her familiar scent backward into a childish feeling I had long forgotten, when all the world was my mama. My head leaning into her, her hands all throughout my hair, and no sound but that of bristles catching air, I drifted past myself, my mother, our room; so when she spoke finally, it was as though she called to me from another country.

"You are all I have in the world, child."

She pressed her cheek to the top of my head and stopped brushing. For a moment, she rested there, and then she stepped away from me and over to my bed, where Jessie had laid my evening dress. I watched in the mirror as she fiddled with the lace at the cuffs, and I understood that she, too, had drifted, but it had been too far for her past comfort, and we were now returned.

"Will you choose a ribbon for my hair, Mama?" I turned from the table and walked also to the bed, pulling at the buttons at my back as I did so. She smiled an answer, unbuttoning what I could not reach, and then walked into the dressing room. Swiftly, I drew off my clothing down to my chemise and splashed water on my cheeks and arms. The water invigorated, calling the life back into my lulled senses.

"Do you know," Mama said behind me, "I had intended to give this to you on your wedding night." I froze. "But I think instead that you must wear it now." I turned and saw she held in her hands the coral choker I knew Papa had given her when I was born. It lay in her hands like a collar of burnished blood, from the center of which hung down a perfect cross of seed pearls.

"Mama!"

"Yes, my girl, let us bend convention tonight." Mama's tone was gay, her smile full and open, a high color in her cheeks. And she placed the choker around my neck, slipping the little gold hook into its eye to fasten it.

I took up my white dress and entered it with a mock ceremony, paying tribute to the necklace. Mama laughed out loud and turned me round so she could fasten the interminable buttons.

"Oh, Maisie," she said warmly. "There is little this life affords that can approach the happiness of giving and receiving affection."

I smiled at the picture I presented in the mirror.

"And should you have the unspeakable happiness," she continued, "of becoming a mother, you will agree with me that a married life is perfect."

I could see it before me—the children I might bend over as they lay in their beds, the cool hallways of my house, a low lamp burning in my hands as I passed into my own room. Everything still and cared for. Everyone sleeping but for me.

"In married life, there is but one head, one heart, and one mind, and you will subscribe to this, I am sure." She stepped from behind me, one hand on my arm, and regarded me in the mirror with a proud smile.

"Whose head?" I asked her half-seriously, picking at the pearls on my neck.

She looked blankly at my reflection. "Whose head?"

"The husband's or the wife's?"

"Why, neither, Maisie—you two will become one. Your voice will blend to his—your hearts beating in time and yearning toward the same destined star."

I thought of Jonathan's opinions and of his ardent letters. To make him happy, to hear his voice always in my ear, to build a kingdom around him for him to return to—this, too, was an avenue beyond the confines of myself. Through him, as Mama said, I would become more than myself—I would become him and also better than him; I would be both. Here is another pathway, Miss Grange, I thought, another shape—and the unexpected violence of my thought against Miss Grange rent in two Mama's soft conversation.

"Your papa's death," Mama said very quietly to me in the mirror, "has left me but a partial thing, a fraction now of what I used to be."

"Let us go down, Mama," I said, turning to her, and took her hand.

She looked at me bleakly for a moment. "I do so want your happiness, Maisie."

"I know, Mama." I smiled, my voice catching. "Let us go down."

And as we walked together down the stairs, the House—my house—drew close around. *My* happiness? Where was that to be found?

VOLUME III

CHAPTER TWENTY-ONE

The following morning, I awoke determined to seek out Perdita's hidden grave on my own, to see if it might speak to me any further. For something had happened here that even the Author did not know. I could not idle any longer. Jonathan was expected within one week's time to fetch Mama and myself back to Brooklyn, where—I could see the ending.

I stood upon the piazza in the great clarity of a blue day and spied Mama in a group of ladies under the canopy on the lawn, and I ventured near enough only to be hailed. For I did not wish to stop in my present mood, and I waved back and smiled into the white-hatted foursome. As I passed by, I heard Mrs. Hunnowell resume reading aloud from the worn House copy of *Evelina,* then saw Mama bend her head again over her work, Miss Burney's story following me into the fields toward the lawn tennis. The net had grown tattered by the season's wear and by the ill usage of the boys. Stuck through the holes of the netting were various treasures of the fields—bunches of grasses, feathers, even the abandoned shell of an enormous crab. The court and its decorated net called to mind the ravages of a midsummer's eve party after the sun rises on what the moon blinked over. I left the court behind and wandered into the woods behind the lawn, half-conscious of the direction my feet took, walking into the woods' dark smells—pine and the dank, damp earth.

I had only a dim sense of how to find that hidden grave again. I tried to recall how Miss Grange had set us upon our path that afternoon last summer, but I could not remember much, save that we had plunged directly into the woods from the back of the House and seemed to walk a path that took the same route as the old road to Middle Haven. When we returned, I remembered, however, we had walked much more directly, straight back to Grange House, as if the grave lay on a compass point stiff-needled by the roof.

I decided to set my course this way, and I retraced my steps out of the woods so as to start off from the back piazza steps of the House and walk forward from that point. But as I emerged from out of the covering shade of the woods back into the bright morning, I heard someone call out, and, light-struck, I pulled at my hat brim to cast more shade and decipher the caller. In the fields, directly in the line of my own prospective path, stood Bart Hunnowell.

I held up my arm in what was, I hoped, an indeterminate gesture. I would not have turned aside his company, yet I had just formulated a plan for myself I rather determined to carry out alone. Bart stood still, awaiting my approach. I gave a shrug to the gods, then followed my own predisposed pathway, arriving at Bart Hunnowell's shoes in the grasses.

"Where are you going, Miss Thomas?" Bart asked, shifting his stick to the other hand and reaching into his pocket for a neckerchief.

I raised my eyes to answer, half-wishing for him to tell me why it was Miss Grange had hold of me so. But his eyes were blue and clear and empty of an immortal prescience, and nodding toward the woods, he offered me his arm. Wordlessly, I took it, his silent companionship for the time being a soothing antidote to the chattering in my own hot and bothery nerves.

We entered the cool shade side by side, proceeding down the wide alleyway of the road to Middle Haven. Last autumn's leaves lay golden over the green moss of summer, and the light wind brushing over recalled the turning tide. We walked in silence for a long spell, my hand still tucked beneath his arm, and as we walked through the deepening woods, I drifted into a drowsy kind of reverie, faintly aware that our steps had fallen in together, as below my thoughts, my feet kept their forward motion in time to his. The long road overhung by the spiraling trees appeared to call us farther and farther down into its dark green distance.

And as we walked in step, the names of the men before me sounded the bass notes through my boot soles: I am Maisie, daughter of Ludlow, son of Ludlow, son of Ludlow, and back and back through Ludlows into nameless time. A litany of solids upon which I close my eyes when I go to sleep, like the familiar furniture in my own dear room at home. But just as the sleeper always drifts elsewhere when he sleeps, the Granges and their story seemed to beckon me beyond my sleeping body—into air. As Bart and I proceeded with silent steps down that cool green alley, I cast about in my mind for visions of what else beside my own thoughts might be loosed from their moorings: hair uncoiling from pins, scent from an unstoppered bottle—and still the dark green firmament, still the warm arm of Bart Hunnowell beneath my own. No, I remonstrated, think of natural things. So geese in a tight autumn V wheeled suddenly free-form, single birds zigzagging cross a previously ordered strip of sky; then umbrellas came to mind, windblown inside out from cap to cup, and then the rooted thing that does not come unmoored—

"Potatoes."

"I beg your pardon?" Bart had stopped short in his tracks.

I felt the hot color flash up. The word had flown out of my mouth as if bowled down from my brain before my lips could close.

"Except potatoes," I said, gathering my skirts up in my hand, and suddenly sprinted off down that yellow road. My sun hat flew from my head as I ran, and, laughing, I looked behind me to see what Bart would do. In that glimpse, I saw he'd set his stick on the ground, and I laughed again, my feet racing faster now, and stretched my arms wide to feel the breeze my running stirred against me. I could hear Bart behind, gaining ground, and suddenly I darted left, scrambling breathless over the stone wall that ran beside the road, and flung myself into the surrounding thicket of red spruce and pine, the pathless woods an almost total chaos—the bent limbs blown down by winter winds lying tossed and skeltered all over the ground. The wildness of those woods whipped my laughter still higher bout me, until I felt I was catapulting through those trees in such a frenzy of motion and hilarity, I did not know how to stop myself, or how it could all end.

At last, I was saved by falling, my foot catching one of the tree roots sticking up into the mossy carpet, sending me headfirst into the unforgiving solid of a tree. I was not hurt, although jolted somewhat, and I slid to sitting, then leaned against the trunk, weak and scraped, but laughing still in breathless little chuckles.

Bart threw himself down on his back beside me, his arms flung out on either side, his mouth open as he caught his breath.

We sat panting in silence for several minutes, until gradually my breathing slowed. I glanced down at Bart still lying flat out on the ground. His eyes were closed and his grass-streaked shirt still rose and fell like a bellows.

"Potatoes," I repeated. And then I pushed myself up and sat on my heels beside him. The rhythm of his chest was slowing, and I leaned over and tweaked his ear as I began to rise.

His hand shot up and grabbed my wrist, pulling me so off balance, I fell forward across his chest, and then he put both arms around me and kissed me. His lips were full and warm, and without thinking, I kissed him back. Once. Then twice. And then a pattern of kisses upon those lips, the quick beat of his heart against my chest.

After a time, I rested my head against his shoulder, unwilling to open my eyes, wanting to continue there in the land of lips and beard and cheek and hand.

"I love you, Maisie Thomas."

I opened my eyes and pushed myself back again on my heels, and he smiled such a smile then, I caught my breath. "You cannot love me, Bart."

"Cannot? But I can. I do."

"You must not, then." And I looked away.

"Ah. Must not. Well, I am stepped beyond the rigors of such a law that says must, must not. Maisie Thomas, you are in my blood; it's you curled inside my heart's room, your little fist that pumps against my chest, keeping me alive."

I stood up, but I could not speak; I could not even think what to say. I had fallen to the ground a girl and risen now as I knew not what. I could think only of flight, and so thinking, I turned and walked back through the thicket of pines, seeking the stone wall's snaking line. I was lost, though the road homeward lay directly in my path.

When Bart caught up with me, he did not speak, but walked beside me until we reached the place where he had dropped his stick. I waited as he leaned over to pick it up, then continued beside him as we walked, still silent, down the remainder of the Middle Haven road.

There is little I can say about what happened, save I would not wipe those kisses from my mouth. Yet, I did not know what to think, and as we walked back to the House, I grew suddenly afraid. What must happen now? I did not know how I could keep such a secret *secret*. And it must be secret, for I had already halfway raised my sails and set out toward another future with a partial promise in my hands.

But why, then, had I returned Bart's kisses? I glanced at him sideways, made shy by how closely he had touched me—and what I saw reassured. He looked no different to me. He remained Bart Hunnowell, the walking stick resting casually on his shoulder now, his hand easy upon it, his gait unchecked by thought. We came in sight of the House.

"I have been asked to finish a story," I said suddenly, stopping.

"Of what?" He threw a stone against a tree trunk and stood beside me.

"Of a lost child." I turned thoughtful eyes upon him. "And of the dead."

He turned to me, leaning his head to listen, and I saw there was only a breath between us—a fine gossamer of restraint. I did not push it aside, and neither, I sensed from him, would he, until I had done so. I fairly held my breath.

"The dead who walk in circles," I continued.

"Beside us, the same as us," he agreed seriously.

I looked down, startled.

"Can't you feel them?" he asked.

"I don't know." The breath eased out between us now.

"I do." His fine face was cast into dappled shadow as the sun shifted in the sky. "I was a child when my sister died. Yet all through my life, she has remained, her feet running below mine; and when I feel that great upsurge in my heart at the sight of something glorious, I know she yearns through me, sees through me toward a glad and earthly beauty."

Beneath the low mantle of the trees, his words recalled Miss Grange's, and nudged me gently toward him.

"Then is this longing in my heart nothing but the echo of another's?"

"Nothing so gray as that, I think." He smiled. "I think your longing is your own, made sweeter by the echo of all those who have longed like you."

"Like me?" I turned to him now and stared into his eyes across the tiny inch between us. "For what? What do I long for?"

He studied me for the space of several heartbeats. "How can I answer that?" His hand found mine between the folds of my dress and pressed gently. "Perhaps it is the whisper of your life, Maisie, your own history, speaking through you."

"There is such thing as one's own history?" I asked a trifle bitterly.

"Just as there is such thing as one's own heart."

I was silent. The words tapped. The words broke open the seam around my heart, and all began to scatter and break loose. "To have?" I asked.

"To keep and give as—"

"Bart," I broke in.

He stopped. "Yes, Maisie?"

"What do you mean to do?"

"Do?"

"Yes, Bart, what is it you mean to do? About what has happened?"

He stepped closer to me, stopped a minute, then shrugged and touched a finger to my heart.

"I mean to love you."

"Oh!" I cried, suddenly maddened by his easy manner and wishing to wipe that distracting smile from his mouth.

"Maisie." His hand was upon my wrist. I looked down at his brown fingers. "What would your heart speak right now?"

"Now?" I repeated. "At this moment?" My eyes filled suddenly as he bent and placed his ear gently next to my chest as if to listen, and my soul expanded then, simply flew. And my hand, seeming of its own accord, rested upon his neck and held him to me, though I could speak no more. "That it was full," I whispered.

"And free," he urged.

I stepped back. "No, Bart—I am not free."

"You are," he asserted.

I was quiet a moment, struggling to speak what else beat in my full heart. "Once, I thought I, too, might be a girl whose proud spirit did not need traffic in the ordinary world— a Brontë girl, who cleaved herself from settee and sitting room and *death,* who cheated *death.*" I fairly spat out the words. "But I am not such a one. I am . . ."

He waited.

"So entangled." I could scarcely breathe in my sorrow, for the double image of Papa gazing up at me in such pain upon his bed and of Mama's relief when I was returned to her from Miss Grange's attic suffused my vision. How might I take up my own heart when their wishes beat so visibly before me?

He raised up his head and kissed the base of my throat. "Here." He put a finger where his lips had been. "Here is where I will rest— where your heart rises up."

"But Bart," I asked, the tears in my eyes, "where do we stand?"

"Where we are," he answered simply.

I looked long into his face. Here was I caught beyond the break-water, in waters toward which I had not meant to travel, and yet how easily, how gladly, I had swum right to them. I turned quickly and began walking homeward; and though Bart called again, "Maisie," I kept walking through the grasses and out onto the cut lawn, across the pebbled back driveway, and around the House. I climbed the piazza stairs, passed through the public rooms, and climbed the main house stairs, until finally I reached my room. I had hardly passed over the threshold before I leaned my forehead against the closed door and gave myself to a hot storm of weeping.

"Maisie?" Mama's drowsy voice issued from her bed.

I sniffed, but the tears still came.

"Maisie? What is the matter?" I could hear Mama sitting up among her covers.

"Oh, Mama." And I turned and crossed through into her room and flung myself, still weeping, into her arms.

Startled, she patted my head, her hands still heavy with sleep. And I lay there quietly in her lap for a time.

"Maisie?" Mama asked again.

I turned my tearstained face to her.

"Dear girl," she said, smiling, "do you miss him so much? Do not fret. Jonathan will be here at the end of the week," and she patted my hand on the counterpane.

CHAPTER TWENTY-TWO

As a winter bird hops from one bare branch to the next, now I could not alight in any one place or in any one activity for long—the House become suddenly a forest of confusion. That evening I remained in my room, claiming myself indisposed. But then, when I descended the next day, there sat Bart at the breakfast table, just as he sat every morning. Blushing, I turned right round and climbed the stairs back to my room, then unthinking, kept right on climbing—until I found myself stopped at the bottom of Miss Grange's stairs. Nothing sounded from up above, no human voice or stirring, though far below I heard the unintelligible murmurs of my kind.

Late that morning, I heard footsteps, and when Bart appeared at the end of the servants' hall, I watched his quiet approach and was calmed. Indeed, he did nothing, said nothing, save to come and sit on the floor below me, stretching his long legs out across the narrow hall. So together, we posted guard.

Three long days passed in silent, anxious vigilance. Dr. Bates paid a daily visit to Miss Grange's room, and I watched him come and go, knowing by his careful, even answers to Mrs. French that the vibrant, troubled soul upstairs was dimming. And I wondered how I was best to do what she asked—several nights starting up from out of a deep sleep as if I heard her call.

Then, the very night before Jonathan was to arrive, at last I received a summons from Miss Grange. "*Come. Please,*" the note read in a shaky hand, and it was signed only "*N. G.*"

I took it through to Mama, who was undressing, and showed it to her. She shook her head, recognizing also the advanced state of weakness that the handwriting bespoke.

"Mama, shouldn't we call for a doctor?"

Mama sucked at her lip, reflecting. "Surely Mrs. French knows best what Miss Grange must want or need. I trust she has been looked in on."

"I am not certain of that at all, Mama."

A hesitant look flew over Mama's features, as if a thought had advanced and then retreated in the space of a breath.

"Maisie, I think it best not to interfere. But do go up and sit with Miss Grange for a little."

I went up. Tapping at her door, I received no response, and so I quietly pushed it open.

Miss Grange lay in her bed, propped up among the white pillows, her beautiful silver hair combed down around her shoulders. Her pale hands stretched along the counterpane. The room had been swept clean and both windows stood open, so the curtains fluttered in and out of vision. My heart calmed. Of course Miss Grange was being watched over—one of the servants must come up and see to her needs. Through the window, I heard the idle slap of the line against the flagpole. Life continued to sound. I crossed into her line of vision.

She turned her face to me with difficulty, and it was with a sharp pain that I recognized the change I'd seen on Papa's face now settled in hers: her eyes were hectic and scattered-looking, as though she had just received some dreadful news. As I read how few hours she had left to spend in this room, I took her hand in mine and brought it up against my cheek.

"So hot you are, Miss Thomas." Her voice still thrilled, though it had slowed.

I leaned close. "Are you thirsty, Miss Grange?"

She nodded. I looked about for water, but there was none near her bed. Irritated by the serving girl's apparent neglect, I ventured over to Miss Grange's desk, where in the shadows I could make out a bottle and a glass. I took them both back to the bedside and slowly poured some of the dark liquid into the glass. Though I did not recognize the bitter odor, clearly it was a cordial of some kind. I held Miss Grange's head up as I tipped the glass against her lips; she drank deeply, then swallowed and motioned for more. Again, I filled the glass with the dark drink.

"Thank you, Maisie Thomas."

And she closed her eyes. I did not let go of her hand, but sat myself on the bed at her side, holding her hand between my own and watching the flickering of the lamp's shadow against the wall behind her head.

After a time, she opened her eyes again.

"Ah, Maisie . . ." But then, as if she heard someone else, she said, "Yes, yes I *must*. She is the one I have chosen. She shall know it all."

I looked behind me fearfully. The soft black of the shadows in the room peered back. Miss Grange pressed my hand to bring my gaze back onto her face.

"Maisie. Stay with me tonight."

I thought of Mama below and something of my hesitation must have spoken from my eyes, for Miss Grange whispered, "We will send down a note to her."

I looked at her who had so little time left remaining and nodded quietly, my eyes filling with tears.

"I will stay."

"Thank you." Her eyes shut again briefly. But the lids fluttered open with difficulty, as if struggling against a closing hand. I leaned down so my face hung above her, so close that I could see how dry her lips had become and could see the gentle throb of life continue its weary patter at her throat.

"Miss Grange, what may I do to ease you a little?"

A trace of her old smile crossed over her mouth like the shadow cast on grass by a fast-moving cloud.

"Maisie Thomas," she said, and closed her eyes again.

We sat for a bit in silence. At first, I imagined that she had something to tell me and was resting before she spoke, but then I saw by the faint movement of her covers that she had slipped into a light sleep. I lifted my head and looked about the room. I had never before been here after the lamps were lit, and the airy brightness the room sported in daylight now had vanished. The room instead seemed cavernous and full of a nameless dread; I resolved not to move again from the bedside and the lamp's dull glow.

Very slowly, Miss Grange spoke again. This time she did not open her eyes, so the effect was of a sleeper talking.

"Maisie, reach below my head. There is a letter beneath the pillow."

I bent over her to find the letter, and as my hand closed on the envelope, her face turned toward mine. "Finish the story, child." I heard, though I had not seen her lips move. And now I was afraid. Had she spoken? Or was the voice inside my own head?

"Maisie—" she whispered.

I faltered. "Yes."

"The way through lies with you and what you do now."

"And that might be . . ." I paused, my heart beating fast, searching her face, so close to mine.

"Anything." She sighed and then, as if satisfied, she closed her eyes and slept. I drew the envelope out from the pillow and sat back again, shaking.

But she did not wake again, sinking, rather, into a deeper place in sleep, a stiller place. Around me, the shadows in the room seemed to hush. The form of Miss Grange remained, but I could see she had begun to steal away, slipping quietly by me at her side. I do not know whether I dozed or slid into a kind of reverie, but the room felt strangely populated, as if, had I really chosen to look, I might have seen what I had never yet seen with daylit eyes. Sometime in the night, I thought a white-clad figure crossed from the windows toward the bed. I started, but Miss Grange's voice, suddenly strong, spoke from out the covers.

"It is all right, Maisie. She has come at last." And she reached her hand out toward the approaching figure, waving her forward, closer and closer, as if to hurry her on. Her face wore such a childish look of anticipation in that moment, such glee, I could not stop from smiling also, and then she gasped once.

Blank followed. I thought someone breathed, and listening closely, I found it was myself. The room was only a room, but there was a hollow in it. When Papa left, there had been so many others with me, watching my face, coming around to hold me in their arms. The living claimed me; we had cried out against the irrevocable silence of his figure on the bed. But Miss Grange had left only me behind in this blank room. It might be I who had died.

Suddenly I feared nothing from the still form or its dim visitor. It *might* have been I who had died. I understood then the slim line between us, that I stood in a room full of my longing for those who had left me behind, haunting them, just as we imagined them to be haunting us. All of us—dead and living—pressing our noses up against the cold transparency of memory between us. Softly, I folded Miss Grange's hands across her chest, closed her eyes upon earth, then leaned to kiss my old friend farewell.

I sat back in the chair. The night stretched open and long before me. What course should I follow now? I did not wish to go downstairs. Her soul was close, I knew—and should she wish to step away, she should have someone to leave, something to step away from. So I remained. My eye fell upon the letter there by the lamp, and calmed by my name in her handwriting, I took it up.

Miss Grange had given very precise directions. I was to reach below the skirts of her bed and pull from it what lay beneath. I was to read her diary then and there. I was not to leave her room until dawn.

Unafraid, I thrust between the linen fabric under the bed, and my hands closed on a waxy package. I pulled it from its hiding place and drew the package up onto my lap. It was thick and tightly bound. Carrying it over to Miss Grange's writing table, I felt a surge of excitement. I cut the cords, and the wrapping sprang back from the contents. Inside were three copybooks. The first was the red book I had seen lying on her desk, and inside, in perfect order, one after another, were neatly written several stories, covering page after page, as if the book were printed. The second was her diary, wrapped in its blue ribbon, and there were loose pages carefully inserted at various points of the book, as though they were additions latterly conceived. I took up the first of these additions stuck within the hard cover of the book and read what was written there. Both the spelling and the clothlike paper made it look to be an ancient receipt for laudanum.

Now a little uneasy, I opened up the third book, which was black and new—and blank, save for these words: *"Here is your book, Maisie. Set us all down in here."*

I clapped the cover shut. Here was I, enacting the very scene Miss Grange must have imagined, for wasn't I bent and leafing through her books, her poor body stretched out beside me, and hadn't I arrived at her command in just the order she had envisioned? I cannot do it, I thought, I'll not take on this part! I stood up from my chair with determined vigor, firmly intending to march downstairs and alert the household.

Then I thought I heard some small stirring. Or did my over-stretched nerves produce a slight whispering? I turned my head to listen more closely. Nothing. I took three small steps away from Miss Grange's bed, then paused. Ah, it was the rustling of my skirts against the bare wood floor. I walked firmly over to the door and put my hand upon the knob. But then, there it came again, from behind, the whisper of a whisper.

Did malignancies hover about? A black-faced demon soared directly into my heart's chamber and fanned the unease burning there. I closed my eyes. There was nothing in the room. I opened my eyes, turned round, and gazed for a moment on Miss Grange beneath her makeshift shroud.

But then, indeed, I thought I heard a step on the stair. I did not dare turn around again. "Mama?" I whispered. There was not another step. Of course, it must be she. "Mama?" I called again. Nothing answered me, and nothing stepped again, and the silence of that nothing grew long and longer, and I opened my mouth to cry out "Mama!" once more, but I could not make a sound against that silence. Nay, I could not breathe against that overhanging quiet, and I closed my eyes, waiting for whatever was to come. And waited. The silence stretched, until stretching so, it snapped and fell back into silence. There was nothing there.

Miss Grange lay among her pillows, and I drew near again to her bedside and gazed at her. Death had smoothed the vital complexity from off her face, and this woman before me seemed simpler, merely worn and exhausted. I put out my hand to touch her shoulder.

And I could not help but think again of my poor papa and how helpless I was as he lay fallen and broken beneath me, and how—could I have called the moment back—I would have stopped him long enough for him to tell the story he never did finish before he climbed those tower stairs. And perhaps—I could not shake this thought—had he finished that story, the heavens might have altered their course and he'd not have fallen, his death to come some other time, Papa alive and breathing even now, downstairs beside Mama. As it was instead, there was his figure walking ahead of me upon the path, then the crashing horror, and then the quiet.

"I will write it down, Miss Grange," I whispered to her. And I took up her diary and began to read.

1 August 1877
> Saturday is baking day.
> Monday is for mending.
> Tuesday is washing day.
> Wednesday is for visits.
> Thursday is sewing day.
> Friday is for cleaning.
> Saturday is baking day.
> And on and on and

On my tombstone shall be writ *Nell Grange—she died on a Saturday*. And the loose-capped mourner of the next era shall stand softly by and look down upon me sleeping below the tall grasses, and she shall know—because ALL WOMEN SHALL KNOW—that with my dying breaths I drew the scent of warm yeast into my lungs, and the mourner shall lean down and touch my headstone gently, her own hands aching a bit from the morning's bake, and think, Blessed are those who slip loose on a Saturday, for they bring to God a bit of their kitchen.

That is the scene if Mrs. Phelps had written it; were I Jane, restless and longing on top of Mr. Rochester's household, I'd jut out my chin and think—

A woman's future stretches before her in a long brown line of loaves: Saturday, unto Saturday, unto Doomsday.

However, I am Nellie Grange, and I say, Mother is herself today, and it is a sunny kitchen when she bakes. This morning I could see the drops had done their good work, for she appeared at breakfast rested and calm and ready. As usual, the bread dough waited our arrival, having sat up the whole night in the back pantry, rising while we slept.

"We'll need the blueberries later, Nell," Mother reflected, looking through the window at the lawn, dried already of its night dew, though it was only just past seven. The day would be glorious, the mare's tails in the sky trailing straight down the full stretch of the sound to Leadbetter's Island, where the quarrymen have long since taken their hammers from the hooks above their cots and trooped out to the implacable stone to make their first cuts. A dry day—light crusts assured for the week's pies. Mother counted up in her head the quantities she'd want while she finished the last of her coffee, and in my heart just then, Reader, it was summer.

SUSANNAH

Even her name is a wild and refreshing sound. When one sees Susannah, one is disposed to think of Antinous, or perhaps Mercury—for she is an abundant beauty of superb figure and stature, who strides, raven-eyed, through our world. But *she* would not have herself described so; were Susannah to choose her own music, it would be a tinkleboard tune, the notes happy jailers to a single melody. And though her arms and hands are glorious, she wears tight gloves in all weather whenever we visit, attempting to appear diminutive, when instead she is grand. She worries she has grown old, and the current vogue in Lady, whose shocking pallor and huge dark eyes gloom out at us from all the magazines, is a great fret to my sister. And though I have pointed out to her that such fashion should be preserved for heaven, when not a one need *work* at such appearance, Susannah studies the Tubercular Lady as earnestly as she did her computation, and lately she has taken to soaking her hands and face in rose-hip water before we sleep—the result of which does indeed lead to a paler, more peaked-looking Sue, as she loses an hour of sleep each evening to her bath.

Yesterday, I looked up from the rocks where I sat and saw my sister striding down the lawn to find me, her dress tossing round her as though she were the very keeper of the autumn breeze. I waved and stood at my position, one arm cross my face to shield the glare as she came down to the water, where it was cool and the breeze had salt in it, and the slap of the waves onto the rock came frequent as the fishing boats passed me by, crossing homeward down the harbor.

But what she had to say was inconsequential, as is frequently the case with her.

I settled back down upon my cushion and gathered the thick folds of my green skirts around my knees, resting my chin there, and looked again upon the white-topped blue. Susannah did not sit, but stood beside me rubbing her boot tip absently against the lichen, so it crumbled and slid away from us down the rock in dry gray clots. And there we paused companionably, the Grange spinsters.

1 September

And yet I see I have drawn her a Romantic Heroine of some proportion, though neither *romantic* nor *heroine* suits. For my sister's worth is not atmospheric—she is distinctly a practical sort. When I say she has nothing consequential of which to speak, I do not mean to imply that she is without consequence. Hers are the quickest hands, her cakes the lightest; her seams use the least amount of thread. Next to her, I am a very abyss of disorder. Next to her, indeed, most would aver I am the one of little apparent consequence.

"Do you know, Nell," Susannah whispered to me last night, "how Cousin Gilroy describes my hair?"

We were tucked up each in our white beds, two great sails becalmed in a windless sea. "No, Susannah. How could I?" I smiled in the dark.

She coughed softly. "You appear to be in his confidence, that is all." Again I smiled.

"How does he call your hair?"

I heard her sit up across the room, and I dimly saw her white gown looming against the lighter dark that came in through the window.

"Well, you remember when I was to go to town with Mother but then in the end went in by myself with Abby's Tom. I had not long been playing with Mary Quail's poor children when I saw Hayden Gilroy crossing over the green on his way down to the boats. Without thinking, I ran to the door and opened it, calling out to him as he passed the steps up to the house. I must have been an arresting sight, for he stopped where he was going and looked up at me there in the doorway, and he did not speak for a full minute.

" 'Where are you going, Cousin Gilroy?' I asked.

" 'Forgive me, I did not recognize you here in town.' He chuckled briefly. 'You present a rather startling tableau.' And he indicated the two children who had pushed themselves in front of me to gaze at the stranger. 'Ah.' I smiled at them. 'These are Mary Quail's children.' He nodded, then seemed about to turn away, when something must have tugged at him, for after a moment's hesitation, he quietly bounded up the three stairs between us and leaned over my boot.

" 'Give it here,' he ordered. And then he took my foot in his one hand and with the other reached to fix the heel, screwing the wood back in tighter so I did not slip off it as I do. I smiled down at his black head of hair so intent above my foot, and suddenly he looked up and caught my smile. Slowly, he grinned in answer.

" 'It is a very apple tree in springtime—your hair all breezing and shaking above me so—like blossoms.' And then, without another word, he tapped my heel, set down my foot upon the granite stair, waved to the children, and descended again to his direction."

She clapped her hands then and lay back onto her pillows.

"As good as a Romance, Susannah," I responded.

"All the better for being true." She sighed.

13 September

Sue is angry with me. Never mind. The rain continued steady throughout the morning, and we worked the new rug, with Abby joining in after her washing-up. Mother read a long while, her voice a pleasing hum to stitch to. Around midday, however, the wind began to rise from the east and the lashings of autumn storms to come spoke behind with new force.

14 September

Another story gathers in the back of this old bureau George has called my brain. Our cousin seems already to be a great boon to George, who—I will admit it here—has floundered these past months in running the business of the quarry. Our cousin understands stone, my brother the men—

Mother has had a slight feverish attack and appears low-spirited.

15 September

Dr. Bates has just stopped in on us and recommended laudanum drops for Mother's moods. It was a blessing to have his amiable presence in our front room talking to Mother, indeed talking Mother into something like herself. But I could not miss the look of worry upon his face when he turned, halfway down the lawn, to look back at the house. And it called to mind a scene I had utterly forgotten, taken place only last year.

A fit of brooding had overtaken Mother, and after four days, Father had gone to fetch Dr. Bates from Middle Haven. I heard their voices in the corridor as they passed by, and heard them once again as they left Mother's room to convene downstairs for consultation. Susannah had fallen asleep long since, but I crept from my covers and followed after my father and the doctor, taking up my own position just outside the study door.

"Do not let her alone long enough to brood, man," he said; "that is the best you can do for her." I heard brandy being poured into the glass tumblers on Father's desk. The glasses clinked. There came a following quiet.

"I cannot abide to see her so."

Dr. Bates coughed. "She has entered the winter of her life."

A grim laugh burst from Father. "As have we all, my friend. As have we all."

But Dr. Bates grew serious, his voice suddenly louder, as if he had risen to his feet. "Nay, Rorie. When the female of the species undergoes the change in life, she drifts free of her moral compass—and if she is allowed to fix her mind too long on one object, her inner guide may smudge, as when the bodily eye dwells too singly on one color and so cannot see the world but through the taint of that dominating hue."

Father was silent. I pressed my ear still harder against the old oak, my hand ready on the knob should either of the room's occupants suddenly wish to exit.

"She cannot loose a particular notion of hers." Father's voice was very calm, as though he had it on a chain.

"Aye? And what is that?"

"It is not based in fact, you understand."

"I understand, Rorie. Of course."

Father did not reply. Dr. Bates said something I could not hear, but then he must have turned back to face Father, for I heard, ". . . been moderate?"

Father smacked the tabletop.

"That is no concern of yours."

"Hush up, you old fool, do not willfully misunderstand what I say. I am speaking to you as your doctor now. At this critical age, too much"—he coughed—"er, love, may produce the gravest disturbance in her nervous system."

Who is this stranger in our midst? Though *stranger* is not the satisfactory word, for he has blurred a bit the borders between us. That is, I believe he has settled into the ways of our house and attempts to please each member of the family (quite rightly). But Lord, he is fitful, popping up everywhere at once, most especially wherever Mother tends. Yesterday, for instance, I watched his close observation of her as she proceeded slowly about the rose hips, appearing and reappearing as she stooped and stood. Before long, he had ventured down to her side, rolling back his own sleeves and, though I could not hear, offered, I think, to help Mother as she picked the last of the fruit, for soon his back also bobbed slowly up and down among the clinging vines.

But I did not think much about his shadowing of her until last night, when George playfully started upon—

AN INTRODUCTION TO THE GRANGES

"Miss Nellie Grange." George bowed to me. "Miss Anomaly Grange is a published Lady Authoress." Then he closed his eyes in a mockery of reflection.

"George!" I protested. "You might at least give me my proper name."

"Though she be slight of stature, Cousin, you must watch what you say about her. Safeguard all the movements you would not wish Posterity to handle with her soft, inquiring hands."

Cousin Gilroy looked over and gave me a tiny wink.

"I mean what I say, good man." George inclined toward Gilroy, his eyebrows raised portentously, though he laughed. "Watch what you do around our Nell."

"George!" I repeated, a bit sharper.

"Our Nell," George continued, pushing the boat out from its berth and jumping aboard, now extending his wild talk into the open sea. "Our very treasure, my own dear sister. I salute the literary hope for the state of Maine!" He stood across the table and flagged his nonsense with a bright wave to me.

"Hush, George. Cousin Gilroy will think he's stepped cross

the threshold of a madhouse, and you a lunatic run amok with the keys," Susannah remonstrated lightly.

"And Miss Susannah Grange"—now George turned to her—"is our Beauty, the undisputed maiden queen of Middle Haven. There she reigns—"

"George! A queen indeed!" But Sue batted his words back at him for the pleasure of hearing them gain in the air.

"Our dear Susannah's beauty," Mother interjected, "is of the inward kind. Hers is a steady presence in times of need."

"Ask Master Joseph Ames, especially," George teased. "He'd give a world for a kindly eye from that beauty."

"Stop up your nonsense, son." Mother's irritation tipped over. She looked full at Susannah then, saying slowly, "No girl possessed of such a beauty was ere so good—or so true."

Susannah twisted a bit upon her chair and did not meet Mother's loving gaze.

"You are fortunate to have such a family around you, Aunt Grange." Our cousin seemed almost wistful.

Mother nodded her head, and at last Susannah raised up and met her gaze. Mother smiled.

"Indeed I am." Then she stood up from her chair, motioning to Susannah and me; but as I pushed back my chair, I noted Hayden Gilroy did not leave off looking at Mother, most hungry as she turned to snuff the candles on the sideboard, and hungry as he continued staring when she turned back about.

"Am I a haint, Nephew?"

He started then. "Nay, Aunt. Do not think me forward. I had a sudden recollection of my first home." He smiled uncertainly.

"Of your home?"

He shook his head as if in confusion. "I hardly can see it, but just now I recalled a miniature in an oval glass hung upon the chimney nook." He looked up at her. "Of you."

Mother stared. "Of me?"

He continued, the child speaking through the man's deep tones. "You were very beautiful—and gone to America!"

"At what age were you?"

He had a faraway expression in his eyes, as though he were sunk again on his knees before his aunt's portrait. "Four, I should think."

"Four!" She spoke so sharply, it knocked the pleasant memory from out the room. She took several steps away from the table but then stood frozen by the door.

"But I had thought—"

We stared at her rigid figure, struck into a fractured pose: While her head was held high, her hands could not keep from smoothing down her black silk skirts, again and then again. I looked at Susannah.

Cousin Gilroy rose into the breach. "Forgive me, Aunt. My childish memory has caused you pain—"

She started but did not turn round. "Aye," she said. And then without another word, she passed from the room. In silence, we attended her slow steps down the front hall. The sitting room door opened and then closed; and then, after a brief time, it opened once more as she crossed the hall and ascended the stairs. Susannah shifted uneasily in her chair. And all this while, our cousin had not turned round, standing in front of the doorway through which my mother had passed, as if he might reach through the velvet portiere and pull her back.

"You wish for a home?" Susannah asked.

Then indeed he did turn round, and another word caught in Sue's throat at the sight of his face; she rose and went to him, taking his hand up from where it hung at his side and placing it gently in hers.

"Do not worry. Here 'tis," she whispered.

The floorboards creaked softly overhead as Mother entered her room, crossing to set the candle upon her nightstand.

(25 drops)

Susannah Fancies *Herself* an Author

This morning, she has entered the room and deposited a small cache of pages on top the table.

"What is it?"

"For your book. A confession." And without another word, she departed, silently pulling shut the door behind her. I have taken up the pages and will read them before I fold them into my own.

When Hayden Gilroy appeared in the west parlor yesterday afternoon, I looked up from where I sat and perceived his heightened color and the damp in his hair, seeing at once that he was agitated beyond measure.

"Please to draw up to the fire, Cousin," said I, "or you will take chill." He did not look at me, but, rather, nodded at the window behind my head, then drew up the footstool to the blaze. But he rose as soon as he sat down, and stood over the fireplace, looking at the popping wood. He took the poker from its hook and gouged at the wood savagely, causing the logs to fall open in a shower of sparks and smoke, which forced me to retreat from my seat by the fire. I did so without comment, for I was a little afraid of him in this mood. I took a spot across the room at the tea table, returning to gather my sewing things as silently as I could. But he whirled as I reached behind his back for my dropped basket, saw I was removing, and instantly knelt to pick up the fallen threads.

"Forgive me," he said, "I am not a great one for gently tending fires." And he stood up with my basket and carried it over to the table for me, where there was nothing for it but to sit and recommence my work. I bent my head and watched his feet crossing and recrossing upon Mother's new carpet, idly thinking about the crimson dye that had not held as firm as it might have had we steeped the wool longer—as I suggested. However, Mother resisted the deeper hue.

For a time he paced and I sewed to the accompaniment of the fire popping and the swishing of the folds in your dress, Nell, the yellow muslin sliding over my knees while I ripped the hem.

"What it must be to have a sister such as yours!" he said, dropping down on a knee beside me. I looked at him to see whether the expression on his face matched the extremity of his tone, and indeed his eyes burned brightly as they gazed at me.

"Yes," I answered.

"There's a whole world abides in that yes."

"Nell is a loving sister," I replied with a flush, uncertain of whither he wanted this conversation to tend. My heart constricted with the unpleasant (I am sorry for it) sensation that Mr. Gilroy aimed to enlist my aid in his suit for your affections! I bent my head quickly and began tearing at the fabric once more. Now I can reveal how much it cost me to converse as I did, lightly treading a path strewn with your attributes for him to walk beside and notice.

"She is original," I offered.

"Original as an uncut stone," he answered.

How did this answer signify? Yea or nay?

"And loyal," I continued.

"As one who would wander holds on fast to his mooring to avoid the tempting tide."

"And canny," I professed.

His voice slowed as he countered, "Your sister moves about the world with spectral eyes."

I raised my head and looked into his eyes then, and for an instant I may have perceived the jester quick-shutting the door behind him. He returned my gaze long enough for me to notice how familiar were his eyes, the blue orbs like those I remembered from a dream.

Oh Nell! I love him. I cannot stop my pen from writing it out in full here. I love Hayden Gilroy. And what is more, I can see that he loves me. His wish to talk about you was a ploy to involve me in close discussion, to sit nearby and watch me as I sewed, demurely and yet with passion as I described you, my very sister.

Do you see? He loves me, and I sideways showed him how it is to be loved by me by making a catalog of your attributes, for, oh Nell, I do love you and your little eccentricities and your vague theories, and though I've never put this all so plainly, here it is in bold letters. Thank you darling, for letting me ease my heart onto this page, and thank you beforehand for reading my poor confession.

But now I have given you something in return. For here is a love scene for your copybook; I know it is hard for you to imagine such things on your own, having little experience, and great distate for the trivial, wed as you are to art and its sublime transcendency o'er our little world.

I think you are very great.

There, I bend and blot this page with a kiss—you are my own best sister, and he who newly lives here beside us is the harbor my own heart did find.

7 October

I have spent the day avoiding Sue, annoyed by her pretensions and made uneasy by her talk of love. "Have you read it, Nell?" She stopped me on the stairs. I looked at her, flushed and beautiful beneath her kerchief, her wide dark eyes clear with hope and the promise of a bright future. "Nay, I have not had the chance," I replied, and proceeded to where Mother waited in her room.

Then after dinner: "Have you read it yet, Nell?"

"No."

"Go to. Go to—I shall finish your sewing."

I departed and returned.

"The scene was good, though poorly executed."

"Executed? Whatever do you mean?"

"The language—the writing of it is not vital."

"What does that matter? That were no scene I practiced penmanship upon."

"Aye? What was it, then?"

"The very life! It was my words and his exact, repeated."

"I hope you do not really love him, Sue."

She flushed up proudly again. "I do."

I could not bear her pride, and poked. "Why does Mother shrink from him?"

"She does no such thing."

"She does. Watch."

"Hush up, Nell. You are manufacturing horrors."

I shook my head. She gazed at me, then nodded slowly as if she understood. "You are only jealous you could not write such a love story yourself."

10 October

A great high sky this morning, like the open palm of a departing hand, then the afterclap came. Storm clouds rolling down the bay all the afternoon, and now we're in the thick of a dark, wet evening. But we're tucked up tight, and just tonight I sat down to this book and felt the premonition of a close winter season. How easy it is to forget the cold in midsummer, and yet how quickly return the habits of winter. There is a quiet to the evenings that settles softly down now; no outside noises penetrate in summer's fashion when windows are thrown wide to catch the night seiners out in the harbor, someone's laugh entering in on the light salt breeze. Now all laughter is our own, muted by the heavy curtains and cast into our group as if Sound herself grew shy.

When old Autumn slaps Summer's fair cheeks, there's work to be done, says Abby, and I'll not disagree. I wove nearly fifteen yards of wool yesterday and today. Sue and Abby were hard at work for a week cleaning the winter pantry, lining the shelves in readiness to take in the squashes, which have begun to bloom big as babies' heads.

Ludlow Thomas sits so quiet there, a book tucked in his hands.

A silence has grown up between myself and Sue, one I find I am not sorry for.

(40 drops)

12 October

This morning's work with Mother began peaceably enough, and the salt air blew gently in among the pages of the German text I set beside my sewing. I gave myself one verb for every seam completed. Susannah sat across the table, one finger on the housekeeping columns, figuring the house expenditures for the month. Mother sat with her needlepoint contentedly in the chair by the window, her face and shoulders tilted toward the breezy, bright morning as she worked upon the new border for the old rug in the dining room. Though she has chosen the story of Telemachus searching midst the brown roses for his father, in truth, he looks a very Yankee boy—resembling George! For a steady hour, we three worked like this, Susannah's pen scratching into the thick pages of the book in countertempo to my own, much slower translation—for every word of mine wrested out of Saxon obscurity, three sums for her and a little smile of satisfaction playing about her face. I caught sight of Hayden Gilroy through the window, crossing the stretch of lawn on his way down to the quarry boat, his fine form striding across the yellowing grasses like a charioteer cutting through the heathens. I paused for an instant, remarking how he went.

"What are you looking at?" Susannah asked so sharply, I started.

"At Hayden Gilroy," I replied, still watching as he ducked his head on entering through the boathouse door.

Susannah leaned across the table without a word and wrote on my page, "Do not." I raised my eyes up to hers in confusion just as Mother spoke slowly from the opposite window, "What manner of man is he?"

"Why do you ask, Mother?"

"I find it peculiar that he has arrived, that is all, and wonder." She leaned into the cloth and snipped off the thread with her teeth.

"Wonder?"

"About him." Mother was finished with cloth and conversation, and she looked at the two of us with a tight smile. "Bring me *Jane Eyre*, Nell, would you?"

But Susannah wished to stay the conversation's shift. "Why does he make you wonder, Mother?"

Mother fixed her quick glance on Susannah. "What is it you have got into your head, daughter?"

Susannah dropped her eyes. I brought *Jane Eyre* and settled back down into my chair, folding away my German in preparation for Miss Brontë. Susannah continued her sums, able to listen and concentrate at one and the same time, Mother's voice providing more music than meaning for her.

As for me, when once another author's words seize hold, I am carried far from the table my elbows lean upon, farther still from the room wherein my mother and sister and I spend our every morning, and out into the atmosphere of wind and sun and streaky clouds. This morning, I was gone in an instant, following Jane's progress upon the unforgiving moors, cast out from her heart's ease by her own stern soul, without money or a friend in the world to lift her up and carry her through her difficulty.

And then, without warning, Mother stopped reading and sat in a musing silence; and though still in Miss Brontë's thrall, a tangible sadness grew larger in the room than the words I still heard about my heart. I watched her thin form, wrapped tightly even on such a warm day as this, the book still open on her lap, and I longed to go to her and stroke her cheek. She closed the book and sat for a bit abstracted, then called Susannah to her, who, also deeply affected, had long since stopped her computations, leaning her head down upon her hands, the better to listen. Susannah raised her head like one pulled from a dream and drew to sit at Mother's feet. Mother did not call me, as there was not nearly enough room for the both of us by her chair. So I stayed where I was, my eyes on my mother and sister.

We did not speak for a long while. Mother stroked Susannah's hair absently, as if my sister were a child again, and I confess the motion became intolerable.

"I think Jane a proper fool," I mused from my post.

"Hush, Nell. You've no thought of what you're saying."

"I do, Mother."

"How can you be so unfeeling?" Sue chimed in. "Jane Eyre has not a soul in the world to turn to," and she sat up.

"It is because she hasn't a soul in the world that she should not turn from the one soul who had offered her his broad, great spirit."

"He offered her a rotted staff—'twould have given her the tumble when she tried to walk about upon it."

"But he loves her—and she loves him."

Susannah looked at me. "You miss the point entirely, Nell. Jane Eyre has her soul to answer to, and her own good self to keep."

"That good self was treated abominably by her fellowmen," I responded, "and she might have died nameless and alone, just flesh and blood in the middle of the field, with no one to know who she had been, or that she had a good self worth saving." I sprang up from the table.

"God watched over her, and did so because what she carried in her was not visible to the creatures around her, but burned bright gold inside." By now, Susannah had also risen and crossed over to stand quite close to me, her cheeks reddening.

"Susannah"—I looked straight at her—"is it not your idea to be useful to those of this world, to your fellow creatures here on earth?"

"Of course it is, Nell." She was growing cross.

"Jane Eyre also wished to be useful, and she was being so at Thornfield Hall—she spread new soil upon the dried roots of that place."

"That is poor logic." Susannah had crossed past me and taken up her seat again at our worktable.

I was keenly aware of the intensity with which it appeared our mother listened, two bright spots burning on either cheekbone, her hands very still in her lap.

I tried to wrest my thinking into shape. "If we are useful here and now, Susannah, then that is the bright gold, I think, for how can we know that saving our souls at the expense of another's heart—two others, in Jane's story—is worthy of any larger plan?"

Mother groaned and put her hand up to cover her mouth.

"Mother?"

Susannah cast me a frightened look, all traces of our dispute wiped clear from her face.

Mother began to shake her head back and forth and now drew both her two hands up to her mouth.

I crept close to Mother then and kneeling down beside her, softly said her name. Still she shook her head and would not hear me. I spoke her name again, this time a little louder. She turned and looked thoughtfully at me and for a long moment—but without a trace of recognition in her face. I sprang up, truly frightened now.

"Mother!" Susannah leapt in between us and took Mother's shoulders in her hands and shook her hard.

"Let her be, Sue!" I cried, attempting to shield Mother, but Sue was the larger and, pushing me aside, would not leave off shaking, or could not is the truth, for she seemed in the grip of a terror beyond her.

Of a sudden, our Mother lifted up her head and looked straight at Susannah for a dreadful moment, and then she laid her head back in the chair and closed her eyes. Susannah sprang back, and I saw she was near a frenzy of a hideous, uncontrollable laughter, her mouth working in horror. Then suddenly, Mother opened up her eyes again. Her hands rose to pat the hair to peace at her temples, then rested there protectively.

"My dear." She motioned to Susannah. "Come here."

But Sue could not take a step, and covering her mouth, she turned away. I drew close to Mother. "I am here, Mother."

She turned and bestowed a weak smile upon me, which lasted but a moment, then turned her gaze back upon Sue, who stood so still, it seemed she was the dim echo of my sister, all living flesh departed.

"My dear, I do not wish you to think too much on Mr. Gilroy."

"*Mr. Gilroy,* Mother?" Sue's face was white as she flashed around.

"Listen carefully to me, my girl." Mother rested her head again back against her chair. "I never heard my sister had borne a child before she died."

"You think he is a stranger?" she gasped.

Mother closed her eyes. "Nay. Far worse. There is something around him I recognize, though I cannot fathom how. He walks in circles in my brain." Sue took a few steps forward. "Do you heed?"

Sue stopped where she was.

Mother closed her eyes. "Heed me, Susannah. Only the wicked walk in such circles."

"Only the wicked?"

"Aye, my girl. The wicked, or the dead."

A shadow darted cross my sister's face, then vanished.

14 October

Frost sparkles upon the stiff ground—it is the first of the year. I do not think either of us will mention Mother's brief vacancy of soul to George, for it was so sudden, and foreign, as if she plummeted downward past us, and then as suddenly returned—with our Mr. Gilroy on her lips. But I could not pretend we had not been witness to a dreadful thing, and I have asked that she not *upset* Mother so.

"I?" She clapped her hand to her chest, astonished.

I nodded.

"Who is it, Nell, who helps her with her drops before she retires?"

I pulled my covers up. "I know, Susannah."

"I am the one who does what Mother wishes." She crossed her arms. "I am."

Again I did not look at her, but studied my two hands there in my lap. She threw back her covers and marched cross the floor to my bed.

"I do not want Mother unhappy any more than you." Then she leaned her face into mine so I must look. There were tears starting round the corners of her eyes.

I was silent, and Sue crept in bed beside me. For a moment, we both lay back against my pillows. Yesterday's scene passed through my mind once more, and then I could not help it—I spoke out again.

"Do more, Sue. Do what she asks."

"And what is that?" In the near gloom, Sue's voice beside me signaled danger, but I plunged into the dark between us.

"Keep from Mr. Gilroy."

She grabbed at both my shoulders and leaned her face in very close to mine.

"Why do *you* ask that?"

Her fingers were hurting me. "For Mother's sake."

She let go of me suddenly and gave me a good shove as she slid out of my bed. "You are so transparent, Nell. I will do as I like about Mr. Gilroy."

"But Mother has asked you."

"I see now that this has nothing to do with Mother."

She had reached her bed and snuffed her candle. I waited until I heard her pull up her covers and lean back again into her pillow.

"You think me jealous of Mr. Gilroy?"

She sat up. "Yes. Clearly. Why else would you continue to be so provoking?"

"Listen to me, sister Sue. I do not like Mr. Gilroy."

"Ha!" She slapped the pillow. I tossed back my covers then and approached her in the dark. "Listen to me," I whispered, "I distrust him. Mother would not behave so strongly without cause."

"Oh?"

"No," I said.

"Ah." I could almost hear the smile in her voice.

(increased to 50 drops)

16 October

Tonight though she tries, Mother cannot attend what she does for long, her hands fluttering down after a time to rest in her lap, her mind elsewhere. I am in my usual spot against the far wall, at our worktable, cleared now of the morning's grammars, the afternoon's patterns, freed for my own night writing. The sofa provides an upholstered barrier between me and my characters—the rest of the room stretching away from me. Mr. Ludlow Thomas appears to be absorbed in writing a letter (to whom?). Susannah sits at the piano against the opposite wall, the two front windows open on either side of her. George slouches low in the chair next to Mother's, reading. Cousin has entered with that ducked head of his, as though every room had a beam too low for his stature. It is a peculiar habit, this—was he raised on nuts and berries in a cave? He crosses to stand behind Susannah, who does not alter her playing one whit, until he stops there. Now he has stood there almost one whole page, and I can tell Susannah is distracted.

There. She's bounced the keys.

"Is there something you would like to hear, Cousin?" She neither turns nor looks into the little mirror in the piano face to see him.

He shifts where he stands. There is a silent pause, and Mother looks up from her work, her fingers keeping their stitches, blind and able. Susannah still does not turn.

"Nay," he answers softly, and moves past to stand at the window.

Susannah drops her hands again into the Beethoven, repeating the phrase where she had left off, and then, as though she is stuck on the branches, she plays the phrase once more, and then a third time.

George raises his head. "Go on, Sue—I am certain old Mr. Beethoven has more than one line in him."

Sue plays it again, *very loudly,* then stops and spins around.

"Don't you like my playing, George Grange?"

"That is not playing, Susannah. That is marching off to war."

She claps her hands. "You are right! I mean to conquer this piece."

"Conquer Beethoven?" Hayden turns back from the window.

She brandishes an imaginary sword and points it directly at the man. "Precisely."

He bows his head to her as if in homage to the conqueror, a gesture that arrests Mother, for even after he has raised his head again and turned back to his study at the window, Mother's gaze remains upon him, and though I see her sidewise, it is as if she is struck by some remembered moment our cousin had pulled up hand over hand from down the dark well of her past, for there she sits still, regarding the place in air just filled by his head.

(55 drops)

17 October

The wind lashes round at the house again tonight, but inside there is no calm whatsoever.

The men sat late around their wine, and Mother had just stood to light her candle and depart upstairs when they all came in to us—in high spirits, I could see by George's cheeks.

"Tell us a story, Nell." He threw himself down at my feet.

I did not answer him, just tapped his shoulder with my boot.

Cousin Hayden came close by to sit beside me at the table. I ducked my head down.

"Why don't you ask me, George?"

"You, Susannah?"

"Does this house consider it holds only one author? I am one, as well."

Hayden cleared his throat. "Are you, Susannah?"

"I am helping Nell with her book. That is, we are writing it two by two."

I raised my head, dumbstruck at Sue's assertion.

"Are you?" George snorted.

"Yes, George. I don't know why you think she is the only one capable of story making in this house."

I stared at her, aghast.

"Are you writing a story as well, Miss Grange?" Mr. Thomas asked.

She dropped her eyes. "I am."

"What a prodigious group to encounter here at the tip of the world!" he said.

I looked up to find his eyes upon me and a gentle look upon his face, which goaded me forward.

"Susannah plays at writing. She makes deposits into my book every now and again."

Sue sniffed. "They are somewhat better than deposits, Nell, and you know it to be true."

"This house is large enough for two to play about with their pens, I think." Mother's voice was very low. "Let us hear no more on this."

And no more did anyone hear from me, all throughout the evening. Nonetheless, after we parted for the night and Susannah and I had wordlessly prepared ourselves for bed, each to her own small cot, each in her own stiff frock, I could not be silent more.

"You shall not steal my telling of this tale."

"Which tale do you think you are telling, Miss Nell?" she responded warily.

"The one of this house."

"Oh? And what is that?"

"One you cannot see—will not."

"Aye. I see very well, better than you at times."

"Why do you think you may trounce what I do, Susannah? Why cannot you keep to your own sphere—"

"My sphere?" Her voice hushed in the low crouch of a beast.

"Yes," I answered coldly. "The mirror. The conversation. The toss of the head. Stick to beauty for your own vanity's sake. Pray, stay there."

"Vanity?" She sat up in her bed. "Vanity! Vain ambition beats in your breast, sister, in place of a heart."

"You misread me."

"Nay. I do not. You will never have a stake in this world, Nell Grange, if you do not soften and let your heart open and beat loudly for the joy."

"That is poor logic, but it works nicely as a speech."

"Oh, how hard you are. And wrong, Nell." She leaned upon her elbow and shot this straight into the dark. "You see wrong."

I sat up now. "But I suspect him."

"Whom?"

"Hayden."

"Of what, pray?"

"I do not know. I cannot tell. He is not what he seems."

"Why must you always see sadness and misery in happiness,

or duplicity and intrigue in a serene face? Why cannot you let things be?"

I regarded her impatiently. "I cannot help what I see."

"Aye!" she cried. "You can. You can, but you will not."

"Hush. You are excited."

"Nay." She was building up now to a scene. "For there is not enough drama in life, not enough *life* for Miss Nell without looking and looking. You create what you see; you look and see sadness, and then lo, it is there!"

I remained silent.

"Do you think *I* cannot feel Mother's dread when he enters the room? Do you think I cannot see how she flushes hot and cold on the subject of our cousin?"

"You do see it, then."

"Aye," she responded coldly. "I do. But I do not think past her behavior to seek a reason, some secret reason, Nell. Have you ever thought that Hayden Gilroy merely reminds Mother of someone, that it is not *he* himself that affrights, but his likeness?"

"Aye, Sue," I answered gravely. "That is exactly what I think."

"Who is it, then?"

"His father."

"And?"

"Who is his father to Mother?"

"Stop it." She shook her head. "Stop it. The ground is solid. The ground is what we walk upon."

Aye, Susannah. But what is neath the ground? Have you an answer?

20 October

A dark, drenching rain this afternoon. We are in the west parlor, and I at my post. Mother remains upstairs with a sick headache. Mr. Ludlow Thomas brings in a thick book and paces the room with it held open in his one hand. Cousin Hayden stands at the window, his back to us all, impatient with the weather.

"I do not think reality can be got from books," Mr. Thomas says aloud, snapping it shut, and takes the seat beside mine here at the worktable. And I write down exactly that, then read this little scene back to him, my laughter bright about my heart.

"That is verisimilitude, not reality." He smiles across at me. "Dictation, rather."

"But she has given you a time and place, a reason for pacing up and down this room with a book in your hand instead of out at work," Cousin says gloomily, "where we all should be."

Mr. Thomas smiles. "Agreed"—he nods to me—"better than dictation."

We are silent for a time; my pen is dipped and waiting. The wind has turned and the rain no longer beats so hard upon the panes. I cannot stand this quiet.

"Tell me, Cousin Gilroy, something I have long wanted to know."

He turned round from the window and looked at me.

"How did you come to hear of us?" At the question, Susannah looked up anxiously from her sewing.

He shrugged. "I received a letter."

"From whom?"

"Your father."

I looked directly at Susannah then. "Our father?"

"Yes, he wrote and invited me to come and work for him."

"When was this?" she gasped.

"This time, last year, I would say."

"And why did you not tell Mother that you had a letter from Father?"

He was silent, regarding me.

Susannah stood up. "Leave him be, Nell. Our cousin has suffered enough without your questions."

"No," he said to her softly. "Your sister asks what she should." But there he stopped speaking.

I felt sick to my soul just then watching the man and my sister, her mouth opening and closing as she tried to cover the silence that grew at our feet. Mr. Thomas remained seated beside me.

"I had sent a letter announcing I would come. But I fear it must have been waylaid, and after I arrived here and saw her state, I was afraid to madden your mother further," Cousin Hayden said finally to me. "She does not like me. And you are—"

"That is enough, Nell!" Susannah cried to me. "Enough." She turned to him. "Do not think you need justify. Do not think you need answer for your own good heart. You came to your family. That is enough."

My cousin's smile to her was deep, and he did not drop the hand she had clasped in his.

21 October

George is just back from town and has crashed the latest wave of science firmly upon our door: A doctor visiting Dr. Bates proposes that all manner of disparate men can easily be classified into four categories merely by studying their faces.

"And these are?" I had one of George's slippers in my hands, while he used my shoulder for a post and stepped into the bootjack.

"Do not rush me," he warned sternly, his face turned from mine as he spoke.

"Nay, my liege lord," I whispered to his back, "I shall remember my place." There came a stifled chuckle, but silence reigned in the front hall.

"Now." He turned, and held his hands out for the slipper, which I curtsied and gave unto him, my brother, keeper of the family name. "Turn your face to the light," said he. I did so, smiling.

"Aha," he whispered. "It is just as the man has written."

"Oh pish! Tell me the categories, George."

"It appears," George drawled, "that the character of each and every one of us may be divined by the quality of our faces, which neatly fall into one of the four categories."

"Those being?"

"Horse, bird, bug, and—" He put his hand upon the sitting room door.

"And?"

"Muffin."

We burst into gales of laughter and swung wide the door, to find Hayden and Mother seated and silent.

But it was not our appearance that had arrested them upon the sofa. From the front bedroom overhead came the low sound of Susannah singing.

(again, 50 drops)

23 October

There is a fever in our house; its name Gilroy. Shy and insidious, the man finds his way everywhere. Mother watches him more and more nervously, as if she plans to send him packing but cannot choose the proper time; every hour crackles with the imminence of that encounter. I watch her: Will she? Will she? When?

S. walks round and round the house. Front room, back room, dining room, parlor. Just a man, I say to her each time she enters, our own cousin, come to us from Ireland. Abby has nodded to me significantly, and pronounced the man "deep." I think the man knows he is a lie.

Beastly day. The fishermen trail one another in—one after the other—back down the harbor, laboriously breasting the whitecapped waves and side wind. I suppose there has been little caught, and the time only eleven. Mr. Thomas is curiously aloof this past week.

10 November

I have not the words—there are no words better than all those written before mine. I have stepped up to the hole and thrown stone after stone down in. The day opens and shuts. Opens and shuts—bright sunlight shining in the midst of a dense fog. We see, we see, and nothing know.

Oh, that my words could spread about them on the page, not as the bare black skeletons they are, but come fully clothed, so that when I wrote the word—*quarry,* for example—instead of then having to spell out what the stones look like, what the workers wore, I might rather sit back and know that the word carried with it all its own noise and color, the sharp smell of spruce deadened by the chalky stink of the black explosive, and the cut granite wall rising like a god over the Italian men, here clambering down the bald face of the white cliff, there crouched in various spots in groups of three, readying the rock for the next blow.

15 November

A diary is but a partial thing.

The trees have shuddered free their bright leaves, and the bent skeletons greet me again, for this is the season I most long toward. All bares itself now. I think at my best in these months, for nothing shrouds the shape of the world in late autumn. The black lines of tree trunks border the stubbled brown fields, and the dark blue of the sky borders the trees, their tops poking into that fabric. Snow will bring shadows and half-buried objects, but for this month, I rest myself within the clearest eye of the land. What I see out here beyond my window contrasts against the newly hidden nature of our house life. I cannot describe what occurs, as nothing seems to—in reality, nothing has changed—but for this feathery inquisitive silence that flutters up as I walk into rooms, as if I seem suddenly to be possessed of a certain knowledge I do not have, and am regarded now with an uncommon attention by Mother, strange for being new, but not at all unpleasant.

(70 drops today)

28 November

Ludlow Thomas is very quiet. Mother unwell.

(80 drops)

1 December

Mother unwell. Abby to town.

(87 drops)

273

We were hard at work unraveling the worn dining room carpet's border and did not hear her enter the room.

"Why are you not at your studies?" she asked angrily.

We both jumped and looked over our shoulders at Mother, who stood above us in her best navy blue silk, like an elegant ghost, her white face floating above the dark collar. I did not know what to answer. Sue smiled at Mother and reminded her of the list of winter chores she had written up for us last spring after the cleaning. Mother crossed the room to slide herself, bustle and all, in between the arms on Father's chair, then leaned her head against its high upholstered back. Susannah looked down again at the work in her hands. I ventured nothing, and did nothing.

"Susannah!"

Susannah shook a little and looked back at Mother. "Yes, Mother?"

"What is your opinion on women's suffrage?"

"On suffrage, Mother!"

"Yes, Susannah." Mother leaned her elbows on the chair arms and pressed her fingertips together before her, looking every bit the schoolmarm then.

Susannah did not immediately respond, hoping, I think, that this question was a passing fancy of Mother's.

"Susannah?"

She squirmed and briefly looked at me. "Women should have the vote, Mother."

"Exactly. Why so?"

A tear fell onto Sue's cheek, though she did not wipe it away. "We are citizens of a democracy," Sue replied woodenly.

"Very good. And the freedmen?"

"And the darkies—"

"Tut!"

"And the freedmen also," Sue whispered. And Mother smiled encouragingly, as if she and Sue were engaged in an actual discussion at which cool Reason sat between and nodded while they spoke. I sat so frozen, I could not unbend my fingers from around the needle. And Mother had turned to me.

"Fetch your book, Nell."

"I beg your pardon?"

"Come along, my girl. Read us one of your new stories."

I flushed. "I have no new stories, Mother. Only my diary."

Mother looked at me long and hard. "I do not believe that is possible."

I looked down at my hands and said very slowly, "It is so."

There was a silence in the room, long enough for my cheeks to stop their burning. I took up the carpet once more onto my lap and began to pick again at the edging with the darning needle. I could not bear to look at Susannah. And then, for an instant— before I understood what it was she had said—it appeared Mother had returned to us in her old, sensible voice.

"How many drops do you have me taking now?"

I looked up. Susannah was a statue beside me.

"How many is it?" Mother's voice was soft and reasonable. We kept silent. In truth, I did not know. Susannah often adds a bit.

"There is a limit, girls." Mother sat forward and spoke to us both. "And I may pass it, 'gain and again"—she giggled—"without any harm, as you can see!" She clapped her hands in the air, then rose to her feet and approached us with her ghastly, wasted face. Mother leaned down between the two of us, frightened in our chairs.

"But I must know of it," she whispered. "I must know how high the bar is set before I leap across."

And then she laughed.

4 December

Mother—

12 December

He is four days gone and still no letter. Stop it! Stop! Poor little brain: You would remember the day one way, while Heart stands fast in her own opinion. He loves you—well, so there it is. But you are a fool, Nell Grange, if you think Ludlow Thomas is made of greatness. He is not. He is all shine and curled sentences, proffered to you on silver plates of thought—but he is rich, so his heart is gilded; he is handsome, so he has felt no slight; and he is gifted with a tongue and a brain such as I have never seen, and yet must come from the south, from the city. Surely he is not alone in his ideas; surely he has merely read them and memorized them.

He cannot feel as I do.

Well, it is nought. Nought. The house quiets at last. We have finally settled Mother down to her rest.

14 December

Have heard nought from him. Mother grows increasingly distracted.

17 December

He has written. He says I become a place. I am a place, yes. For him, I am the wild woods calling. I am calling him.

18 December

Cousin Hayden came downstairs and found us in the front room, listless, the mending basket unturned between us. The poor man, for so he is, could not look at either one of us, just resolutely studied the mantel above our seated heads.

"I must leave this house and find my lodgings in town."

Susannah raised up her head directly then.

"What has happened, that you should leave?" I asked.

"Your mother and I think it for the best," he said.

Susannah flushed and looked down again, but she said softly, "I am sorry you should think it so."

He frowned at this but did not reply. None of us spoke, and after an awkward silence, he clapped his hands together soundlessly and turned to leave.

Susannah pushed her sewing from off her lap. "Why is it best?"

He did not turn to face us and his hand remained on the knob. "I cannot say."

She nodded at Mr. Gilroy's bowed head, as if she suddenly had understood something, and then she shot such a look of fury at me, I rose up from my chair and moved a little distance off. But she shrieked and came after me, whirling me round to face Mr. Gilroy, who, astonished, had turned from the door.

"Have done with it!" she cried out to him.

"Susannah!"

"Now. In my sight and hearing!" She had hold of me so tightly, I could feel her fingers down to my bone.

"Stop it, Sue!" I whispered to her. "You do not know what you are saying."

She gave me a good hard shake. "Hush up." And she pushed me toward Mr. Gilroy, who stood before us, all color drained from his face, his eyes on Susannah.

"Tell her what is in your heart." Sue's voice quivered.

Hayden Gilroy looked at me in confusion and then stepped forward toward us with his hand outstretched. "Susannah?"

I looked down at the ground between us, but Susannah was possessed by some scene she must have envisioned, and still holding me tightly with one hand, she reached round with her other and tipped my chin up and held it, forcing me to stare directly into Mr. Gilroy's troubled countenance.

"Let me hear it." Susannah trembled behind me, though her voice did not waver again.

"Susannah, I cannot fathom what it is you wish me to say." Hayden Gilroy stood quietly before us. "But I do not like to think I am somehow the cause of this treatment of your sister."

"Ah . . ." Susannah let go her breath slowly. "So, you are concerned about my sister?"

He took a wary step closer. "Please, I think you might be hurting her."

Susannah let me go so suddenly, I almost stumbled against Mr. Gilroy, who rushed forward to catch Sue in his arms as she fainted there on the spot.

Frightened, I ran to fetch some water from the dining room.

Returning quickly as I could, I thought I heard a low murmur of voices as I drew nearer to the room, and I stopped upon the threshold of the scene. Susannah had awoken, though Mr. Gilroy still held her fast in his arms. She lay below, looking up into his worried face as he bent over her, and she slowly smiled. And he leaned farther down and kissed her. I stepped into the room then and came to my sister's side, leaning over her to put a damp cloth upon her forehead, and without a word, she reached up and covered my hand and held it there upon her brow. A glad sob rose in my chest at her unexpected touch. Hayden held her for a moment more, and then he gently lifted Susannah up to a sitting position, where she placed her arms around me then and laid her head against my shoulders. With a pained look at me, he rose from the place and started for the door. But he could not leave, so turned again, with this to say:

"Your mother"—he cleared his throat quickly—"thinks me to be someone other than the man you see before you." And then he opened the door and passed through.

We sat together on the carpet and listened to him gather his bags in the hallway, heard the front door open, then close behind him, his boots descending slowly down the porch stairs. Then came the quiet.

The two of us remained on the carpet, Sue's arms about me and my cheek against the top of her head for a time. The sun stretched across the room to us along the gray floorboards, nearly reaching to our hems. I felt Susannah's fingers loose their grip from off my shoulder and she put her head into her hands.

"I never loved him, Sue."

She shook her head. "You have teased me unmercifully."

"Nay." I leaned in and tried to open the gate of her hands.

"Yes." She dropped her hands and looked up at me. "You have."

"I only meant to tweak you at times, Sue."

She shook her head again.

"You angered me," I said simply.

"I?"

I smiled despite myself. Susannah drew herself up to her

knees, adjusting her skirts around the crumpled bustle. A bit of lace was caught on one of her back buttons, and I reached round to help her guide the fragile stuff off the shoals of bone and iron.

"Nell . . ." Sue sat still while I unhooked the buttons.

I did not answer.

"Do you think he loves me?"

I paused. She turned her head round to see me. I looked at her.

"Yes," I answered truthfully.

She crossed her arms and whispered, "Then it is all made fine."

"Nay, Sue." I let go the buttons and moved to sit in front of her, but she would not meet my eyes. "Now say it, Nell," she uttered very slowly. "Say the one true thing: that Mr. Gilroy loves me, and all your other thoughts about Mother are but fictions."

"Oh Susannah," I cried. "Hush now. Let us be friends again."

Later—

I cannot sleep. Mother has just come in to bid Sue and me good night and left us shivering instead. She was frightened by something, and walked about our room agitated, not pausing to look at us, nor even to finish a sentence, but moving from window to mantel, to bookshelf, and then back again. Once she stooped transfixed above the tiny needlepoint rug between our two beds. "Mother," Sue begged. "Come sit down." And she patted the side of her bed. But Mother gave no notice she had heard, and continued her aimless pacing about our room. Then, she stopped suddenly, as if commanded by someone we could not hear. She nodded in agreement and then turned to us and smiled.

"Can you hear it, girls?"

"What, Mother?"

"Listen. There is a child crying."

"Where?"

"Out there." She put her hands over her mouth.

"Out in the woods?"

"Yes," she said firmly, and threw up the window. The frigid air swept in with the buoy bell's clang. I listened for such a sound between the scraping and sighing of the trees. The bed creaked as Susannah sat up. And Mother had turned her head, pressing her ear against the upper panes of glass, her hands on either side of the window frame, an awful midwife to a ghostly delivery.

And then I heard what might have been a tiny wail, as a sleeping child first calls for attention on waking. And then it grew louder and larger, as though the child walked forward toward us through the trees; still, it was just sound, a long wave of sound, until it built up one more notch and the word began; the word came clear to us finally through the window.

"Mama!" And again, "Mama!"

And then the cry was cut off.

In the silence that followed, Susannah moved again in her bed, and the sharp snap of the wooden bedstead gave me a start.

"Did you hear it?" Mother's voice was low and insistent.

I nodded in the half dark, unable to trust myself to speak.

"No, Mother," Sue said very gently. "It was only the wind in the trees."

Mother closed the window and drew the curtains once more across the glass. Then she turned to Susannah.

"Why cannot you hear?" she asked in amazement.

Susannah shook her head, fingering the blanket up around her chest. For an instant, I thought she meant to speak, but a great sob shook her, and she suddenly buried her face in the blanket.

"Oh Mother!" she wept. "Mother!"

No child could cry as pitiably as Susannah did that night, such wrenching sorrow as I have never heard from my sister. And our mother stood transfixed by the sight, seemingly unable to step forward and comfort her, her firstborn, her best-loved.

Neither did she leave the room, but stood still and waited as Susannah's sobbing lessened, then weakened and finally ceased. Then did Mother move forward to Susannah upon her bed, and pulled straight the covers, smoothing the rumpus in her old way, as comfort had come to us when we were very small, wordlessly. Susannah laid her head back upon the pillows and let Mother cover her.

And then Mother turned round to look at me where I sat, knees up against my chest; I saw she did not need to ask the question, for my face must have left imprinted there the certainty of my belief. She nodded once at me and then took up her candle from Susannah's night table to depart our shared room, putting her finger to her lips to cover her smile.

"Hush, hush now." She turned to go, opening our bedroom door quietly. But through the closing crack in the door, she gave me a single warning nod, then vanished backward into the dim light of the passage.

19 December

Winter draws around us, the mornings rising dimly through the fog. Mother seems herself once more—though the drops are so increased! Tonight, Susannah has said she gave one hundred.

I doubt, however, that this can last. I sense she plays a part; there is too little ease in her walk. And last night as I bid her good night, her eyes lingered on me, so that I turned again to see what she might utter. The look remaining was not the one with which she had bidden me good night—the light smile stood upon her face like the stump remaining long after a tree is cut. But Sue's step in the passage erased what I saw.

I am distracted from thoughts of Ludlow.

20 December

A half hour past, I awoke in utter darkness, my head raised above my pillow to listen to a sound that must have reached me while I dreamed. There was nothing. I lowered my head. But there came a little rustling in the passage, and then a faint groan of wood, as though someone pushed slightly against our bedroom door. For a long while, there was silence all about. I imagined what I thought I heard was the echo of my dream hovering in my ears. I closed my eyes again.

And now, I am sure of it, I heard somebody softly breathing

on the other side the door. For what seemed a long time, I listened to the breathing; then the clock struck on the stairs. The breathing stopped and I heard faint footfalls departing down the passage.

I do not like to wake Sue only to frighten her, so I have written this down.

21 December

Again last night, I woke to the sounds of footsteps passing by our door, and swiftly as I could, I slipped from my covers. The footsteps continued lightly down the passage, then passed from hearing. I stood, my ear pressed to the door, and heard the footsteps return, then slow and stop in front of me on the other side of the door. The wood pushed against my shoulder as she whom I listened to leaned also into the door to listen. I barely breathed. Then she moved away, advancing again down the passage.

I eased open the door. Bathed in what little light the stars cast through the window, my mother's nightdress wandered out of sight. I opened the door wider to watch her go, wishing to make sure she reentered her own room and found her night-walking way back into her bed. But she did no such thing. At the end of the passage, she turned and glided back toward me, her white figure passing through the darkness like an unhitched star. Again she stopped before our door, and again she leaned forward as if to listen, so I swiftly closed the door. Now came the familiar pressure of the wood against my own body as my sleeping mother pressed to the door and listened for our breathing.

"What are you doing there, Nell?" I jumped in terror at the voice, unsure at first who spoke to me.

"Nothing," I whispered back.

But I had hardly answered when I felt Susannah's hand on my shoulder, and her voice again spoke into my ear.

"Is it Mother?"

I nodded and pointed to the door, my finger on my lips. Susannah drew closer to me, and together we listened to Mother.

There came a low cough on the other side, and then she moved away.

I quick flung back into my own bed. Susannah followed more slowly and perched herself on the edge of my bed.

"I am frightened, Nell."

I nodded.

"Nay, listen to me." I looked up.

"There is something wrong with Mother."

I smoothed the covers over my knee.

"We must do as the doctor has said," she whispered sadly.

My eyes flew open, and now I sat up. "We cannot give Mother more drops."

"What are we to do, then, Nell? Mother is not herself—it is clear—and perhaps more tonic will coax her wandering spirit to rest."

"Nay, Sue." I put my hand out to touch her. "How might it help poor Mother if her two girls contrive against her?"

"Not against."

"Then how?"

"*For* her, Nell. The old her—the one who does not keep midnight vigils in the passage."

But though Susannah uttered this with surety, she remained seated where she was upon the bed a long while, neither speaking nor moving, nor trying me again—and for my part, I listened to her silence, waiting for her to break it, as she perched there at the end of my bed in her nightdress, gazing over the harbor waters that stretched incessantly away outside our window. I think I did not love her more than then, Reader—and though I closed my eyes, I think I dreamed she sat upon my bed the whole night long, and then, at dawn, I woke. And Mother's footsteps still beat up and downward in my head, like a slow rain coming on.

24 December

We sat quietly in the window seat of the dining room, our heads resting against the warm glass. All of the downstairs was swept and all the cushions had received their weekly beating, and now we dreamed a little in the winter sun. I did not want to look out the window; rather, I felt the slight heat on my shoulders and imagined us backward into summer, when I might lift my eyes from the work on my lap and see a tall man walking to me from down at the boathouse. Susannah hummed beside me, and without opening my eyes, I know she played with the cuirassed lace border that circled her waist; and the sound was almost like a wave slapping against a rock on a breezy day, the silk of her dress rustling as she shifted the lace forward, backward, forward, backward across her lap. I am a little glad this morning. George is to arrive back any moment.

(100 drops)

Christmas Day

On Mother's tray, there was a little jagged smile bitten in her toast. "See there"—I pointed to Abby triumphantly—"her appetite has returned."

George is delayed two weeks by hard snows down south, the board meeting postponed. I am so uneasy.

27 December

We have between the two of us, and without speaking of it, taken up most of the tasks about the house now—with Abby, of course. Susannah bakes, I am in charge of the fireplaces and the stove, and I empty the earth closet and keep the hopper full of earth—I have become a prodigious digger in the ground, carrying shovelfuls of the stored unfrozen ground in the root cellar up the stairs to feed the hungry hopper. I wonder, Would Ludlow recognize me?

28 December

Now I am frightened. Today Mother descended to us in her brown silk with the papillon collar and cuffs, though her hair hung down unbrushed and wild about her waist. Susannah asked if she would like it brushed. "Nay," said Mother without stopping, then went directly to sit in her chair.

"Bring me the basket!" she motioned. I went to find the basket in the back pantry under the drying rack.

"There has not been so much since George and Mr. Thomas have gone," I remarked on returning, and presented her with the mending.

"And Mr. Gilroy!" she added. "Let us not forget Mr. Gilroy!"

I looked quickly away from Mother and nodded. Susannah said not a word, but turned back to gaze out the window. Between them, I did not know what to do, so I drew to my usual spot at the table and opened a book.

With a start, I realized I had arrived myself at the end, having flipped through the pages vacantly as a—vacantly, and we shall leave it at that. What stared at me in bold black print were the words *THE END,* and the words—nay, even the very print— comforted me somehow, for here I was, vagrantly arrived at a firm stop. The end, I thought to myself. That is good. There will always come an ending to every story, and Mother's moods are merely chapters. In the distance, perhaps in another volume, Mother will return to herself, put up her hair, and smile again at me in her old way. I lifted up my head, gladdened by the possible future, and saw Susannah pressed against the window glass.

"What do you see out there, Sue?" I called to her, a bit desperately. "Your future?"

Her arms dropped to her sides as though cut from a string, and she turned round slowly.

"What will it be?" she asked me gravely, and she left the window and came to sit by me at the table.

Just then, Mother clapped her hands aloud and turned round in her seat to regard us. "Your future is clear to me, Susannah!"

I stiffened.

"What is it, Mother?" Susannah clasped her hands across her chest as though to prepare.

"Well," Mother drawled, "you shall marry."

"Who?" Susannah whispered, and I saw that she was shaking.

"Who?" Mother blinked. "Why, Susannah, you shall marry a man as fine as Mr. Thomas; and though he is betrothed, he is your match in every way—more beautiful, more intelligent, and richer by far."

Susannah gasped, and I opened my mouth to stop Mother from speaking further, but she turned back to concentrate on the undergarment in her hand, delivering a lecture to the linen.

"Women should always strive to marry higher than themselves. Always. A lesser marriage partner would never know how to appreciate all the value in a woman's heart, and one such as you, Susannah, requires a lord among men." She held her needle up against the window and threaded it with a sure hand. "Think of it this way. Your hair is your crowning glory—were such a jewel to be fingered by a common sort—an Ames, or, worse, a Quail—the fingers would begrime the very luster simply by not knowing, by not comprehending"—she slowed to knot the thread—"how such natural treasure should be cared for. Within a decade, your silk would turn to tatters and all the color fade to a murky and uncomely gray."

I cast a glance sideways at Sue, but she sat rigid beside me, her eyes straight forward.

"Mother," I began.

"Do not joke so." Susannah stood abruptly, knocking the stool to the ground behind her skirt.

Mother stopped midstitch and looked round. Perhaps she saw the tears threatening to spill over Sue's eyes, for Mother put her sewing down and gave a little smile to reassure.

"Dear girl. Do not be afraid. It is where we all of us end—at the altar with fine flowers and a man."

"Mother!" Susannah pleaded.

"And then will I bring home my own dear Johnny after the wedding, at long last."

I grew cold. We neither of us spoke, and Mother, suddenly distracted, stood up, letting her sewing slip to the floor, and moved over to inspect the lambrequin upon the piano top.

"Who is Johnny, Mother?"

But she had begun humming, and the bustle of her dress swayed slowly, as if there played a waltz tune in her head.

29 December

From time to time, Mother will lift her head and consider us, vagrantly—her attention on us and away all at once; I have to fight the urge to clap my hands or call out "Mother!" And just now, it came to me that perhaps this may be how it is to have lost a mother. For she is not here, divided from us by an invisible hand, and yet there she sits. She is as absent already as if I only remembered her.

Who is Johnny? I have a dread about the answer. I have a deep and everlasting dread.

Thank God, George returns within the week, though he will find a house sorely lacking in warmth and the gladdening spirits of a feminine hearth.

I put down the pen each night and cup my hand around the candle flame—and think of Ludlow Thomas's eyes. That is all I can allow myself. He is far from here. And I fear his one letter is but a golden clasp he has snapped shut upon our story.

30 December

Drab and drear, the day is close about us. We have not been able to keep abreast of the washing without Mother's help, and so I am writing with cuffs smudged by last week's ink, and soon to be blackened further, but I do not care! Abby worries none of us is eating enough, none of us, that is, but myself—for I am prodigiously hungry and dine on nut cakes and apples all morning. Susannah has begun to look indeed like the paper ladies she so admires. And Mother—

I was glad to be home last evening after the trip into town. I thought a curious quiet followed us up the street as we made our way to Brown's. I cannot be certain of this, but a watchfulness seems to have replaced the usual neighborliness. We are isolate at Grange House, to be sure, but I do not remember having been made to feel it so before.

Perhaps, however, I only shift the silence from one basket to another—I have grown used to the creeping silence within the house—but in town, the silence seems more strange, and it frightens me a little. It is as Dr. Bates has said: My eye has too long focused on the strangeness in this house. And now the very world seems altered when I lift my eyes and look about.

1 January 1878

The wind commenced this morning—early, I heard it as a whisper sifting between the trees, and when I rose, I saw the spare branches cast about as if thrown by childish hands, though the sky remains sharp and clear. The woods are entombed in their snow casing.

I am a quiet thing. I do not think of him. And how should I? He has not written.

2 January

Just as I fell to sleep, in the state when I still imagined I saw the contours of the room with my day-lit eyes, an orange cat advanced on me from the darkness at the door, and the closer it came, the faster it went, so that when it leapt onto the bed, it seemed to hurtle into me. And then just as I thought it would land on my face, its head split into two, the two faces surrounding my own in the instant before it vanished. When I awoke, I was panting as if I had been chased from one world into the next.

From Mother's end of the house, I heard a call. My heart pounding, I lifted to my elbow in the dark of our room, unsure whether or not I had heard my name called into the night. But then it came again, her call, and I stood and wrapped my coverlet about me, then softly turned the knob so as to leave Susannah where she slept.

All down the long passage, I stepped toward Mother's voice. It seemed she, too, called from a dream, for now I heard what I had thought was my name brokenly sent out, repeated into some other word I could not fathom.

"Hush, Mother, I am coming," I whispered, my hand upon her door, and pushed it open.

288

Lord, there stood my poor mother facing the mirror, her hair all about her, her long arms reaching toward her own figure standing in the glass. The candle burned brightly by her bedside, casting shadows across the ceiling of her room, making the very air seem lively. I stood stock-still on the threshold.

"Mother," she implored, while her hands clasped either side of the oak frame and she leaned in close—so close, her lips touched upon the mirror's cold surface—and then she started whispering directly into the mouth of that wide-eyed figure in the glass.

"Nay, nay, Mother. Let me hold him now." There was a little pause, and then Mother replied to her own self, "You canna. Save yourself."

"I must take him with me." Mother's voice was unswept and broken.

"Nay, girl," came her other voice from out the mirror. "You will have to bury him at sea."

"Is he dying, then?"

"The ship leaves. Go now."

"Is he dying, then?"

"Go."

"Mother! Is he dying?"

"Go."

Mother kissed the glass again and again, her eyes frantic, her hands grabbing the oval frame. "Mother!" she cried, sobbing out against the picture she saw cast into the glass. "Mother!"

I turned and ran.

4 January

I entered the woods as usual to collect kindling. The day rose drear, what light there was tentative below the insistence of a cloud-heavy sky. From the east, the soft tips of morning stretched across the whitened horizon as though groping their way in the dark, an old woman shuffling down a passageway. The tops of white pines swayed in the low wind gravely as church elders—I felt a sudden pang of fear in me, made vaguely uneasy by such chill silence—and the wind played tricks, shifting so as to erase what we would ordinarily hear—ice fishermen on the harbor, or a gull's cry. It is the waiting for a dread to occur that most provokes me—I can run straight into the arms of terror if I see it, but beforehand, the chill premonition weaving its lithe fingers in my hair strikes me impotent and restless.

5 January

It is well Mother is so ill, else my mind would turn and stare down the long tracks to Brooklyn, where he sits—silent.

6 January

Last night, she called for me once more, and this time I did not go gladly, but, heavy-limbed, I dragged from off the bed to wander down that lonely passage to her room. But she wore an entirely different aspect then, and she had stirred up the fire, so the room was snug and cozy. She smiled at me as I came in, and that unexpected sight arrested me on the threshold.

"Come in, Nell. Why do you stop?" Her voice was clear.

I crossed into the room and drew up the chair by her bedside. "How do you tonight, Mother?"

She turned her head on the pillows, so the light of the fire fell full across her face. "I am lonely, Nell."

I did not know what to reply.

"Read to me a little."

"What shall I read?"

"What you will." I cast about for the stack of books Ludlow had left behind, and seeing them on the chaise lounge by the fire, I quick chose the top one and sat back down with it, opening it in the middle—an old habit.

Lord Tennyson's poem lay there. I began to read, and Mother gave a tiny nod in approval. I read on, my voice a basket into which I gathered all this fineness. For a long while, I read, not quite lost as usual in the words, but not fully attentive to my ailing mother, either. After a bit, I looked up from reading by her bedside, to find her eyes on me—a look that sought me as if a shore. She smiled when I met her gaze, and I smiled back gently, not wishing to loose this hold. But she closed her eyes.

I leaned forward a little in my chair. "Would you like me to read again?"

She turned her head away.

I sat back and looked down at my hands holding open the place in Lord Tennyson's book. My fingers framed a small section of the poem, making a little picture on the page. Idly, I spread one finger, opening a wedge of another stanza, and then, finding it intriguing to see what lines flashed out from under my pink screen, I spread the finger of my other hand and read at first:

> But who hath seen her

I stole a quick glance at Mother, but she had turned her face from me and appeared to have fallen back into a sleep. I lifted my fingers from off the page to uncover the rest.

> But who hath seen her wave her hand?
> Or at the casement seen her stand?
> Or is she known in all the land,
>   The Lady of Shalott

I closed the book with a sharp clap, wanting to waken Mother, suddenly and inexplicably frightened by that question. Who would hear my voice and think me living in this dark house, not some shattered fragment of a dream?

"What was that just then, Nell?"

I smiled at her to reassure. "Only just the book closing."

She started up in terror. "What book, girl?"

I held up the red book with its gold lettering twined all round it. "Lord Tennyson's book, Mother."

She flushed and put her hand to her hair. "Yes, of course it is."

I slid off the chair on which I sat and knelt down by Mother's covered knees. "Mother, what ails you?"

Her hand dropped down into her lap.

I laid my cheek against the bedside and stretched my hand

along to touch hers. She did not take my hand up, but did not remove hers, either, and I grew emboldened.

"Mother, who was the child you heard crying in the woods?"

She shuddered and snatched away her hand. I stood up and leaned over her to try and calm her, but it was as if the one fit had crashed a shuddering ocean over her body, for she could not stop her shaking, and her face grew suddenly white, her teeth chattering in bloodless lips. And from her chest came a strange keening.

"Stop, Mother!" I begged, a terrible shivering beginning deep in my bones. "Stop!" But now she began to point wordlessly at a spot behind my head, and, fearful, I looked round to see where she pointed. "It is nothing, Mother." I turned back to her in the bed. "There is nothing there."

"Look!" She pushed away her covers as if to stand up.

"No, Mother," I pleaded. "No, I won't. Please, get back under your covers."

But she pushed me away and stood up, though she still swayed and shivered, her one hand clutching the folds of her nightdress while the other pointed past me again.

"Look!"

"Mother." I grabbed hold of her from behind, my arms around her waist and my face pressed against her shoulders. "There is nothing there."

For one terrible minute, she strained forward, and there was little I could do but to hold on to my own mother pulling against me as though I were a chain. And then she suddenly stopped, her arms limp at her sides; and in the quiet, all I could hear was her heart racing inside her, beating against my arms.

"Mother, I am right here."

But the sound of my voice was not a tonic, for Mother closed her eyes again, and I saw a tear start up in her lashes, then another, and slowly then a weeping, soft and steady, drop after drop pushing through her lashes, then falling away, trailing across her temple and into her hair. Gently, I turned her back round to the edge of her bed, and quietly, she did what my hands asked her to do:

She sat down and let me draw her legs up onto the bedclothes, and then she leaned her head back again onto the tossed pillows.

"Forgive me," she whispered, and I would have answered, but what was once the rush of tears now gave way to this steady, awful whispered patter. "Forgive me," she murmured again. And she would not hush as I worked round her, nor after I had her tucked up tight and covered snugly once again. "Forgive me," she said as I eased her cap from off her feverish brow, her hair matted and damp. "Forgive," she repeated as I measured out the drops of laudanam into the waiting glass at her bedside. "Forgive me." I loosened the lace at her neck and around her shoulders, then held the glass up to her still-moving lips. "Forgive." And then she drank and drank, and finally she seemed to quiet, though her eyes remained open wide and staring.

I stood over her for a long while, uncertain whether to seek Susannah. But after a time, she glanced up at me with a frown, as though she had come to a decision.

"I called you for a purpose." She handed the drink back to me. "Can you guess it?"

I shook my head, clenching my jaw to stay the tears that threatened. Suddenly, she reached up and cupped my chin with her hand and looked at me for a long moment. My tattery heartstrings wove round her fingers then, stretching a fine, taut note between us. I could not help the tear that splashed over and onto her wrist. She nodded once, as though I had spoken.

"Is the door closed, Nell?"

I shivered. "Aye."

"Then take out your book."

"My book?"

"Yes, my girl. That great book you write in."

"I do not have it about me."

"Fetch it then, and come quickly back in here to mè."

I did as she bid me, and when I returned, I saw she had composed herself then, too, her hair pulled back and her sleeves pushed all the way down around her wrists, so her fine white hands rested plain again upon the coverlet.

And now she has told me. All of it.

2 Pierpont Place
Brooklyn, New York
6 January

My dear,

I have not had a word from you and I worry. Last night, I had a waking dream in which you came to me and stood beside my bed. You did not reach out your hand. You did not lie beside me. Only gazed down upon me. I tried to speak but found I could not open my mouth. For a long moment, we stared at each other, and then you turned and walked back through the door.

I feel cold and uneasy—I fear I am dead in your heart. Please send me a few words, at least to know that all is well with you.

Ludlow

15 January

Ludlow—

   We have lost Mother.

   Dr. Bates said her heart burst from the strain of keeping up with too unquiet a mind. We are in a strange state up here—too strange.

   Go to her to whom you were bound—let her be the place upon which you build. Let me not be your history, Ludlow. Mine is a gaunt, unexplainable thing.

Nell

15 January

Here is his letter by my page. There are his words by mine. His hand lay warm upon this paper. And yet, I cannot—

I am place, Ludlow. A mad place.

27 January

A fine sheath of snow and ice covers the granite back, and the hush and white of the winterland made me feel a very ghost haunting my summer days, the green path stretching gray now through strict, unbending trees. I looked behind at my own footprints softly whispering into the silent terrain, and I marked the spot I stood upon, scratching my name into the snow with the tip of my boot.

30 January

George considers Hayden Gilroy to have been unfairly treated and has asked him back into the house. How am I to prepare the others?

I cannot think. What course must I keep to? What must I best do?

1 February

I dreamed of Mother suddenly, standing upon our wharf with a lantern in the fog, and I was little and returning home with Father from the town, and held the bow painter in my hand, my body pressed into the triangle of the bow and speeding forward toward home, though we could not see it, and Father's breath as he grunted was all I heard. And all in the dense fabric of the fog—the world stood so full, so silent and so waiting— behind me my father and the oars, and there ahead the light that meant Mother but was not Mother. How had Mother known to come just then and meet us? But indeed, she had only just come down that time and was hanging the lantern on the dock sprit and making ready to return, when she heard the oars, and so turned round. But before I knew this, before I knew what was actual, what was reason, there it was—all that was. I leapt up with the painter and passed it into Mother's outstretched hand.

I see. I am the woman between. I shall be the one who holds her secret and passes it on.

3 February

It is a glum, drear morning. I can barely hold up this pen, I feel so ill. Often of late, I look up from what I do and find Sue's attentive gaze on me as though I were the portal through to what she would enter, but does not know which part to push against. And lately, I look back direct at her, so see the trace of my own face cross in hers, like the shadow of a swallow flying down the lawn.

5 February

Tonight, the sky muddies upon closing. The fierce, bright clouds underlit by the dwindling light in the west have suddenly collapsed, the one into the other.

I think I can hear my heart once more start her patter. I have taken his two letters and smoothed them flat beside me. Here is no ordinary love story, I think. No ordinary lover. I can turn to him, now, a little—and begin to hope again. There are days I think to see beyond my sorrow, my soul racing out into that clouded aspect, singing above the waving tops of the trees: Let me live out this glory!

Let me love. Let me love *and* let me be able to write it down. All of it. Let me write.

Ludlow,

All is cleared.

I will be your history. I will be your place.

Nell

15 February

I have no letter from Ludlow Thomas.

A winter sky this morning, clear and cut, and cold as my heart. The frozen waves round-stitch the shore in binding loops of water, curling their icy arms about the rock.

17 February

No letter. A ghastly countenance of sky. George brings wild summer into this frosted room, the balsam logs in his arms holding the sharp, glad calls of wood swallows and the shade of the deep trees, though my brother does not smile.

I have sent him another letter, saying *"Come."*

18 February

Gray fog all about—as if the spirits breathe upon the glass of the afternoon. I was ill again this morning. Glad to have her lord returned, Susannah plays the lady of the house, organizing us all into the ordinary patterns that replicate a life, a family—*no*.

How am I to tell my sister?

27 February

The black water of the harbor. He is to come. Perhaps I will sail away with him after all.

5 March

Tomorrow.

6 March

I did not like to smile too greatly, but when I heard his voice in the hallway, I did lift my head up like a wren upon her bough. He entered and at first could not see where I sat, back here against the window, and so, thinking the room empty, he softly pulled shut the door behind him. I sprang from off the seat and was halfway to the door after him, when, lo, it swung open once more and George appeared.

"Hallo! Where are you off to?" he asked. "Look who has

returned to cheer us." I raised my eyes and looked directly, Reader, into his.

But he was formal. "Miss Grange," he said, but did not step toward me.

I pulled back my own hand held forth in greeting and nodded at him, waiting. George coughed.

"Leave us, George. Please," I asked. And so we were alone. I crossed in front of him and pulled my skirts round me to sit. The clock ticked.

"I am sorry about your mother."

"Yes." I was shaking.

"Are you well?"

"Yes," I said, then corrected myself. "Nay. I have been sickly." I could not keep from shivering, such a cold breeze blew from where he sat. "Tell me, Ludlow"—his jaw tightened as I said his name—"what you have come to tell me."

"After I received your letter in January, I saw my dream had been prescient after all. I knew—" He broke off. I watched him, drawing my shawl tighter around my shoulders.

"I knew you had departed somehow from the ordinary verge of the world."

"And?"

"I married."

Tick. Tick. Tick.

"I beg your pardon?"

He did not look at me, nor speak. I was chill, stone. *Tock. Tock.*

"Tell it me, again," I whispered.

"You wished me to be—"

I stopped him. "Yes, I did." My two hands spread protectively across my lap.

"Elsewhere, I thought," he burst forward. "You did not wish for one such as me, one so ordinary."

"What! Again ordinary?" I could not hide the small tremor of voice. "This is a precious place, this ordinary, where you and the world reside."

There were tears in his eyes. Again I looked down. Our feet

pointed directly across the carpet at each other, one to one. I heard Susannah's brisk footfall crossing down the hall. I looked up, aware he watched me carefully.

"You are magnificent."

"Magnificent!" I sprang up. "Magnificent. Poor split companion of ordinary—the two could never share a coach now who once were trot horse, bridle and spur."

"Listen to me, Nell." In one step he was before me, his hand upon my wrist. "In these months—"

"*Three* months."

"In these three months since we parted, I walked round my ordinary world"—he almost spat the word—"ordinary, yes, for it is so—with your lips pressed to my ear, your voice murmuring in my chest. And I saw my world cast back through your brave eyes, you who see so clearly."

He had turned my hand over and with his two fingers stroked the soft part. I did not speak, could not, listening to this anatomy of departure, for he had one foot already in the leaving boat; though he still rested his hand on mine, his fingers still remained ashore.

"At first, I was jubilant, remarking on how small my world had grown, and making plans for all the vast future—myself become so large, so reaching."

I looked up at him, startled by the power in his voice. And he shook his head. "But it was as if I heard the music and could not play the notes, could not even make manifest an orchestra—and saw my triumphant vision, my large self"—he smiled sadly—"nothing but a shadow. And my world reasserted herself in the old dear habits, and I crept back into myself—my smaller self."

I gently withdrew my hand. "To her. You crept back to her."

"You are touched by genius. You are made of different stuff than she," he whispered. "And of different stuff than I," he finished.

I could not speak, could not think to speak, but turned from him and walked to the window, but there was the sea—no—

back to him where he waited—no—I sat down finally, back in my chair. The room was so quiet. The room was so empty, though we stood inside. I shuddered and could not look up.

"Nell?" he whispered, and placed a hand on either arm of the chair.

"Yes," I replied. He stood above me. For one moment then, the whole world rested there within the circle of that chair, my head bowed against his, his arms about me where I sat—we were, for an instant, a house.

And then he was gone.

12 March

As I walked this morning, I looked up through the gaps in the tops of trees and thought I peered through the broken slats in the roof of the sky. It is a freezing-cold day, the ice thick across the harbor. Early this morning, gray streaked over the pink clouds and I watched the weather snatch up the bright morning and carry her off, her hem leaving a line across the sky—a small reminder of a day in summer, the dawn and the blue and the high white clouds floating up above.

Is gray a countless color? There is the black-gray of the water, granite gray, this ink's black will turn to gray with time, and I, too, am a gray thing, for I am the shoreline now; I am rock beat by the cold tide. Now the big flakes fall into the sea—water unto water—and what was white darkens in that cold single kiss. In the hour of snow—

He had said, "Nell," and I looked down where he stood among the rocks waiting for me, though we had not appointed for each other. And though we had no meeting, I had stolen from the house into the white coverlet falling over the day—I had walked straight out into that dim scraggle and hush, the snow emptying her silence into the sea's regular beat, and though I searched for him, I did not think I searched, so that when he called and stepped from below the boathouse, where he stood, I looked down into his upturned face and saw how the snow fell on him—and I smiled. And that was but December.

13 March

Susannah slips loose each afternoon. I am so weary these days, I cannot watch her as I should. But today I mean to follow where she goes. Ah, there is Hayden Gilroy emerging from the boathouse. And there, behind him, is my sister. I must go.

He nodded once and then left her, walking straight up the lawn and past the house, toward the woods. She waited a few moments, looked about, and then followed after in his direction. Her slight, hurrying figure with its fugitive motions propelled me fast as I could after her. Something about the manner in which Hayden had nodded—the assurance, perhaps?—suggested a compact between him and Susannah that worried me terribly. Susannah moved deftly ahead of me, and I am grown so weary lately that I had a hard time of it behind her. I am struck again and again by her fleetness, a single-mindedness borne in her every gesture.

She neared the edge of the field and slipped between the new pines into the darker stretch of the woods. I followed at a distance, though I am not certain now as I write this that she was unaware. It would be like her to flaunt her secrecy. Deeper and deeper we wove through the trees, all hope of a path obliterated by the wreckage of the winds and the season. Soon, I saw where she led me. The whitened slats of the old blacksmith shop shone slightly out between the spindle trees.

When Hayden turned round at her approach and saw my sister coming to him, the great glory of his heart shone up into his smile and he stretched his arms out and she came running.

I cannot watch. I must tell them who they are.

30 March

At midnight, the ice in the harbor began to break up. We could hear the dreadful cracking from our beds. I crept to the window, but the glassy plate did not show its strain. Now in the warmer afternoon, the black waters border the unmoored icy chunks, like little cards of mourning floating past.

3 April

No one comes here to visit anymore, and today something curious has occurred. Hayden drove us into Middle Haven for some necessaries (his every move a caress of my sister, though they do not touch in front of me), and the two of us were packing the flour and sugar into the back of the wagon, Hayden being nowhere in sight. Suddenly I felt eyes on my back, eyes sweeping over me like warm hands. Trembling, I turned—but there was no one.

"Why, Hayden, you are shaking!" Susannah exclaimed. And I turned, to see our "cousin" strangely changed and standing quietly by. The rich brown of his face was suffused by hot scarlet.

" 'Tis nothing," he said, and shook off Susannah's sympathetic hand. Susannah shivered as if brushed by a wind, then pulled her cloak tightly about her, climbing into the wagon. No word was heard from any of us, each wrapped in our separate thoughts, the new green in the trees quaking above us, like women shaking loose their brushed hair.

Mother watches. I cannot wait longer.

3 April

I have told Hayden.

"Is it true?"

"Yes, Brother."

His face went ashen at the sound of that name upon my lips.

"What shall you do?" I asked him. Poor man, he held his great brown head so stiffly upon his shoulders, and looked at me for an answer. But I have none. I have nought to give.

8 April

April proceeds fitfully along, now gusting in between us, now delicately suggesting the warmer tones to come. Snow slides off the banks of the brook, falling in heavy, blanketing thuds into the newly released water. We are a land in between. In the ashy dawns, the lobstermen, cooped and restless during the winter months, nudge their thin-prowed boats severally into the widening mouth of the harbor, released at last to the open waves of the sea. Their nets hang off the bows, the pots like slat bricks piled atop the port and starboard gunwales. Now when I rise, I have companions in the early drab, the men's voices drifting over the water, separate and short as the slap of their oars, the high whine of the oarlocks a light song.

This morning, a tightening fog shrouds the men, and listening to their calls, I feel I have reached the end of a chapter. They row from pot to pot, pulling their blue-black cargoes up. Today, their familiar grunts and laughter bespeak such purpose, I see I am on the far bourne of their world, no longer moving with an idea burning clearly in my head. I have begun to rise and listen only, listen for the crossing of my sister's footsteps, the latch of a door eased open, my own heart thudding steadily.

10 April

The crisis is past, and so quietly. Hayden has gone to the quarry at Leadbetter's Island. He will live there, he told us this morning, until the autumn, by which time George can find a suitable replacement for engineer. I did not look at her face.

"What do you mean?" George cried. "Where are you going in autumn?"

"I must go back to Ireland."

"Certainly you must, but not for some time!" George finished his coffee. "I refuse to look for your replacement."

Hayden was silent. It was as if George were the only breathing being in the room. "I will, however, come out shortly myself and join you. Now is the time to get the men back up into their paces." And then George clattered out of the room.

We three sat. I would not leave them. This was the hour of danger. Abby sang out belowstairs.

At last, he stood—and left.

11 April

Quietly?

She came to me with a note from him held in her hand, bidding her to ask me why he must leave. At first, I looked at his handwriting and could not see the meaning of the words, so frightened was I of her face.

"What does he mean?" Susannah spoke so quietly.

"I have told him something Mother told me."

"Mother?"

"Yes."

"Tell it to me." And so I told her—all of it—simply.

"Am I to believe such a story?" she half-whispered. "This mongrel vision of our life, with a blot put upon it that need not exist?"

"Yes." I nodded.

"Why?"

"Because it is the truth," I answered fiercely, glad to have it burst out finally into the air between us. "Our grandmother nursed Hayden—our brother!—back to health, rather than to the grave, as Mother had thought, and told our mother not a word."

My sister watched me as if weighing when she might leap. "Go on," she said.

"Father knew, Susannah. He knew, and he kept the secret of our brother's life—"

She sprang and grabbed me round my waist and gave me a good shaking. *"Lies!"* she cried out, pushing me from her. *"Lies!* You are bursting with lies—" She stopped abruptly and ran her fingers down the seams of my dress on either side.

"Are you fat, Nell?"

"Susannah!" I tried to push her hands from me, but she held fast as any devil, repeating twice more, "I think you are grown fat."

"Stop it, Sue! What are you doing?" She frightened me terribly.

Her hands encircled my waist now and she measured, thumb-to-thumb. And then she held her hands spread wide as my widened waist in front of our faces. "Do you see?"

Her wild visage suddenly recalled Mother at the end, and I batted her hands away from me and covered my eyes. "Stop it, Sue!"

And then she whispered into the gap, "This lunacy comes from your condition, Nell."

"What?"

"You are unstable." She pressed harder now—oh Lord! "Because you are with child."

"Nay," I moaned, and turned to leave the room.

"Yes. You," she called after me. "You are to be a mother. *You.*" I kept walking, determined to reach the door. Why should she say it out loud? Why need it be mentioned? A sob broke out behind me, and I reached for the knob, my heart dead in its casing. I turned the cold ball and then the darkness crashed about me.

12 April

I am Mother's echo even in this. I see it now. I am to follow behind her—telling her story to any who will listen (though Sue will not believe it). And I am to carry a child—a child!—without a father. Like Mother. I am just like Mother now.

George is kind. He came to me up here and sat beside my bed and said nothing for a long while, and strong comfort grew in his silence.

"Do not fear the town's reaction," he said. "I will protect our name against any and all who dare speak."

I looked at him uncomprehending. "Thank you," I said.

We sat together quietly and I knew he wished me to unmask Ludlow, but the longer we sat, his hands hanging between his knees, his feet shifting upon the floor, the more I saw he could not ask that question.

"I am not Father," he finally said.

"Yes," I answered, and leaned forward to kiss him, for there was a world in that admission. He smiled wearily. We were silent again. A cardinal dashed by outside the window, stopping upon a branch, then lifting—a scarlet apparition. "Susannah has told me the story."

I nodded, my eyes filling. Why did he use the word *story*?

"But we should not have allowed Hayden to take himself off. This is his home, and how deeply must he have longed for

307

a home all his life. Do you recall his face that night when he remembered Mother's portrait?"

"Yes," I said uneasily. "But—"

"And how Susannah sensed it even then—and gave him her hand?"

"George." I was suddenly frightened. "Susannah has given him her heart also. She is in great danger."

A queer expression crossed over my brother's face. "She said you might claim such a thing."

I saw it all then—how my sister meant to keep her love pure, how she might hold it a bit longer, intact. Oh, it was dreadful how she believed and denied with one and the same breath! And it would be my . . . condition, that she would creep behind for a covering shroud. She might never be the broken one, with me beside her.

"George," I pleaded. "You must believe me. Do not bring Hayden back to the house."

But on this point, he grew hard. "Why are you so cold upon the man?"

I flushed.

"Is it he?" George stood up, horrified.

"Nay!" I looked up at my brother, struggling to make the jagged pieces mesh. "Nay," I said again, softer, and held out my hand. He stared down at me. "Nay." I shook my head. "Do not worry so." And slowly, he took my hand in his. I did not speak again.

15 April

The men are all gone to Leadbetter's now. All gone. Abby clucks. Susannah has not spoken to me in nearly five long days. My heart. It seems mine was an old, old story, after all.

16 April

As I put down the book, I saw Susannah watched me in the mirror. The clock on the mantel chimed the eight softly, then resumed the steady ticking. There wasn't a sound between us.

Still she looked at me in the glass, and then suddenly, she took up her brush.

"You thought I would break upon the truth, is that it?"

I did not know what to reply. She continued brushing her hair and watching me in the mirror.

"Susannah," I whispered.

"But that was not as it was. I know it was not as you say."

Speechless, I sat still and watched my sister.

She swept her hair up with one hand, neither looking at me nor into the mirror. "Your imagination was lurid. Mother's story was far more simple than that."

"You believe me then, at last." I smiled sadly.

Now she looked at me in the mirror, and I saw what the words had cost her. And with one hand, as if to forestall any more conversation, she leaned and opened the top drawer beneath the mirror and carefully pulled forth a baby's curl tied in a blue ribbon, a wedding ring, and a spoon, all three of which she laid on the dressing table before her.

She lifted her eyes to meet mine in the mirror. "These tell the same story as what you have told. But they speak a plainer, sadder truth."

Now I was a little stung. I folded my arms across my chest. "Do they? I do not hear them."

She shrugged. "That is because words do nothing but clamor, they are so greedy for attention; they bid Truth lie down within their windy chamber and tell her to hush."

I burst out laughing.

She shrugged and swept the things back into her hands, then swiftly replaced them in the drawer. "You are more wed to your precious story than to the truth these tell."

I flushed.

"It must be so," she finished quietly. "You did not even ask whose ring that was."

"Whose ring was it, then?"

"Mother's."

I took the three steps between us in one and swung Susannah

309

around on her seat. For a long moment, we stared at each other, until Sue flinched beneath my grip upon her arms. I softened my hold. "She gave it you?"

Now she could not keep the triumph from off her face. "Yes."

"What did she say, then?"

Sue paused and looked away. "She said, 'For your book.' "

"Nay," I said sadly.

She sat, rubbing one hand against the place where I had held her too tightly. "I do not know what the ring means, only that it is Mother's and that she did not wish it to be lost, nor for it to be explained."

"Nay," I repeated.

19 April

The grass struggles out from under icy patches in the back field and the earth is a sickly color, as if someone had knocked the breath from out the green—though there is a bluish sky.

April the thirtieth—

The hungry birds are returned; the titmouse hops with the finch upon the short grasses of the lawn, and there is the flutter of wings beneath the eaves up here beside me. All in the world is wet and surging from the moon tide—yesterday, three dories drifted past our wharf, burst free of their moorings, the snapped lines slipping from the bow. Ah—

10 May

Abby's shriek began it. I lifted my head from off the page to listen, and it came again, a deep, wailing cry this time, long and awful. I rushed to the door, pulling it wide. "Susannah?" I called out. "Do you hear?" Overhead, I heard her come running even as I also ran toward the dining room to find our Abby. But through the long windows of that room, facing front, my eye caught sight of her figure hurrying down the lawn—and then I saw it all, too.

The men from the quarry were carrying him up from the

landing, wrapped in Father's old green tartan. There were four of them, their faces still white with dust, and Mr. Philbert walked ahead. I could not move from my spot in the window, could not speak to my legs to move, nor tell my hands to let go their grip upon the sill. Up they came, slowly up the porch stairs, silent and steady and into the house. Sue waited in the front hall and greeted the men—thanked them! I watched through the doorway as she put her hand upon our brother and said, "You are home, Georgie," and then kissed him, though he did not open his eyes.

Still I could not move or speak.

"Nell?" I heard. "Nell?" I looked at Susannah upon the threshold. She held her hand out to me and the string between us quivered, and I walked forward to her, my only sister. "Let us put him in the front room," I suggested. "The couch is widest there." She nodded and we turned together back to the men and took this new hell into our hands.

"What happened?" I asked Mr. Philbert after we had settled George comfortably as we could before the fire.

"Your brother tried to save a man from falling."

"But he was not able to?" I asked quietly, sensing another horror.

"Nay." Mr. Philbert shook his head.

"Who was the first?" Susannah could not look up. I think we both knew.

"It were strange," the foreman reflected, "for him to have been up there at all—it were not like him in the evening—"

"Speak!" Susannah cried. "Who was't?"

The man raised his eyes to her slowly. "Mr. Gilroy, miss."

The cloth had fallen from Susannah's hand. "Where is he?" I asked.

"In the boat behind. The men'll have him up certain."

The slow tramp of heavy feet sounded then upon the outer stairs.

14 May

We have buried Hayden next to Mother. Sue and I walked down the hill together, side by side—and at the bottom, she

311

tucked her arm in mine, and I covered her hand with my own. So we walked slowly homeward, our tears slipping down unheeded.

16 May

Each night have I thought he would not live to see the morning, and yet he lives. Yet he lives! My poor George.

But he is badly broken. I hear an ocean in his chest where I lay my head to listen.

22 May

I wish I had not heard what he has told. I wish I had the moment back to switch the course of what did happen. Were I leaning over him once more and could see the struggle in his eyes, I would not say again, "Tell me, George." But I thought it would be comfort for him to speak of it.

For several days now, he has been restless, crying out and then relapsing suddenly into a horrified silence, his eyes staring right through me. "There, Georgie," I have tried to soothe him. "There, there." But this morning, I thought to take a different tack and urged him forward. Once shown the way, he burst over.

"Hayden was working like a man possessed when I arrived, seemingly at every site in the quarry, overseeing Mr. Philbert, even filling in a hand when the teams were short."

He coughed and grimaced. "At nights, we'd take supper with the Philberts, and Hayden drew out detailed maps of the rock face, tracing out the strongest fault lines. Computing how much explosive would be required." He took some water, and Sue had come into the room, as though she had some sense of what was being told there.

He gathered some strength and continued. "For nearly two weeks, we worked this way, never speaking of what we knew. Indeed, hardly talking of anything save the business of granite. I did not like to cause him pain. I thought the best way to bring it up was not to speak of it at all, and so kept silent. I found myself wandering more and more out into the quarry at night. Eerie—quiet. That rock staring over me." He paused then, clearly tired out. Susannah and I sat silently on either side of his bed.

"Some nights, I fancied I was not alone there, for the quarry, empty of its workers, becomes a kind of amphitheater." He closed his eyes. "Some nights I thought I could hear voices."

We waited while he rested. He began again, having gained some wind.

"That evening, I walked out to the quarry before supper— why, I do not know. To my shock, I saw a man standing there at the rim, dressed in his black coat and hat, his arms now raised above his head, now stretched in either direction, as if to make of his body a compass. I drew closer. I saw it was Hayden."

George's words strained forward against the braces of his poor breath. "For several minutes, he stood like that, mute, speaking to the rocks. I felt I must reach him quickly." George choked. "I thought he meant to do himself some harm."

"Hush, dear," I said, the tears starting in my eyes.

"I clambered up to him, and at first when I saw him, I thought my fear was fancy, for he greeted me with a smile"— he swallowed—"and then—" But George could not go on.

"What? He did what?" Sue's frightened question drew George back to her.

"He drew one step closer to the edge of the quarry, his back facing the hole, and asked me what I was doing there.

" 'I came to call you Brother,' I replied without thinking.

" 'How do you call me "Brother"?'

" 'With all my open heart,' I said, glad at last to bring it out between us. But he shook his head, as if the cause for my joy gave him only pain.

" 'I cannot be your brother.' He spoke low, then stepped the last bit to the edge.

" 'Yes!' I cried, coming a little closer, my hand reaching out to him in my eagerness. 'You must! We are a family. Grab hold!'

" 'You are a family,' he replied."

George closed his eyes.

"What did you say then, George?" Susannah whispered.

For several moments, he did not speak, but lay with his eyes closed against the final sight.

" 'I said, 'We must stand together. Our sister is with child.'

" 'Nay!' he cried, looking at me with horror, and I grabbed hold of him to stop him, but he stepped—and we both fell."

And then poor George covered his face with his hands, shaking his head back and forth upon the pillow as though he'd loose what he had seen from out his head. I shuddered at the sight of our brother stepping off that ledge as though it were a stair, his dark-coated body plummeting down across the white rock face, pulling Georgie behind; the men's startled cries and hurried footsteps in the half dark of that twilight as they crossed the quarry floor to reach Hayden and George. And all around them, Hayden's desperate *Nay!* still echoing against the rock, repeating the last breaths of his sad life.

25 May

George is worse.

27 May

Today no better. Dr. Bates rests here.

30 May

This morning, George smiled at me and died.

3 June

Susannah stood above me, very quiet—and then she pulled an envelope from her pocket. "Just look at this," she whispered savagely. "Now you will see how foolish is your brain!"

I reached up and took the piece of mail into my hand. It was from Ireland and addressed to Hayden Gilroy.

"Where did you get this, Susannah?"

"It arrived this morning."

I raised my eyes to her, uncomprehending.

"Read it," she hissed.

Trembling, I pulled the thin official piece of paper from the envelope and read the death certificate in my hand.

Johnny Gilroy died on this day, 16 August 1840, age six months. Typhus.

"You see how your imagination did break our house?" she wailed, and then she sunk to the ground before me.

Our mother's story is the hole through which we are all fallen.

June

Clouds trail overhead, picking down the sky with purple hems—if you are going to him, my sweet duchesses, please to let him know—I am Sorrow.

June

I am sole occupant of this room, left behind to the great wide table where I am writing this in daylight, for Sue will not enter while I am in here. Last night she whispered at me, "Nell," and came to the foot of my bed to put a shaking hand upon the stead. She has grown terribly thin and pale. "Do you think you might change into your nightdress now, Nell?"

I looked down at my walking costume, a little soiled but quite adequate. "Nay, Sue. This does me well."

She struggled only an instant. "Well, tomorrow, then. Perhaps you might wear your blue?"

I smiled again at her in the gloom. "Nay, Sue. This one suits me."

June

There in the silence, Mother's smile in her olden days crossed her face, and she held out her hand to me as we walked through the woods into town. I stood up in my strange between state and walked to meet her there across the hall, shyly stretching my own hand to touch hers.

But my fingers met cold glass, and with a start, I recognized this mother as myself, forlorn and sad, my eyes starting out from the gloomy hallway as I caught my image in the mirror.

July

I have moved my bedding, and a desk and chair, into the attic room that stretches the length of this house, establishing my residency there. The stair ascending to the room is fearfully dark and narrow, so that as one climbs, one has the sense of tunneling upward in an unknown direction. Yesterday I came up here to find Susannah waiting for me, and her head appeared at the top of the stairs, drooping over the banister like a bud. I had the strangest sensation I had seen her in this fashion before, but then later I recalled this is how I imagine a mother appears to her newborn child, as a distant flower peering down into the small cradle.

Oh! I am uneasy.

Susannah—but never mind. I write now, just to pass myself through this eyelet in the morning. I am the damp guard of the day.

July

Susannah breathes so softly when she sleeps, she would not trouble air. I have just stood over her for a little and watched. It calms me to have her so beside me, her face unshuttered, as it used to be when we were heedless and we talked.

The baby knocks a tight-closed fist in me.

August

Smooth white faces of birches stare back at me this afternoon, insolent and quiet. It is a damp, hot day emptied of color, the sky a drab hue, windless and lonesome. Susannah disappears each day now before dinner and is gone until sundown. I sit here at my window, like the lighthouse keeper, watching a small craft hurl itself into wetter and wetter weather.

And I? I stare at the face of my page and ask it to speak as it used to, but the swift singing in my head is hubbub now—I cannot write as I used. I have only the insistence of those I carry.

August

A miraculous perception that all occurs simultaneously and in an uninterrupted stream flashing below the habits of our house serves to disavow the call to mark off minutes, hours, even days. It is as if I have stepped through the fog and to the other side, at last.

The world holds whispers in it. I cannot but hear others' voices underlying my daily sounds: women in the birdcalls, a child beneath the twitch of branches at my windowpane. I am their captive listener. In the market, I look into the faces of boys and see below the lineaments of their adult faces. I see also the twelve-year child in the cheeks of old men, and the prance and twinkle captive in the feet of the tired women who drag themselves in a weary line from home to the public well. I understand now what I had early learned: There resides a kind of sight in books; the men and women there are more real than the four walls in which a reader sits. I had long ago heard the words of those I read in the tones of my mind's voice, but this new crossing over, this simultaneous life and underlife, is unlike all I have ever imagined.

September

I am strangely apprehensive and cannot concentrate on tasks. There is a wind in the trees, like to keening. I will walk out.

September

There was a breeze begun to whistle slightly, or it was my mother already reached the old blacksmith shop and singing to herself as she did. I turned in the direction of the music and fixed my attention on the way through the trees, picking over the thick roots and marking the bright tops of mushrooms looming above the moss. My skirts rustled in the needles behind me, almost, I felt, as if I walked over a wood floor strewn with the rushes cast off at threshing. I closed my eyes, instinctively yearning away from what now I see I must have known awaited me.

The closer I drew to where my mother tended, the higher pitched grew the wind, until, just before I turned the bend to step into the clearing where sat the blacksmith's shop, the sound of the wind rose to a shriek, high and sharp as the cry of a gull, but with the undernote of a moan. I clutched at the mantle around my head, endeavoring to muffle my ears in wool. But I could not keep myself from walking farther toward the sound.

The shack sits against a giant granite boulder, like a jewel inset in a barbarous crown. In the summer, Spanish moss hangs down, winding its way through the gaps in the abandoned roof, affecting the appearance of hair brushed back on either side of the roof's pitch, falling lightly away. The moss now wore the aspect of torn veils around an elderly lady. I stepped past the well-known sight to glimpse where my mother had taken herself. My hand traced the corner of the shack, fingering its old boards and lightly holding on to it for balance, my eyes again cast down to concentrate on my footing.

So I was not prepared for what I saw there behind the shop, in the stone theater made by the bowl of quarried rock.

There sat our mother, a white form punctuated by the gray of her mantle and her gloves.

Around her, in various postures, sat also—

Sat also white forms around her on the snow gray rocks, their white faces several round moons, skin a milky blue—as though I gazed at them through the surface of a pond. The figures indeed looked the watery reflections of themselves. Mother did not sense my presence, so I heard her broken words as she carried on what seemed a one-sided conversation. I could not make out any answer from the forms, but I noted some of them bent and nodded in liquid acquiescence.

Then she turned to me.

"Can you see them?"

"Yes," I whispered, and stole closer. "Who are they?"

"Visitors." She smiled. "From the other side."

One of them rose as if to give me his seat. A great tearing pain caused the earth to crack open at my feet, and Mother loomed high above me. I dimly perceived her hand reaching down before I fainted dead away.

When I revived, it was with the faint sensibility of swimming upward toward a bright hole at the top of the water's surface. I opened my eyes, gasping. Susannah stood quietly by. She leaned over me and tenderly adjusted the coverings at my neck.

"Can you sit up?"

I struggled to do so, wanting to leave this gray place, wanting the solid of our house, the trim white sheets of my own bed and the cold window glass between the inner and outer worlds. I rose to my feet, swaying a little into her encircling arm. She turned us toward the home path. We walked side by side in silence. Around me, the trees leaned to listen. I promised nothing. As the woods thinned, as we approached the wide back field that stretched behind our house, my heart eased somewhat. But Mother was not finished. She put her lips up to my ears and whispered into them, her breath hot in my hair.

I have named my little one—Perdita.

There is my baby crying at the back of the house—I can hear her tiny little wail. I raised up my head, but all about me is darkness, and when I try to move, I cannot swing my legs from the bed, I am grown so weak and feeble.

"Susannah!" I called. But I cannot even hear her, and since I have written this, I do not hear the baby's call.

I woke with a start, my heart beating wildly. "Where is my baby? Where is my girl?"

Susannah's face bent near. "Hush now."

I turned to her. "Where is my baby girl?"

She patted my hand, though there is such coldness in her face!

"Sue," I cried, and I lay back, weak as a child, weeping. "I thought I held her little body in my arms as on that first night. I thought she lay beside me—I was digging."

"Hush now." And my dear sister stroked my cheek, her face a bit softer.

"Try to think it for the best," she then said, though her voice was strange.

"What is for the best?"

"You never wanted a child."

I closed my eyes.

"That's right," she said. "Think of that."

I turned my head upon the pillow, away from her voice, and slid back into the welcome darkness.

"Mother!" I cried another night. "Oh, where is my mother?"

Susannah's chair fell backward with a thud. I opened my eyes. Only the light burned low in the room, and Sue's face leaning over me seemed half of darkness, half of light.

"How do you speak of Mother?"

I think I did not know my sister. Something buried had risen in her eyes.

I moaned. She patted my hand, though her touch was heavy, not gentling.

"Do not speak of Mother more. Do not speak of them who are gone. I cannot," she cried fiercely to me, "I will not, bear it!"

My baby had bright black hair and eyes shut tight—

Three months are passed, and the gap on this page a silent witness. I have been lost to myself, to my sister. I do not recall Mother's face any longer—only the smooth round of stone we placed upon it.

We are grown used to the split house, Susannah below, and I hardly go downstairs to her region. The attic suits me.

And today, I have seen my little one's grave.

"Are you strong enough?" Sue's voice trembled as she asked me.

I nodded and handed Susannah her wrap. It was a gray morning—snow already upon the ground, and the sky heavy with more. I leaned upon my sister's arm and we walked out, down the steps and out across the white fields to the woods. Arm in arm we walked, without speaking, and for the first time in a long while, there was the old capacious ease.

Slowly, we tended toward the place where a part of me lies buried. And at the moment when the clearing appeared through the deep trees, my heart raced forward and I dropped Susannah's arm and ran to the spot.

It is so little after all, the place. The stone, the mound of earth, the name.

PERDITA GRANGE
Pray for Her

CHAPTER TWENTY-THREE

When I put down her book, there was scarlet in the sky. All through the night I had read, turning page after close-written page without looking up, so absorbed in the story, I hardly moved in my chair. So long had I lived in Nell Grange's world, looking outward through her heart and mind, that when I raised up and saw Miss Grange's shrouded body before me, I could not affirm with whose eyes I now saw.

I stood and drew to her window. The morning lifted slowly higher, drawing darkness from the waters until the harbor shimmered a reply to the down-turned face of that peach-and-golden sky. The first of the morning's boats slid past Grange House pier in silence, the long double oars dipped in and pulled, dipped and pulled, past the breakwater and out to sea. How simple, how beautiful the dark boat passing by appeared. And the dark outlines of buoys upon the flat sea mapped a particular world of lobstermen, reefs, and catches, so the fever of those last words upon the page cooled in the dim calm. Here was water marked. Here, ordinary answers clung to the bottom of those long lines where solid weight and flesh slunk and snapped into the rope nettings resting there at the harbor's bottom. I was a young woman. I was Maisie Thomas. I pressed my palm flat against the middle pane and leaned my brow into the clear glass.

As she had done. The thought flashed up and I shivered, suddenly made cipher—not Maisie, but an echo; not Maisie, just another, like Miss Grange, placing her hand upon the cool glass and looking out. I raised my arms to catch hold of either side of the window. A man's harsh shout crossed the water. Small and blue, a second fishing boat approached, and in the stern stood a man waving—to me, the figure in the attic window. Had a girl started forward just then from the dark mouth of the boathouse and walked up the lawn, raising her hand in a small salute, I should not have been at all surprised.

Dazed, I turned back to where Miss Grange lay, and took up the book. Once more I opened to the pages, worn silky by the steady pressure of the writer's hands—writing, reading, then smoothing them back. In the beginning, her penmanship was beautiful, the tails of the g's and j's curling deftly below the faded lines of the page, and not a crosshatched line to stem the flow. The tops of her letters tilted right, as though she could not keep from racing forward, one line pushing into the next and the next and the next! And then, almost imperceptibly, the writing changed, growing nearly illegible, and descending unto a kind of desperate slanted scratching upon the white—indeed, there were places at the end where the nib of her pen had torn cross the paper, wild dashes and exclamations cataracting through.

I raised my arms to stretch; and then I saw the words. Scratched into the soft old wood above my head, in the eaves slanting away from the window, were names; and I drew closer with a kind of dull smile, for I thought I knew what I should read. There they both were: *Susannah Grange, b. 1847—; Amalie Grange, b. 1848—*. I reached up my hand and traced the firm cursive of their names dug deep into the wide board, then stopped upon that final dash.

And Susannah? I looked at the name of the girl who was rendered a proud beauty by her sister. Where was she now? Buried, I imagined, up on that hill in Middle Haven, next to Rorie and Cassie Grange, next to Hayden Gilroy, next to George—

Grange. Even the name palsied the comprehensible world. My hand rested upon those several thick cuts into the roof, and I had the uncanny sensation of standing inside a living thing: the House become a great body upon which was writ the names of all who had lived within. There was its face below; and then up here lodged its character, its breath and blood, the names tattooed upon the inner skin.

My eyes came to rest upon the captain's chest in the opposite corner, below the eaves. I crossed to stand in front of it and with one motion knelt and pulled up the lid. But it was no chaos that greeted me this time. Now three neat stacks of paper, of varying height, sat squarely at the bottom of the dim upholstered interior. And upon each stack there newly lay a covering page:

PERDITA GRANGE
A Novel in Three Volumes

Staring back at me from the depths of that trunk in triple boldness, my sister's name repeated upon the white page was far more eerie than upon the lonely tombstone in the woods, a sad testament to just how Miss Grange had stuck. The needle paused above the cloth, the hand abstracted, the mind stung. Miss Grange had told me the pages in the trunk held everyone's story, yet she had gathered them together and called it a novel—a novel she had titled *Perdita Grange*. Perdita. Perdita. My sister proliferating, my sister never ending. My head was thick in the morning light. Thick and tired. Sometime in the night, it was I who had been lost.

Downstairs, the shutters were thrown back, their wooden slats clapping into the still morning air; and it was this distant, ordinary sound, a tiny sign from the world of the living, that caused my heart to race once more within my chest. With a cry, I sprang up and made for the door, longing to return to the known regions of a summer morning.

But someone opened the attic door at the bottom of the stairs, and I heard the accompanying rattle of crockery upon a tray. I looked about me for some place to hide, and sought the protecting cover of the old window screen at the end of the attic just as Cook crossed the top of the stairs, a tray in her hands.

There was not a sound. For several long moments, there was not even a breath. I lifted my eyes above the screen and saw Cook holding the tray, utterly still at the foot of the bed, a profound sorrow clearly written upon her mottled face. Indeed, in those few moments, a transforming sorrow blessed her stern features with such a gentle look, she grew almost sympathetic, and her bearing softened. After a time, she gently set the tray upon the coverlet at the end of the bed. Again she stood motionless for a long while, looking down upon her mistress, until seemingly coming to a decision, she moved round the big bed and stood directly over Miss Grange.

Such a paroxysm of emotion crossed over Cook's face as made me cover my mouth with my hands. She bent and pressed her lips to Miss Grange's cold brow. And then she laid her own head down on the pillow beside the dead woman's cheek and closed her eyes, her one hand resting on Miss Grange's chin in what was an almost childlike caress.

I thought this touch too familiar, and I must have made a noise, for suddenly Cook looked up from where she stooped, and she straightened instantly, a strange, uneasy expression upon her face, as though she had been caught at something she should not have done.

"Who is there?" she whispered into the shadows around me.

I came forward from the screen, and as I approached, all softness vanished from her person, and the habitual look of slanted pride slid back over her features.

"I thought you had descended."

"Nay—no," I corrected myself, the diary's hold still strong.

She walked around the side of the bed to me, her one hand still holding the coverlet, causing the sheet to slide from off Miss Grange's head and shoulders. "Stop!" I cried out, horrified, and motioned to the bed. Cook turned her head slowly, not taking her eyes off me, but upon seeing what she had done, she dropped hold of the white coverlet immediately.

I brushed past her and pulled straight the sheet once more, tenderly drawing it up over Miss Grange's face, all the while aware of the silent and steadfast attention Cook paid to my every gesture. I turned quickly round and looked at her standing beside me. There was the most peculiar expression on her face as she returned my gaze, half of wonder, half of fear. Uneasily, I stepped backward, too swiftly, for I stumbled against the copybook lying on the floor and lost my balance, tripping over my own skirt and falling against the chair behind me. Clumsily, I drew myself upright and sank into the chair. Cook did not move to help me, nor move to leave her post at the bedside.

"Shouldn't you go down and alert Mrs. French?" I asked her somewhat peremptorily.

The question recalled Cook to her proper place, or so I thought, for the glazed look in her eyes vanished. But I saw that she looked at me now with a tiny smile of contempt.

"Aye, and what should I tell her?"

"Why, whatever do you mean? Tell her that your mistress has passed during the night!"

Cook took one step toward me, then stopped and crossed her arms over her chest. She regarded me for a long instant, and then without a word, she turned and walked to Miss Grange's writing table, where the bottles of her medicine sat upon a wooden tray. I watched as Cook drew forth the bottle from which I had poured out the tonic for Miss Grange last night, then held it up to the morning light now streaming through the window. Slowly, she shook its contents, tapping against the green glass sides as she swirled the bottle in the air, as if she considered something. I watched, vaguely disturbed but unsuspecting of what she did. Abruptly, she set the bottle down on the tray, unstoppered it, and, still without a word to me, poured a large draft of port into the bottle, nearly filling it to the brim.

"There," she whispered to herself. "No one shall know." And carefully, she replaced each bottle on the tray, wiping the lip of the one she had newly filled, and then she pushed the tray backward on the table so that it sat against the window, a pretty ornament of green and blue and crimson bottles in the light.

Cook turned around and once again regarded me. "Were you with her when she passed?" she asked with a quiet authority; and perhaps her inexplicable attention to the levels in the bottles, her air of familiarity with this sickroom, called forth the quiescent respect I then paid to the Grange House cook.

"Yes," I answered.

"And did she go"—Cook hesitated—"gently?"

I nodded, remembering the joy upon Miss Grange's face.

"Why do you smile?" Cook's voice was unfamiliar to me, verging on a haughtiness I had never heard before.

I shook my head and smiled gently back at her, unwilling to disclose Miss Grange's last moments to this woman.

But the woman would not be denied. Swiftly, she crossed the distance between us and stood over me, her hands on her hips. "Why do you smile?" she repeated.

I looked up into her face, which was disfigured now by an intentness bordering on mania—her dark blue eyes frightening me by their fixed gaze. "Why do you smile? Why do you continue smiling? What did she say before she passed?" Cook bent closer to me, and I shrank farther back into the chair.

"Nothing," I answered, "nothing. She seemed glad when the end was come."

"Did she speak of someone meeting her?" Cook's voice had dropped to a monstrous whisper. I trembled.

"Yes," I whispered back. "Yes, at the very end—" My words sprang forth now. "At the very end, she spoke of someone else in the room, one whom she expected."

Cook smiled slowly, then straightened. "Aye." The softer Cook returned, and I unclenched my hands from around the sides of the chair. She stood looking off into the blank room behind me as if considering something, but then the rustling of my skirt drew her reflective eyes back down upon me.

"Do you know, Miss Thomas"—she lingered for an instant—"how much of the cordial you gave her?"

A nameless dread crept in beside me. I was so tired, suddenly, so weary—I thought the question cast us back into the diary, and I could not remember at which point exactly I stood.

"What she asked," I replied without looking at her. "There was very little in the bottle."

"There was very little needed to ease her end."

My head jerked up and met her eyes. "I think perhaps your wits are unsettled," I said stiffly.

She gave me a long stare in return. "Well now, Miss Maisie Thomas," she uttered slowly, "I see you are your father's child through and through."

All fear vanished now at yet another familiarity taken by the cook, and I was pricked to anger by the woman's boldness. "How dare you speak of Papa! How dare you?"

"How dare I?" Cook whispered, her face gone bloodless. I closed my eyes against her, my heart pounding against my chest, and she burst forth into a soft laughter. Wondering at this sound, I opened my eyes. Again she leaned toward me, but this time I simply returned her gaze. For several instants, we stared at each other in silence.

"We will speak again," she finally declared.

"Never," I vowed stoutly, and turned away from her, gathering my books up into my arms, shaking despite my brave countenance. But just as I stood at the top of the attic stairs, she spoke again behind me.

"Sooner or later, you must seek me out."

I did not answer. I fled.

CHAPTER TWENTY-FOUR

D own the attic stairs I dashed, my feet hardly touching the boards, so eager was I to put her behind me then, and on through the empty servants' hall, down and down that next flight. Only when I had reached the second story did I slow my footsteps. All was quiet here save the ticking of the passageway clock. It was not yet seven. I paused where I stood, my hand on the newel post. The new light of the morning washed across the well-tended passage, and I felt doubly the calming influence of order. The straight-backed chairs along the wall gleamed in the sunlight and the floor bore the mark of many hours of mop and polish. Here was custom. Here was cleanliness. Downstairs, the House itself soothed. Downstairs, the House itself dismissed to ether the harsh words of the woman above.

I stepped slowly along this passageway to descend the last wide stairs, making no sound, and walked across the front hall through the open doorway into the front room. The sun stretched along the dark green carpet at my feet. I looked down at the dull crimson roses entwining a border around the room and, without thinking, followed their pattern.

And there it was: the forlorn brown face of Widow Grange's Telemachus staring back at me from the full bloom of a rose. With a sharp intake of my breath, I leaned farther down to examine the image. The brown eyes and curling hair set upon a little round face tipped in the direction of the cosseting flowers. And in tiny stitches below him was the legend: *Find me, Father, for I am lost.*

With a strange thrill of recognition, I whirled round toward the center of the room. I had descended the stairs into the memory of the House, held here in the curve of the pillows in the enormous birch chair by the mantel, there upon the cracking ivory of the piano keys. There stood the heavy old round table as it always did, covered with a mauve shawl fringed by beige tassels. I lifted a fold of the shawl to examine the tabletop—never uncovered, in my memory—and saw the marks and tickings of years and years of use before its decorative purpose in the present. Tracing the grooves and tiny scratches upon that table, I recalled the conversations I had read upstairs—words that had been written, here. Pressed here, like one of Susannah's keepsakes, were the diary's words, which beat softly now inside my head.

And for the first time that morning, there came to me a kind of quiet akin to privilege as I regarded my surroundings. Down here, the House did not importune; the furniture merely recalled within it the shapes of their backs and arms, the imprints of their hands. For they were here, all of them; here where the diary had set them into motion, crossing the pages to me—the sole deposit of their voices. At the table and at the piano sat the Granges of Grange House. And, though it were a cracked version, still it was my Papa at the mantel, standing with his back to me and delivering a swift kick to the log, then turning round and crossing time, come toward me. Me alone.

In the fresh gloss of that morning, the House had never seemed to me so beautiful, or so full. Softly, I walked through all the rooms downstairs as if my feet took possession: into the dining room, where the couple on horseback still kissed in midstride; entering the large library with its rows of shelves rising on either side of the great mantelpiece, upon which sat an antiquated pipe stand of fine black walnut; and back across the front hall and into the small sitting room for ladies' writing. There was the secretary, and in it—I put out my hand to count—Susannah's seventeen black scrapbooks carefully shelved, books I had never thought to open, though they had rested there before me all the while. And staring at the row lined before me, again I wondered what had happened to the sister who had gathered artifacts instead of stories to keep a history of her days—the sister who had been with Miss Grange when she had borne her child, and had led her to Perdita's grave.

What was before me—the sharp lines of books and chair backs and the deep rich colors of cushion and sofa—mingled with the scenes that thronged in memory and on the page. The diary had granted me fresh eyes. The diary made me the hinge upon the gate between the present and the living past: I could swing open—or shut—at will.

And must I open it? I asked Susannah's scrapbooks, and crossed my arms. Must I indeed?

A serving girl passed by, carrying the first of the tea trays upstairs, and smiled pleasantly at me. With a start, I was recalled to the day. Mama! I had forgotten Mama. Another of the girls passed me on her way upstairs and I darted after her, thinking to catch her up and take the tray she carried to Mama myself.

Morning glowed softly into the room, the curtains still pulled across the windows. One of the shades lifted and lowered in a small breeze. I put down the tea tray and threw wide the curtains to let the light in. Then I turned round. Mama lay stretched upon the bed, still fast asleep, her head turned to the side, her long, pale neck gleaming out of her lacy collar. Her hands lay open on either side, perfectly still and cupped, the slender fingers slightly bent.

I crossed back through the door, eased myself out of my dress and slippers, and sought my own pillow for sleep.

Mama did not wake me before descending to her breakfast, and when I arrived below, flushed and hungry, her pale face greeted me like a cold and distant moon from the middle of the deserted breakfast room.

"How does Miss Grange?" she asked.

"She has died," I replied with a small tremor of voice.

"Ah," said Mama, and sipped again at her tea, her eyes set upon the middle distance of the room behind me.

"Two years ago, I should have welcomed the news," she mused aloud.

"Mama!"

She looked up and saw the tears in my eyes. "Why, Maisie, I am sorry."

"But now?" I asked crossly.

"Now?"

"Now you do not welcome the news?"

She shook her head sadly. "Now it seems that yet another part of him has also died."

"Another part of whom?" I asked, shaken.

"Why, of Papa, of course." She replaced the butter knife upon the dish.

"Mama?"

The toast stopped halfway to her lips, and she regarded me an instant. "Do not mistake me for an utter fool," she said quite low, and then returned to the toast upon her plate.

I sat silent in the glare of this new light. She gave me an odd pinched look as she swept the crumbs from off the cloth into her cupped hand and then rose to throw them in the dying fire. "Ah, and here is Mr. Cutting!"

I would not have been surprised if she had uttered "to save us" beneath her breath, for now I distinctly saw she was uneasy, incapable of sitting down again once she had ordered more hot coffee for the latecomer, standing at the top of the kitchen stairs and ringing the bell upon the chain there. Ringing it long after there was any doubt it had been heard.

"Mama?" I repeated softly. She turned round. "Shall we walk out?"

With a swift glance at Mr. Cutting, who was thrust deep into the pages of his journal, she looked at me, and this time her eyes did rest upon me for a touch longer than an instant before they shifted by. A seagull's sharp-voiced *toy toy toy* passed overhead.

"There is something we must speak of, Maisie." She was sharp, although reluctant, almost fearful.

I rose and went to stand by her.

But she could not meet my gaze, indeed could not keep from

glancing back to see what Mr. Cutting did, as if the world's answers lay within that bald dome; within or nearby, for she set her eyes upon the place just slightly to the left of his seated figure.

"Just look at that Lady Rose, will you please?" Her gaze fastened upon the vine climbing up one of the verandah columns, and through force of habit, I looked where she looked; indeed there was a new rose bursting into bloom.

"Yes, Mama." I did not shift position.

"So late in the year." She grew thoughtful.

Irritated, I touched her arm to bring her gaze back round. "Mama"—I broke my morning resolution and cast off the anchor— "Miss Grange wished that I—"

"Miss Grange wished!" she repeated sharply, turning right round so her words might be heard in the full breadth of the room. "Not only did you disobey me—"

"Disobey!"

"Yes, Maisie. You never came down."

"Forgive me, Mama," I said quickly, hoping to mollify. "I forgot myself."

"Indeed. Indeed you have forgotten yourself. Look at you: You have become a regular servant to the servants."

"Mama! Miss Grange was never a servant."

"She ran a hotel, Maisie," Mama responded very quietly.

"Yes." I nodded. "But it was once a great House, and her father once was Papa's partner, and—"

"Maisie!" Her voice thinned. "Why must you invent such non-sense?"

I looked at her carefully. "I do not think it is nonsense, Mama. It is the truth, and I must grant that truth its due." I smiled to re-assure her and moved a step away. "I promise I shall see you at lunch-eon."

"I rather think, Miss Thomas, that your mother might wish a bit more notice than an announcement." I started at the sound of Mr. Cutting so close.

"An announcement?" The insufferable man stood just at my shoulder.

"In my day, no young woman would dare to speak to her own

333

mother this way, telling her what she intended rather than asking leave—as she should."

I looked from him to Mama, but she was staring again out the window.

"Thank you, Mr. Cutting," I said to him stiffly. "I am glad always for a touch of historical perspective." And I excused myself, my heart pounding, fully aware as I crossed the verandah and marched down the steps at the front of the House that Mama and Mr. Cutting still stood at the window, regarding my departing form.

How dare he speak to me so? How dare he? I made a blind turn round the corner of the House, wishing to vanish from their sight. He was a fool. A despotic fool. A ridiculous figure. Papa had never liked him. Never. My feet hurried through the dew-sopped grasses alongside the House. How dare he presume to speak as if I did not know my place beside my own mother? As if I intended her disrespect, or harm? My feet slowed, rounding the back corner. I never did wish my own mother harm. How could I? She understood so very little of what went on—certainly she had to be protected. I sought to know the full truth so that Mama need never know.

I looked up. The back porch bore the force of the morning sun, the wide, clean boards bared in that light. But the possibility of a second agitating encounter with Cook caused me to turn round and retreat from the kitchen stairs. A spot of movement and color flashed between the trees. I closed my eyes, then slowly opened them once more. There was Bart, walking from out the woods into the dry grasses of the field, a battered brown cap upon his head, his red kerchief around his neck. So casual, so familiar was he just then, ambling across in my direction, it worked upon me like the turning of a page. With him in my eyes, I could let the trouble rest.

I stood upon the back porch and waved to him, crossing my arms up above my head. With a shout, he greeted me, then walked faster toward the House. I had the sensation of reeling him in, of having put my hands up and taken hold of a line I must have cast but only now discovered; and sure at last, I grasped its heft in my fingers firmly and pulled and pulled as he bounded up the back steps and took my hand in his. I rested there with him, my hands caught and held.

"Oh, Bart," I whispered. "So much has happened."

He squeezed my hand in his. "I have heard," he answered. And neither did we speak of her again, and neither did we need to.

After a time, we slowly descended, slightly apart once we were out of the shadow of the back porch, and walked round the side of the House to the front. I saw Mama's head and shoulders rising from her usual rocker faced out to sea, the band of morning shadow slanted cross her. Mr. Cutting stood beside, his one hand upon the back of her chair, the other thrust into his pocket. Some slight communion had joined them now; I could see the silence they shared had notes within, something they could hear, together. I broke off that last Lady Rose as I passed the soft scent, and gently shook the dew from its head.

"Good morning," Bart greeted the pair, and threw himself down upon the topmost stair, facing me. There was an instant when I stood, my one foot on the bottom stair, looking up at the trio, each in their own fashion staring down upon me. Bart's eyes rested on my face and hair, his lips parted as he gazed, a look soft as the breath I imagined escaping him. I could not look directly at Mama, but noted how she worked on, her fingers quick with the thread, the tiny needle glinting in and out of shadow.

"Miss Thomas," Mr. Cutting greeted me gravely. I looked at the precise nature of his hand just to the left of Mama's shoulder, the nails well cut and polished. I nodded briefly, then turned round to regard the bright triangles of sailboats cutting across the smooth surface of the bay.

But Mr. Cutting was involved in machinations of his own. "From which direction do you think the wind blows this morning, Mr. Hunnowell?" he asked amiably.

"From the left," Bart answered.

"The left?" Mr. Cutting sputtered.

"Yes," Bart admitted, "I have a ghastly sense of direction."

"But it means nothing to say it comes from the left." I turned round. "If you move, then your left is someplace entirely different."

"What does it mean to know the direction, exactly?" Bart replied, apprehending a deeper conversation.

"Well, young man, I am sure you know that if the wind is blowing from the north, you're in for a cold snap."

"You know where you stand," I put in slowly.

335

Bart nodded to Mr. Cutting but answered me. "And does that information make an enormous difference to you on a summer day stretched wide and open before you?"

He had managed. He had nudged me clear of the rocks. I could smile at the easy picture he painted. "No, indeed, it does not matter which way the wind blows as long as I am warm. But it matters—in the abstract—in the world of commerce, say."

"Of commerce?"

"Yes," I continued. "If the wind blows from the north, men's ships take longer to enter New York or Boston harbor, and tender cargo may be lost, and a sailor's babe may be born without the father seeing the first blue eye open, and sweethearts may turn fickle."

"That is a very fleshy abstract, Miss Thomas," commented Bart. There was that sound again in his voice, a murmur, a low, low sighing, and I trained my ear upon it—a rapid beat I wished to touch, but could not. "All that human sorrow because of the way the wind blows?"

"Yes, Mr. Hunnowell," I said with mock severity. "How little you know the world."

He almost made to reach for my hand, then remembered just in time who sat behind. So the caress came in his answer and sang from his tone. "I little value that knowledge of the world."

"What other sort of knowledge is there?" Mama broke in impatiently, rattling the colored spools of thread in her basket as she sought another strand, still refusing to look at me.

"Well," said Mr. Cutting into the breeze above Mama's head, "I think I'll pursue the one certain form of knowledge"—I believe I saw his hand rest upon my mother's shoulder just slightly as he stepped away—"to be found upon the morning steamer. Mr. Hunnowell"—the man looked at Bart—"would you care to come and get the papers?"

It was not a question. But Bart would not leave until he had a kind word from Mama, he said. I drew in my breath. And he began to banter her there upon the step, coaxing her to look up at him and smile. "Hush your foolishness," she said, finally relenting and smiling at the piece upon her lap, "and please go down with Mr. Cutting."

And for the instant she smiled, we three were joined. For that

336

instant, I forgot it were a broken joining—from the first. For when Bart did rise finally to follow Mr. Cutting, walking swiftly down the lawn in the direction of the wharf, Mama's voice behind me was bare, all the woolly laughter shorn.

"Maisie, you must stop this."

"I am sorry you are distressed, Mama." I took one of the steps toward her, advancing near where she sat. "But I do not think Miss Grange's story will require much time."

"I do not mean that." Now she looked straight at me. "I am sure you will tire of all that soon enough."

"Mama—"

"No, Maisie, I mean this flirtation." Her words rapped out. "You must stop this flirtation."

A sickening draft blew through me. "With whom, Mama?"

She took the steps between us with surprising vigor, putting her hands on both my shoulders to hold me in place.

"Do not think to playact with me, Maisie." She rested two fingers beneath my chin. "You have made a promise—no"—she took a breath—"you have made a vow."

"I never vowed," I answered stiffly.

"Not in words, but in gesture"—she tipped my chin up, forcing me to look at her—"and in kind."

"Mama." I struggled under her gaze. I would make her understand, I would tell her. "Everything is suddenly altered."

She dropped her hand from my chin but still held fast to my arms. "It is you, my girl, who has suddenly altered. Who do you think you are, Maisie Thomas, to snap your fingers and break a man's heart?"

I could not answer; the tears welled into my eyes.

"You do not know what you do. You do not know of what you speak when you speak so lightly about things . . . altered."

"Mama," I whispered. "I think I can see something new—" But the cold panic in her eyes stopped me dead.

"What is it you think you see?"

I pushed forward into telling, though I trembled under the grip of her fingers. "My life," I said miserably, "not as foretold, but as—" I looked up at her, pleading with her. "Mama, someday you might think me brave."

She took her hands from off my shoulders suddenly. "There is no bravery in casting away a promise you have made. You do not know what you say. We must leave this dreadful House at once," she said, and raised her hand to touch my hair, but the chill of her voice iced over the gesture. "At once," she repeated firmly, and started down the stairs, nearly pushing past me.

"But we cannot leave until I have done," I whispered.

She wheeled round upon the lawn, her two hands knotted into the folds of her skirt. "What is it you think you must do?" There, the unfamiliar hard tone crept in again between us.

"I must settle the past."

"Ah," she answered softly, and squared her shoulders. "Why don't you ask me, then?"

I stared at her. "You, Mama?"

"Yes." There was that smile upon her lips. I saw the effort in the thin line she set. "I am your own mother, after all. All that you need to know, all that concerns you, I have." She paused. "I bore you; I raised you. Why need you look elsewhere? Why need you look . . . past me?"

"Mama," I asked softly, "do you know about what Miss Grange has written?"

Very slowly, she let loose the folds of her skirt. "It has nought to do with you, Maisie."

"With whom, then?" I quavered.

"None whom I knew," she answered me firmly. "None whom *I* knew."

She had cast him down. She had cast him away.

"I see I cannot make you understand," I blurted back angrily, "what you have not the breadth of knowledge to grasp."

She smiled at me then, a tiny tight smile, as if my words were meaningless as a child's—a child who does not understand her own desire.

"I know your father once loved someone other than me, Maisie." Mama's face forbade a reaction from me, so I stood mute before her. "She was an outside sort of girl, I think, and he was drawn away from me for a time." She crossed her arms before her. "But nothing can change this fact—there are those who can call a man out to what feels like freedom among wild rocks and trees and bright air—but eventually all men long to come inside and hover round the lit windows of a house."

I opened my mouth to protest, but she cut through me. "Because freedom is not found out-of-doors—one is cold there, and finally, hungry, too. And your father"—she shook her head at me—"your father came to know that. He came to me."

I stared at her.

"That is the breadth of *my* knowledge." She regarded me, two small spots of color fastened to her cheeks, her chest rising and falling with short, harsh breaths.

"Listen, Maisie," she said. "You are in the grip of some strange lunacy. Else how am I to understand you would rather believe the rantings of a sick old woman?"

"I cannot help it, Mama," I gasped out, "her words speak truth!"

"Truth!" Mama took two great strides to stand before me. "Here." She grabbed my hand in hers and pressed it to her face. "Here, Maisie," she murmured, "here is truth."

I swallowed.

"Yet I do not know who you are anymore, Maisie Thomas," she said slowly, and turned right round away from me to stare down the lawn and out to sea.

"Look at that," she whispered. "He has come early."

I followed where she looked, to see the tall, inevitable figure of Jonathan Lanman flanked by Bart and Mr. Cutting, advancing up the gangway from the dock. And without another word to me, Mama began to walk away down the lawn. As she left, her back was a remonstrance, and the cord between us tightened. I felt the knot it made within my chest pull against me, pull and pull, so that I almost cried out at the pain. She walked and walked, so slowly, it seemed illusion, this rip inside my breast—so slowly, she seemed to fade from sight even as her absence loomed.

At the bottom of the lawn, she turned round and regarded me still standing in the lee of the House. But she made not a motion. She made not a gesture toward me. She simply picked up her skirt and turned once more, vanishing through the dark doorway of the boathouse.

CHAPTER TWENTY-FIVE

Once upon a time, I considered the most frightening moment of my life that in which Papa lay below us in that shattered hole, down, cast down so far from our help; but as I watched Mama vanish from me, only to emerge again upon the wide platform of the dock to take Jonathan's hand in hers in greeting, it was as if I lay down with my father in the black hole and saw my mother step up to that pitiless rim, her head floating above us like a flower upon the surface of a pond. She peered down at us there, the two of us fallen and broken open, and shook her head, withdrawing. For she would save only part of the man, my father. She would read but one history. She would pull only the one in her heart back up through the timbered hole and keep him there, and she would dare me to rescue the other. She would dare me, and she would leave me where I lay.

I looked at the blank spot through which she had passed. All the dis-ease of the dawn upstairs in that prolific speaking attic surged forward. I could not open or shut the past at will; no more could I answer the simple question, *What is it that you wish?* I watched Jonathan accompany Mama up the lawn, and when he caught sight of me watching from the verandah, he raised his hat jauntily.

All about me now, the House spoke. I had seen. I had lived and seen through the diary's eyes another world, the world before my own, a world past the bourne of my own body. I could not rest or remain silent after all. My eyes were stolen, and I stood and watched this new beginning as if through Perdita's eyes. For if Perdita had not died, would I have inherited this sight?

I descended the steps of the verandah, one by one, frozen and fleeing all at once, and Jonathan, with a happy pat upon Mama's arm, broke from the others and walked briskly ahead, so he arrived at the bottom of the stairs just as I did.

"Maisie!" he exclaimed, stretching his hand out to take mine.

"Miss Grange is dead, Jonathan," I answered quietly.

He stiffened, but the forward motion of his joy trundled over my incomprehensible reception. "I am sorry, dear," he whispered. And then he turned round, for the others were just behind.

"Shall we row, Maisie?" Mama spoke out gaily, as if nothing had been said between us. "Mr. Hunnowell declares it is an admirable tide."

"Mama?" I stared at her, a little dazed.

"A row, Miss Thomas!" Mr. Cutting joined in merrily. "Your tutor proclaims you have an admirable stroke; perhaps you can learn still more from mine."

I blanched, and realized my hand was still in the strong grip of Jonathan Lanman. The world seemed to me to have dipped below sanity. And my heart no longer seemed to beat.

So it was that the four of us, Mama beaming with the success of her persuasion, proceeded down the lawn to the boathouse, bound for a morning row. Mr. Cutting got in first, and from his seat, he directed Mama and myself into the stern and then, after Jonathan had handed us down, instructed Jonathan to man the bow pair of oars and push off. To my surprise, Mr. Cutting proved a nimble oarsman, and he set the stroke for Jonathan, the long oars gliding above the surface of the water like low-flying birds, the men falling into an easy rhythm, shooting our boat forward into the wide harbor, busy at this hour with a mix of fishermen and other rusticators like ourselves.

A little breeze fluttered the skirts of Mama's parasol, and I dared not look at her, afraid of what I might see there. Instead, I leaned against the back of our seat and closed my eyes for a spell, listening to the wooden oars scrape against the iron oarlocks as though the boat itself hummed to our progression. I heard drops trickle off the tips of the flat blades as they hung above the water between strokes, and Mr. Cutting tapped his feet to keep himself in time. Farther and farther we went into the harbor, the four oars speeding us toward the breakwater.

"Isn't this lovely." Mama sighed.

The men rowed in silence. Mama and I sat in silence. The morning waters were placid. The boat. The women in white and shade. The men's strong arms revealed. Here we all were.

Save Papa, I thought, and opened my eyes. Save Papa and Nell, and all the Granges—and Bart. There were too many missing from this boat. I stared at Mr. Cutting bending and leaning, his mustaches perfect. And Jonathan, behind him, saw me watching, and he smiled at me.

"Shall we turn round?" I said to him directly.

"As you wish!" he answered, happy to take my request of him as a sign of our connection.

But when we pulled back into the dock, I grabbed hold of the landing ring and swiftly climbed out with the boat's line in my hand, eager to tie it up and flee.

"Thank you, Mr. Cutting," I said while they all three still sat in the boat. "Thank you, Jonathan," I cried to him also. And then I turned and made my way up the gangplank, aware of the stunned silence I had left behind me.

"Maisie!" Mama called at last when I had reached the top. I looked down. Jonathan and Mr. Cutting had climbed onto the dock and were preparing to hand Mama up.

"I *must* speak to Cook," I said to her quietly. And then I turned and did not look round again. But her voice on the air and the certain tilt of her head as she had called my name made me a child again. And in my sore heart, her words—*I do not know who you are*—pealed a vast, repeating sorrow. The gap between us had widened as surely as the swath of water grows between a boat departing and the shore. She was going from me; yet it had been I who cast her off. Up the lawn I walked, then climbed the stairs to the verandah, then across the shady, breezy station and into the House. I sought Cook now—myself shattered into pieces—no longer frightened of her fury.

When I emerged into the front hall, there was no one in sight, and I wandered through the dining room and suddenly found myself pausing at the top of the kitchen stairs. I stood looking down into the dark well, one toe out in the air, making ready to descend. The sound of rushing water came through the pipes beside the door, and for an instant I felt the House spoke out a little. Perhaps this thought nudged my toe downward, and then the next down still more, as I stepped to where she worked.

She stood alone at the sinks, pumping up water into the pipes overhead, her back to me. The sun blanked out the windows before her as it streamed low and bright straight across the kitchen floor, rendering her edgeless for an instant, an enormous dark spot at the center of such light. Blinded, I stopped where I was, the kitchen dizzyingly alive and seeming to spin about this thick old woman whose arm worked the pump in regular strokes, a counterpoint to the steady stream of water rushing through the pipes above us with a motion nearly elemental.

Her arm dropped and her enormous frame wheeled round. "Ah. Maisie Thomas."

"What have you to tell me?" I could not quash my nerves and my voice skittered out from my mouth.

She considered me for an eternal moment and then replied quite calmly, without a trace of her former violence. "Ask me the question."

"Cook"—I had lost all ability for nicety, though my voice was soft—"please tell me. Are you Abby?"

She started, an unguarded expression upon her face—one almost of sympathy. "Abby! Nay, nay, she is dead long ago."

"Mary Ames, then?"

A shiver swept across her frame, and she appraised me from the other side of her table, the several spoons and ladles drying on the towels between us. This time she could see I would not fly, and neither would I bend.

"Cook," she replied in a queer, high voice. "I am Cook."

One of the iron servant's bells rang out, but she did not appear to hear as she advanced, fearful in her earnestness, indeed as if she did have something particular to convey. The bell rang again, louder this time. She looked up into the corner where the bells hung, and then back at me. The impatience in her face just then recalled someone— though read or remembered, I could not say.

"Janie!" she snapped, still looking at me. "There's the front bedroom calling for you."

"I am coming, Cook!" the girl replied from the back bowels belowstairs.

"Go on," Cook invited me.

I looked at her. "I must finish this story." I crossed my arms at my chest. "I must finish the story Miss Grange gave me before she died."

"A sight more than a story is what she gave unto you, my girl." Cook also folded her arms above her heart.

"Yes," I amended quietly, "she has given me Grange House."

She watched me a little. "And what will be lost if you do not, if you cannot, finish this story?"

"I will," I answered.

"Aye? And what are you?" Her face softened.

"A girl."

"All girls are lost. They marry. They become women."

"Yes, but that is terrible."

"Is it?" She folded her arms. "Why?"

"I cannot help but think of it as a sort of drowning."

"I see, and you a sort of savior?"

She was scoffing at me. "Yes," I said.

She turned away, wiping her hands upon the cloth still in her hands. "How little you understand."

She must look at me, I thought. I walked round and stood by the side of the sink. "Then help me."

"Why should I help you?" She was gazing out the window, but still, the hard woman of the attic was not in evidence now. Her question this time seemed really to seek an answer.

"Because you know the ending."

She lifted her chin and gave a harsh chuckle.

I drew in my breath. "Tell me," I begged, pressing against this reluctant. I stepped forward suddenly, causing her to jump, the ring on her left hand clinking against the lip of the sink. "Tell me," I urged gently. She turned her spent face from the window toward me. "Tell me what you know. You need not fear that you have been disloyal to Miss Grange." I paused.

She clucked then and shook her head. "Child," she began, but she hit the word too heavily and it clattered in the air between us. I stiffened, again on my guard against her. She straightened, opened her mouth as if to continue, but then closed it and turned away from me. "It has begun," she said, speaking so low, I thought she did not speak to me. The words grew in the silence, grew too heavy, it seemed, for she faced me once more and gazed upon me.

"Have you seen the little grave?" she whispered.

"Yes." I could not keep my eyes from off her face, it was so changed, so inexplicably weary.

"Miss Grange showed it you?"

I nodded.

"Then"—she breathed a long sigh—"go with me there tonight. The thing can explain the plain truth far better than I."

In a daze, I climbed back up the kitchen stairs, through the empty dining room already set for luncheon, the light from the windows catching the crystal glasses like indoor stars upon the dark tables. I caught the tip of my mother's voice through one of the open windows that gave onto the verandah. Her voice and several others swatted and hung within the clear air, the words indistinct.

I wandered into the writing room, but it was occupied by a man standing with his back to me, facing out the window. I stole out and softly crept toward the stairs.

"Maisie?"

I turned round.

"Hello, Jonathan." I smiled weakly, but did not move, as if frozen to my stair.

"Hello, my love." He held out his hand to me, smiling. "I had hoped to find you alone."

"Jonathan." I swallowed, but I could not take his hand. "Jonathan, I fear you think me very strange."

"No, dear." He dropped his hand. "A little tired perhaps. Your mother has explained that you sat up the night with Miss Grange."

"Yes, and did Mama also tell you that I have a charge from Miss Grange?" I was suddenly unspeakably angry at Mama.

"No."

"Miss Grange has asked me to finish a story. One she could not write."

"Why would you finish a story of hers?" He had drawn very near to me.

"Because," I answered, "because she was my friend."

He put his hand upon my shoulder and shyly caressed it. "I should think you would rather concentrate on one of your own."

In anguish, I looked up at him. "I think her story is my own," I whispered.

He stared at me, speechless.

"Pardon me," I gasped out, then fled, my skirts high in both hands, my face rigid, the only sound my heart beating to the tune of my feet racing through the passage to my door.

Once there, I collapsed upon my bed. A sob rose and burst forth like a foul taste, and there followed one harsh cry after another.

I woke in a shining darkness; a single long beam of light stretched through the window to me across the floor from the risen moon. I rose to stand in the window. The moon shone so brightly, there were shadows on the great white granite rocks at the shoreline, and the stretch of lawn appeared gray until it foundered at the water's edge. Across the top of the boathouse, across the moon-brushed water, the tops of the trees on the answering shore etched a ragged line of black into that eerie, windless pale.

Some other light moved from out the doorway of the boathouse, the reddish glow of a cigar held in Bart Hunnowell's hand, his form washed also to a chalky gray by that insistent moon. He sprang lightly onto the largest rock to the side of the boathouse, then walked down the broad ledge until he stood upon the ridge, his back to the House, facing out to sea. He paused for a moment there, and then the arc of his cigar's red ember flashed briefly before it was swallowed by the watery gray. I leaned my brow against the cool glass of the window and watched him turn, cross the ridge once more, and leap down onto the grass.

He had taken but a few steps when he stopped where he was, and he seemed to look directly at me in the window. I drew back, startled, still in a half sleep. But then I leaned forward again at once to see if he still stood on the lawn. He did. And when he saw my face again in the window, he raised his hand to me and waved.

Without thinking further, I turned from the window and reached for my shawl from off the easy chair, and covering my face and head, I made my way noiselessly to the back stairs. I paused at the top, listening. Two floors down, there came the clatter of pots and the sound of washing-up.

I stole down those narrow stairs to the kitchen passageway, where I crept past the overcoats and shawls and turned the knob to pass onto the small verandah at the back of the House.

All was quiet under the broad wash of moonlight, and for an instant I was unsure how I came to be suddenly outside, my heart beating fast. The night seemed strangely altered. I descended the back stairs into the too-bright night, intending to stay within the covering shadows of the House so as to watch if Bart might approach. There was something I wished him to do. With one hand at the covering round my throat, and the other tracing the lines of the House, I rounded the back corner and slipped along the dark green wood at the base of the verandah.

I paused at the front corner, then peered round to observe the lawn before me. Bart had disappeared. Where he had stood looking up at me and waving was nothing but flat gray lawn. A shadow crossed over the white rocks at the edge of the water, but it was that of a cloud. Perhaps he had withdrawn again into the boathouse.

"Maisie Thomas," came her voice behind me. I whirled to face Cook's tall figure standing there in the moonlight, the kitchen fire shovel in her hands.

At first I would not answer. And then I found I could not. There was something final in her appearance beside me, something terrible in her position. Without another word, she took up the shovel and began to walk directly into the trees. Once through the dark perimeter, she slowed, as if uncertain of her direction, and cast a sideways look at me as I stood at her shoulder. I cannot say what she saw upon my face, but she stiffened. She picked up her skirt with one hand, the shovel in the other, and began to walk in earnest upon the narrow, worn path that diverged from this green alley and led directly, I remembered, to that hidden grave.

The moon shone even in there, and we walked briskly, arriving before long at the familiar spot.

It appeared smaller to me this time, less terrifying. Now I could see that the letters upon the marker had been carefully chiseled into the stone by an unprofessional hand. PERDITA GRANGE, and then the tender plea: *Pray for Her*. The ground around the grave had been kept clear of fallen branches, the undergrowth picked from the mossy bed. I recalled Miss Grange's mushroom harvest here, and my throat closed, thinking of her keeping vigil in this lonely spot.

The night wind drew through the inland pines, swaying them back and forth, so that their deadwood creaking gave the eerie sense of doors opening and closing absently. What might she have been, this sister of mine, had she lived? I tried to imagine her—like myself, yet wholly other. Someone who might have stood at her window wishing to see past the dampness and the fog of an ordinary morning all the long, long way down to me, her sister at her window. We might have been companions. I patted her stone. No. For it had been chance that I discovered her; had Papa lived, I never would be standing here, a witness to his long-buried secret.

Cook stood and turned round to me, and I saw her features had grown finer in the light—and for an instant, transformed, almost beautiful, almost—but I cast away the thought.

"When Nell was delivered of her baby," Cook began, the moon rippling in the folds of her cloak, " 'twas as if a madness had dropped across her." She traced the rim of the shovel blade with an idle finger. "Nay, not madness, more a blankness—as if her mind had fallen to sleep. Morning after morning, I entered her room, to hear the babe's poor, weak, hungry cries, and Nell upon the bed, unheeding, her eyes fastened upon the door as if she expected a visitor at any moment. Even I went unrecognized, and so I passed in and out of that doorway like a ghost. After four days, I simply took the child with me, and filled a sac with new milk and took up the feeding on my own."

She stood beside the grave straight as the silent marker that rose to her waist. The square set of her shoulders, the cast of her head upon her neck reminded me suddenly of Miss Grange.

"And then"—she considered me—"there was a dreadful time, worse than the oblivion into which she was cast that first week."

I looked past Cook's shoulder to a sound, a soft snap in the trees beyond us.

"She had begun to walk, Maisie Thomas," Cook continued, reeling in the past so careful, so slow, I think she never heard what cawed around us, nor hardly even saw me—seeing through me, it seemed, to that other time.

"Night after night, she would walk. And as I lay in my own chamber with her baby snug and close to my side, I heard her footsteps wander up and down the dark passageway. And heard the sound of her hands." Cook gripped the shovel still tighter.

"The sound of her hands?"

"Pressing into the walls of the corridor, pressing them softly as she passed along." Cook let the shovel drop and raised her own two hands up before my face, placing one thumb to the other to achieve a terrible bird of hands, the fingers stretched in broad, bent wings.

"But one night, I heard the footsteps in the passage stop outside my door, and then saw the door swing open, and Nell stood there for a minute, a wide and staring half sleep upon her face. Without waking, she advanced to the room and took her child from where it slept beside me, though I do not know how she knew where to find the baby— she had not shown a flicker of interest all the many days since the birth."

Cook stopped speaking suddenly. There came again a crack, another small snap between the trees. We both turned in the direction of the sound and listened. But it was nothing after all. I turned round.

"And then?" I prodded.

"I followed her at a distance, out into the woods, keeping to the edge of the old rock wall."

Cook kicked softly at the blade of the fallen shovel and would not venture forward, even as the picture of Miss Grange's night walk crossed in the air between us.

"And when she arrived here—" Cook sighed, stopped abruptly, and looked at me.

"Yes?"

"She set her baby carefully down and took from her pocket a teaspoon."

I stared. But now Cook rushed forward with the tale. "And she began to dig with her spoon, steady as a workman, into that rocky ground.

"At that, I stepped forward, for I feared her, even sleeping as she was. 'What are you doing?' I whispered to her. But she did not look up. She did not pause. 'I must find her. I must find her,' she cried. 'Hush.' I replied. 'She is gone.' "

"Who?" I interjected.

"Her mother," Cook burst forth, anguished.

"The Widow Grange?"

"Aye," she whispered, and closed her eyes. "You would call her that."

Tears started up in my own eyes at the vision of Miss Grange's misery there in the dark, her baby asleep beside her as she dug to find her own mother in the ground.

"What did she mean to do, do you think?"

Now Cook looked directly at me and did not quail. "To bury her own child."

I stepped back, horrified. "Never."

"Aye, Maisie Thomas, she did. Nell Grange—your Miss Grange— intended to bury her own child."

I could not stop then, but roamed to the far edge of the wall marking the end of that cleared spot, then round the other side to the end once more. My eyes widened: Hadn't I myself seen what the cook had told me? The woman in a white gown, frantically digging, tearing at the earth beneath her fingers, the silver spoon useless in that ground as a toothless jaw upon a hasher of meat—though still she dug, and dug, and made a little hole. But it could not be Miss Grange who would dig like that, like a mad animal in the dirt.

"How can you be so hateful about Nell Grange?" I gasped finally, turning round to Cook.

"Hateful?" she hissed. "Hateful!" She spun from me as if she could not bear the sight. For several long seconds, she remained still. Then she turned round fast as a snake uncoiled, her dreadful meaning clear upon her face and in her hands. For she had swooped and taken up the shovel. She plunged its thick blade deep into the mossy cover and the surprised cry of a heron lifted suddenly from the trees behind us, as if Cook had struck the dirt to sound.

"Stop!" I whispered, horrified. Cook continued to dig at the foot of the grave, four feet from where I stood, my hand still upon the leaning marker. I sprang at her, snatching at her cloak and grabbing her by the arm to stop this desecration, but she shook me off easily, her great girth throwing force behind her mad determination. Still she did not speak to me, and I was forced to stand back and watch as the shovel bit farther and farther into the dark ground, where it soon must meet the coffin lid. I turned from the scene and covered my ears. Never again did I want to hear that heavy, thudding *clank* as the dirt fell backward upon the coffin, *clank* as the shovel scraped the leaden top. I raised my eyes and watched the trees round us leaning this way and that in the sea breeze. For an eternity, it seemed, and even through my hands, I heard Cook's heavy panting and the steady *clop* of uncovered ground deposited behind me. Suddenly, all was quiet.

"Maisie Thomas."

I would not turn. Yet neither could I run.

"Child," she whispered, and this time she hit the note with such an unexpected gentleness, my heart beat softly in response. The sorrow in the woman sang out in the simple word, and the sorrow in me answered. I turned.

There lay before me a black and empty hole. I took a step forward, my hand to my mouth. Below that careful marker, below the earth, there lay a blank Nothing. *Nobody.* I stared and stared down into that hole as if I might see it into some kind of sense. Along the sides, small cascades of dirt tumbled down. There were chips of granite cast up into the light.

"Tonight is the second time I have unearthed this . . . grave."
Cook spoke low, as if to pull me back slowly toward understanding;
gently, easily, she came and stood by me.

I stared down into the empty hole, hardly hearing her words, just
the quiet of her voice, the quiet steel of her voice.

"Where is the body of Perdita Grange?"

Now Cook faced me squarely. "She was given to her father."

I could not lift my eyes from the gaping hole, a blank eye staring
back up at me, unmoving. "My father?" I asked, trembling.

"Yes."

"Then—"

She did not move.

"Where is my sister?"

She did not answer, only watched while I struggled to understand.

"Please," I asked her again. "Have I a sister?"

"Nay," she said with a sorrowful kindness, and looked back
through the trees.

"But she was there on the page."

"There was nothing on the page." She shook her head at me. "It
is all in here." She tapped upon her heart. "Can't you see, my dear?
It was I gave you life."

I sprang from her, my heart pounding.

"All my life . . ." She gazed upon me. "All my life, I disbelieved
her, and now I must atone, by teaching her own child—"

My heart beat fast and thick and all my leashed senses strained
forward, waiting for the flick of her words upon my flesh.

"To see true."

I raised my eyes to hers.

"When you were born, it was I wrote your father, and later I took
you from your mother's arms—when she would bury you alive—and
wrote him once again."

"And?" I hardly breathed.

"It was I knocked down his weightless objections and formulated
the plan; and when he came, it was I delivered you into his arms."

"I don't understand. I cannot understand." I stood before her,
utterly quashed, my voice smaller and smaller as I spoke.

"But you must see at last, my girl. You must see: I am your Author." She smiled sadly. "I wrote the story that brought you from the ground. It was I, in the end, who told Nell you had . . . died."

"But I am my Mama's child," I protested. "She told me herself of her sickness after bearing me."

"Your mother never had a child," Cook replied slowly. "It were hysterical from the first." She nearly put her hand upon my shoulder, but stopped her hand between us in the air. "*She* were hysterical. A weak and ordinary woman."

Speechless, I took a step backward from the hole.

"Do you see? When your mother was brought to bed, she delivered nothing—nothing at all. But by then, your father knew of your birth. He knew!"

"But why would you cleave a child from her own mother?" I cast back at her across the grave.

"She said she did not want a child." Cook shuddered. "I decided, at last, to take her at her word."

"Then you are—" I could not finish.

"Susannah," she answered simply, though the name seemed forced through her lips.

I shook my head, still disbelieving, but wishing to hear it all said aloud at last. "And Miss Grange?"

"My sister. Your mother."

"But—I am Maisie Thomas."

"Oh, my dear"—she gave a thin smile—"that is only just a name."

In the milky sky above her head, soft clouds had succeeded the fierce brightness of the moon.

She sighed, as one who has finished with sighing. "You are Perdita Grange," she declared.

I shut my eyes, but her voice with my name upon it continued, above me, around me.

"Then this is *my* grave?" I sobbed.

She nodded. "Two months after your birth, I 'buried' you here."

"And she did not see the ruse?"

"She was too ill."

"So she never knew—" My throat closed.

"She never knew you were hers," Susannah finished, the tears in her voice finally loose.

I spun from her and ran. Through the spectral trees I ran, blindly, my feet moving while my brain snagged on the name, Perdita. I could see the path before me, the moon shone down so bright, and though I did not think, I followed, panting, wishing only to leave my aunt behind with that hollow grave, wishing only to press on out of the woods and into the bare grasses, out underneath that clarifying moon. I ran to the tune of *Perdita, Perdita, Perdita,* and the closer I drew to the clearing, it was as though I heard an echoing patter of footsteps, as if someone followed me in my anguish, as if someone came along behind.

At last I cleared the woods and emerged into the back field. Across the grasses I ran, past the House, down the lawn, and through the dark boathouse, out onto the dock and the boats. Breathless and intent, I knelt to untie one of the dinghies, my fingers struggling with the knot, and still the words bobbed free: *My sister. Your mother.*

CHAPTER TWENTY-SIX

Footsteps clattered upon the wood above me, and I wrenched at the rope, sobbing, desperate to leave. The footsteps stopped. I looked up, and there was Bart, silently watching me, and waiting. I turned back to the knot in my hands.

"I heard it all."

I stopped what I did, my heart thudding, and looked at him. Tears sprang into my eyes.

"Let us row," I pleaded.

He came quietly to my side, gave a practiced tug on the rope, and loosed the boat from its ring. I did not look at him again, nor care to, and stepped down into the body of the rowboat, sitting at the first oars seat.

"We will need two pair."

He nodded, drew out another pair of oars from the boat beside us, then stepped in himself and shoved us off. I slid my oars through the locks, and without a word, he began to row. I heard him placing his oarlocks in their slots behind me, and heard the oars slide through on either side, then came the doubled surge of our boat forward as he fell into my stroke.

Out and out we rowed, our oars dipping and stroking in perfect tandem, leaving behind us the dark hunch of the boathouse and the low outline of the dock across that widening flat white of moonlit water. The longing to move and move and not to halt gave strength into my arms, my blood echoing dully, coursing round and round my body. In and out we pulled, and pulled.

Until at last, I had to rest. And as suddenly as we had begun, our voyage calmed. Grange House was but the stark outline of roof and shutter beneath the moon. And somewhere, still, I was sure, she stood, watching me propelled by her claim outward onto the dull surface of this sea—who I was cracked open: my mother not my mother; myself not myself.

"Maisie," he began very quietly.

I did not answer.

"Maisie," he said again.

I turned round in the seat and faced him, my hands holding tightly to the oars pulled into my chest. He slapped at the water. The quiet resumed around us, then lengthened. I wished then for the whole great silence of the sky to wrap round me and draw a shadow between me and the moon's watching white eye.

"I am Maisie no longer," I whispered sadly.

He did not answer me.

"What I have known, what I took to be mine, my life before this, was a pretty nothing, grounded on illusion."

He leaned forward and whispered in my ear, "Perdita."

I had not known I waited for his lips to frame my name, but it was as if the word passed from his mouth and swept through my body, nudging open all the chill corners and turning what was gray to very sunlight. "Perdita," he repeated, the name nestled deep in his throat; and then he put out his hand and gently traced a circle round my cheek. "Is this an illusion?"

I shivered, smiling, and replied, "No."

He touched my lips with that same tracing finger. "Or this?"

I shook my head again, no, nearly overcome by the great feeling that threatened to pour from me at his gentleness.

He leaned still closer, so his face was nearly against mine. "What is a name to the wind?" he asked me. "What is meaning to the stars and this great sea?"

I watched him. "Nothing." He smiled and cupped my cheek in his hand. "Nothing."

I closed my eyes, and for the second time that night, I let another's voice possess me. But this one filled me, as though he breathed his soul directly through my blood, so his love coursed round in my own body, and it was his soaring great spirit that pumped the bellows of my heart.

"This moment is your name. My lips on yours, your name." He kissed me. "There is no other story but this one."

I kissed him, lulled. And indeed, I felt as if this moment my soul had stretched newly forward with uncertain steps, treading lightly toward some fresh vision. As if he sensed this, he whispered again into my ear, "Let your mother set to sea. Cast out her language. Cast away her words. They are not yours. Her story is but her own."

For answer, I leaned my cheek against his cheek and felt the vital warmth of his body enter into mine. I closed my eyes and let him comfort me, his arms stealing round my shoulders and his mouth against my hair. "Write down your words, my love," he said softly. "Take your great heart in your hands and write your own name upon its door."

"My name?"

"Your name, and—"

I turned my head, the better to hear his low whisper. "And?"

"And mine. Write your own name next to mine."

A voice clapped out across the water, and there came the distant splash of oars.

"Quick!" I gasped. "They must not come upon us here." I leaned forward and grabbed hold of my oars, sliding them back through the locks and into the water. Bart did likewise behind me, and our little boat surged forward as our oars drew water. I could not discern the figures in the boat, nor their purpose in setting out, like us, in the middle of the night, into the middle of the harbor; so at first I watched them without interest as we stroked, Bart navigating us around the point where at least we should not be so easily visible. We rowed hard for several moments into the choppier waters round the point, the tide against us and a wind from off the Atlantic blowing broadside as we left the lee of the harbor. A great cloud settled upon the moon, casting the sea into a welcome shadow.

I had not looked again to see where the other boat lay, so hard was I concentrating on keeping my strokes in line with Bart's behind me, my back and hands become rude mechanicals, my eyes set on a point in the stern of the boat. But when I lifted my eyes to reassure myself there was nought but empty water behind us, I saw to my horror that two boats, not one, followed us and were clearly now in pursuit.

A lantern hung in the prow of the first boat, casting the identity of the rower into black darkness and giving the uncanny effect of an unmanned vessel advancing through the clouds. The breeze slapped the chill of the water against us and I shivered under the thin cover of my shawl. The boat kept coming, that eerie cloud of yellow light obscuring and illuminating all at once. Bart had stopped rowing altogether, and his breath came in short bursts as he rested. "Who the deuce is that?" he whispered to me.

"Cook," I said, convinced by the surety and the strength with which that boat had followed; a leaden certainty gripped my limbs, such that even had I wished, I could not have lifted the oars again to take another fleeing stroke.

"There!" came a man's voice across the water from the second boat fast advancing.

Bart stood suddenly, sending our dinghy rocking violently, and I grabbed the gunwales for balance. "Who are you?" he shouted over my head at the approaching lantern. But the wind, which had easily borne the other's words to us, had as easily carried Bart's question out to sea.

Now they were closing in behind us, and the moon again shone down, casting what had been shadow into that unearthly brightness; then I saw who sat in each boat.

"Maisie!" Mama cried out. "Maisie!"

Still standing behind me, Bart chuckled and said, "I do believe this is a rescue party for your honor!" Then he called back to them across the water, "She is all right, Mrs. Thomas. Do not fear!" And he sat down again, laughing.

"How ridiculous!" I shoved my oar back into the water, angered by Mama's melodramatic pursuit. "Leave us be!" I called back, and took a stroke with my oar, spinning the boat round.

"What are you doing, Maisie?" All traces of laughter had fled from his tone.

I turned fiercely round. "Here is our beginning, Bart. Let us take it."

He whistled slowly but sent out his oars. "Aye. Let us, but I did not mean a future to have begun in flight."

I looked at the pursuing boat for a moment, then splashed at the water. "I am lost from them."

"Do not say that," he replied softly.

"It is the truth."

"Only a moonlight truth."

I wrenched round once more. "As were your words?"

He swore softly under his breath while he looked full into my face, and then he leaned forward and kissed me.

"Maisie!" Mama shrieked.

I opened my eyes again and saw there was now only fifty feet between us, and, horrified, I saw also that my mother stood in the shaky little boat. Her white dress shone preternaturally bright beneath the moon, rendering her figure horribly distended and unnatural as her arms reached for me. Again she cried, "Maisie!"

Bart stood up behind me and, unthinking, I stood suddenly also, causing the boat to wrench violently, knocking Bart from off his feet so that he fell backward against the narrow prow with a heavy thud. I wheeled round and saw he lay as if stunned, unmoving, his arms sprawled over the gunwales and his face upward, his throat bared to the sky. "Bart!" I gasped, stumbling in the still-rocking boat and tripping over my soaked skirts as I tried to reach him in the bow.

"Maisie!" came Mama's voice behind me now, very close, the lantern light casting its yellow glare across the painted oars in our boat, and across Bart's closed eyes. He moaned weakly.

There was a splash as she fell into the water. "Mama?" I whispered, unbelieving, afraid to turn round. I sat stalled at the middle seat, Bart's form lying in front of me.

"Elizabeth!" Mr. Cutting cried into the white night.

"Mama!" I shouted, and her two names crossed the water to echo round our boats, carried by a gentle caprice of wind. We stood waiting for her to reappear. From the corner of my eye, I saw Cook wheeling round and moving forward to give help. A terrible minute passed, and still I could not see or hear any evidence of poor Mama. Bart raised his head groggily in the bottom of the boat. I threw off my shawl and leaned over the gunwales once more, desperately searching the water for some sight of Mama's head. Bart sat up beside me, holding the back of his neck. "What is it?"

I turned, frantically unbuttoning my vest. "Mama has fallen into the water."

Without a word, he rose to his feet, shaky but determined, and then dove in after Mama. "Bart!" I whispered. I thought I saw him shoot past the oars into the waters between the boats, and standing to mark his progress, I caught sight of Cook suddenly halting in mid-stroke.

Incapable of moving, Mr. Cutting stood in the opposite boat, holding his lantern aloft in echo of my own solitary terror. We watched for several moments and then there was a faint splash on the other side of him, and he swung his lantern round after the sound. "Elizabeth!" he shouted. I heard another splash and, I thought, a soft moan in the distance.

"Mama!" I cried out, unable to see past the bright glare of the lantern. In answer, there came a second sigh, though this time from very close by. "No! No, Mr. Cutting, she is here!" I called out, and crouched low again to search the water.

In that instant, I saw Bart slip off the oar onto which he must have clung silently this little while, then sink slowly under the surface and vanish from sight. I sprang down with a cry and stuck my hand into the spot where he had sunk, gasping as the bone-chilling cold of that water grabbed hold of my wrist. But my hand touched nothing. Backward and forward I splashed in that water, but still nothing. With a sob, I pulled my hand up and tried to dry it on my skirt for warmth, but I had begun to shake miserably now, and found I could not command my limbs to do my bidding.

It was then I heard the commotion by the other boat, as, with a great shout, Mr. Cutting seemed in truth to have found Mama. I looked up and saw in the moonlight the dark figure of the man straining as he pulled the lifeless white-clad body of my mother into the boat; he laid her down in the stern, carefully pulling her limp arms in by her side and covering her in his thin jacket.

"Come on, girl," he shouted at me as he sat quickly back down and thrust his oars into the water.

I could not move, nor speak, save to shake my head back and forth. No. No. No.

"She must have the doctor!"

There was a crack in my head, as if someone had opened a door to peer into a very dark room, the yellow sliver of light slanting cross to my eyes.

"I cannot!" I whimpered.

"Pick up your oars and row," Mr. Cutting commanded.

"But he is here, he is down below."

"He is lost, girl. He is lost. Here is your mother!"

I sat rigid, still unable to move.

With a disgusted sound, he began to row against the tide as swiftly as he could. Sobbing, I watched that little boat carry Mama's unconscious body across the water toward Grange House, the rapid splashing of the oars beating an uneasy countertempo to my torpid heart. The white upon the water impressed my mind, as if the boat crossed over the brow of the moon and we were all, all of us, borne from ourselves, pulled along behind the body of my mother.

It was then a low moaning began, coming to me from very far away, from a far-down place, and I bent my head to listen to him calling me, calling to me from where he lay, and I stood up in that little boat and stretched my arms out so he could see how open was my heart then, how wide was the world I meant to offer him, myself a new-made creature, opened for his touch.

There before me, it seemed a dark body was carried swiftly upon that moon-laden sea, the tide turning it gently first this way, then that. I stepped one foot upon the seat to reach it as it passed—but it was nothing but a shadow. I looked down into those whitened waters and felt I could see down, away down through the surface to the bed upon which he lay. For an instant, I looked and saw my heart, and then the waters closed again, replacing his form with the silver face of she who shone above. Now I stood up straighter, the low moaning still ringing in my ears, and made to step up the other foot, when I heard from that liquid glass a voice call out, "CHILD!" I looked down into the clear face of that white reflected moon and whispered to her, "I am coming."

"Stop!" Cook's urgent cry cut through. "Step back from there, child!"

And then a cloud dropped down across the moon, and in that instant I was plunged into a halfish nighttime, and the boat grew suddenly unsteady beneath my feet. I dropped down onto the seat and put a hand up to my throat, which was raw, as though some dreadful word had been pulled from it. And indeed it seemed that I returned to myself, for in the silence I heard the echo of my own voice coming to me cross the waves.

Cook had come athwart and we bobbed gunwale-to-gunwale. "You must go," she urged.

I shook my head.

"You must. I will find him. I will bring him home."

Distinctly, I could hear several voices at the pier, then saw a line of lanterns suddenly flare up.

"Go!" she whispered, and gave a shove to my bow.

With a sob, I took up the oars and pushed them silently through their locks, making ready to row back.

"Love," I whispered to him who lay below me, but the word was too heavy in my throat for speaking. So I left him. I left him, not calling aloud his name into that dreadful night. The great song of him I had begun to sing, laid silent, final beneath the rocking of the blackened, implacable sea.

I rowed the distance between his grave and the House in a state somewhere between sleeping and waking, my arms and back pulling the long oars through the water. And though my eyes remained fixed upon the spot I departed, my traitorous body remembered far too well what Bart had taught me, and I shot the dinghy forward, steadily forward, carrying me into whatever lay ahead.

Jonathan waited at the pier, his ragged face horrible to see.

"Come quickly," said he. "It is possible she will still revive."

Wordlessly, I shipped the oars and took the cold hand he offered. Never the once did he look at me, then, holding his lantern up so I might see the lip of the gangway and the gap between the dock and ground, he assumed himself in his old position: my helpmate, and my guide. Dumb with sorrow, I let him lead me up the lawn, grown black beneath a perpetual cloud that had finally blotted out the moon, and into the House. The conversation ceased in the front room as I passed the open doorway and followed Jonathan up the wide staircase to Mama's room. There, too, the door was open, and I approached the dismal scene slowly. Softly, I took a step forward, and then another, until I stood at Mama's side.

She lay upon her pillows, her long hair loose about her face, still damp, and a streak of water slid slowly, like a forgotten tear, down the side of her neck. She had sunk a ghastly shade of pale, so white that it was almost lightness—as if she had traded places with that moon and it lay now upon her pillow, shining up at me. Mr. Cutting stood by on the other side of the bed, watching as Jessie held the bottle of hartshorn to Mama's nostrils. She moaned very softly, and Jessie patted her cheek. "There it is, ma'am. That's right." Still I moved as if what I saw had nought to do with me, for I could neither lean forward to touch her nor aid in her comfort. Behind Jessie, Dr. Lewes had hold of Mama's wrist; I saw her long white hand hung limp below his doctoring fingers, and I caught the infinitesimal shake of the man's head as he listened for my mother's life slowly running through her cold body.

Hovering this way, it was then I heard the very faintest cry from down the boathouse, and without a word, I turned from the bed and moved to listen at the threshold of the bedchamber; again came a cry, and so I fled.

"Maisie!" Jonathan called after me.

I cast myself down the stairs and out the front door, plunging back into the darkness below. Down the lawn I ran, sick with fear that I had missed him just as he had arrived. My footsteps pounding against the old floorboards of the boathouse, I reached the top of the gangway above the pier, breathless.

But nothing, and no one, was there. The three dinghies floated upon the water, loosely tied to the dock. I heard Jonathan approaching behind me, but I did not move until he was at my side. Then, still not looking away from the water, I said to him, patiently as I could, "I cannot leave here."

He put his hand on my shoulder and pressed it gently, trying to cause me to turn round.

"He may come back," I whispered to him.

"He is drowned."

"Nay. Nay. It may not be."

"Maisie," he began.

"Stop from me. Who are you to me now?"

He drew off his hand, answering stiffly, "Your husband, I hope."

"You cannot be. You do not even know my name," and I walked a little farther down the dock to lean against another of the black pilings.

"You are Maisie Thomas," he said urgently, "and, my love, you have had a great shock." He moved a bit closer to where I stood. "Maisie," he whispered into the night, "let me help you. Let me—"

I turned round upon him. "Jonathan Trumbull Lanman, I—" But I could not think what to say next.

"Yes?" he responded eagerly. "Yes, Maisie. I am, yes, for you."

I shook my head. "You cannot be for me, Jonathan."

"Why not?"

"Because my heart was drowned tonight." My voice was ragged. "Because my heart, my name, my very self was drowned, and—" The breath felt grabbed from my lungs, and I could not speak for grief.

"Well," he observed quietly after a time. "This was the day I was to bring you home." I could but nod. But he did not venture closer. Yet neither did he leave. Sometime later, I roused, to find Jonathan had placed his jacket round me as the night grew chill. All through the rest of that night, we waited; through the first birdcalls, until the telltale streaking in the pale sky.

At dawn, Mr. Cutting came onto the dock.

"What do you do here?" His voice was curiously calm.

I did not answer him, could not.

"How is Mrs. Thomas?" asked Jonathan.

"She sleeps."

"Ah." Jonathan sighed in relief. "So all has not been lost."

Mr. Cutting came to my side then. For a moment, he looked where I looked at the waters shimmering just beyond the point. "Miss Thomas." He cleared his throat.

"Yes," I answered him, not turning my head.

"Your mother is very ill indeed."

I did not answer. He watched me, I think, for a little time; and then, confounded by this stone statue of a girl, he turned abruptly away and walked the remaining paces to the top of the gangway. The foghorn blew its single note from off the breakwater. He struck the wooden railing with his fist.

"The Deuce, Miss Thomas! Where is your duty?"

Numb, I looked at him. "Who am I to help her?"

"She is beyond help. And, I must say, your inexplicable behavior smacks of disregard, of violent disregard!"

"Sir!" Jonathan's shocked voice rang out behind us.

"No," I said softly to Mr. Cutting. "You cannot understand. How am I to help her, when he could not?"

"She is going to Him," Mr. Cutting replied.

"You misunderstand. Bart dove to find Mama. He has not returned. Mama will not return. I must wait for him here." I turned from the sight of the man's face. "And then we two will come up to see Mama." And I smiled at the pink face of the sea.

I think Jonathan moaned then, although I do not recall, for suddenly the world went blank.

CHAPTER TWENTY-SEVEN

I awoke to whispering just near, and upon my closed lids the quiet flicker of candlelight danced black flames. Perhaps I had crossed over, at last, and when I opened up my eyes, there would be those who might call me by my certain name, instead of these who had a partial hold of Maisie, Maisie. "Maisie?"

I opened my eyes. Jessie's anxious face bent close to mine. "Ah. There you are, child."

"Is he found?"

"Who?"

"Bart," I whispered.

She shook her head. I closed my eyes again and turned my head from the light.

There was the rustle of silk close by, and then a cool hand closed over my own. "Maisie," I thought Cook whispered into my ear, "I am here."

A tear forced its way over my lid, and then, unbidden, another, then another. "Cook?" I said brokenly, still not opening my eyes or moving.

"Yes?"

But there was nothing to reply. She sat beside me, remaining quiet for a long while. Finally, however, she leaned close again and asked, "Do you want to see your mother?"

I shook my head.

There was a long silence beside me.

"Why not, Maisie?"

"She is dying because of me."

Cook patted my cheek and leaned close again. "No, girl."

I opened my eyes then and sniffed. "She came for her daughter, but I am . . . not her." I could not speak again for a short while, just lay there against the pillow, weeping. And when I had done, though the sorrow did not lift, I closed my eyes again and dozed.

When I awoke, Cook still sat by my side, and Jessie was nowhere about. I had the impression Cook had watched me as I slept, and I pushed up against the bedclothes so I could sit. She gave me water to drink, and then, still watching me, she said very carefully, "Nell was not your true mother."

"She was."

"No, Maisie. That was a book."

"It was she who wrote the book."

She shook her head firmly. "A book about the past, about what is past."

"What is past is fiction. Who I am is not who I am."

Cook was suddenly impatient. "Did *she* nurse you in your sickness? Did *she* teach you how to read, or how to dress your hair?"

I was silent.

"Maisie!" Cook bent her face close to mine. "Maisie, you had a mother. You had one, and now you would toss her away because of a story in a book!"

"But what does it mean—to have a mother?"

Cook took my hand, the tears welling in her own eyes. "Someone who watched you, Maisie." She blinked. "Someone who watched what you did, who saw you as you moved from room to room in your childhood. Someone who saw . . . you."

I turned my head upon the pillow and saw she was speaking of herself—and Halcy. And my own eyes filled.

Then the bemused look in my mother's eyes, the slight twitching of her mouth as she waited for me to speak came to me. Waiting—the two of them turned round and waited for me to follow, their eyes upon me. But now there was the third pair of eyes watching me from the window, the eyes that had seen me but not known what they looked upon. In Miss Grange's room, I had felt most . . . wide, most possible. In her eyes, I was become multiple.

I looked back at Cook bleakly. "Can't you see? That woman in the diary—she belongs to me. *She* was my mother, more my mother in kind than my own mother. Had she lived—"

"Had she lived, you never would have known what you do now."

It was true. This present moment was the child of my parents' deaths, my knowledge nursed to being by departed ghosts.

"What would you have me do?" I asked her dully. "How am I to speak to my heart?"

"Tell it to remember, Maisie," said she. I shook my head, biting my lip to stop its shaking. "Tell it to recall—"

"There is nothing to recall but another girl's childhood," I said simply, and closed my eyes wearily. "Had she lived, *she* would have guided me. *She* would have known what I should feel."

Cook let go my hand. "It matters little, Maisie, when she who raised you lies next door—and waits for your farewell."

I shook my head mournfully. "Who am I to bid her farewell, when I cannot even call her by her name?"

"I tell you, a name means nothing, Maisie Thomas," Cook said. "She was Mama, once."

When I heard the door shut to, I pushed aside the bed curtains. A child looked back at me from the glass: the little white face and wide eyes staring from beneath the shock of hair. I could not see it. I could not imagine the long carriage ride home from Grange House after Susannah had given me into Papa's arms. The big man and the baby cozed tight against him. The stops in Portland, Portsmouth, Boston, Providence, New Haven. Down the long, fingered coastline between Miss Grange and Mama, down he traveled with me. When did he decide not to tell the whole secret to Mama? When did he think it best to leave the lie buried beneath the rocky topsoil of Maine?

When I woke again, sunlight streamed through the sheer curtains, and there was no one by my bed. I rose upon my elbow and looked out the window and down the lawn. An old woman stood alone there in the middle, as if she had forgotten whether her direction lay up or down. She looked weary, from my post, and a little lost. For several moments, she stood in the midst of that bright, shining green lawn; then she turned, and I saw it was Mrs. Hunnowell.

With a cry, I sprang from my bed and pulled open the door into the passage. Cook was hurrying up the stairs toward me.

"Come!" she said. "They have brought him back." She took my hand and led the way to Bart's door, then flung it wide, and we stopped upon the threshold.

He lay upon the bed, a sheet pulled up to his chin, his hair combed from off his face, and his hands crossed upon his chest. I stood unmoving for some time, afraid to venture closer, my eyes riveted to his beloved face, stilled upon the pillow. It was all I knew to do, my poor heart formal, implacable, and my brain reciting: *Dead. Dead*. I watched because my eyes simply refused another task. And the grave that was my heart stirred its soil. My father and Miss Grange lay in me, entwined, as would Bart. As would Mama also. In me, there need not be dividing lines, my own body a graveyard without the little plots. What did it matter who had borne me? All of them were gone.

Cook still held my hand in hers, and just then I grew sensible of her abiding touch. "Come," she whispered, and she pulled me forward to where my love lay upon the bed.

My heart saw the sweet lips. My heart saw the strong hands resting upon the coverlet. "How did he come here?"

"Night seiners pulled him from off a drifting spar."

I turned cautiously round, not daring to understand what her words promised.

A weak moan escaped his lips, and I whirled back to him upon the bed and saw one of his hands rise, then fall again swiftly down. I froze. "He lives?"

"Yes, Maisie. He will live." She turned me from him to face her. "But your mother will not."

A hot jolt reached me then from her fingertips straight through to my heart. I regarded her a long, speechless moment. "I do not understand you."

"Your mama—"

"Nay," I broke in. "I do not understand *you*. You who took my mama from me and now"—my eyes filled—"you who would give her back."

"Ah." She almost smiled as she reached a mechanical hand to nudge the shade above the bed back into place. "Me."

"Why did Papa never tell Mama?"

"I forbade him."

"You!"

She leveled her gaze upon me. "Every summer, you returned here, Maisie Thomas. And every summer, you grew beneath both—" She stopped. "Your mama *and* Nell might both have you, might both see you, though they were unknowing what they saw."

She spoke it as if it were a gift, as if her logic were a treat. I stared at her, unbelieving someone could foster such an enormous lie. She drew in her breath, her eyes never leaving my face. "Ah." She exhaled slowly. "I see you are a Grange after all."

"Tell me," I demanded quietly, "why?"

I do not know where the high, proud voice emerged from in me, but I spoke as if I were a justice upon a mount, and the woman answered me so, for she did not balk then, or turn away. She continued to look at me, and nodded when she saw I had comprehended it at last.

"But—Nell wished to protect you, I think."

She gave a ghastly broken smile in response. "Aye, that were a dark protection. One that broke our House."

"Then why did you stay and torment her so? Why did you not leave her?"

"Leave?" She shook her head at me, unbelieving. "How might I leave?"

I crossed my arms.

"Nay!" she whispered. "Nay, you will know." She stared at the miniature hung behind my head for a long while, a great struggle upon her face as the words crossed through her, and yet she could not speak. It was as if I watched a drama played without the curtain falling in between, without the actors and their signal voices—yet I saw the scope of it in my aunt's hard face, as if her face were the stage. And I needed none of the voices then, for the pantomime stirred in me an answering sorrow. When she finally opened her mouth to speak, I was startled by the clarity, the vigorous simplicity of tone—here was Susannah come through at the end; here was the woman who lived inside the cook. In the diary, she had been tall and proud and capable.

"I did leave, Maisie. Nay—not a leaving exactly, but a flight. I tossed myself into the arms of Joseph Ames, who had sought me since he was a boy, and departed Middle Haven with him on a whaling ship."

She looked at me. "A whaling ship? Ho! Do you know what the life of a first mate's wife is upon a ship? Within four months offshore, the cook took sick and died. And I—proud Susannah Grange—cooked and slopped for the crew."

I stared.

"And all that year"—her voice quieted—"it was this House that was my firm horizon, and Nell's face I thought of to soothe myself to sleep."

She crossed her arms. "How could I leave," she asked me directly now, "what was my own memory: my history walking, and remarking in her?" She stopped a minute. "Nell need only cock an ear in the family manner and that whole rich year of my love"—she looked quickly at me, wary again, but seeing my steady face turned to hers, she continued—"that thick love that came on so slow, so achingly slow, reappeared in the slant of her cheek and chin as she listened."

She paused. Neither of us moved.

"I did try, Maisie, to strike out anew. But my sister's story of our life—nay, my sister's stories—held me close. I could not tear against them; they were imprinted in me as those tiny hands upon the fictitious walls." She shuddered quietly and folded her arms before her, finally looking up at me.

"So I returned to the House I had renounced—a widow"—she shook her head—"with my baby in my arms." Her voice broke, but she said, "With Halcy. And I took up here as the cook—not daughter, never daughter again. For I could not think how else to mark the rupture."

I reached forward and took her hand.

"You see a woman's story is not single, never a lone tramp toward the end."

"Why?" I whispered.

Susannah smiled. "Because there are the voices of her house. The lit rooms, peopled and cushioned, that she carries. And though she may travel—" She broke off, considering. "Aye, that is the horror of it—she may never travel from the house that made her."

My aunt dropped my hand and looked at me. "I once thought the past to be a faint thing I must paste down in my scrapbooks, so memory might endure." She gave a bitter smile. "But do you know, my dear? It never avails. What is written, or collected, is but a glance, the flash of a cheek as it turns elsewhere. Nothing speaks correctly for the past. Everything lies."

"No," I whispered, "not everything."

She cast an eye on me and shook her head sadly. "They are gone. All of them gone. And you, who are left, who look at me now, do hardly see me."

I put my hand upon her arm. "Nay, Aunt," I said simply.

And her name upon my lips did not soften the thick woman before me, thick and slow with the secrets she had wrapped round her year by year.

"Aye." She nodded again, still sad. "You cannot see me, though you look. You see Susannah of the diary." She nearly laughed. "And then you see Cook of Grange House."

"There is a vast gap between," I admitted.

She pursed her lip, studying me for an instant. "There, then. Look there in that gap. Look there—for me."

Slowly, she took my hand from off her arm, but she kept hold of my hand in hers.

"Now. Go to her," she uttered.

*　*　*

372

And so, at last, I turned my feet in the direction of Mama's room. I stood a long while in the passageway outside the door, my hand upon the knob. My hand? And hers, and hers, and hers, and all of them written into these walls; we finally turned the knob on her door. Jessie slept in the chair beside her, and the lamp was low. I looked again at the bed, my eyes filling with tears at my poor mother's frail white form. For there she was after all: the hand I had held, the cheeks I had kissed, the shoulder I had sobbed my childish pittances upon. It was as little as this—her body was all that remained behind to remind me of my own small self. And I understood then what Susannah had said. For there, before me upon the bed, lay all my past—suspired within her bosom, the gentle casing of my own heart.

Like the quarry, like the ocean—there is the surface, and then the deep. Who they had been, these women before me, was all round me in that room. The Widow Grange, Miss Grange, Susannah—even Halcy, my own lost cousin. I had seen. I had sat beside. I had considered that I knew.

And yet the attic story was my mother's story, the one I lived beneath and never knew. I was a grave, repeating. It was I my mother buried by her words. And then set free.

"Mama," I whispered into her ear, "it is Maisie." And then I could speak no more; I laid my forehead on her still hand and wept.

All through the rest of that long day, I held her hand and whispered to her who I was, whom I had buried, who had buried me, wishing her to pass it along, to carry it to those I could no longer tell. To tell all the whispering dead what I knew. And her quiet was a blank letter upon which I could write what was, and what might be, her face unmoving, though I knew she listened; my voice was a steady sound in the dark room. Into her silence I poured my philter, and stirred it round, speaking low and urgently at first, then slower, in time to her breathing.

It came slow and slower, then so slowly, it was as though the gaps between breathing were a little sleep. And then finally, it was the gaps that came more freqently than breath. Just at twilight, a change fell over the room; I looked up into her face and saw she stared at me, wide awake, it seemed. "Maisie?" she asked.

"Yes, Mama?"

"You have come."

"Yes, Mama."

She smiled. "I thought I should die alone."

I took her hand and pressed it between my own, the tears streaming down my face. "Nay."

She swallowed. "Maisie," she whispered. I bent my face close to hers. "Yes, Mama."

"All your life——" She passed a hand across my forehead as though she checked for fever. And she opened her mouth once more, but this time could not find strength for voice. I could not keep my eyes from hers. I could not keep from feeling as though we both had begun to drown.

"Hush, Mama," I soothed. "I am right here." But her mouth would speak, and her silent lips said, "I did love you." And then she breathed out, "Maisie."

There was no sharp break, no sudden plunge away. Mama sailed from me as if over a calm sea. For when it came, the final change was slight as the first breeze catching cloth, the sail opening—opening and then the gentle drop.

And the word set adrift from her lips had been

Maisie.

AFTERWORD

But what did it matter?" I asked Bart tonight. "What would
have been lost had I not written it all down as I could?"
"A lasting pleasure," said he, quietly shutting this big book
and turning round. "For that was just how it was."

"How it was?"

"And greater," he said firmly.

"Ah, then it wasn't at all how it was." I smiled.

"Regardless"—he patted the book on his lap—"here is your legacy."

I laughed then, but after he had departed, I took up the book and
wrote Bart's words down. I suppose he is right.

Here is my legacy, then. My book, my boat. One of you will find
this after I am gone.

22 June 1924
Grange House

ACKNOWLEDGMENTS

I am indebted to the following works: Harold B. Clifford, *Charlie York: Maine Coast Fisherman* (International Marine Publishing Company, 1974); Eleanor Motley Richardson, *Hurricane Island: The Town That Disappeared* (Island Institute, 1989); *Victorian Women: A Documentary Account of Women's Lives in Nineteenth-Century England, France and the United States,* Hellerstein, Hume, and Offen, editors (Stanford University Press, 1981).

I am very grateful to the MacDowell Colony for the time and space given me.

I want to thank Elinor Blake, Melanie Braverman, Alan Brown, Jane Brox, Michael Cunningham, Carolyn Dever, Catherine Havemeyer, Bridget Hughes, Laurie Lindop, Alexandra McGovern, Heather McGowan, Diana Phillips, Claudia Rankine, and Heidi Jon Schmidt for all their comments on various drafts.

My heartfelt thanks to the frank, the supportive, and the funny Leigh Feldman, without whom I would be lost. And enormous thanks for the clear-eyed advice and copious attention of my editors, Reagan Arthur and Doris Janhsen.

And then, there is Joshua Weiner—for whom my thanks are but the smallest part.